Passions

SHERITTA BITIKOFER

MOONSTRUCK WRITING

Published by Moonstruck Writing

ISBN: 978-1-946821-63-8
EBook ISBN: 978-1-946821-64-5

Cover Art by: *Covers by Combs*, www.coversbycombs.com

The characters and events portrayed in this book are fictitious and a product of the author's imagination. Any similarity to real persons, living or dead, is purely coincidental and not intended by the author.

Contents

Dedicated to those passions that burn inside, waiting to come to light.

Prologue

Mary Anne quickly locked up her home and glanced to the nurse who had come all the way from Savannah to help her. In her mind, the help was entirely unneeded, but with how unstable her life had become, going without a companion was out of the question. The young lady with her blonde hair pulled back into a ponytail, gave a nod as if to give her permission to give one last goodbye to the house.

Her wrinkled fingertips lovingly grazed over the smooth wood of the front door. It was likely that she would never see this place again. She would never see Gavin again – except perhaps in her dreams. And even then, she didn't know if the medications would twist her mind. Would he be erased forever by her declining health and the tricks of the doctors on staff?

The assisted living home had been her idea, but she hated to do it. She hated how her friends all thought she was crazy and how her own sister had forsaken her. Her niece, bless her heart, was the only one who held a decent opinion of her anymore, but she hadn't seen Chloe's smiling face for so long.

Mary Anne felt forgotten by the world, pushed aside as a useless old crone who talked about a man living in her basement. Gavin had been her only friend for so long that she sometimes forgot that he couldn't be real. But, he did seem real. He was flesh and blood. She had touched his face and talked to him for hours into the night when she should have been sleeping. Now, she was leaving him.

She turned and with the nurse's help, she eased herself down the uneven steps of the front porch to stand on the gravel pathway.

"Is everything settled with the real estate office?" she asked, her voice withered and fatigued by the sadness of this parting.

"Yes, ma'am," the young nurse drawled out. "And the lawyers have your will."

Mary Anne nodded her approval and let the girl help her into the passenger side of the car. The back seat and trunk were load down with her suitcases. Only the essentials were allowed at the facility, but she'd balk every step of the way so she could keep her knitting supplies. She needed something to occupy herself on the long, lonely days.

Through the windshield, she looked up at the cabin and how the tall pines and spruces closed in around it, shielding it like a precious gem. This home had belonged to her family for centuries, and before that it was Gavin's. She could only hope that Chloe had become more sentimental in her young adult years and would come back to receive her inheritance. Passing this priceless heirloom off to the next generation had been her wish for some years now, but she was a spinster and without children of her own. Chloe was their only hope for continuing the legacy.

The car pulled away and wound down the mountain path and Mary Anne strained her failing eyes to watch the last of the house disappear in the rearview mirror. Swallowed up by the forest to be reclaimed someday.

Chapter 1

Chloe was still sitting in her car fifteen minutes after pulling up the gravel drive. She stared out her windshield to the cabin before her, still in disbelief that she was actually here.

It seemed only a few days ago that she received the call from her aunt's attorney when it actually had been over a month. Once the grief subsided from the news that her favorite – and only – aunt had passed away in her sleep, Chloe was thrown into a whirlwind of life changes. She regretted nothing regarding her decision to move into the cabin.

Along with a sizable trust fund that her aunt had been secretly stashing away into for decades, she received this cabin. It had to be at least a couple hundred years old but she could tell it had been renovated within the last few years. No doubt to accommodate tourists who wanted to rent out the cozy cabin for their vacations. When her aunt had been told she could no longer live by herself, she had moved into an assisted living home in Savannah while renting out her former home here in the Blue Ridge Mountains.

Chloe immediately told the real estate company that she had no intention of letting the home remain available for weekend getaways. They were also dismayed to hear of her aunt's passing. She was a beloved woman in the small town of Carter Lake. Everyone knew her and the cabin well. It was old enough to be declared a historic landmark, but Chloe had other intentions for the home.

She took a deep breath and finally slid out of her silver sedan. Her stylish leather boots crunched against the gravel walkway as she made her way slowly towards the front steps. She had taken several trips to Carter Lake since the news about her aunt, but she had never stepped foot into the cabin. Her scouting trips had been consumed by settling affairs with the realtors and acquainting herself with the town a couple of miles away in the valley.

Carter Lake was a modest town with only one school, one grocery store, a bank, a few diners, a gas station, and city hall. The town had grown since she was a child, but not by much. The mere presence of an ATM was a major improvement.

The cabin was quaint, sitting upon a sloping hill that crested to the right of the house. The pathway had been leveled for the convenience of the temporary tenants, but Chloe remembered a time when she had a hard time keeping her balance while making the trip from the car to the porch. But that was many years ago.

Childhood images flashed in her mind of winter afternoons spent riding a plastic trash can lid from the front steps down to the creek that bordered the cabin's property to the south. Her girlish squeals could probably be heard for miles around as she steered her makeshift toboggan around tall pines and fallen logs.

The porch had been reconstructed, the old squeaking floorboards replaced by new planks. A carved log railing with balusters now skirted the edge of the porch, where it used to be open years before, giving the cabin an even more rustic, homey feel.

Even the column supports for the second story had been replaced with brand new beams, free of carpenter bee holes and jagged cracks in the sides. The old rusted tin roof had been refreshed, too.

The second story edifice hadn't changed much, still retaining the two dormers that jutted out from the upstairs bedrooms. However, Chloe knew that behind those lacy curtained windows would be a whole new interior, much different than what she knew before.

Such improvements were necessary for safety regulations, but a part of Chloe wished that everything could have remained the same; a little piece of her family's heritage serving as a time capsule for her in this dismal hour of her life. Instead, there were only the memories of its former self to remind her of a time when she didn't have to care about anything beyond having a good time.

Things had certainly changed since she last visited in her youth. But then again, Chloe had changed a lot, too.

She fished out a single brass key from her jean's pocket and unlocked the front door. The lock was new, too, sparkling like it had been recently polished.

But she froze there, her hand gripping the cool golden knob. This shouldn't have been so scary. Chloe had faced worse things. Why should this place, an icon of her childhood, prove so terrifying?

She steeled herself, squared her shoulders, and opened the door.

Her chest squeezed tight as her dark hazel eyes surveyed the inside.

Stepping into the living room, she breathed in the earthy scent of wood and musty furniture. One thing she was glad for was the fact that the cabin came fully furnished. This was a relief, because she would have hated to ship her apartment furniture from Atlanta. She doubted a moving truck, no matter how small, would have been able to traverse the miles of winding mountain roads to make it to the cabin.

Even she had a hard time making the trek in her car. She had made a mental note earlier that she would need to get a more efficient vehicle such as a jeep or truck to get up these steep, winding turns. The idea of her, a born and bred city girl, driving a truck made her shiver. What a change.

Light streamed in through the front windows, filtered only by the gauzy curtains that framed the panels. None of the furniture was the same. The couch was no longer the vintage sofa with coarse cushions, but a piece reminiscent of cabin life with a carved log frame, much like the balusters on the front porch, lacquered to a smooth finish.

The upholstery was a dark burgundy, almost brown hue, with a throw blanket draped over the back. It was woven, depicting a moose and its offspring in the early winter forest. Chloe recognized it as something anyone could buy from Wal-Mart, not the hand-sewn quilt that her aunt had cherished as a family heirloom.

Catty-corner from the sofa was a single armchair made in the same fashion, and both were pivoted around the fireplace, the focal point of the room. Only a coffee table separated them. Underneath the living room furniture was a thick rug spread over the hardwood floor. The patterns on the rug reminded Chloe of Native American art with their symmetrical shapes and vibrant colors.

The stone hearth of the fireplace was just as she remembered. At least one thing hadn't changed. She used to spend hours sitting by the warm fire, listening to stories the adults shared and roasting marshmallows after supper.

Chloe's eye was drawn to a corner stone on the hearth that was cracked down the center. The ghost of a smile passed over her lips as she remembered how it became chipped like that. She must have been only five years old at the time, playing with the fire poker while her mother and aunt were baking in the kitchen. Chloe, though a small child, got too rowdy in her pretend game and smacked the stone, causing it to split. Her mother was furious, but her sweet aunt only laughed. She could still hear that bubbly laugh echoing in her mind.

The same stones that made the hearth also decorated the flue, climbing up the wall to the ceiling. Just above the firebox opening was the hardwood mantle, decorated with a stock photo picture frame and a stuffed black bear in the corner.

Chloe noticed that the real estate company had failed to take most of their decorations, and she was fine with that. It made the place feel a little more like home and not as barren.

Her cell phone buzzed in her pocket, shattering the stillness inside the cabin with her violin concerto ringtone. Chloe jumped at the sudden noise and fished it out to see her mother's smiling face on the screen. She bit her lips together, debating whether or not to tap the green button. If she did, it'd mean spending the next hour or two talking when she had a car to unload. Not only that, but she hadn't told her mother about this huge decision.

"Sorry, mom," she muttered. "I'm not ready to chat."

She let the call go and ignored the voicemail notification. Her mother was probably just checking on her, wanting to know if she was all right after everything that happened in Atlanta. Chloe wasn't ready to talk about that either. She needed to continue down memory lane for a little longer.

Past the living room, she could see into the cozy kitchen. The positioning of the counters and cabinets hadn't changed, but the doors had been replaced with new polished oak panels carved with leaf patterns. A small island separated the kitchen from the dining area where four spindly chairs were pushed under a matching round, mahogany table.

Straight ahead from the front door was the back door in the kitchen, leading out to the deck that overlooked the snaking creek and tall pines that hid the cabin from the rest of the world, almost in perfect isolation.

Another window illuminated the dinette area and the space between. Stairs lined the other adjacent wall, leading to the second floor.

Taking slow, deliberate steps, she ascended the stairs. The treads no longer groaned under her weight as they had before. Undoubtedly, a tenant had complained about the creaking and had the realtors fix it, just like they fixed the rest of the cabin.

The hall twisted around, leading to the only bathroom in the house and two bedrooms. The bathroom was tastefully decorated in everything black bear, whereas the bedrooms were inhabited by moose and deer; definitely a tourist rental. Chloe knew she would have to remedy this before long. She could only take so many beady eyes staring at her.

And just as she had predicted, the bedroom furniture matched the sofa and chair from downstairs. What used to be the old guest room she slept in as a child when her family visited was nothing like she remembered. The furniture was arranged differently. Unless she moved the dresser and nightstand back to where it used to be, she'd stub her toes in the dark until she became used to the new arrangement.

But she didn't have time to move anything right now. There was still a carload of luggage that she needed to bring inside. And there was also the dilemma of what she'd have for dinner. The fridge downstairs was bare, as were the cupboards.

Taking a soothing breath, she whipped out her elastic tie and pulled back her long, wavy, brown hair into a tight ponytail and then headed back downstairs.

Chloe had almost forgotten how heavy her suitcases were until she began lugging them, one by one, up to her room. She counted her blessings that there was only one flight of stairs to climb instead of four like at her apartment in Atlanta. Of course, it was easier to drag luggage down steps than up.

The job would have been easier if she had someone to help her. But Chloe was all too painfully aware of why she had no one to assist her with the move, and she didn't want to think about that now. All she wanted to think about was the chance of a new life stretching out ahead of her in the months and years to come.

She loved her cushy desk job as a receptionist at the dentist office in Atlanta, and she loved her apartment. Chloe would miss the stores, the convenience of civilization, and the great Chinese takeout. And even though her parents raised her in the big city, her heart yearned for the mountains, whether she realized it or not.

The mountains offered something that the city could never give her; the fresh air, the friendly faces, and best of all were the memories. It was the memories of fishing by the creek and hiking in the woods with her parents; the memories of campfires, crafts, and getting lost in piles of autumn leaves; the cheerful holiday vacations spent away from the hustle and bustle of city life.

Chloe berated herself for neglecting her aunt in her teenage years.

Like all teenagers, she brushed off the offers to visit family, especially if it meant being away from her friends for more than a few days. Her parents had been lenient with her in those times and let her recalcitrant attitude slide under the radar. If Chloe could have done things over again, she would have been the first one to jump in the car with her backpack filled with books and pajamas.

She would have given anything to undo all the terrible mistakes she had made in the last decade of her life. But the past was the past. It couldn't be changed. All there was left to do was to move on and learn the lessons that foolish choices had forced her to experience.

Once all of her luggage was upstairs, she sat down heavily on her mattress. Despite the cool breeze outside, a thin sheen of sweat coated her forehead. Even after stripping off her brown canvas jacket downstairs, she still got a good workout from the task. She was used to trekking up flights of apartment buildings stairs, but the added weight of all the clothes she owned was too much.

Chloe fell backward onto the downy comforter, threw her arms above her head and sighed. Now that she was still and mentally unoccupied, she finally noticed how deathly silent it was.

In the city, traffic noises were constant, only interrupted by the occasional shouting match in the apartment down the hall or car alarm going off in the parking lot. But out here, there was nothing but peace. It unnerved her at first. She never thought silence could seem so loud in her own ears.

She let her gaze wander around the vaulted ceiling. There was still unpacking to do, but it took a moment for her to fully register that the hardest part was over. All the paperwork, the move, and the flowers she left in the cemetery during the funeral were all behind her now. Now was the time for her to rebuild her life and do what she had always wanted to do. And nothing was going to hold her back anymore.

"I can't believe I'm really here," she whispered, feeling both pride and anxiety building in her chest. She had never done anything so impulsive.

Chloe had yet to tell anyone what her real motive was behind quitting her job and moving into the middle of nowhere. She knew they would all laugh and give her weird looks if she confessed she had dreams of becoming a writer.

For years, she had compiled stories and fictitious characters that had become as real to her as anyone else. They became better friends when the bottom fell out and she was suddenly alone in the world.

She never really told anyone about her secret passion. Not even her mom or her closest friends growing up knew the truth. They all just assumed she had an overactive imagination. Only her aunt, Mary Anne, saw her true potential and didn't ignore it.

Her aunt knew from the time Chloe was little that she was a natural-born storyteller. Every Christmas and birthday, she gifted Chloe boxes of books. Some were priceless and old, while others were second hand from the local bookstore in Carter Lake.

She had given away a lot of the books and had loaned many others out to unfaithful friends who had not returned them. The rest were located in her Atlanta storage unit, and she knew she would need to get them before long

She carried only one book in particular with her, nestled safely between layers of clothes inside her suitcase. It was a priceless and extremely rare copy of Mansfield Park by Jane Austen, printed in 1857. It was her most prized possession, a gift from her aunt when she turned sixteen. The pages were so delicate that Chloe didn't have the heart to open it and read the story that lay inside the cover. Instead, she purchased a brand new copy and read it while the 1857 copy lay inside its protective plastic case.

But there was still the matter of procuring a bookshelf. She couldn't find a single one in the cabin to accommodate her treasured collection.

Chloe's laptop bag sat downstairs on the sofa along with an external hard drive that contained all of her story files. Between work and other life obligations, it was hard to find time to write. But, now she could. With her aunt's trust fund to hold her over until the royalties started flooding in, she would have plenty of time to dedicate herself to the stories that had been mulling around inside her, bursting at the seams and screaming to be told to the world. Whether or not the world wanted to hear them was another matter entirely.

That thought reminded her that there was still another person who knew about her writing dreams. Brent used to talk about how the world was clamoring at her door to hear what she had to say. But, he was always saying things like that. It wasn't until later that she realized the bitter truth. Chloe would never forget the moment she woke up from the delusion she had been living for years.

That wound was still too tender to touch yet. She blinked hard and long as if to push back the unsolicited thoughts. She wouldn't think about it. Not about Brent, not about her old job, her old friends, and nothing about Atlanta. She was done with it and everything it represented to her. There was only this cabin, Carter Lake, and her stories. That's all that mattered now. Returning here may be the best decision she'd ever made. It was a new adventure.

Chloe opened her eyes and took a deep breath as if it were her first. It was clean, new, refreshing. And only then did she notice something.

Apart from the silence, there was a presence about the house. Some spiritual types might have told her it was the imprint of those who lived there before. Chloe was too grounded to believe such things. It was just the oldness of the house, the memories, and the familiar warmth of childhood that she had almost forgotten amidst the craziness of adult life.

With a stiff push, she rose from the mattress and planted herself heavily on the wooden floor. Some eerie auras weren't going to keep her from doing what needed to get done.

Chloe made her way back down to her car. Her new adventure still needed food. If her written words alone could sustain her, she would never be in want. But, her growling stomach was a good reminder that even artists needed to eat.

With the grocery list in hand, she drove down the mountain into Carter Lake. She took it slow around the twisting, hairpin turns, passing by countless different specimens of trees and shrubbery on the way. She couldn't remember if there were any wildlife in the area besides the birds, squirrels, and occasional skittish deer, but she was mindful to watch for anything that dared to dart out into the road. The last thing she wanted was a guilty conscience over a flattened turtle or squished chipmunk.

Chloe wondered how nerve racking it would be to traverse these roads at night. Checking the time, she knew she would have to set herself on a schedule to ensure she was back at the cabin before the sun began to set. Hopefully, shopping wouldn't take too long.

Once at the base of the mountain, she drove past several plots of farmland bordered by split rail fences before reaching the main road. Carter Lake quickly came into view, heralded by the old gas station that only had two vintage pumps and an old dented Coca-Cola sign hanging on the storefront. Parked at one of the pumps was a rusty truck, the bed full of hay bales and the driver dressed in dusty farm clothes.

Driving on, the rest of the town became visible.

The town only had one main street with two lanes bordered by red brick stores built at least half a century ago, if not earlier. Old advertisements for products that weren't even on the market anymore were still nailed to the sides of the buildings. Titles like "Murphy's Antiques" and "Carter Lake Hardware Store" were painted in white on the storefront windows, shadowed by the canvas awnings that fluttered in the afternoon breeze.

Only a few pedestrians sauntered along the sidewalks while she passed perhaps only four cars on her way to the grocery store on the other side of town. It was a modest establishment, nothing like the supermarkets in the big city. They sold strictly food products, but Chloe was unsure if they would have everything she needed.

She received her answer halfway through the shopping excursion. They didn't have all the big name brands that she was used to, but she found adequate substitutes. Her next fear was that someone would recognize her. Chloe hadn't been back to Carter Lake in years, but she wouldn't be surprised if someone spotted the resemblance between her and her late aunt.

Her mother always said that they looked similar, especially in the almond shape of their eyes combined with her sharp nose and cheekbones. Flattering friends said she would have made a great model if she were skinny enough. But Chloe loved food too much to live such a lifestyle. And for that, her mother was grateful. Chloe wasn't overweight by any means, but she wasn't a fragile twig of a woman, either. She had curves in all the right places, which made it a little difficult to shop for jeans sometimes.

While perusing the canned foods aisle, she heard it.

"Ma'am?" a gentle voice came from behind her.

Chloe wanted to lean against her cart handle and pretend she didn't hear anything as she hurried along. But, that was the old Chloe—not the new Chloe who was a writer. Running from people wasn't an option anymore. The voice didn't belong to someone she had wronged, and there was no need to fear it. No one in this town would insult her or give her dirty looks for no reason.

She straightened and turned to see who was speaking.

A slender, elderly woman stood there, clad in a brilliantly colored flower dress that reached down to her knees, holding a hand basket in front of her. The woman's silver hair was pulled back into a bun, but small tendrils had escaped and framed her wrinkled face. She had the clearest blue eyes Chloe had seen on a woman so old. She must have been a knockout in her younger days.

"Excuse me, but are you new in town?" she asked, her slow, thick southern drawl gracing Chloe's ears like a timeless lullaby. It reminded her so much of her aunt's accent and the one her mother had all but lost after moving to the big city decades ago.

Chloe nodded and put on her kindest, most genuine smile. "Yes, ma'am. I just got settled in today." Her own accent was faint, not near as heavy as this old woman's.

The woman peered at her, bright red lips tightening into a thin line. "You look strangely familiar."

There it was. Her whole new adventure may have just been ruined. Chloe had never been good at lying, so she might as well come out with it. "My aunt used to live here a few years ago. Mary Anne Hilton."

The old woman's face lit up, making her suddenly appear a decade younger. "You're Mary Anne's niece? I thought I recognized you. I saw you at the funeral, but before that the last time I saw you, you were yay high." She held out one of her bony hands to about her hip level to emphasize her point.

"You'll have to forgive me if I don't recognize you," Chloe replied, maintaining her pleasant grin.

The lady gave her a dismissive wave and shook her head. "No, no. I wouldn't expect you to. Your aunt and I used to play cards together years ago before Mary Anne got too old to make that trip up and down the mountain." She offered her hand to Chloe. "My name's Rosie."

Chloe gingerly took her hand and shook it, careful not to crush Rosie's fragile bones in her grip. "I'm Chloe. But, I guess you knew that already."

The wrinkles around Rosie's eyes deepened with her smile. "Yes, I remember. So, where are you staying?"

Their hands dropped and Chloe nervously slid hers into her jean pockets, fiddling with an old paperclip she had never bothered to take out. "At my aunt's cabin. I inherited it from her."

It seemed a bit morbid to take pride in the fact that she was now living in her deceased aunt's home, but somehow the excitement of having a place to call her own overshadowed the sadness of losing her relative. Not only that, but the cabin would stay in the family for at least one more generation.

Rosie's expression suddenly shifted from merry to wary. "Really? Do you like it up there?"

Chloe was a little disconcerted by such a question but only shrugged. "It's OK so far. The real estate office was nice enough to leave all the furniture in there, so I didn't have to bring my furniture from Atlanta."

Rose inclined her head, eyebrows raised as if she were trying to have a serious talk with a child. "But, do you like it?"

A frown formed between Chloe's eyes as she tried to decipher the old woman's question. "I haven't spent a lot of time in there to really form a good opinion yet."

Rosie nodded and made a sound in her throat like Chloe's answer was satisfactory. "Well, just be careful up there."

Chloe wanted to attribute this behavior as mere eccentricity, but there was something in the cryptic warning that intrigued her.

"Why?" Chloe asked. "I used to spend a lot of time up there as a kid. Is there something wrong with the house?"

"Not really." Rosie didn't seem convinced by her own admission. "Just, every time I went up there, I never felt safe—like the house was haunted or something."

Out of respect for her elders, Chloe did not roll her eyes like she wanted. Perhaps this old woman really was eccentric. She was a friend of her aunt's after all. Part of her wanted to keep an open mind for a potential friendship with this old woman. The other part wanted to bid her a good day and keep rolling through the grocery store.

She gave Rosie an encouraging smile and shook her head. "I can assure you, it's not haunted. I understand it was a pretty popular spot for vacationers. The real estate office was sad to give it up."

Rose leaned in, her voice dropping a bit. "They were probably sad to see it go because they were concerned for your safety."

Chloe was growing impatient and a little offended. There was nothing wrong with her aunt's house, and there was certainly nothing to worry about. There were no ghosts, no spirits, and no monsters hiding under the bed. Even as a child, as perceptive as children normally are, she felt nothing when in that cabin; nothing but happiness anyway. However, she would indulge the woman. It had been a long time since she'd had a lengthy conversation with anyone that hadn't involved her late aunt's affairs. And, despite the fact that their discussion was less than sensible, she wasn't willing to cut it short just yet.

"Did the renters complain about something?"

"Not that I've been told."

"I'm sure it's just how old the cabin is. If it was good enough for my aunt to will it to me, then she must have been certain that it was safe enough to live in."

Rosie heaved a sigh and nodded. "I suppose. But, if you find that house is too much for you, take my advice and have it torn down or condemned."

Torn down? Condemned? She couldn't be serious. The home was a piece of Carter Lake history. It might have been one of the first homes built in the area, and she had the gall to suggest she demolish it just because of a little creepy feeling? Chloe didn't want to despise this woman for her late aunt's sake, but Rosie was slowly crawling up her long list of people with whom she'd rather not associate.

Chloe flashed another fake smile. "I surely will, Miss Rosie."

After a cordial invitation to a game of Bridge the following Tuesday night, the two ladies parted ways, and Chloe continued her shopping trip.

With every step across the white tiled floor of the grocery store, Rosie's words floated back to her. What did she see in the cabin that Chloe and her aunt didn't? Or more specifically, what her entire family didn't.

Before the cabin was in her aunt's possession, it belonged to her grandparents and her great-grandparents and their grandparents before them. Though the last name changed a few times, Chloe was a descendant from one of the founders of Carter Lake. Somewhere in the attic were old land deed documents, photo albums, and memorabilia that her aunt had cautioned the real estate company not to leave undisturbed. Chloe knew she would need to take a visit up to the place she was never permitted to go as a child and see if a reason lay there.

Chloe couldn't help but feel a fiery indignation for the suggestion to take down the home. She knew Rosie meant well by it, but burning down the place that had become her refuge was the last thing she wanted to do. She'd sooner move back to Atlanta than see her childhood memories get blown to bits or torn down board by board.

She drove back up the mountain, nearly panicking every time her tires spun on the roads. Finding herself once again parked in front of the cabin with her backseat packed with groceries, she took a long hard look at what was now her home.

Even in the orange glow of the sunset, the cabin was the picture of peace. She could faintly hear singing birds in the surrounding woods, mingled in with the rustling of the autumn wind through the trees that towered over the property. She squinted her eyes against the harsh golden glare of the tin roof, but otherwise the house was unimposing.

She hated to think it, but maybe Rosie was just blowing smoke. Chloe had never heard about the cabin being haunted until Rosie mentioned it. It was completely possible that Rosie was either senile or simply mistaken. Maybe this wasn't even the cabin she was talking about, but somewhere else on the mountain and she was confused.

Chloe scolded herself for being the least bit worried about it in the first place and hurried to get her groceries inside. Tonight, she'd have a simple meal of spaghetti using her mother's famous sauce recipe and sit down for as long as she could keep her eyes open to continue writing her first story.

As she stirred the noodles, her mind buzzed with the words she would say first. How would she grab her future readers? With an action scene? Dialogue? Maybe a dream or just skip right to when her characters meet for the first time. Every story she had ever thought of was always a love story. Her thoughts were consumed by nothing else.

Even as a child, she dreamed of her handsome prince coming to sweep her off her feet and whisper gentle words of love and affection. While most girls were forming the "No Boys" club, she was daydreaming about new crushes in school.

It took a few years for her friends to catch onto the boy craze, but it was worth it to have others with her swooning over buff football players and young handsome teachers. She spent many weekends giggling at slumber parties when she could have been here at the cabin with her family.

Quite ironic, actually, that she of all people would think herself an authority on romance. Out of all the crushes she'd had, and all the unrequited loves she fawned after, only one man ever bothered to return her affections. And it had turned out disastrously.

Memories flared up, ones of an afternoon spent in the park and late evening dinners in her apartment. She could see his brown eyes smiling back at her. But then, the memories turned sour and a handsome face morphed into a scowl. Spiteful words echoed in her ears once more, words that she never wanted to hear again, words that she wanted to forget.

Chloe shook her head and took a steadying breath to fight back the tears that gathered at the corners of her eyes. New life, new adventure, new Chloe, and no more Atlanta. She hoped it wouldn't be this hard when she actually started writing.

Sitting down at the little writing desk under the stairs, Chloe set up her laptop as the meat sauce began to simmer. The real estate company had never hooked up the cabin with internet service, but Chloe was able to use her mobile hot-spot to check her email. Nothing was there, as she had suspected. She wasn't expecting anyone to contact her for anything. But it was worth the time to check at least.

Chloe plugged in her hard drive and scrolled through the dozens of folders marked with novel titles that were waiting for her. Character profiles, plot outlines, and picture resources swam before her eyes, and she couldn't help but grin and squeal like a child. It was all too exciting.

With a plate of steaming spaghetti next to her mouse, she opened up a fresh word document and began.

Chapter 2

The morning sun slanted through the thinly curtained windows of Chloe's bedroom. Bathing the room in a golden glow that she wasn't used to after living for so long in the big city. She rolled over under her silky comforter and stretched her arms high above her head, letting out a tired groan as her eyes took in the room in all its chaos.

Suitcases were piled haphazardly in the empty corner of the room, and the clothes she had worn from the day before were strewn across the woven rug at the foot of the bed. She'd only had enough energy last night to strip and change into her flannel pajamas before collapsing on the mattress.

Her sleep wasn't anywhere near long enough, but there was a feeling of contentment in her gut when she closed her eyes, knowing that she had accomplished a lot the evening before. She had managed to crank out three chapters before her mind refused to form the right words for a scene.

It took a moment for her to remember where she was as she surveyed the tongue-and-groove wood walls and ceiling that boxed her in. She wondered how long it would take for her to get used to her new surroundings. Days? Weeks? Months? Would it ever truly feel like home?

Then a feeling settled in that was unwelcoming. It was something she'd been able to fight off for weeks. With all the business of the move and settling her aunt's affairs, she'd had no time to feel lonely. But now, lying in her bed, knowing that she was miles away from another living soul, she felt it all too keenly—that aching in her core that longed for the presence of someone else. It was enough to knock the very breath from her lungs.

Chloe never gave a second thought to the fact she would be living alone with not so much as one neighbor to rely on for company. She should have been used to such loneliness in Atlanta. The week preceding her aunt's death had been nothing but loneliness. But at least she still had her job and a place she could go to hear human voices.

Out here, there was nothing but birds and squirrels. Perhaps now would be as good a time as any to get a pet; a dog, or perhaps a longhaired cat, to talk to and take care of. Her apartment had strict rules regarding pets, but Chloe was no longer under such restrictions.

Her troubled heart began to take comfort in the notion that perhaps a farmer down in the valley was trying to get rid of a litter of puppies. That would surely cure her loneliness.

She let out a tight breath and struggled to push herself up. Before she went scouting for a companion, she would need her morning cup of coffee. The familiarity of her favorite blend would make this cabin her own as its aroma filled the air.

Chloe threw back the blankets but recoiled the moment her bare feet touched the freezing floor. She had been accustomed to carpeted floors that were the perfect temperature, no matter the season.

After slipping her feet into some socks, she ventured downstairs to the kitchen, her mind still a bit foggy with sleep.

The same warm sunlight beamed through the downstairs as it did upstairs with only the shapeless shadows of the trees to hinder it. Chloe made her way to the kitchen and mechanically started the coffee maker with the only thought in her mind that she needed to wake up. She filled up the pot a little more than usual, knowing that she would need more caffeine than normal. If she played it right, she'd make the brew last all day.

The water in the appliance began to boil as she started up the slightly used electric stove. Placing a cast iron pan coated with oil on the eye, she pulled out two eggs to scramble from the fridge.

It was when she closed the fridge that she first noticed it. By her computer was her yellow notepad that she used to jot down random notes. Last night she didn't write anything on it at all, but Chloe could faintly see a few sentences scrawled out in neat, almost perfect cursive penmanship between the lines at the top of the page.

Chloe froze as panic flooded her body, gripping her chest like a vice. The oil in the frying pan sizzled in the background, and the coffee pot chimed from the far counter, but she hardly heard them. Her vision zoomed in on the note as her hands began to shake. She was more awake now than she had been in days.

She hurried to the notepad, her weak legs tingling with sudden fatigue, each step feeling heavier and heavier. The chair creaked loudly as she dropped into the seat, letting her eyes pour over the carefully scripted words.

Your beginning was acceptable. However, the descriptions were obscure, lacking flair that adequately paints the scene. You should consider revising. I am interested to see if Mr. Johnson will pursue Miss Alleia after such a rude introduction. Also, there are several spelling errors that will need your attention during the final editing. Because of the sheer number of mistakes, it would be more efficient to correct them now, rather than later.

A critique? The note was critiquing her story? Chloe snatched at the mouse to activate her laptop screen. The open document of her story appeared at the exact place she had left it the night before.

Who left the note? Who was in my house?

Glancing back down to the notepad, she saw that they didn't sign the bottom.

Chloe checked the front door and found the knob was still locked. The same was true for the back door in the kitchen.

She ran and checked her purse. Credit cards, keys, driver's license and checks were all still there, not even her pack of gum or expired library card were missing. There were no televisions in the house and the only thing of any value was the laptop, which they obviously didn't take.

None of the windows looked to be damaged or even opened. She checked the driveway and saw the car was still parked there. And from what she could tell, it hadn't been disturbed, either.

The stench of burnt oil snapped her out of her frenzy long enough to take the pan off of the stove. Suddenly, she had no appetite.

Chloe sat down in the chair and read the critique again. Her first initial reaction was pure panic that someone had broken into her home. But, there was absolutely no sign of such a thing. She hadn't checked the upstairs yet, but she had the feeling that she would find nothing there, either. She was a light sleeper, and if someone had decided to sneak in through an upstairs window, she would have heard it.

This childhood place that she had loved for years, the place she thought she would have been safest from the outside world, had been violated. Someone had tread upon her sacred ground, and there was nothing she could do about it. All she wanted was a little solitude, time to regroup and start on this new life she had dreamed of. But now, as she looked around, all she could feel was the pounding of her terrified heart screaming out for peace and answers.

This feeling of helplessness was exactly what she had wanted to escape; the feeling that maybe, even now, some hungry predator was watching her, waiting for a chance to steal her money, her possessions, her life, and her peace. She had already had so much taken from her in the last few months. Why else did she possibly have left that they would want?

Her second thought was about the note itself. Did they really read what she had written so far? So the beginning was fine, but there were all these other errors to fix? She felt as if she had already submitted her work to a publisher and had it torn to pieces. But, whoever it was had voiced their interest in the story, so she couldn't have been doing too badly.

Chloe chided herself that she would even care about the opinions of this trespasser. She should call the police and get a security system set up for her home. She should panic at the very thought of a stranger walking through her home while she slept, rummaging through her laptop and God only knew what else.

She knew one thing; sitting here and fretting was not the way to handle this situation. She had to act, but she also knew that she couldn't call the police. They probably wouldn't come on such a crazy request and a security company couldn't risk losing one of their vans going up those steep slopes.

After taking a quick survey of the windows and rooms upstairs, she discovered that nothing had been touched, and the windows were still intact. Chloe put the eggs back in their carton, turned the stove off, and made her first cup of coffee to go, her hands trembling the entire time. It was a shock to her that she could pour her coffee without spilling it all over the counter.

She had seen a hardware store in town and it would be a sorry excuse for a store if they didn't have locks. Leaving the note where it was, she dressed in a pair of comfortable jeans and long-sleeved, navy blue shirt, grabbed her purse and headed out the door with her mug in hand.

Chloe inspected the outside of the house and found nothing to support her fears that someone had broken into her home without her knowledge. Below the house was what she perceived as decorative stone walls to conceal the support beams so the house could sit so precariously on the side of the hill.

Now, more than ever, she wished she could read the ground like a hunter or trapper could. She'd be able to tell if anyone had wandered around outside the house by the broken twigs or disturbed grass.

Chloe slid into her car and pulled away from the cabin, sipping her scalding coffee. She realized a little too late that she had completely forgotten to put sugar and cream in with her morning wake-up juice, but she wouldn't bother with that now.

Taking one last glance at the cabin in the rearview mirror, she breathed a quick prayer that it would be safe against mountain prowlers and sped on into Carter Lake.

On her quick trip to the hardware store, she purchased a brand new set of locks for the cabin. Killing two birds with one stone, she found that the owner of the store was selling a jeep and arranged a trade to be made with her car. They were to settle the transaction sometime later that week, but scratching one more thing off of Chloe's to-do list helped calm her tremendously.

In an effort to eliminate one possible theory of who this intruder might have been, she called the real estate office. No one had been up to the property since she moved in. Another dead end and she still had no answers.

Angling out of the car with her hardware store purchase, she walked up to the front porch and listened. After peeking through the windows and satisfying herself that no one was currently in the home, she went inside and set to the task of installing the new locks.

Nearly three hours later, the new door knobs, deadbolts and door bars were mounted to the best of her limited abilities. She had even purchased swivel locks for the old windows. No one was going to get in that house without her knowing it.

While she fixed herself a sizable lunch, half starving since she hadn't taken the time to eat breakfast that morning, the mysterious note caught her eye once more.

Chloe let her eyes skim over the suggestions again as she bit into her turkey sandwich, already contemplating the changes she would need to make to the manuscript to accommodate this intruder's critique.

Part of her wanted to wad up the note and burn it. It was another reminder of what had happened the night before. But the other part of her wanted to savor the note. It was the first real piece of advice she had ever received regarding her writing. It gave her hope that perhaps her calling really was to become a writer.

Her imagination wandered as she began to imagine who this burglar was. Obviously, they were not illiterate, judging by the eloquent wording of the letter. And they had a solid grasp of literary concepts of what was good storytelling and what wasn't. But was it a woman? A man? Were they in her house to steal something and got distracted by the writing? Why were they there at all?

Chloe sat on the couch, note in hand, and read it a hundred times before finally setting it down and returning to her computer. She'd apply the changes and continue. With luck, the new locks would keep out any other unwanted literary critics.

Chapter 3

Chloe awoke late the next morning, after spending half the night writing. Her lower back felt sore from hunching over her laptop keyboard, and her neck was still stiff. Regardless, she slid out of bed with her feet already clad in warm wool. But despite this extra measure toward comfort, the air inside the cabin was chillier than she had expected.

Having not taken the time to put away her things yet, Chloe hobbled towards a suitcase in the corner of the room and pulled out a plush cream-colored robe that she'd owned for many years. It was a birthday gift from her parents when she was a teenager. The hem of the garment used to drag the ground, but now in her adult years, it tickled the back of her calves. Wrapping it around her shoulders, she ran her fingers over the velvety fabric.

She took a quick survey of her belongings, making sure that everything was accounted for, and then turned to go downstairs. Her heavy footfalls on the treads were the only sound in the house that morning. Not even the usual warbling of the wood thrushes and blue jays could be heard twittering outside.

Glancing towards the living room windows, she saw the sun was already pretty high in the sky. It was no longer time for breakfast, but for lunch. But, regardless of the time, she would have her cup of coffee. Because despite sleeping in, she knew there was a long day ahead of her, filled with plans to write and maybe go look for that puppy she was thinking about the previous morning.

Her eyes shifted toward her desk on her way to the kitchen, and her heart jumped against her ribcage as she saw more writing on her notepad.

Another letter. This one was longer.

Chloe was jolted awake once more, just as she had been the day before. The disquieting thought rammed through her sleepy head that the locks hadn't worked.

Without taking the time yet to read the letter, she checked the windows and the doors. Again, there was no sign of forced entry.

Chloe's eyebrows furrowed as she thought it over. With the locks on the two doors, there was no way the intruder could have broken in, written that note, and then returned the locks to their original positions on their way out. The same went for the windows. How were they getting inside?

She sighed heavily and ran a set of long nails through her dark wavy hair, snagging on a few tangles at the back of her head. There was nothing she could do about it now. Perhaps there was nothing she could do to prevent this from happening time and time again.

Shuffling to her desk, she sat down and read the perfect cursive writing, feeling mixed emotions as her eyes followed the words.

I thought you would never go to sleep. I do not appreciate waiting. Next time, do us both a favor and get to sleep at an earlier time.

Chloe's jaw dropped. Had they been watching her the whole night? They knew when she was still up writing? A cold chill ran up her spine at the thought of someone spying on her. Wrapping the robe around her chest a little tighter, she continued.

As for your manuscript, I noticed you made the changes I suggested. Excellent work. You have a firm grasp of dialogue composition. Their conversations are believable. But, I do suggest that you avoid writing from the male point of view. This is not meant as an offense to you, but you obviously do not understand the inner workings of the male mind. As a writer, if you narrate strictly from the female's perspective, you will sound more competent in the genre you have chosen. Nonetheless, your story is coming along just fine. I look forward to reading more. Yours sincerely – G

Chloe was stunned. She leaned against the slatted back of the chair and stared dumbly at the wall.

She didn't know what to think. Whoever this was had noticed the changes as well as read through the additions she made the day before. Not only that, but they commended her for it and exonerated her dialogue style. She took no offense to their comment about writing from the male point of view. It was difficult and uncomfortable to put herself inside the male brain and try to figure out how their thought process worked. It had always been something of an impossible task, and she took no joy in it.

Deducing from that comment alone, she assumed her mystery correspondent must be a man. Why else would he be so knowledgeable on how the male mind does or does not work?

If she adhered to this instruction, there were many changes she'd have to make to the story. There were several scenes with only her male protagonist present and his thoughts on the female. She'd have to change the whole book to an omnipresent perspective if she wanted to keep those scenes. But wasn't that pretty much the same thing she was already doing?

Chloe groaned and held her head in her hands, propping her elbows on her closed laptop. She hated herself for taking these notes so seriously. The thought that a complete stranger was somehow breaking into her home, just to write these silly critiques, was far from her mind. All she could think about was obeying the suggestions as if his opinion was valid and worth her consideration.

Then it occurred to her that she wasn't writing for this stranger. She was writing for herself. Why did she have to change her entire story just to accommodate him, of all people? A stranger she had never met and was forcing his way into her home somehow without any trace or reason.

She sighed and thought that maybe a cup of coffee would help clear her head.

Chloe brewed her usual blend, generously stirring in cream and sugar to offset the bitterness. She'd been drinking coffee for years, but there was something different about this cup. The coffee from the previous morning got thrown out after growing cold in her car while she was in the hardware store. Chloe didn't care for the blackness of the raw brew anyway. And in the heat of writing, she never poured herself another cup.

But the tawny liquid swirling around in her bright green mug had a special appeal to it. It would be the first cup of coffee she drank in her new home. Perhaps it was a way of christening her new life. This cup of coffee would be the first of many she drank in the cabin. Chloe could already see herself a few years older, drinking coffee while looking over her royalty reports from all the books she'd published.

Gripping the warm ceramic mug in her hands, she moved to the window that overlooked the back deck and forest beyond. The sun warmed her skin, seeping through her pajamas to warm her very soul.

The mountains were a beautiful place. She'd been a fool as a child to not want to escape from the big city. Chloe was glad she had seen the light and made the decision to come back. Often times she wondered what made her decide to return to her ancestral home. Was it really to write or an excuse to flee Atlanta and all the things she hated about the city? But she didn't want to think of that now and spoil the serenity of the late morning scenery.

A soft, contented smile crept across her lips as she watched the still woods. Just beyond, she could see the glittering waters of the creek where she had spent many happy hours as a child.

Why was she still inside?

Without a second thought, she slipped on the pair of boots she had left by the door for just this occasion. There was no time to change into more suitable clothes for walking around in the woods. The wilderness was beckoning her to return to that special place in her memories. Just for a moment, she'll be the old Chloe again; the one with bright eyes and an imagination as big as the mountain this cabin sat upon, the Chloe before puberty consumed her and the hardships of life broke her down.

Stepping outside with her coffee in hand, nature contradicted itself. The sun still shone down bright and warm, but the chilly wind whipped at her long, slept-in hair and seeped through the fibers of her robe to give her skin momentary goose bumps. It took her a while to get used to such contrasting effects. But her flesh warmed and the breeze felt good upon her brow.

She nearly slipped on some fallen autumn leaves after stepping off the deck, but she gained her footing quickly and continued down to the creek with an eagerness she hadn't felt in years, leaving behind the confusing mess she had somehow gotten herself into with her mysterious literary critic and the notes he left for her.

She left a path of crumbled dead leaves in her wake as she approached the creek. Chloe heard the trickling sound of ice-cold spring water cascading over the smooth stones, and she stood on the creek bank and watched as the sun shimmered in the rippling tide. It was just as she remembered it. The town may have changed, the cabin changed, but this creek was timeless and untouched.

Just below the crystal-clear surface of the water, Chloe spotted schools of little fish fighting against the current to travel upstream. A turtle basked upon a protruding rock just a little distance from where she stood on the shore.

If she weren't wearing her favorite robe, she would have sat down on a nearby log or squatted in the rich, damp soil to watch the water break against the rocks further upstream. The creek wasn't deep enough to swim in, but she remembered a time when she'd take her shoes and socks off, roll up the legs of her jeans and wade into the shallows.

Chloe still remembered how it felt to have the cool current flow past her, wrapping around her ankles, and how the mix of prickly and smooth rocks felt on the tender undersides of her feet. She'd have to come back and do that one day. Maybe every day. But not right now. There was too much going on right now.

Taking a sip of her coffee, she watched as two birds flitted and twirled around each other in the open space above the creek. They chirped a few times and then disappeared into the branches. Chloe swallowed, letting the warm liquid wash down her throat. Was there anything more tranquil in all existence?

The scenery did wonders for her nerves. She was able to think clearly, more rationally.

Maybe there was a friend of Aunt Mary Anne's who lived on the mountain near the cabin that was delivering these notes and sneaking in. They could have seen Chloe move in and were curious. But where was that secret entrance into the cabin? Then again, she saw no other driveways on her way up the mountain, and her cabin's driveway was at a dead end. If there was any other way up or around the mountain, she didn't know of it.

Somehow, in the train of reasoning, Chloe thought of Rosie's warning. When they met in the grocery store the other day, she mentioned that something was wrong with the house; that it was haunted.

Chloe was a grounded person. She didn't believe in ghosts, spirits, or paranormal phenomenon of any kind. But the more her mind played Miss Rosie's words, mixed in with all that had happened in the last two days and the uncanny presence she felt in the cabin, the more she began to wonder if there was some validity to what she was saying.

Maybe the reason there was no evidence of a break-in was because there wasn't any break-in to begin with. Whoever or whatever was leaving her the notes lingered somewhere in the house, unseen and undetected. It was an absurd theory, but what else could it be? Locks were still intact, nothing was stolen, and she now had two letters written to her from some anonymous critic. She took that back. The critic was not anonymous. He signed his name with a "G". G for Ghost? It was ridiculous all around.

But in the silence of nature, Chloe came up with an idea. She would debunk this haunted myth and play along.

Hiking back up to the house, she began to mentally form the words she needed.

Chloe took the last swig of coffee, set it down in the sink and then hurried to the notepad. She would beat this ghost at his own game.

Grabbing the big yellow notepad, she sat on the couch, pen in hand and began to formulate her response to his second letter.

Mr. G,

Thank you for the advice. I am struggling with putting myself into Ben Johnson's shoes. But how can I change the whole perspective of the story now? If I change it to strictly the female's perspective, I lose a lot of scenes I had planned for later in the story when only Ben is present. Might you have a suggestion to remedy this problem? If so, I'd love to hear it. If not, I might as well scrap this story and be done with it. I have plenty more I can start writing. If you've poked around on my laptop, as I suspect you have, you'll see all of the folders on my hard drive just waiting to be started. I'm glad you have enjoyed it so far, though. You may feel privileged to know that you are the first person to ever read my work, let alone like it. I hope to hear from you in the morning.

Your resident aspiring author, Chloe

P.S. Forgive my terrible handwriting; it's chicken-scratch compared to yours.

Chloe sat back and examined the letter. Perhaps it was too light, maybe a little teasing, but it would have to do. She had no confidence that she would receive a response. And if it was, she didn't know how she would react. She wasn't sure what exactly it proved. That she was crazy?

She didn't want to think about that right now. She still had plenty to do, but none of it included writing. She didn't want to continue writing if she'd just have to scrap the story in the end, if Mr. G suggested it.

There were still plenty of her things left in Atlanta that she needed to pull from storage and a man to call in Carter Lake about a jeep.

Chapter 4

A smile pulled across his face as he read Chloe's reply to his letter. He had never imagined that she would be so receptive to his criticism. And never had he felt such joy; the first hint of it in years. Decades

It had been a sheer gamble to write at all. No one knew he was here, and he didn't want to risk such a relatively peaceful existence just for the chance to communicate with someone he barely knew. Actually, he knew her quite well. He knew her father, her mother, her grandmother, and so many others who had passed through this house. Though, except for one instance, he had never revealed himself.

There was so much that could go wrong; so much to somehow explain if this simple correspondence grew into something more. He wondered if he would have the nerve to stand so openly in front of her, disclosing his identity. He had done it once, but could he do it again?

But when he realized how much raw, unpolished talent she possessed, he had to reach out to her. A letter was the most subtle way, at least for now.

Though he had not heard her voice in years, he could somehow imagine how adulthood had changed it. He could tell simply through reading her reply. It was light, but not too airy; husky, yet with a playful bounce as was evident in the way she casually teased him about his handwriting. It was not flirting, but it tugged at something within him that he hadn't felt in a very long time.

He lifted his head and listened to her steady breathing coming from one of the upstairs bedrooms. How he would love to meet her now, to see if his preconceived impression of her held any truth. He hadn't even seen her face yet, but already he felt captivated. He didn't want to think that it was because she was the first bit of excitement that had walked through those cabin doors in so long. If her writing style was any reflection of her personality, he wanted to know her more than he wanted anything else.

He turned his gaze down to the notepad and penned his reply, carefully wording it so that she may not be frightened by what he had to offer. There was a fine line between the two of them—one that he dared not cross. Not yet.

Holding the third letter from the mysterious Mr. G, Chloe thought she would have gotten used to seeing the beautiful cursive letters waiting for her in the morning. But her nerves failed her now, just as they had the first two times. This man, ghost, thing... was no physical threat to her, but she was terrified nonetheless.

Dearest Chloe,

It takes great courage for an author to say they struggle with writing. If you had replied with anything else, I would have thought you prideful and too inept to continue this book. In contrast, I say that you should not discard the novel. It has a strong start and deserves a strong finish. I did not previously see your numerous manuscript folders, but after taking a peek through each of them, I believe you made a fair choice in beginning this story as opposed to the others.

To address your aforementioned concern about telling the story from a different perspective, I can understand your dilemma. If those scenes with Ben Johnson truly matter to you, I would gladly offer my services as a ghostwriter. This way, you can continue the story from Rebecca's point of view, and I will substitute for Ben. If this compromise agrees with you, we can start immediately. You need only to stop and write a note to let me know you are ready for me to take over. I have also read through the plot outline you constructed, so I can follow the storyline fluidly. You'll find that no editing is necessary for my part. I will do my own.

And thank you. I do feel privileged to be your first audience. I sincerely hope you have many more.

At your service, G

P.S. Your handwriting is indeed deplorable, but readable.

Chloe sat there, trying in vain to remain calm. Her lips twitched violently in an attempt to smile, but she wouldn't allow herself.

Last night as she fell asleep, she had hoped that he would agree to scratch the story and move on to something different. It would have been the easiest option and one that she almost preferred. Instead, he was offering to go out of his way and help her with the novel.

How could she possibly credit him for his work? It would throw her readers off if the dedication page listed her aunt, parents, and English teachers, and then at the very bottom of the paragraph say, "Oh, yeah. And thanks to that ghost in the cabin who wrote the guy parts for me. Great help, Mr. G!"

No publisher in their right mind would accept such a thing in one of their books.

The ridiculous became real as Chloe sat there, racking her brain, trying to find a more logical explanation for this. Now in possession of three letters, she still had no clue as to this man's identity. She wasn't even sure if he was a real man or a ghost. Or were they the same?

Chloe shook her head, and tangled locks of hair tumbled against her flushed cheeks. She must be losing her mind. Nothing else could explain this. She wasn't even in the cabin for a week and already the isolation was getting to her.

She set the letters on the coffee table and then let her eyes wander over the numerous boxes that crowded the wooden floor. They were filled with books and other personal belongings from the storage unit. That job had been tedious, to say the least, cramming the boxes into the back of her sedan, filling it to the brim. Chloe managed to make them all fit, but she still had no bookcase. She resolved that they would just have to remain packed away until something could be made to hold them, but she dreaded the task of hauling them upstairs just yet.

After letting out a great yawn, Chloe shambled into the kitchen for her coffee, and perhaps this morning she would have some breakfast.

As she heated up the oil in the frying pan for scrambled eggs and let her coffee pot brew, Chloe caught herself mulling over Mr. G's offer.

It would sure be a help to her if he wrote the part for Ben. She never understood the male mind, not even when she was with Brent. His very name still sent her heart and mind into a dizzying turmoil that was hard to pull out of.

Not having to worry about those bits of the story that terrified her would make writing this novel so much easier. And the easier it was to write, the quicker it could be finished. Then, of course, the sooner she could send it off to a publisher.

Ben's parts were just about half of the book anyway. And if Mr. G could write a chapter a night, and if she could write a chapter a day, it'd be done in no time. Sure, there was still the task of editing, but the hard part would be done.

Chloe felt like a fool to be thinking of such things. But she couldn't pour enough of herself into making a simple batch of scrambled eggs to forget about the letters and the strange affair altogether.

She ate breakfast and sat down at her writing desk to work, but the words just wouldn't flow. Her creativity was clogged by her bizarre correspondence with Mr. G. But what else was there to do but write? She brought no movies with her, she still didn't have a fast Internet connection to stream her favorite Food Network shows, and God knows there was nothing to do in town.

She had already taken care of a lot of business the previous day. She emptied the storage unit in Atlanta and after unloading her car, she traded it with the hardware store clerk for the jeep she had seen the other day. It was now parked outside the cabin, and she hadn't had to pay any extra except for the documentation fees that she settled with the DMV the afternoon before.

Bobby's wife was tired of the bulky jeep and wanted something nicer to drive through town. The trade was a blessing for both of them. Bobby had a happy wife, and Chloe had a car that could handle the mountain terrain.

The rest of the previous evening was spent putting her clothes away and moving her bedroom furniture around to her liking. Besides the books, there was nothing else to sort or organize. And there was certainly nothing to clean yet. She'd only been there a few days and for once, she was careful not to let dirty dishes pile up in the sink.

She stared at the new blank chapter and sighed. Maybe a shower would do the trick. She could wash away everything that was bothering her and start fresh.

She came out of the bathroom smelling sweetly of magnolias, her hair in a wet tangle down her back. But, even after a steamy bath, it changed nothing. She still felt confused, paranoid, and a little like she was losing her marbles through the cracks in the floorboards.

She lay in bed clad in her bath towel and stared at the ceiling as if it held all the answers she needed. In that moment, more than ever, she wished that her aunt were still with her today.

Aunt Mary Anne never had the perfect words to say, but she was a comforting presence, like a second mother or young grandmother. When Chloe was upset over something silly, she offered a turkey sandwich or chocolate sweets. It was a superficial response to a troubled child, but it worked. After guzzling down so much chocolate that she felt sick, Chloe completely forgot what she had been worried about.

Her aunt spoiled her, plain and simple. But the older she became, the more a perfectly made sandwich did not look so much like a Band-Aid anymore. It was a cure-all for inadequate childcare. Maybe that's why her family stopped taking so many trips to the mountains.

It seemed like every other weekend was spent at the cabin until she was about halfway through junior high, and then her family stopped going for nearly a year. By the time her mother was ready to visit her sister again, Chloe wasn't interested in spending a weekend in a place that didn't have cable.

Chloe remembered asking her mother why they couldn't visit Aunt Mary Anne one weekend before the attraction of sleepovers became too much to resist.

Her mother's response was that Aunt Mary Anne was too busy. But as time went by, Chloe caught tail ends of phone conversations and heated discussions between her parents.

She heard things like "Mary Anne has lost her mind" and "Mary Anne can't be serious about this". It was only when they stopped talking about her that Chloe's mother decided to visit again.

Looking back now, it must have been out of pity rather than a genuine desire to visit. Chloe wondered if Rosie felt the same way about Mary Anne's sanity. That card game night was coming up soon. Maybe she'd go just to talk to the old woman about her dearly departed aunt and discover what was going on.

Even as an adult, she didn't know the full details of why her aunt was put into an assisted living home. Whether she checked herself into the home down in Savannah was another mystery entirely. Did it have something to do with the hushed whispers behind closed doors and the rumor that this cabin was haunted?

Lying in bed, letting the dampness of her hair soak her feather pillow, she began to feel the loneliness harder than ever. She knew that living out in the middle of nowhere was going to be very different than living in the city, but she never imagined that it would be this different. She had no friends to call up for a chat, no work to eat up most of her day, no exciting new restaurant or store to visit in town. All she had was this cabin and Mr. G.

The ache in her chest didn't ease at the thought of her resident ghost again. He only came around at night when she was asleep. A lot of good that did her now. It was still a long while to go until the sun went down and even then, he never appeared to her.

In the meantime, she could initiate her own investigation.

She didn't know much about the supernatural, but from what she understood, a ghost was a spirit of a dead person that did not move on into the afterlife for whatever reason. Maybe this Mr. G had some unresolved business in the world of the living and was stuck in Limbo until it was finished. But who was he?

Chloe could almost feel the light bulb materialize above her head and flicker to life. She knew just where she might find the key to his identity. She quickly dressed into something comfortable and tied up her sopping hair so it didn't get in the way, pulling it back tight until the strands tugged against her scalp in protest.

She roamed around the upstairs level, searching for the pull cord into the attic. Finding it inside the guest bedroom, she gave a firm yank and released years of dust and light debris onto her clean hair and shoulders. She'd sweep up later and probably take another shower. But, right now she needed answers. The situation was still too ridiculous and absurd to believe, but Chloe was falling into the craziness of it all too easily.

Chloe unfolded the wooden ladder and ascended the steps into the attic space. The odor of mildew threatened to clog her sinuses, but she pushed through the cloud of dust to peer into the dim light. An octagonal window flooded the room with gray tinted light, washing over a few dozen boxes labeled in black marker. Dust coated the floor, and she could see the dark speckles of rat droppings all around. How long had it been since another living soul was up here?

She crawled on her hands and knees, unable to stand up straight in the cramped space. The labels did not give her many clues as to the contents. Some were labeled "Tax Records" when they were actually filled with antique dolls or toys that looked to have been made a century ago.

Rifling through every box, she stumbled upon children's books, more toys, vintage china, and then finally found a box that contained family photos and albums. It was a treasure trove of family heirlooms, and Chloe could feel her heart skip beats as she ogled each precious piece. Who touched these things last? Who did they once belong to? What tiny hands played with these dolls decades ago?

She flipped through some of the photo albums a little carelessly, growing impatient with the lack of clues so far, but soon Chloe's eyes snagged on a photo she couldn't easily set aside. It was a picture of her aunt and mother outside the cabin. It had to have been taken at least fifty years ago, but the bright smiles were the same as she remembered. Chloe felt nostalgic tears sting her eyes as she gazed at the two sisters embracing one another.

Her mother appeared very young in this picture, perhaps no more than six years old, and her two front teeth were missing. Mary Anne was at least ten years older, but her aunt's hair was a tangled mass of curls atop her head. They both looked precious.

Chloe had always wanted a sister, even when she was older. Envy grew in her each time she witnessed the special bond of sisterhood amongst her friends and even with her mother and aunt when she was young. Chloe never understood the kind of connection that sisters or siblings shared, but she wished desperately that she did—if not for her own sake, then for her stories. Some of her heroines had sisters or older brothers, and when it came time to write those stories, Chloe would be at a loss to describe such a relationship.

With a sigh, she designated two piles for her search. One was for photos she found that she'd want to take downstairs and possibly compose into a scrapbook. This pile contained pictures she wanted to cherish or ones that might yield a clue. The other was for all the other pictures she didn't deem important at all.

The first pile grew steadily as she discovered pictures of her mother, her aunt, and grandparents. Hidden between these family portraits were photos of the cabin that predated the turn of the century. She found old frames that held the likenesses of men straight out of the Civil War and pencil portraits of women with haunting stares. Some were dated on the back; others were not.

Then she found something that she didn't expect to see in a box of photos. There was a scattered stack of documents at the very bottom of the box, buried beneath all the pictures and cameos.

This box also happened to contain the true tax records, as well as the original land deed for the property and cabin. Most of it was gibberish to her; legal talk and swirly calligraphy upon delicate parchment. Many of the documents looked like they belonged in a museum. Dates she read were as far back as 1790 when the original deed was drawn up in what she assumed was her ancestor's name.

It was all very surreal, to discover such a jackpot of family history. Perhaps there was a historian in Carter Lake that she could contact regarding these priceless documents. If nothing else, she could trace her lineage back to the very beginning. There was something fascinating and tantalizing about discovering one's heritage that Chloe had never known to appreciate until recently.

But there was one document that appeared even older, dated from 1733. It was a royal land charter from England. She was a bit shoddy at historical dates, but she knew for a fact that this was before the American Revolution, probably when Georgia was a meager colony rather than a state.

But it wasn't the date that intrigued her. It was the name. Out of every single document, not one name had any first initials starting with a G. This was one did.

The land grant was issued to Gavin Caras from Devon, England in the Hatherleigh County. He was to settle in Georgia with this land grant. Could this be her ghost? He was certainly dead, and if he was the original tenant of the cabin, it was completely possible that he could be haunting it. There was a significant time gap between this land grant and the first deed that was written up nearly sixty years later. Perhaps it had lain vacant during much of that time after Gavin died.

Finally putting a full name to the ghost was a relief. He no longer seemed so enigmatic, so out of reach. She could address him now without the formality of a pen name. And he was from England, too. How exciting. If this ghost really did exist, maybe she could interview him for a book later.

There had to be a way to find out if Mr. G really was Gavin and if he, in fact, was her ghost.

Chloe, eyes full of wonder and intrigue, searched for anything else with Gavin's name upon it but found nothing.

She took a deep breath, gathered up the photos and land documents in her arms, and descended from the attic with her mind a little more at peace.

Chapter 5

C hloe's eyes snapped open at the harsh cry of a crow on her porch outside. The house was bright with the morning sun as she lay on the sofa in the living room. Her gaze swept over the high wood paneled ceiling, frantically searching her memory of why she wasn't in her pajamas, or in bed.

A hardback copy of Moby Dick lay open across her stomach, and all at once she realized what must have happened.

The night before, she resolved to wait up for her ghost, her Mr. G, whom she suspected was really named Gavin Caras from England. The coffee table was littered with photos and old documents, along with his three yellow notes. Chloe had planned to confront him about what unfinished business he had that made him into a haunting specter.

Even as the clock tolled midnight, she felt foolish, like a child waiting up for Santa Claus on Christmas Eve. But she had to know. Mr. G only appeared when she went upstairs to go to sleep, and despite his previous chiding that she should get to bed at a decent time, she prepared an extra pot of coffee to help keep her awake.

But the last thing she remembered was reading a particular sentence in the fifth chapter over and over again, her mind unable to grasp the meaning of the jumbled words as an unexplainable drowsiness took hold. And before long, her eyes refused to stay open. Chloe passed out and judging by the typical birdsongs drifting through the morning air outside the cabin, she had completely missed Mr. G's arrival that night.

Without even a twinge of grogginess about her, Chloe flipped a bookmark into the volume and turned around to look at her desk.

Her laptop was still there, and next to it was another note with the familiar slanted cursive of her British ghost. Chloe groaned in frustration, mostly at herself.

It didn't make any sense why she would have fallen asleep. At her last count, she had three cups of coffee before dozing off, which would have been more than enough to keep her awake. When she was in Atlanta, she used to stay up all night with her friends on less coffee than she had consumed hours ago. Perhaps her mistake was in reading a book. Chloe should have done something more stimulating like exercise or baking countless batches of cookies.

She pushed herself off the couch and retrieved the note.

My Dear Chloe,

You will have to try harder than that to catch me if that was indeed your intent. I was disappointed to see that you had not written a single new word for the novel. Nor did you respond to my offer to help. If I have offended you in any way, I apologize.

I also saw that you found the land grant that was issued to me in 1733. Let me convey my sincerest gratitude. I thought it had been lost to the ravages of time. And I suppose I can no longer hide my true identity from you. This is just as well.

I shall return with the night, but until then, I encourage you to write more. Or, at the very least, allow me to assist you. It would not be an inconvenience in the slightest.

You obedient servant, Gavin

P.S. I admire your choice in literature.

Chloe's head was reeling. She didn't know what bothered her most; the fact that he thought she was offended or that he had leafed through, not only her book collection that was still packed away in boxes, but also possibly her family photos on the coffee table with his land grant. The two things she held most dear in the world had been practically laid at his feet, and she wasn't there to supervise. Once more, Gavin had violated her space without her permission. She thought British men had better manners than that.

But now, she knew who he was. He confirmed it himself in the letter she held in her hand. The unknown had been brought to light and, somehow, the thought that he had been through her stuff didn't matter so much anymore. He must have been bored, and she would have been, too, if she were over three centuries old and trapped in this cabin.

She ran her fingers through her hair, feeling the strands a little silkier than usual since she took two showers in the span of twenty-four hours. Then a scent caught her attention.

Coffee.

Chloe went to the kitchen and saw that a fresh pot was steaming and ready for her. Even one of her favorite mugs had been set out in preparation for her morning ritual. And this was not just left over from last night. That pot had been half empty by the time she fell asleep.

Gavin must have done this.

And with that thought came the violent shaking of her whole body. She was not only terrified by this strange and wondrous thing that was happening to her, but also by the effect it played on her soul.

Somehow, knowing that Gavin wasn't an intruder, but a spirit whose presence was technically always there, made living in this cabin alone a little more bearable, not that it wasn't before. But the idea of having a ghostly roommate made the mild case of loneliness seem smaller.

Making her coffee was a friendly gesture, but not one done lightly. None of her old friends back in Atlanta knew exactly how she liked her coffee to be brewed. And just by the smell, she could tell that it would be perfect. Not even Brent could make her coffee just right. To Chloe, this might as well have been flirting.

Gavin cared enough about whatever kind of superficial relationship they had to go out of his way to make her coffee. Chloe appreciated the favor, but would this lead to more? First, he offers to help her writing and now, he was making her coffee. Where would he stop?

But she didn't want to rely on Gavin for companionship. Perhaps this is what her parents had whispered so covertly about before. Did her aunt go crazy because of Gavin? Did he drive her to a madness that could only be remedied by leaving?

Chloe didn't trust herself to pour the coffee without spilling, so she sat down heavily in one of the dinette chairs and buried her face in her hands.

Maybe this wasn't such a bad thing. Maybe Gavin was her ticket to becoming a famous author. And perhaps, in the end, she could help Gavin ascend out of Limbo so he would no longer be bound to this cabin. Then she could have the solitude she had been wanting all along.

But her mind bucked at the notion. Part of her held tight to the idea that ghosts didn't exist and that she was crazy for thinking so. What if a few of her screws were coming loose?

The stress of the move and the grief of losing her aunt may have proven too taxing. One gentle mind could only take so much, and Chloe knew where her breaking point was. Brent had pushed her there on more than a few occasions.

But then, on the other hand, what if she wasn't insane? What if ghosts and goblins of fairy tales really did exist? Then, that begged the question if everything else of myth and folklore were real? Chloe squeezed her eyes shut against the idea. She wasn't a child anymore. She was an adult; a perfectly rational adult who held a correspondence with a ghost that may or may not be a figment of her deranged imagination.

The last weakening hold on her sanity released, and Chloe felt almost relieved. If she accepted that Gavin was real, perhaps that would make things easier. She wouldn't be so stressed and torn between two realities. This might not have been the wisest choice, but it was better than returning to Atlanta and sacrificing the future she could have by sticking it out in the cabin.

For the time being, she would let Gavin be real, at least until proven otherwise. But there was still one way to find out if he were truly real or just a product of a stressed out psyche.

Chloe had yet to confide in any living soul about all she had experienced. And, until further notice, she would hold fast to that ultimatum. However, she could still fish around to learn who Gavin was and what truly happened to her aunt. And, in order to fish, she'd have to go to a prime fishing spot.

Checking the calendar hanging on the kitchen wall, she confirmed that it was Tuesday. Rosie would be hosting her Bridge game tonight in Carter Lake. Her mind raced to remember where she had stowed away that card with the old woman's number on it. Chloe had no intention of being late.

Chloe pulled her black jeep up along the grassy shoulder of the road and peered at the mailbox. Even in the dim evening light, she could make out the house number that Rosie had given her over the phone.

The narrow street, nestled just off the main road of Carter Lake, was lined with tall shady trees and an aging concrete sidewalk riddled with cracks that were filled in with sprouting weeds. Beyond the sidewalk was a white picket fence that could use another coat of paint. But beyond that was a very cozy looking home with deep-set porch and white shutters.

Rosie's home was like many on that block, probably built at least a few decades ago, aiding the small-town feel that Carter Lake exuded so well.

The walkway that led up to the porch steps was hedged with flower beds and lush bushes to hide the lattice paneling that wrapped underneath the house. The orange glow of the porch light illuminated the pale blue front door that was only a slight shade darker than the vinyl siding. Topped off with a gray, shingled roof, Chloe wished for a split second that this could have been the home her aunt willed to her instead of the cabin.

Two other vehicles were parked in front of the house. Chloe took comfort in the knowledge that she wouldn't be the only other person here. It wasn't too surprising that Rosie had friends. Aided by her sweet demeanor, Rosie must be on good terms with everyone in town.

She wanted to think that her aunt had been the same way at one point in time before she left for the nursing home. But Chloe's memory was spotty when it came to remembering how Aunt Mary Anne interacted with other citizens of the town. She couldn't recall if people gave her dirty looks or smiles. In fact, she couldn't think of a time when she saw her aunt leave the mountain at all. Chloe was sure that she did, but she just couldn't remember.

Chloe slid out of the jeep and nearly tripped on the way to the pavement. She wasn't used to the drop from the driver seat, which was much higher than her old car. That was something she would miss sorely. Other than that, the vehicle was in great condition, just like Bobby said at the hardware store, and it drove like a dream around those mountain roads.

Making her way up the porch, she could already hear laughter coming from inside. It then occurred to Chloe that this was the first time she had been to anything resembling a party in such a long time. Would she know how to act? Even her last party was nothing like this. Her last party involved alcohol and dance music.

She rang the doorbell, interrupting the riotous laughter. Rosie appeared in the doorway a second later, wearing a pair of dark slacks and a loose, flowery shirt that flowed with every subtle movement. A long, beaded necklace hung down from her slender neck, silver hair piled up on top of her head in a stylish coif, and lips painted a bright red. Chloe likened her to an elderly Hollywood movie star, glamorous even in her golden years.

The two women smiled brightly at one another, and the younger presented a dish of peach cobbler to the elder.

"I wasn't sure if I should bring anything," Chloe began hastily to explain herself, "so I just decided to go ahead and bake something since I had the time."

Not only did Chloe have the time, but she needed the distraction.

Rosie seemed pleasantly surprised and touched by her offering. "That's so sweet of you, honey. I wasn't expecting this at all," she crooned in her rich southern twang.

Chloe just shrugged and was quickly invited in. The air inside the house was a few degrees cooler than the evening air outside and smelled distinctly of peppermint. She was thankful for the decision to wear her warm off-white sweater and jeans; otherwise, she'd be freezing.

Stepping into the living room, wood creaking beneath her boot heels, she was amazed by the collage of pictures on nearly every wall. The walls were so arrayed with baby photos and wedding portraits that Chloe had to really look to see what color the wall paint was behind the frames.

The furniture was truly vintage, complete with wooden rocking chairs and flower print upholstery on the sofa and wingback chair. Knick-knacks cluttered every surface of the home from end tables to the mantle above the fireplace, while a coo-coo clock ticked away on the far wall, its pendulum swinging rhythmically. The inside reminded Chloe of her paternal grandmother's house in Idaho.

Sitting on the sofa was a man and woman of similar age to Rosie, making Chloe the youngest attendee thus far. They both smiled to her in warm greetings. The woman was dressed in a long skirt and button up blouse, while the man wore a pair of khakis and a bright canary polo. If she hadn't known any better, she might have thought they were dressed to go to church rather than a game night with a friend.

"Marge... Jeff... this is Chloe. She's Mary Anne's niece."

The couple lit up at the mention of her aunt's name. They both began to exclaim over Chloe's prettiness, suggesting that she looked just like her aunt. To give her cheeks enough time to pale out again, they went into how unfortunate it was the Mary Anne was no longer alive.

It was apparent that they all knew each other, and upon further listening, she learned that Mary Anne had been another frequent member of Bridge Night at Rosie's and a beloved member of the community. That set her mind at ease given what she had just been thinking about earlier.

They began to reminisce on how the house used to be packed with friends from their school days. But, as the years came and went, attendance slackened due to health limitations and the general hindrances of daily life. Some moved away, and others were laid to rest in the local cemetery like Mary Anne. Only Rosie, Marge, and Jeff remained.

Chloe found it exceedingly sad and hoped that perhaps youthful presence would brighten their gathering a little. But she soon found that their aging bodies were facades. Underneath, they were like children with energy and a zest for life.

Marge and Jeff began to sort out the cards while Chloe trailed behind Rosie, following her into the kitchen that was overly decorated with roosters and fat pigs dressed like chefs.

Rosie set the cobbler down on the counter and went to pull out some small dessert plates from the cabinet.

"My doctor was just getting on my case about having too much sugar in my diet," Rosie said, a hint of humor in her voice.

Still, Chloe blanched a bit. "Oh, I'm so sorry. I didn't know."

The old woman laughed and took out a wide spoon from a drawer on the other side of the kitchen. "No, no. Don't worry, honey. I haven't had peach cobbler in years, and a few bites won't kill me."

Chloe gave a breathy laugh and leaned back against the counter to hide her unease. She watched Rosie dollop junks of warm sliced peaches and crust onto four porcelain plates bordered with pink cherry blossoms painted around the border. Her fingers were restless against the counter, nails tapping sporadically against the laminate.

She wondered if now would be a good time to ask about her aunt and the cabin. Bringing up the idea that the cabin is haunted and that her aunt was crazy might not have settled well with Marge or Jeff, seeing how fond they were of Mary Anne.

"So how are you liking the cabin now? You've had a few days to form an opinion, I suspect."

Chloe was silently thankful that Rosie was the one to bring up the topic first. Giving a thoughtful nod, she said, "I'm really liking it. I spent a lot of time there as a kid. I'm just sorry the real estate company changed it so much to accommodate tourists and renters."

Rosie snorted and shook her head. "That cabin was gorgeous before those idiots tampered with it. There wasn't anything wrong with it when your aunt lived there—besides the obvious, of course."

"The obvious being that it is haunted?"

The clang of metal on porcelain stopped, and Chloe felt Rosie's hard stare on her instantly. If there were a way to reword her question, Chloe would have taken the words back into her mouth and swallowed them down.

"I know you must think it silly of me to believe the place is haunted, but I'm only telling you what Mary Anne confided in me years ago."

Chloe stood perfectly still as if the slightest wrong move would send the whole moment off kilter, and waited for Rosie to continue. This was exactly where she wanted the conversation to go.

"What did my aunt say?" she asked.

Rosie sighed and slid the spoon into the peach cobbler dish. Planting a fist on her bony hip, she turned to Chloe and wagged her head disapprovingly. "She talked about so many things. And I guess that should have been a red flag to all of us that she wasn't all there anymore.

"At first, it was little things." Rosie flipped her free hand back and forth to address her point. "One night, she didn't wash the dishes and left them lying in the sink, but the next morning they weren't there. Someone had come in, cleaned them, and put them away. Mary Anne thought it was a burglar, but she didn't do anything about it."

Rosie's brows furrowed together. "And then things got stranger. She said she heard footsteps around the cabin in the middle of the night. But when she got up to look, no one was there. Things turned up missing all the time. Mostly books, paper, pens, and other office supplies, you know.

"Mary Anne tried to talk about it with your mother," Rosie said with a shrug, "but she didn't help the situation by refusing to visit again."

Chloe slumped a bit and realized her assumptions had been true. They stopped visiting her aunt because her mother thought Mary Anne was going crazy, and no self-respecting parent would want their child to be under that kind of influence.

"She got really lonely," Rosie continued. "And she even disappeared for a while, staying locked away in the cabin for days at a time."

An unexpected laugh bubbled up from Rosie. The lilt of it suggested more disbelief than amusement at what she had to say next. "Then, all of the sudden, she was talking about a man named Gavin."

Chills skittered up Chloe's spine at the name that had consumed her life for the past few days.

"Mary Anne wouldn't stop talking about Gavin, but I never met him."

"She had a boyfriend?" Chloe asked, playing dumb as if she had no clue who Gavin really was.

"You know, I'm not sure. She never talked about him as if they were intimate, just very good friends. They talked all the time."

Chloe gripped the counter tighter as if she expected the room to turn upside down any moment. Her life was doing just that, so why shouldn't this lovely house? She took a deep breath. "What else did she say about Gavin?"

Rosie opened her mouth as if she were going to continue but then froze. Something in Chloe's face caught her attention, and the old woman tilted her head curiously. "Are you feeling well, honey? You look a little pale."

Chloe touched her cheeks and found them a little cold. She just smiled and shook her head. "I'm alright. Maybe I just need a little sugar."

Rosie chuckled softly and handed her a plate loaded with the delicious dessert. "This will fix you up right good then."

That was when Chloe knew she would get no more information tonight. Miss Rosie proved to be an invaluable help, however.

The two ladies took up the plates and headed back into the living room where the others were waiting. While passing out the servings to Marge and Jeff, Chloe couldn't help but think about what Rosie said in the kitchen.

No doubt, Gavin was the one causing all the strange happenings in the cabin. Chloe felt a little envious that her aunt had personal conversations with Gavin, while she was stuck passing notes like a grade school student. Although, she didn't know what there was to be envious about. The idea of coming face to face with a real ghost wasn't appealing in the least. Maybe it was the idea of finally meeting Gavin in person that made her stomach churn with suspense.

Going over the order of events, and if Rosie was telling the truth, that meant Gavin had been communicating with Mary Anne even when Chloe was a little girl. It wasn't until the happenings became too disturbing to keep secret that her mother stopped bringing Chloe to visit the cabin.

It was all so extraordinary. And there was still the mystery of why Mary Anne went to live at the assisted living home. Chloe still wasn't sure if it was because of Gavin. From what Rosie implied, Gavin's presence was a Godsend to her aunt. He kept her company and gave her someone to talk to. Rosie described their relationship as strong friendship rather than intimate. In her old age, living alone, Mary Anne would have wanted a friend like Gavin.

It was then that she found similarities in their situations. Mary Anne was lonely when her sister stopped coming to visit, and Gavin showed up to keep her company. Chloe had just moved to the cabin without a friend in the world when she received the first letter from her ghost pen pal.

Was Gavin merely there to comfort lonely women? Was that his purpose? At least Chloe was not the only one to experience Gavin's manifestation. Then she knew she wasn't crazy. This had all happened before.

She found it hard to focus on learning the game of Bridge while all these thoughts swelled in her mind. But the carefree chatter of the elderly people was enough to make her forget her immediate troubles.

Chapter 6

The darkened windows reflected the glaring glow of the jeep headlights as Chloe pulled up close to the cabin. She'd completely lost track of time at Rosie's, and it was a little past midnight by the time she arrived back home.

The bright moon, not yet full, shined overhead, casting the forest in a cool silvery blue. Choruses of crickets and other nocturnal critters filled the air and almost drowned out the roar of the engine.

Chloe shut the car off and killed the lights, letting nature illuminate the cabin in all its eerie glory.

All at once, she wondered a million things. Was Gavin inside waiting for her? Had she missed him completely? Or had he always been there, lurking in the shadows? It was a disturbing thought that he might have watched Chloe while she slept—or watching her right now.

But he'd never done anything to bother her. He had never hurt her or stolen her personal belongings. Not yet anyway. She was sure it was only a matter of time before he became a nuisance. If he was what drove her aunt away—which was doubtful—then it would be for the fact that he had become too clingy.

Chloe was too tired to think so seriously about the answers. All she wanted to do was go inside, slip into her pajamas and crawl into bed. With luck, she'd be unconscious until noon the next day so she could be well rested enough to catch up on all the writing that she neglected to do today. Gavin was sure to have some nasty words prepared for her if he found out she hadn't written anything like he suggested. She never even wrote a reply note to accept or deny his help yet.

She made it to the front porch, her boots making heavy scraping noises across the rocky path. Chloe managed to unlock the door before pausing for a moment of reflection.

Her extended stay at Rosie's was not only attributed to the fact that she lost track of time. Chloe hadn't wanted to come home. It had become a place of mystery and supernatural hauntings that she could scarcely explain.

And her bed was not the only thing waiting for her inside. Chloe could sense something different about the cabin. Even standing on the porch, the cabin didn't feel empty. Maybe Gavin really was waiting for her.

The idea made her shiver. She'd never faced a ghost and never wanted to. It was easier just to write letters. Somehow, she wished it could go on forever like that—just passing notes and refusing to face each other. But did Gavin want the same? She could avoid the house all she wanted, but he could manifest himself at any moment without her permission. If he wanted to be seen, there was no stopping him.

Her imagination tried to fill in the many gaps of what he could be like. Maybe he was tall and lanky, clean-shaven and dressed in old English garb. Or perhaps he was short and fat with a mustache. Letters could not describe one's voice. Did Gavin have a deep voice or a shrill one that made him sound like a woman rather than a man?

Chloe pulled back her hand from the doorknob and waited for any sound. Could he sense she was home? Did he even know what went on outside the cabin? Was he confined by the walls of the cabin? Was the presence she felt coming from behind her?

Spinning around, she squinted in the darkness and found nothing unusual. The jeep sat alone in the yard, the moonlight glinting off the metal frame. Chloe listened to the forest that surrounded her, the hairs on the back of her neck prickling up against her collar.

If Gavin was not the friendly ghost that she believed, no one was around for miles to hear her scream for help. She was isolated from the world, cut off. That feeling was constant. Chloe could be in a crowded room and still feel like no one knew she was there. The old fears rose up like poltergeists, straight from Atlanta to give her grief. Brent was so far away, and yet he still had a grip on her. Chloe didn't want to believe it, but in this moment of hysteria, as she stood alone in the darkness of a place she hardly knew anymore, she didn't know what to think.

Tears stung at her eyes as she began to wonder why she even came to Carter Lake. Yes, the cabin needed to have a more permanent tenant, and she wanted to write. But something tugged at her heart, insisting she could have rebuilt her life in Atlanta rather than come here just to spite her old friends and colleagues. She could have gone anywhere else but here. But how was she to know that things would turn out this way?

Was this all for nothing?

Chloe took a stuttered breath as a raging storm of conflicting emotions swept her up. She needed to get away—to escape somewhere that wouldn't give her pain.

Through the din of night noises, she heard the gentle trickling of the creek down the hill. As if an angel had announced her salvation, she dropped her keys on the porch and began to run down the steep slope towards the creek.

Perhaps there she could be free of this torture and get a hold of herself again.

But it didn't take long before Chloe slipped on damp autumn leaves, and her sprint down the hill turned into a tumble of flailing of arms and legs. Her hands failed to grasp anything to slow her down as she plowed on towards the tree line.

Twigs and sharp pine needles tore at her exposed face and hands, and Chloe was positive that her sweater was ruined with soil stains. She heard the softest of ripping sounds through the rustling of grass and a draft in her pant leg.

Dark tree trunks came into her dizzying view, and she let out a shriek. Her arms shielded her face as the rest of her body slammed against the rough bark. The tall pine had halted her descent down the hill with barely a shudder, but Chloe lay groaning at the foot of the tree.

Everything ached, and minor scratches began to make themselves known with stinging pain. Hissing through her teeth with each little movement, Chloe pushed herself off the ground and looked up toward the cabin.

She'd fallen a long way from the porch. All was still and silent as she assessed the damage. It was foolish to go running down a hill so carelessly like that. Chloe should have known better. If her mother were there, she would have berated Chloe and thrown that "I told you so" in her face. She couldn't count how many times she'd been told as a child to be careful going down that hill.

Nothing appeared to be broken. But when Chloe brought her right foot underneath her to stand, hot searing pain shot through her ankle. She whimpered and extended her leg behind her.

Flipping onto her backside, she tried to inspect her ankle in the dark. It wasn't bleeding, just extremely sore, and there was no way she could put any weight on it right now. Chloe reasoned that she must have sprained or twisted it during the fall. She also noticed that the left knee of her jeans was torn and showed her milky white skin underneath.

She sighed and looked around for anything like a strong stick she could use to assist her up the hill. But it was useless to look for such a thing in the dim light. And there was no way she could get back up the hill by hopping on one leg. Crawling was always an option.

But, for the moment, Chloe would rest. She managed to get herself upright and leaned against the tree. The world went on as it had before she fell. The night was oblivious to her accident, and that was alright.

Chloe felt silly for the whole thing. What had she been so upset about? Being alone? She'd practically been alone for over a year now, and it never bothered her so much before. It must have been the night that brought on the sudden panic.

Or maybe it was Gavin, her ghost. Gavin was proof that she wouldn't be alone anymore. He'd always be there, watching, waiting, and reminding her of his presence every day.

It scared her to think she would be right back where she had been in Atlanta—trapped by someone who may have the best of intentions, but who didn't really care about her as a person.

But Gavin wasn't just any person. He was a ghost. And from his letters, he did seem to care, at least a little. Maybe it wouldn't be the same as with Brent. At least Gavin knew how to make her coffee.

Chloe's thoughts were interrupted by an unexpected sound coming from the cabin. She saw the silhouette of the back door opening and a figure stepping out onto the deck.

Her blood froze in her veins, and she held perfectly still. Chloe tried to steady her breathing as fear gripped her core, refusing to let her relax.

The figure was undeniably masculine; tall with broad shoulders, but a long coat concealed the rest. Or was it some ghostly mist that obscured his figure? He closed the door and moved without a sound, his motions languid as he descended the steps on the back deck.

His face was cloaked in shadows. In fact, he might as well have been a shadow. He moved with such fluidity like a silhouette on the sidewalk or a wall. Not even the light of the moon made him more visible at this distance.

But Chloe's intuition confirmed her initial suspicion. This must be Gavin.

As if his name had been called out into the darkness, the shadow paused, his head tilted up, and turned towards the tree line. In that moment, Chloe knew she had been spotted.

Her hands trembled in her lap, and she could feel every nerve in her body scream out to move, to flee. But she was too petrified, and her body refused to obey her commands.

Time passed like an eternity as the black phantom stood there, staring at her with that blank face, too shrouded in darkness for her to distinguish any features.

Then, he took a step towards her. And then another. Almost gliding down the hill, he approached her, and she could see him clearly at last as if a fuzzy image were finally coming into focus.

She could see the moonlight gleam upon strands of dark damp hair that were loosely swept back, the ends grazing his shoulders. The same light that shined off his hair twinkled like stars in his thin almond eyes. His irises were the color of the forest, deeper and brighter than emeralds, burning through the dark in a preternatural glow.

His other features were sharp with a bit of a long nose and a bold, square jaw that was covered in dark thin stubble that contrasted starkly against his pale complexion.

As he came closer, the coat he wore billowed out from his frame, revealing the rest of his body. He wore a black button-up shirt with the top few buttons undone to reveal a smooth and pale muscular chest underneath. The shirt was tucked into a pair of equally black trousers, accentuating his trim waist.

Chloe felt even more breathless than before, but not from fear. Her muscles stayed taut beneath her skin, but there was a quiet that settled over her soul that she couldn't explain.

This couldn't be Gavin. Gavin was a ghost, and the man walking toward her was all too real and solid. She imagined a ghost to be transparent with soft edges and a chilled presence. But whomever this was barreling toward her brought with him a radiating warmth that wasn't natural. And she saw him open her back door. Wouldn't ghosts simply pass through barriers like walls and doors?

He stopped a mere few feet from her, staring down calmly upon her. But the eyes that she felt so inexplicably drawn to told another story. They flitted over her body as if unsure of what to do now that he was so close. They held a bit of fear, a bit of confusion, and a bit of wonder as well. His eyes were so candid and full of expression.

Chloe couldn't bring herself to speak first. What would she say? If she opened her mouth now, she'd ask a string of questions that probably wouldn't even make sense.

Luckily, she would not have to worry about that just yet.

"Are you hurt?" he asked.

His voice was deep, vibrating in her flesh as the words tumbled from his perfect lips. Through the haze of fear and puzzlement, she caught the hint of an accent, though she wasn't quite sure of its origins.

Her first instinct was to brush off the fact that she was sitting on the ground in the middle of the woods with her hair riddled with twigs and leaves and her clothes disheveled. She wanted to say that she was fine and simply enjoying the lovely night air.

But there was something about him that wouldn't let her lie.

"I... I fell down the hill." Her words were raspy and faint. She would be surprised if he could hear her at all. "My ankle... I think it's twisted."

He ventured a few steps further, and before she fully realized it, he was beside her and squatting down to examine her ankle.

"May I?" he asked, holding his hands out towards her foot as if to scoop it up.

The dark side of Chloe's mind wanted to give him permission to do anything he wanted, but she could only nod her consent.

The man reached out and unzipped her boot with deft precision. Even the task of slipping the boot from her foot was quick and nearly painless. His hands were warm as they gingerly gripped around her ankle and tested its maneuverability.

Chloe was not too skittish to let him know when it hurt, letting out little whimpers here and there. His brows pinched in apology each time, but his eyes were focused on the task at hand.

Finally, he replaced her boot and fastened it back into place.

"I believe you're right, it is twisted. Can you walk?"

Chloe mutely shook her head, her eyes unwaveringly fixed on his handsome face. There was something else in his voice that pulled at something deep in her memory, but it was too obscure to pinpoint just yet.

He glanced over his shoulder at the cabin and then back at Chloe. "May I have permission to carry you back up the hill?"

"Carry?" Chloe asked, the question coming out a little shrill from shock.

"Yes. It would be more prudent and less effort on your part."

Having this man, whoever he was, carry her up the hill and inside her home-made her head swim. She should have said no. She should have rejected any help from this stranger.

But before she could stop herself, Chloe uttered, "Ok."

With one swift movement, he scooped her up and cradled her against his chest. Chloe was drowning in his scent of pure masculinity and pine needles that made her melt. Muscles, all at once, ceased to work, and she felt light headed.

Burying her face in the place where his neck and shoulder met, Chloe lost all sense of reality. She hardly felt like she was being carried up a steep incline but rather that she was ascending into heaven, wrapped in the strong arms of an angel.

When they came to her porch, she made the slightest move to wiggle free of his hold, but he only held her tighter. Chloe didn't notice if he had reached down to open the door or if it opened by itself. Her mind was blanketed in a fog, almost as if she were floating in and out of consciousness without any explanation why.

The sounds of the night dimmed away, and the moon no longer beamed down upon them. The cabin was tranquil, the emptiness overwhelming. The man moved up the stairs as Chloe felt herself get higher and higher on this blissful sensation of weightlessness. She wondered if he had somehow slipped her a drug or if that tumble down the hill had killed her.

Before she knew it, she was in bed, and the stranger no longer held her close. His absence jolted her awake. But as suddenly as she was awake, Chloe felt herself plunge into a deep and dreamless sleep, void of thoughts or feelings that troubled her.

The last thing she did remember in the brief moment before her heavy eyelids shut for the last time that night was the stranger's face gazing down at her with those piercing green eyes. Those eyes filled with a mix of mystification and awe as they studied her with a ferocity that she'd never seen before in any living soul.

Gavin watched Chloe fall into the comatose-like sleep he had induced upon her. It was safer this way. When she woke, she might think this was all a dream, nothing more than a fantasy. He should have made her sleep long ago, but he wanted her conscious, if only for a little while, just to hear her voice.

Her voice was just as he had imagined from her letter. It no longer held the high pitch ring of childhood but had been deepened by the cares of adulthood and rounded by her femininity to make it a little more than alluring to his senses.

Chloe was the first young woman he had seen in years. She was, in his opinion, the spitting image of her aunt but at a much younger age and even more beautiful. He was initially shocked by how pretty she was.

He was drawn to her eyes, especially, because they reminded him of better days. There was no innocence in her eyes. But there was an obvious fear there when he came into her view. The last thing he wanted to do was frighten her. However, when he drew closer and made himself known in the light, she seemed to relax. How strange that they had never met, but finally meeting the unknown made her more comfortable.

He knew that she was comfortable by the subtle change in her scent and by the way her voice softened and barely quivered as they spoke. Any other human might have tried to escape from him. Perhaps she didn't know or hadn't guessed what he really was.

Gavin bent down low and drank in her scent, so full of life. Her perfume and body wash had faded but still retained the faint scent of magnolias. His keen eyes swept over her body and ended at her sprained ankle.

Yes, there was still that to resolve.

He sat down at the foot of the bed and slipped her boot off as carefully as he had before. Gavin wrapped his hands around her ankle, feeling the coolness of her skin pressed against his warm palms. He hadn't touched a human in so long. Holding her close was an experience he would not soon forget. Feeling her breath on his neck, and her scent enveloping him like a pair of heavenly wings, was enough to shield him from the darkness around them, if not the darkness within.

His body gave a shiver of pleasure, and he shook his head to chase away the thoughts. He couldn't grow attached. Not now, not ever. She did not belong to him, and she never would.

The world passed by like a silent observer to his strange talent as the muscles beneath his grip began to mend and heal to their rightful state. When he was satisfied with his work, Gavin released her ankle and slid her shoe back on.

It would be so easy for him to stay there for the remainder of the night, watching her peaceful face frozen in sleep. But the primordial needs that afflicted him would not let him take solace in her company. As much as he wanted to stay, there was no way he could.

He stood and moved across the room without as much as a whisper of sound. When he reached the door, he turned and regarded her once more, watching the way her chest rose and fell with each breath. It was a natural function, an involuntary movement of the body to inhale and exhale that which gave it life. It was something he hadn't done in ages; to breathe; to have a heart that beats.

Gavin turned and drifted through the darkness of the cabin as he always had, as he had for generations.

Chapter 7

Chloe's head listed slowly to the side and she let out a groan. Even with her eyelids shut tight, she could tell there was a sunny morning outside waiting for her. Her arm lifted to cover her face. She didn't want to get up. The bed beneath her was too plush and comfortable. In fact, it was the most comfortable it had been since she arrived at the cabin.

Her leg slid against the wrinkled sheets, and Chloe noticed something. There was the faint inclination that her ankle should hurt, but it didn't. Through her grogginess, she rotated the joint a few times and found it perfectly fine.

Chloe moved her arm away from her eyes and looked around the room, so bright with a golden glow that filtered through the window. It looked the same, but it didn't feel the same. Just like a house never felt the same after knowing that someone had been born or died there. It completely changed one's ideas and feelings about a place after knowing something marvelous or utterly tragic had happened there.

Then, all at once, her sleepiness dissipated, and she remembered the night before. She remembered running down the hill towards the creek and twisting her ankle when she gracelessly fell. There was the pain, and then there was the shadow that took the pain away.

But it wasn't a shadow. It was a man. Chloe could see the burning green eyes shining through the dark night like two beacons. She recalled his handsome face, so elegant in its lines and contours that he almost seemed unreal. But he certainly was real.

Then there was the warmth that seared her bones when he touched her. How her heart and blood had raced as he'd carried her into the cabin and up the stairs. It was all a jumble of words and feelings, but there was no mistaking what happened.

Chloe pushed herself up and looked around for her rescuer, but he was nowhere to be seen. Taking strength from the drive to find answers, she swiveled her body out of bed and bounded down the stairs, feeling more fit than ever despite her fall.

She didn't find the man downstairs, either; not a single sign of him. Chloe remembered when she first saw him coming out of the back door onto the deck, but the door was locked tight. Although she had a feeling that nothing was amiss, she checked around the house anyway.

Everything was in order, nothing was missing – save for Chloe's sanity. Standing in the living room, she gazed around mystified as she reached up to comb her hair back from her face with her fingers.

She found the strands to be caked with oil and sprinkles of dirt. She even found a twig or two stuck in her hair behind her head. Looking down, Chloe realized she was also still wearing her now dirt-stained sweater and torn jeans.

A hot shower and some clean clothes would be good, but how could she go on as normal after what happened the night before? A handsome stranger had whisked her off her feet, and her ankle was miraculously healed without the need for modern medical equipment.

Outside, the cabin seemed normal. Birds sang, the sun was beaming down, and the air inside the cabin was pleasantly cool. But within Chloe raged a panic, and combined with everything else from the past few days, it threatened to swallow her up completely.

Her throat tightened as desperate tears gathered at the corners of her eyes. Who was the man, really? Was it Gavin, her ghost from England? Or was it some stranger who had broken into her home and then happened to help her back up the hill? Had she imagined the entire thing? But that didn't explain her dirty and disheveled state.

None of it made sense, not until she noticed the new note sitting on top of her computer.

It was the one bit of familiarity that Chloe needed right now. It didn't matter if the words were comforting or chiding, but coming from Gavin, they would be welcome nonetheless.

Perhaps Gavin saw the stranger lurking about her cabin. What if Gavin was the reason that the stranger was no longer here? How heroic of her ghost to have frightened away her rescuer to protect her.

But as Chloe's eyes drank in the letter, she began to realize that this was far from the truth.

My Dearest Chloe,

I hope your ankle is feeling better. I apologize if I frightened you last night. I hadn't expected to find you sitting outside in such a manner. In any other case, I would have passed on and avoided confrontation at all costs. But I could see you were in distress, and I couldn't ignore you.

I also apologize if carrying you upstairs was a little too untoward. As I said last night, it was more prudent to carry you rather than act as your crutch.

Let me encourage you to spend the day recuperating from your injury by writing. I am eager to read more. You truly are a talented writer. I hope you know that.

Always at your service,

Gavin.

Chloe's shaking hands made the yellow notepad paper crackle from the strain. Gavin was the one who rescued her. But, that couldn't be possible. Gavin was a ghost, and the man who came to her aid the night before was anything but a ghost. He was real, solid, warm, everything that a ghost should not be.

She had always imagined that a ghost would be transparent and perhaps emit a glowing aura of light or mist. She didn't expect a bulbous headed mass like Casper, but she certainly didn't expect what approached her from the shadows last night.

She read the letter over and over again, searching for any hint that Gavin only witnessed the man carrying her up the hill. But it was plain as the black ink in front of her eyes that Gavin, her English pre-revolutionary ghost, had been the same man who scooped her up into his arms like a small child and carried her effortlessly up to her room and laid her in bed. How she wished she could remember more.

The idea was mind shattering. Her whole preconception of ghosts and everything mythological had been systematically blown out of the water. If ghosts could present themselves as tangible and as real as people, there was no telling who was a ghost and who was not anymore.

Chloe didn't know where to begin to process everything she had discovered, nor did she want to. A hot shower was looking more and more appealing now; that and a cup of very strong coffee.

After standing in the shower until the water ran frigid cold, Chloe dried her thick hair as best as she knew how without a blow dryer, then slipped into her flannel pajamas and warm socks.

With last night washed away, she walked lightly back downstairs to brew her usual pot of coffee even though it was very late in the morning. Whilst waiting, she looked down at the clutter of family photos on the coffee table. Images of her mother, aunt, and grandparents gleamed back up at her with bright smiles. If only she could return the gesture.

Life was not turning out to be as simple as she would have liked. Moving into the middle of nowhere to seek solitude was supposed to be easy. The loneliness was hard to cope with, but at least she was doing what she always wanted to.

But Gavin was ruining it all for her; Gavin, a ghost who didn't look like a ghost; Gavin, who seemed caring, thoughtful, and polite beyond what any contemporary man would even try to achieve. Chloe hated to admit it, but she was growing fond of him, not only for the letters but those eyes that were burned into her memory. If she ever saw him again, even if she lived to be over a century old, she would remember those eyes.

Finally, Chloe took the time to connect the two--the Gavin that wrote to her practically every night and the Gavin who she met face to face.

According to the land deed she found in the attic, he was from England, and the accent that was so prevalent in his voice testified to his origins. She had no photographs or sketches of Gavin for obvious reasons, but somehow it seemed to make sense that he would look so handsome and sophisticated.

But those eyes, Chloe swooned, those eyes that so perfectly matched the evergreen leaves of the forest around the cabin. They sent her heart into palpitations and made her breath freeze in her lungs. How could such a pair of eyes belong to any being, dead or alive?

Remembering those eyes made Chloe not only appreciate him for his sincerity but also admire him for his handsomeness.

Just about the time the coffee pot chimed, Chloe realized she was standing on the border of being morbid. She was fantasizing about a man who had been dead for nearly three hundred years.

She shivered and then poured her first cup, hoping that the warm liquid would fight back the odd sensations that settled in her gut like a heavy stone. But no amount of coffee would erase what happened last night. Coffee could help her in the present and maybe make her future look a little better, but it couldn't change the past.

With hesitant hands, Chloe unlocked the back door. The thought came to mind that Gavin had touched this doorknob, and she shivered again before stepping out onto the deck. As a matter of fact, Gavin had probably been everywhere in the cabin, touched almost everything in some way or another. She knew that she was sharing her house now, but it became a little more real each time she thought too much about it.

Chloe leaned against the deck railing and sipped her coffee, feeling its rejuvenating effects already as she gazed out into the wilderness. She could see the creek down below the hill, its waters flowing as they had for ages.

Chloe wondered if the creek had been there when Gavin was alive. Did he enjoy watching its glittering ripples too? Was that why he built his cabin here instead of in the valley?

Then she began to wonder something she hadn't thought about before. How did Gavin die? It was obvious that he was dead. No one could live forever. But what caused him to be a ghost?

Perhaps he had drowned in the creek. If the water level was higher back then, it wasn't hard to conceive of a grown man drowning. Maybe that was why he had such pale skin.

Chloe was surprised her thoughts had taken such a macabre turn over the last few days. Seeing obvious proof that ghosts were real had surely changed her way of thinking.

Was this what led to her aunt's downfall? Rosie had said she talked about Gavin a lot. Maybe it was an obsession with the ghost that led her to insanity. It was not a far-fetched idea to Chloe. She had felt her own grip on sanity weaken since she moved into the mountains.

Chloe knew probing Rosie for answers might seem too conspicuous. Plus, she wouldn't see the older woman for another week until the next Bridge night.

But there was one other person she could turn to for answers; someone who knew her aunt better than anyone else in the world.

She hadn't spoken to her mother in weeks.

Chloe's parents were traveling the country in the RV they bought a few years ago. After Mary Anne checked into the assisted living home, and Chloe seemed to have dropped off the face of the planet, it only made sense for them to spend their retirement years seeing the North American continent.

Sometimes, their phones were not in service, and most of the time, her mother would let her know by giving her one last call before hitting that dead zone where no one could be reached. But that hadn't happened in a while.

Taking a chance, Chloe finished off her coffee and went back inside to fetch her cell phone from upstairs. It'd been sitting there for days, constantly charging even though it had a full battery.

Chloe, unlike most adults her age, chose not to spend all her time with her eyes glued to her phone, browsing through social media and texting friends. Who did she have to talk to anyway? She had no one to call or text, no one to reach out to besides her parents who were off living their second childhood.

She flopped down on her bed and dialed her mother. Her fingers splayed out over the soft fabric, and she wondered if Gavin had ever once lain in this bed or sat on the edge to watch her sleep. A cold wave washed over her, and she withdrew her hand to rest it on her stomach.

After a few rings, Chloe heard the willowy voice of her mother answer, "Hello?"

"Hey, mom. It's me."

There was a bit of rustling in the background as if her mother were standing up. "Hey, honey! How have you been? I haven't heard from you in a while."

Chloe played with a strand of damp hair as she talked. "I've been alright," she lied. "I finally got all of Aunt Mary Anne's affairs taken care of."

"Well, that's good." There was a twinge of sadness in her mother's words. Chloe knew that she was still taking her sister's death hard. She hadn't been able to attend the funeral because they were over three thousand miles away in Washington at the time. Not only that, but her mother was the last living member of their family apart from Chloe. It was a sobering thought to think that she was all alone now. Chloe could identify.

"Did I tell you I'm living in the cabin now?"

Her mother gasped in delighted surprise. "No, you didn't!" she exclaimed. "How is it? Did the real estate company keep it in good condition?"

Chloe could have told her all about the changes they had made to the porch, the walkway, the kitchen interior, and furniture. "It looks great. No leaks, no damage. They even installed new locks."

"I'm glad they changed your locks. Those old iron ones weren't safe at all. Your aunt liked them, but I always thought they were too flimsy. And Carter Lake, how's that old town looking?"

Chloe told her all about the old gas station and Main Street, the grocery store, and especially Bob and Rosie.

"Sounds like it hasn't changed too much. That's a good thing. Your father and I drive past these old towns that have been totally deserted, and it's a shame. And then we stop in these big cities that look like they were once boomtowns with old housing districts, and we talk about how horrible it is that the modern age has destroyed these old relics. Why can't people just keep things the same?"

Chloe had to admire her mother's viewpoints. She didn't share them to such an extreme because she was sorely missing the convenience of high-speed internet, but she did hate it when old historic landmarks were torn down to make way for shopping malls. If people forgot where they came from, they would lose their future as well. Any philosopher would say the same.

"I don't know, mom. But the cabin looks great."

"I'm glad. We're making our way back east and we'll stop by. We'll probably have to get a rental car to go up the mountain, though. The RV won't make it."

Chloe shook her head as if her mother could actually see her. "No, I'll come down and get you. There's a little hotel you can stay in, I think, and I can pick you guys up there."

"Is your car big enough?"

"I actually traded my car in for a jeep. The guy at the hardware store was selling his."

"Oh! Was it Bobby? He's so sweet. So is his wife. We knew their family growing up."

And there was the wonderful part about living in a small town; everyone knew each other.

"Yeah, his wife wanted a smaller vehicle, so we traded. I like the jeep. It runs well."

"That's good. I'm glad."

A long pause of silence passed on, and Chloe was finally able to distinguish the slight rustling in the background. Her mother was folding clothes. It was familiar from her childhood, something she heard every day growing up.

Chloe took a moment and closed her eyes, envisioning her mother methodically folding shirts and pants while propping the phone between her ear and shoulder. It was soothing, and all she wanted to do was listen to that rhythmic sound all day.

"You ok, baby?" her mother asked, a bit of her southern drawl leaking out.

"Yep. I'm good. This cabin just has me thinking about Aunt Mary Anne a lot."

Her mother sighed. "I know. There are a lot of memories there, huh?"

"I kind of wish there were more."

"I know, baby. But that's just the way it goes sometimes. We can't turn back the clock and do things we wish we had done."

"Or stop ourselves from doing things we wish we hadn't done," Chloe added thoughtfully. Lord knows, she had plenty of regrets.

"How are you holding up in that department?" her mother asked. She'd always been able to see past Chloe's cryptic remarks.

She was the first person to pick up on what was really going on when the fallout happened. And she was the one to convince Chloe to make the changes she needed for her own emotional health. Then, Aunt Mary Anne passed, and everything seemed to fall into place. It was the right piece of advice that came at the right time.

Chloe heaved a heavy sigh and nodded, mostly to herself. "I'm alright. It's not near as hard as I thought it would be. Getting away from Atlanta really helped."

"I told you about how your father wants to skin Brent alive, right?"

Chloe giggled despite herself. "Yes, you told me."

"And he can do it too."

"Yes, I know."

Chloe's father loved to hunt. Her parents met back when they were teenagers in Carter Lake. At the time, he could skin a buck in record time while leaving very little mess behind. It was the kind of thing that a country boy could be proud of, and Chloe knew her father was itching to break out his set of knives again, especially after word leaked out about what Brent had done to her.

"I have something to ask you," Chloe continued, almost forgetting why they were on the phone in the first place. "It's about Aunt Mary Anne. What happened to her? I mean, I remember when I was little we would come up here all the time, and then, all of the sudden, we stopped."

"I told you. Your aunt was too busy."

"I don't buy that, mom." Chloe did her best to not sound too offensive. She simply wanted the truth. "I heard you talking with dad about how she was going crazy."

The sound of folding clothes stopped, and her mother sat down heavily on the side of the bed. Chloe could hear the squeaky springs groan under her weight. "Listen, your aunt wasn't crazy; she just was going through some things and getting older. When people get older, they start to have problems remembering things, and sometimes, they make up stuff. And that's what happened to your aunt."

Her mother's tone was level as if she were giving a lecture about something mundane. But Chloe could pick up a tremor of emotion. It told her that there was no way to logically explain away what her mother witnessed over the years. It couldn't have been easy to listen to your own flesh and blood wilting in old age.

"Like dementia or Alzheimer's?" Chloe asked.

"Exactly."

"So what was she saying?"

Her mother took a deep breath and let it out slowly. "Lots of things. She talked about how staying alone in the cabin was becoming hard. She wanted us to move in with her, but with your father's work, it just wasn't going to happen. She called constantly, and we visited all the time. I thought she was just lonely. She never married, you know."

"Yeah, I know."

"But then she was started to sound scared over the phone sometimes. Like late at night, she thought someone was watching her, and stuff was going missing. I remember that happening when we were growing up, but never to the degree that she described. Again, I thought she was just lonely and was trying to get us to visit more by making stuff up. Guilt trips never worked on me, anyway."

"You said those things happened when you were growing up?"

"Oh yeah, all the time. My mother, your grandmother, would lose things all the time. Mostly, it was books. They always showed back up in the oddest places later on. And your grandfather, bless his heart, had clothes go missing."

"Clothes?" Chloe asked laughingly.

"Yes! All the time. I remember him screaming at your grandmother that he had underwear and trousers that had gone missing, but they weren't in the wash. It was little stuff like that. But your aunt took those stories and blew them way out of proportion. She started saying that the house was haunted."

Her mother paused, but Chloe knew there was more to this. She was so close to finding the answers she needed. "But we didn't stop visiting just because she thought the house was haunted, right?"

"No. We didn't stop visiting because of that. We stopped after one trip around Thanksgiving time. Your aunt pulled me aside and said she'd met the ghost that stole all those things when we were growing up."

Chloe's blood ran cold. "Met him?"

"Yes. I remember she said his name was Gavin. She went on for hours about him and all the things they talked about. I admit that I was a little freaked out about it. Your aunt was always the rational one. After that trip, I talked to your father, and we decided that it was best to not let you be around her for a while until she got out of this ghost phase. We didn't want her to fill your head with stories and things that weren't true. You were so impressionable at that age."

Chloe let this new information settle for a moment. Her aunt had met Gavin. So far, the story was checking out—from what she found in the attic to what her aunt had told Rosie and what her mother was confessing now. There was no mistaking that he was real.

"Did she ever say what Gavin looked like?" Chloe asked, trying to keep her voice steady. If she could fool her mother into thinking that everything was alright, she would get all the answers she wanted without the unnecessary worry.

"Oh, I don't know. Tall, dark, and handsome, I suppose. The way she talked about him over the phone sometimes, I thought maybe he was actually her boyfriend or something. I knew Mary Anne had lost it when she changed her story all of a sudden and said that Gavin was a vampire and not a ghost."

Chloe dropped the cell phone and let it tumble onto the mattress. Through the stunned daze, she heard her mother call out to her over the line.

She blinked away the shock and picked up the phone again. "Sorry, I uh... She said a vampire?" Chloe asked with heightened incredulity as she sat up on the bed.

"Yeah, a vampire. She even told me how she caught him drinking the blood of a squirrel one time out on the back deck."

Chloe suddenly felt dizzy and pressed her free hand against her forehead to keep the world from spinning. With this new piece of information, nothing was simple anymore.

Rosie never confirmed that it was a ghost that Mary Anne met. And Chloe really had no solid proof besides the idea that the place felt haunted. She had no doubt that Mary Anne was in her right mind the entire time while she told these stories to her mother and Rosie.

So, she must have been telling the truth when she said that Gavin was a vampire. Unbidden, the distorted image of Gavin's pale face and fierce green eyes came to mind. In her imagination, she could easily see his lips and chin coated in dark blood. Yes, it wasn't hard to picture Gavin as a vampire as opposed to a ghost. It explained why she never saw him during the day and how he felt as real as any solid human being rather than a misty ghost.

But there was that warmth about him. Weren't vampires supposed to be cold? And how did he become a vampire? Was he the same Gavin who the land deed was issued to? Could vampires live forever like that too? Was he even dead?

Once again, Chloe knew nothing beyond what pop culture taught her in passing about monsters and folklore.

"You still there, baby?" she heard her mother ask, though her mind was miles away.

"Yeah, I'm fine. I just didn't know any of that stuff. Did she check herself into that place down in Savannah?" she asked after swallowing a few times to compose herself.

"Yeah, she did. But she would never tell me why. I did notice that she stopped talking about Gavin a few weeks before she left Carter Lake. So, I think she was beginning to get a hold on reality for a while towards the end."

"Did you ever meet Gavin?"

Her mother laughed. "Of course not. He didn't exist, Chloe. Yes, we did go to visit her a few times when you were a teenager, but we never met him, and Mary Anne never offered to introduce us."

Chloe could tell her mother was finding this all a little hilarious. If only she knew the truth—that Gavin certainly was real. She had a fantastic memory of the night before and a small stack of letters to prove it.

"What's this all about, honey?" her mother questioned after a long pensive pause over the line. "Nothing. Just all the memories here made me wonder about it. That's all." Chloe took a deep breath and finished with, "I should have visited her."

"We all should have, dear. But that's just the way things are."

That was her mother's favorite saying. She said it whenever she knew that she couldn't change things or go back to the way things were. She said it when Chloe broke the priceless vase her father brought back from Europe one summer. She said it when Chloe lost her best friend to a silly argument in junior high. She said it when everything in Atlanta came crumbling down. And she said it now talking about all the things they should have done for her late aunt.

Chloe wanted to just forget and move on with her life the way her mother had. Her grandmother always told her to let horrible things be like water off a duck's back. But Chloe had a hard time letting go. She couldn't just forget this place, Gavin, or her aunt.

Moving to the mountains to escape Brent and all the mistakes that followed was futile when Chloe could never truly forget. And she wouldn't let herself off the hook when it came to her aunt.

"Did I tell you that I started my first book?" Chloe asked, changing the subject more for herself than for her mother.

"No! You didn't!" she exclaimed and Chloe didn't have to see her face to know that she was smiling with pride.

Chloe then began to tell her all about the novel she was working on. She wanted there to be someone besides Gavin who knew about the book. Her mother sounded interested, but it was a passive interest. Romances were not her favorite genre, and Chloe knew it. But while her mother served as a captive audience, she figured there was no harm in boring her.

Once that conversation was over, her mother took her turn in telling mind-numbing stories to Chloe about their many adventures out in the Midwest. She was glad her parents were finally getting out and doing the exciting things that they always talked about doing, but Chloe liked the idea of being settled and stable in one place too much to up and travel across the country. Maybe a few vacations to Disney World here and there, but nothing like driving for days on end to see the Grand Canyon and all that came before it on the road.

The chatter did help for one thing. It distracted Chloe, just for a little while, from the heart-stopping anxiety about Gavin and the cabin. She'd rather think about her imminent death in the years to come than about the fact that a vampire had offered to help write her book.

Chapter 8

C hloe lay awake in her bed, moonlight filtering through the lace curtains of her bedroom. She was listening so intently, she thought she could hear her own heartbeat in between breaths.

After getting off the phone with her mother, she devoted the entire day to two things: one, learning all she could about vampires according to what her slow internet connection could provide, and two, writing a short story for Gavin.

It was a little something to entice him to open her laptop and keep him there. Chloe had shut her computer down just before going to bed, something she hadn't done before. She made sure to turn the volume on high so that when Gavin turned the computer on to check for any new stories, it would chime and alert her all the way upstairs.

It was a cunning trap as she thought it. Not only would his arrival be heralded throughout the cabin, but he would be forced to stick around and read what she'd written in the hopes that he hadn't woken her up. If she knew anything about Gavin at this point, it was that he was eager to read something new from her. That might give her enough time to slip out of bed and catch him in the living room.

But, as she lay in bed, her mind raced with all she had learned. Vampires, as everyone knew, drank blood and needed it to survive. Gavin, if he really was a vampire, would be no different. It gave her chills to think that she had been so close to death itself, and yet he never bit her. How many nights had she been in a vulnerable position, and not once had he given in to his primal need for blood; not only with her, but with the other tenants of the cabin over the last few years who came and went.

Then, there was the idea that her entire family line had lived in this cabin, yet no one had been drained dry by the vampire—not to her knowledge anyway.

But her aunt had told her mother that Gavin was caught red handed—quite literally—feeding on a squirrel. Was Gavin the vegan version of a vampire, or did he have an acquired taste for the type of humans he preferred? If he really wanted to, he could ensure that no one else lived in that cabin except for himself. But he didn't.

The mystery of his origins still remained. He was from England and had been given a land grant to settle in Georgia before the Revolutionary War, but was he a vampire in England? Did he turn when he came to America? How did he turn? The internet gave her many different ways that a human could become a vampire, but which ones were true?

Chloe was left with more questions than ever before.

Her naturally curious and over-active imagination ran wild with images of how he looked when he fed. Not only did she research on blogs and web pages, but she watched how Hollywood depicted vampires. She saw everything from sparkly hotties to skinny, bat-like men dressed in suits. Some were portrayed as vicious beasts, and others were hopeless victims of an eternal curse. What was true?

She was determined to find out tonight.

Her whole body convulsed when she heard her laptop turn on. Her heartbeat pounded in her ears, thudding against her chest. Gavin was in the house. He was sitting at her computer.

She could hardly move and barely breathe from the mix of terror and excitement building up in her core. Though every muscle in her body protested against it, she swung her legs, slowly but silently, over the edge of the bed and lowered herself to the floor.

The floorboards creaked against her weight, and she winced, hoping he hadn't heard her. One wrong move and he could vanish.

She read how vampires could dematerialize into smoke, which could have been why her locks had proved useless. Then again, a vampire was supposed to be invited into a home. But this was technically his own home almost three hundred years ago, so did that apply in the same way?

Chloe waited for a moment and then took another step towards the door. The rest of the way towards the stairs went much of the same way. Step, wait. Step, wait—until she reached the top of the stairs.

The living room light wasn't on, but she could see the blue glow from the computer screen reflecting on the smooth stones of the fireplace. Chloe listened and thought she could hear the faint stroking of fingers on the mouse pad on her laptop as Gavin scrolled through the document.

What she wrote wasn't more than a few pages, so she didn't have much time.

Chloe took a deep, muted breath and began to descend the stairs. For once, she was glad that the third step from the top didn't groan with the slightest weight.

Who knew that the improvements the real estate company had made would turn out to her benefit?

She made it halfway to the bottom, right to the point where the wall would no longer conceal her from the place where her desk sat in the living room. After taking another pause to make sure he was still there, she bounded down the last few steps and flicked on the lights.

Sitting at the desk, slightly hunched over in order to read the laptop screen, sat the same man who had come to her aid in the woods the night before. But now, in more ample lighting, she was able to paint a full picture of him in her mind, filling in the gaps that the darkness and disorientation had created for her.

He seemed to be wearing the same outfit as the night before, the trench coat draping down around the seat of the chair to graze the floor. But in this light, she found that he wasn't all cloaked in black as she had previously thought. His slacks were indeed black, but his button up shirt was a rich navy blue.

Not only his clothes were different than she remembered but his hair as well. Despite the moonlight, his hair that had appeared black was actually just a very dark brown. It was like seeing a black and white photograph in full, high definition color for the first time. But even in the yellowish, fluorescent light, his skin was a pale, milky white and his eyes a blazing green.

She froze at the bottom of the stairs, gazing at the eyes that were not focused on her yet, but soon would be. For one silly moment, Chloe thought she'd burst into flames under such a stare from him. Could she handle the intensity? Night had diluted its effects before, but now she could see him more clearly.

After a few agonizing seconds, Gavin turned his head and looked at her. His expression was carefully blank, but a world of feeling was hidden beneath that she could see very plainly. She felt if she could just reach out and touch his pale cheek, his defenses may shatter. But did she dare to get that close?

Chloe stared, lips parted and eyes wide with a mix of fear and wonder at the creature before her. Still moments passed, and he patiently waited for her to speak first. She hadn't prepared for this meeting. Yes, she made sure that it would happen, but she never really thought it would work. Gavin was cautious, that much she could tell. She half expected that we would have vanished into mist by now if such a thing were possible. Was he still able to do that, or did he stick around for her? Did he want to see her for a second time as much as she wanted to see him?

Before she could stop herself, the words tumbled out. "Here I come down to get a snack, and I may end up being the snack." Her voice was breathy and light as if she had little voice at all.

When she finished speaking, she realized how much of an insult that must seem to him. It was unintentional.

Gavin, in one graceful movement, stood from the chair. He was much taller than she remembered, towering at least a whole foot above her meager five-and-a-half-foot stature. He was intimidating. Predators had to be, she supposed.

But her knees went weak when he gave her a smile. It was a good-natured smile, with one side tilting up more than the other to show one of his long, sharp incisors. Her stomach lurched at the sight of it.

"If I wanted you as a snack, you would have been gone a long time ago."

Chloe's heart seized at the accent she had almost forgotten. She wanted to hear more words flow from his perfectly formed mouth, but she hardly knew what to say. All the questions she had fled her in this moment while his eyes stared so fixedly into hers.

They were still a good eight feet from each other, well out of arm's reach. But if all of the facts on the internet proved true, distance was no match for him. He could close that gap in less time than it took her to blink. And still he stood firm, not making any movements at all. Not even breathing.

"You needn't have any fear," he said, a little softer than before. "I will not harm you."

Surely he could hear her pounding heart, her quickened breaths as they seeped out between her lips. Could he smell her fear? Could he sense her every emotion? Or even read her mind?

"Do you know that I know what you are?" she asked, tilting her chin down a bit in an effort to make her neck less appealing if it was at all.

"I do," he said with an affirmative nod.

"And now you're not hiding?"

Chloe remembered all the near misses she had with him like that time she'd tried to stay up all night to catch him. Thinking about it now, she wondered if he had used some sort of mesmerizing trick to make her fall asleep so they would never meet. Is that what happened last night, too?

Gavin shrugged. "I see no need to."

She marveled at how such a human gesture seemed so incongruent with the fact that he was a creature of the night, a thing of myths and lore. And yet, he shrugged just like she would.

"Then why didn't you just tell me from the beginning? You had your chances." Chloe heard her voice rise with an indignant fervor. It was the one question that had truly weighed on her mind all day.

She appreciated honesty and abhorred cowardice. At least, she did now. In any other circumstance, and with a human who was hopelessly flawed, she would have been even angrier. But Gavin only annoyed her with his secrets and mystery. She wouldn't have talked this way with a stranger, but she felt like she knew too much about Gavin to be coldly polite in that way.

He blinked and opened his mouth as if to answer, but he donned a thoughtful look as if he were sensibly choosing his words. "I thought it would be easier to continue our correspondence if you remained unaware of who I was."

Chloe, feeling slightly more comfortable in the flow of conversation, snorted an impertinent laugh. "You kind of blew that out of the water last night. I would have rather you had been honest. Do you realize how freaked out I was the whole time? I thought you were a burglar when you left that first note." Without her conscious effort, she began to gesture around the room as if to make her point. "Then, I was pretty content with the idea that you were a ghost. Imagine my surprise when I had to hear from someone else that you're a vampire. I'm still pretty freaked out all around by this."

Chloe gripped her arms and shielded her chest as if such a move could block out the madness that she had unwittingly walked into. It felt good to finally voice how she'd been feeling over the last few days. She couldn't confide in anyone. But as soon as she was done with her rant, she wanted to take every single word back.

He looked at her, so pained and distraught by her admission. She had unintentionally struck a raw nerve and that judiciously formed defense he had been sporting since God only knew how long, had been shattered. Chloe wanted to throw herself off the nearest cliff without a parachute. The last thing she had ever wanted to do was hurt him with her words. She knew how it felt to be on the receiving end.

Gavin lifted one foot as if he would step closer but then pivoted and swerved around the computer chair to walk towards the kitchen. "Then I'll leave you to write your novels."

Chloe was torn. The idea that he wouldn't disturb her again was tempting. But if he left, she knew the loneliness could return and she couldn't stand being alone again, not in that way.

She took a few bounding, sock-footed steps forward to catch up, though making sure that she stayed a little farther than arm's length away from him. "No, don't leave."

Gavin stopped, and his hands slipped into his coat pocket before he turned around to face her once more. She'd seen that move before with Brent. But Gavin didn't turn around with a proud and haughty look on his face as if he'd won some game they were playing. Instead, he still looked wounded and defenseless.

They stood a little closer this time, and Chloe was once more trapped in his gaze. She lifted her hand, enticed once more to extend her fingers and let them touch the skin that looked so soft.

She saw his eyes dart to her hand and there was a subtle twitch in his posture as if he'd shy away from her touch. After noticing the change, she withdrew her hand before she could make contact and gripped her arm once more.

"You're not going to hurt me?" she asked, sounding like a frightened mouse now, as opposed to the feisty minx she had been a moment before.

Gavin shook his head but held her gaze. "I would never do such a thing...to anyone."

Chloe felt his statement to be true, and she could feel her shoulder muscles release with relief. "Then how do you live?"

His mouth, which had been drawn into a thin line before, looked to be struggling to smile. "How do you think I live?" Perhaps he was enjoying this bantering.

She felt the answer might have been a stab at sarcasm, but his tone was all wrong, so filled with regret. "You don't drink blood?"

Chloe watched the slight tremor that flashed across his body, making the hem of his coat quiver. "I do, but not the blood of humans."

It was odd how they talked so casually of blood and humans as if there were other races besides them. Keeping her eyes fixed on him, she moved around to sit down on the sofa, angling herself towards the kitchen. "How do you get in here?" she asked.

The tension eased between them as she took a more relaxed position on the couch, ready for deep conversation. Gavin even appeared to soften with another dazzling, yet faint, smile. "If I tell you that, how can I be sure you won't try to kill me while I sleep?"

Chloe saw his point. "But how can you be killed?"

His smile deepened. "Again, why should I reveal so much to you?"

It was disheartening to think that Gavin didn't trust her. Yet, she found it perfectly logical seeing as they knew practically nothing about each other except for the obvious.

She nodded slowly and turned her face away to look at the fireplace. "I understand."

Immediately, she spotted her foolishness and snapped her head back to look at him. Sure enough, he'd vanished without a trace, except for the slight sway of the back door window blinds.

Chloe's mouth remained open, ready to speak again before she realized he was gone. Without a second thought, she bolted up and ran out onto the deck.

The night was colder than the previous evening, and tiny mist-like droplets of rainwater splattered on her cheeks.

She called out his name into the darkness. Not even the moon above, so blotted out by storm clouds, could give her enough light to search for him.

Totally mystified by his sudden departure, she turned back inside and locked the door behind her, more out of habit than in an effort to keep him at bay. If he wanted to get in, he could, and there was no stopping him.

Chloe rubbed the soft sleeve of her pajama shirt on her face to wipe away the moisture before returning to the living room.

Her nerves still rattled by all the excitement, Chloe took her place back on the sofa as if he were going to return in a few moments to continue their talk. She wondered what he could possibly be doing out there in the dark.

He said that he didn't drink the blood of humans. And, from what her aunt told her mother, he was seen eating a squirrel. So, he must feed only on animals to survive. Was that an adequate substitute? He didn't seem ill or fraught with malnutrition, apart from his pale skin. But neither did she know anything about vampire illness or what their bodies needed to survive.

Chloe unconsciously rubbed her hand over the side of her neck, glad that she was able to survive her first real confrontation with a vampire without losing her life or a single drop of blood. The night before didn't count because she was unaware that he was a vampire at all.

Gavin said he would never hurt her. Even when she was injured the night before, she would have been a prime target for feeding if he chose. But he didn't, and she was still alive. Her trembling hands were a fine testament to that.

After taking a few moments to compose herself, listening to the drizzling rain patter against the porch's tin roof, Chloe knew he wasn't coming back anytime soon. She stood, finding her legs a little stronger now than they had been before, and climbed the stairs once more to her bedroom.

She left the light on just in case Gavin wanted to come back inside. Although, he probably didn't need a light in order to see his way around.

Slipping underneath the cool sheets, she now realized how feverish she had become. Not only was officially meeting Gavin for the first time terrifying, it was thrilling. Those eyes, that hair, the outfit—everything about him was dashing, dangerous, and utterly attractive. She wondered if it was just the nature of being a vampire that made him so, or if he'd always been that way.

As she tried to sleep, Chloe struggled to keep a level head about Gavin. Each time she remembered how it felt to be held in his arms, she tried to picture him tearing apart an innocent deer with his bare hands.

But it was hard to put Gavin in such a light. That wounded look, the pained expression in his eyes when she called him out for being dishonest. There was no way that he could be such a vicious monster.

Chapter 9

Energized by a long nap in the afternoon and three cups of coffee, Chloe waited anxiously in the living room. She paced back and forth from the front window to the edge of the kitchen, slowly shuffling her socked feet along the wood grain. She tried to focus on how the ridges of the planks felt beneath her toes as they skimmed across the floor, but nothing could keep her mind off of what she had planned for that night.

Driven by a determination to learn all she could about Gavin and his vampire nature, she constructed an orderly list of questions. And she would not go to sleep until she had the answers.

The night before proved to Chloe that she needed to take the reins of them getting to know each other. Judging by the way Gavin ran off when she wasn't looking, he must have been skittish around her. Or, at the very least, hesitant to form that connection that he had been so eager to make when they first started communicating through notes. He didn't even mention a word about her novels or the idea of helping her. Granted, there were far more pressing matters in front of them that needed addressing.

She regretted the things that she had said initially. Perhaps that was why he was so reluctant to stick around. Chloe would do anything to make amends, even put on her big girl panties and stand up to a blood-sucking creature of the night.

Glancing out the window for the thousandth time, she sighed. Her hand pushed back the curtains so she could get a better look at the sky. The final moments of sunset had come, and the cabin was becoming increasingly dark.

She hardly even noticed the difference before flipping on the lights. Gavin didn't need them, but she did.

Minutes ticked by, feeling like hours as Chloe waited. She could hear crickets outside begin their nightly calls, and she could have sworn an owl was not far off in the woods around the cabin. Still, he hadn't shown up.

He may have been avoiding the cabin for her sake. Or perhaps he decided to go search for a meal before coming. Chloe ran her fingers through her hair and tried to calm her nerves with pleasant thoughts. But every thought led back to Gavin in some way or another, and she was worse off than when she started.

Afraid that she would wear down the wood flooring or the bottoms of her socks, Chloe decided to busy her mind with something else. She climbed up the stairs a bit until she had a good view of the living room.

The furniture was arranged tastefully, but Chloe wondered if the sofa might look better facing the kitchen rather than the fireplace. Would it open up the room a bit? She never had an eye for interior design, but reorganizing the furniture was a better option than tiring her legs out by walking around the cabin.

Chloe moved the boxes full of books first; the ones that still had no place in the cabin. She pushed them off to the side towards the writing desk.

She pulled out the armchair next, freeing up the space in front of the window where the sofa would go. Being a girl of little strength, she couldn't lift the heavy wooden armchair by herself. Instead, she dragged it across the floor.

The most obnoxious groaning sound filled the cabin when the blunt legs of the chair skidded against the wooden floorboards. Even Chloe winced at the noise, but there was little she could do to remedy it. The store in town might have had furniture pads—small felt circles to tape under the legs—but it was far too late in the evening for a trip to town, and she might miss Gavin in the process.

Sliding the chair to the foot of the stairs and well out of the way, she positioned herself against the far arm of the sofa and pushed her shoulder against the polished wood.

The sofa made the same racket as the chair had, only an octave deeper since it was heavier. The process was slow, and Chloe's feet slipped several times, causing her to fall and bang her knee on the floor. She knew bruises would form by the end of the night, especially after falling repeatedly on the same point on her knee.

Chloe managed to move the sofa about halfway to where she had originally planned before she paused to catch her breath. In that same moment, she heard a soft creaking sound come from somewhere behind her in the kitchen.

She turned and was suddenly face to face with Gavin. He was closer than she might have liked; close enough to touch and breathe in his masculine scent that seemed to pour from every part of him. A gasp of surprise slipped out as she met those green eyes that had haunted her dreams the night before.

But the look on his face was anything but the caring, sensitive expression she'd fantasized about all day. He seemed annoyed, his brows drawn low over his eyes and nostrils flared. If looks could kill, she would have been struck down in an instant.

Chloe was momentarily stunned by his appearance before glancing behind him to the back door. It remained locked tight, chains and bars all in place. "I didn't hear you come in," she remarked, her hands gripping the arm of the sofa and leaning against it for support. "How are you getting in every night?"

Gavin's face softened a bit. Evidently, whatever he was angry about couldn't keep his attention for long. Either that or he realized whatever intimidation tactic he had tried to use had failed. "That's something I'd rather you not know yet."

She couldn't help but give him a faint smile, loving his British accent more and more with every word he said. It was lyrical compared to the normal southern drawl she was used to.

"Do you materialize or something?"

She saw his eyes skate over her briefly before peering at the furniture behind her. "What are you doing?" he asked, a thread of curiosity in his tone.

Chloe glanced over her shoulder to the chair in the far front corner of the room and was thankful that when she looked back, Gavin was still standing there, looming over her. "I was waiting up for you and got bored. So I started rearranging the furniture."

"Waiting for me?" Gavin asked, his chin lowering a bit with an expression that was too guarded for Chloe to read. Was it surprise? Appreciation?

She nodded. "Yeah. I...What are you doing?"

"Where did you want the sofa?" he asked as he moved around her while she was still in mid-sentence. Chloe caught a whiff of him as he passed by, then deeply inhaled his masculine scent.

It took her a moment to come down from the high his scent had given her. "Below the window," she replied.

With a slackened jaw, Chloe watched Gavin take the sofa in his arms—one gripping the top of the back and the other anchored beneath the seat—and hoisted it up into the air as if it were a giant feather pillow. He let it down just where she said without as much as a grunt or drop of sweat.

Gavin straightened up and turned to her as if he were awaiting instructions. Chloe had to snap herself out of the daze. Part of her was in disbelief that this was truly happening. A vampire was helping her move furniture.

Pressing her palm to her forehead, she assessed the room again.

The sofa now blocked the front door by at least six inches. She hadn't accounted for that.

"I'm sorry, but can you move it over here instead?" she asked, motioning towards the space between the kitchen and living room. She had turned the sofa ninety degrees one way, and now she'd try the other.

Gavin didn't complain at all as he lifted the sofa up again and toted it across the living room, being mindful not to hit the fireplace mantel or stair railing in the process.

Chloe could immediately tell that she'd be in the way and scurried towards the writing desk over on the opposite wall. Leaning against the cool wood paneling, she watched him start to angle the couch into position.

But it soon became clear that the sofa would not fit there either.

"The sofa will be blocking the way to the kitchen," Gavin simply commented.

"You're completely right," Chloe acknowledged with a slight blush to her cheeks. She'd been silly to think that there was any other way to arrange the furniture at all. Even her aunt had placed the sofa the exact same way years, ago and it had worked fine then.

"Should I put it back where it was before?" he asked, looking at her from the corner of his eye.

Chloe gave him another weak, but approving smile and nodded.

He obeyed and set down the sofa exactly where it had been before. Without being asked, he put the armchair back as well.

"Thank you," Chloe said, folding her arms over her chest. The notebook filled with questions was sitting on the coffee table and far out of reach. If Gavin looked down, he would see it for sure.

Once more, she found herself lost in his presence, unsure of herself and what to do. What could one say to start such a conversation with a vampire? Now she wished she had bought the eBook version of *Interview with a Vampire*. Perhaps the key was somewhere in there.

When she saw Gavin begin to look over his shoulder to the coffee table, Chloe went rigid.

"While you're up here," she said, hoping to get his attention, "do you want to join me for dinner?"

Gavin turned to her, ignoring the notebook. His face wrinkled with confusion before he replied, "I suppose. But if it's all the same to you, I'll watch you eat instead."

Chloe's face turned ghost-white, and a cold flush surged down the skin of her back. She hadn't meant the invitation in that way, but she was thankful that he took it the way it was intended.

In all reality, she never intended to invite Gavin to share a meal with her. It was a spur of the moment question to get him to stay; nothing more. But her mind went to work to figure out what exactly to prepare.

She'd already eaten dinner, but a snack wouldn't hurt. Gavin hadn't moved or taken his eyes off her for a second while she stood by her writing desk, looking like a silly girl who didn't know what she was doing. It was the truth, but Chloe didn't want him to know that.

Awkwardly, she let out a tight breath and headed to the kitchen. She turned her back to him and rummaged through the fridge for the ingredients she needed for the thing she didn't know she was cooking yet.

Her eyes fell on a head of lettuce, a ripe tomato, and a bag of sharp cheddar cheese. She grabbed them all, along with a mostly-full bottle of ranch dressing and moved towards the counter, dumping it all out a little too loudly.

Chloe glanced towards the living room, and Gavin was still there, wandering around aimlessly, his eyes calmly roaming on everything but her. She pulled down a cutting board, knife, and bowl, wondering if he had any idea of the effect he had on her.

Her fingers were trembling violently as she began to tear up bits of the lettuce to make her salad. His voice caught her completely off guard.

"Did you write anything today?" he asked. She half expected him to be right behind her, considering how silently he moved. But upon searching, Chloe found him standing beside the desk, staring down at the sleeping computer.

"No," she answered. "I slept for most of the day."

"Are you ill?" he asked.

She could sense the sliver of concern in his voice, and it made her want to smile. With her eyes still focused on the lettuce, she couldn't tell if his brows were furrowed with worry, but she fantasized that they were. It would fit with how he had cared for her so far. This proved that nothing had changed. Revealing that he was a vampire did not change that.

"No, I'm fine. I was just making sure I could stay awake all night for this."

Chloe bemoaned her candidness. Now she sounded more like a silly fangirl than someone who might have been casually curious. Upon thinking, she probably fit the profile of a vampire fangirl perfectly with how obsessed she had become over this man, so shrouded in mystery and intrigue.

She pushed aside the head of lettuce and brought the tomato to the cutting board. She sawed at the plump flesh of the tomato, a bit of pinkish liquid seeping out as she sliced.

"You needn't change your schedule for my sake," he said. She detected a quiver of a laugh in his voice, and it made her weak. "I would have preferred that you spend that time working on your novel."

A frown formed between Chloe's brows. He spoke as if he was her tutor or mentor rather than a colleague or—dare she think it—a friend. "Why is that so important to you?" she asked.

Just as she finished her question, her clumsy hand made the serrated edge of the knife slip across the smooth skin of the tomato and straight into her left index finger. Blood had been drawn.

Chloe hissed and dropped the knife in order to grip her finger. And all at once, the room began to spin. She wasn't squeamish at the sight of blood, and the wound wasn't deep enough to cause any debilitating pain.

What made her feel faint was the knowledge that Gavin was in the cabin, and fresh blood had been drawn just several feet away. Chloe's whole body trembled, knowing these few stuttered breaths may be her last.

She had no idea what kind of control Gavin had over his hunger, and this was not part of her plan to find out. In fact, she never wanted to find out at all.

Chloe turned and looked to Gavin, whose full attention was fixed on her. The lines on his face had gone hard, and his muscles tightened like a predator ready to pounce. But he didn't pounce. Instead, he took gliding steps forward, his shoes finally making the soft tapping noise that she had expected to hear all along.

As Gavin drew closer, she knew the smart thing would be to move away. Instead, she felt as if her body was not her own. Her legs moved without her bidding, turning her whole body to face him. And there she froze, fixated in one spot.

Chloe had never experienced a heart attack, but she imagined it felt similar to what was going on in her body at that exact moment. Not only because of how intimidating Gavin was, but also how handsome and still unabashedly captivating. She felt her heart would explode with the intense feelings that swelled in her constricted chest.

But she didn't explode or even implode. She just stood there, shaking and holding her finger as blood oozed into her palm.

Then she noticed a change in Gavin's eyes. The once brilliant green was growing darker and darker until his irises were completely black and expanding out to plume over the white around it. He was nearly on top of her when she saw the red ring, as bright and fierce as a roaring flame, take the place of the green she'd come to love.

What stared back at her were not the eyes of a handsome man but a vicious vampire. His lips parted ever so slightly and she could see his saliva glisten on his pointed fangs.

If Chloe had any control whatsoever, she would have lost it completely anyway. If it weren't for the mysterious force that kept her standing, she'd have fallen into a puddle on the kitchen floor.

She couldn't breathe, she couldn't think. Her core tightened for a few seconds as if to squeeze out the small tear that trickled down from the corner of her eye.

She felt it glide over her cheek, cold and leaving a moist trail behind it. Could he see her cry? Did he care?

He was so close now; close enough to see the pores on his skin. Would he bite her now? Rip out her throat? Or just suck on her finger until there was nothing left in her whole body?

No. He did none of those things. Instead, he reached out and peeled back her hand that was holding her injured finger to reveal the mess beneath. Both palms were covered in her blood; the deep cut pounding sore and stinging. His touch was hot on her skin, burning and tingling with every stroke.

He took her injured hand and eyed it with an otherworldly fascination as if he hadn't seen human blood before. Perhaps he hadn't. Or maybe it had been too long since his last human meal that he'd forgotten.

Something broke the spell over his concentration, and Gavin looked towards the counter. There sat a roll of paper towels. He reached out and tore off a sheet, then began to clean up her wound.

"Do you have a first aid kit?" he asked.

Chloe was perplexed, her throat too dry to respond. All she could do was glance down to the cabinet below the sink. Gavin understood and bent down briefly to retrieve it.

She watched as he leafed through the contents, pulling out gauze bandages and antiseptic. He rinsed the sheet of paper towel he had previously used and cleaned up the dried blood before applying the medical ointment on the cut.

It hurt, but Chloe couldn't think to react. He was so gentle, his touches feather-light. He began to wrap her treated finger in the bandages, his movements so careful and deliberate that she was mesmerized.

Why didn't he attack her? Why didn't he feed? The least he could have done was lick at the open wound, but he didn't. Instead, he was helping her even though he must have been hungry. Those menacing eyes were evidence to the fact he probably hadn't fed yet.

As if he had read her thoughts, Gavin said softly, "I'm not a monster." His tone was laden with such sadness, such palpable remorse, that another tear fell from her eyes. "I'm just a man, trying desperately not to be."

Chloe had never openly accused him of being a monster, but, somehow, he still felt like one in her eyes. It convicted her so harshly that she wanted to crawl away and die. She had never intended to make him feel that way.

Those questions on the coffee table would have only served to make him feel cornered and put under a microscope. She had no right to probe him like that.

He taped off the dressing and repacked the first aid box. When he straightened back up from placing the kit back under the sink, she could see the red and black colorations in his eyes begin to fade away. The threatening colors swirled back into his pupils, leaving the emerald gems sparkling down on her once more.

Gavin cleaned up her other hand and tossed the blood-stained paper towel into the trash. When she heard the rustle of plastic from the trash bag, Chloe felt her legs begin to buckle beneath her.

But Gavin saw her begin to sway and gripped her arms to steady her. "Perhaps you should sit down," he offered.

Chloe nodded, still unable to speak but now able to freely move as she willed. Gavin escorted her into the living room and lowered her to the sofa before he turned and hurried through the kitchen and out of the backdoor.

Without another sound, he was gone, possibly for the whole night, and she wouldn't see him again until tomorrow.

She had so many questions, so many thoughts and wonderings that she knew she couldn't keep to herself. But how was she to get the answers she craved? Chloe knew that bombarding him with those questions would do nothing but harm and cause friction between them.

He must have hated what he was. Why else would he not seize the chance to drink her blood and restrict himself to feeding only upon animals? The vampires she'd read about and watched on TV shows were bloodthirsty killers with no shame for the crimes they had committed.

Yet Gavin had a soul; he knew what true sorrow was, and perhaps he was trying to atone for what he was.

Chloe knew so little, but she could infer so much from those expressive eyes and the hints dropped in his voice. For a man who concealed so much in their conversations, his body language was far more expressive.

One thing was certain; Chloe wasn't going to give up, not this easily. She would try to reach him again and build the bridge between their worlds. Even if she had to drink three pots of coffee during the night and sleep all day, she'd do it. She'd do it for him.

Chapter 10

After the near emotional and mental breakdown that had taken place in the downstairs kitchen with Gavin, Chloe had tried her best to sleep. But it wouldn't come. Her mind was alive with too many thoughts.

Mostly, she'd thought about what Gavin had said about being a man who was desperately trying not to be a monster. What did he mean by that exactly?

She tossed and turned, unable to get comfortable because of the caffeine that was still working its way through her body. Her eyes felt heavy, but the rest of her was all too awake.

Admitting defeat, she wrapped herself in her plush robe to cover her pajamas and went back downstairs. As long as she was awake, maybe she could get a little writing done. That would certainly please Gavin.

She was still torn over whether to let him help with the novel. She could surely use his help, but now the circumstances had changed. He was no longer the distant ghost who came in the night to leave her encouraging notes. He was the vampire who had scared her out of her skin and made her ache with a desire she had scarcely known before.

Flipping on the lights, she took stock of the room and found that Gavin was still missing. The clock told her it was almost midnight, about five hours after sunset at least. She wondered if he was still out hunting or had gone to wherever it is that he hid during the day.

Still set on writing, she shuffled into the kitchen to brew a new pot of coffee. Though it'd be her fourth cup in the last twelve hours, she could use another to help her eyes stay open.

She grimaced when she saw that the lettuce, cheese, and tomato were still sitting out where she'd left them hours ago. She'd been in such a befuddled state that she had completely forgotten about the snack she was going to make. The leaves were already beginning to brown around the edges, and the cheese was room temperature.

With a mutter of frustration, Chloe tossed everything in the garbage and rinsed off both the knife and the cutting board in the sink. By then, the coffee pot chimed, and she could smell the wonderful roasted blend.

She pulled down one of her favorite mugs. It was powder blue with a white snowflake painting on the side. A much younger Chloe had done the artwork with the help of her mother, and it had earned its place on the special list of treasures, right below her rare copy of *Mansfield Park*.

She poured the coffee, added four and a half spoons of sugar, and sipped on the warm brew, letting it refresh her body

When she turned to go towards the living room, she was surprised to see Gavin standing there, no more than a foot from her, an amused smile gracing his face.

Despite the pleasant expression, Chloe was startled nonetheless. She shrieked and jumped, consequently spilling her hot coffee all over Gavin's shirt and the waistband of his trousers.

Chloe covered her mouth, but it didn't stop her from letting out a noisy gasp. She was mortified. Not only by the fact that Gavin had suddenly appeared from out of nowhere, but that she just soaked his shirt with steaming coffee.

For a few seconds, she didn't know what to do besides stare at the way he looked down at the mess, hands slightly raised out to the sides. And she watched as the faint smile broadened into a toothy grin and he let out a chuckle as if he found all this utterly hilarious.

Chloe slammed down the mug on the counter, spilling the last of it on the surface and grabbed at the roll of paper towels while sputtering out incoherent apologies.

She tore off a few sheets and stepped towards him to help him clean up, but she stopped cold when green, smiling eyes landed on her. Her hands jerked back and forth, visibly debating on whether to willingly touch him in that way.

Beneath the damp shirt, she could see the fine definition of muscle. If she were to press the paper towel onto his shirt, she'd feel those muscles. It'd be the first time in her life she'd ever come into contact with such a figure. Brent was soft, but not overweight, and still nothing like Gavin.

"Chloe, it's alright," he said, and she felt as if she'd turn into a gibbering adolescent standing in front of her crush. The way he spoke her name was so unique, so warm and lilting. She would have given everything to hear him speak her name for the rest of her life.

Without thinking, Chloe brought the paper towels up and covered her own face in embarrassment. She groaned and stamped her feet like a child. "No, it's not," she whined. "I just ruined your shirt."

He laughed. The sound was so deep it vibrated in her bones. "No, you didn't ruin it. It's been stained with worse." Chloe cringed, knowing that something worse must have been blood. "It just needs a turn in the wash."

With the paper towel still masking her face, she took a breath and let it out in a big huff. When she finally uncovered her eyes, she found that Gavin was undressing in her kitchen.

The trench coat was thrown over the back of a kitchen chair while he began to unfasten the buttons of his shirt. Chloe felt her eyes go wide at the sight as smooth, flawless, pale skin was unveiled to her in the most erotic way possible.

Gavin wasn't even looking at her but had his eyes focused on the washing machine in the far corner by the back door. He peeled his shirt off, tugging the tails out from his pants and wadding up the material in his strong hands.

Chloe leaned heavily against the counter, knowing her buckling knees wouldn't be able to support her weight for much longer. Gavin had the body of a model with large pecs and chiseled abs. She watched as his arm muscles flexed and bunched with every movement.

Her own muscles tensed, especially low on her belly. She'd felt this feeling of attraction before with Brent, but never anything this intense. Gavin was magnificent.

Mesmerized by his half-nakedness, she barely noticed that he was starting the washer. The machine sputtered to life and poured out a little bit of water but then died unexpectedly.

Chloe made a move to assist him, but she was shocked to witness him give the appliance a good hard kick with the tip of his boot. The water began pouring once more.

He turned and regarded her look of confusion. "I've learned how all these contraptions work over the years," he said as if answering her silent question.

She blinked and realized that she'd been slowly tearing at the paper towel with her nails while she ogled Gavin's perfect body. The thought that he was a vampire didn't even come into the romantic fantasy that was playing out unbidden in her head.

As her eyes drank him in once more, she recognized that her previous belief that his skin was flawless was totally wrong. She saw the faintest of scars streak across his right bicep.

"What happened to your arm?" she heard slip out.

Gavin squinted at her in confusion. He probably expected her to mention how pale he was or something related to his vampire nature. But she took notice of this unremarkable scar.

He glanced down at the blemish. "It happened a very long time ago," he replied, putting emphasis on the adjective. But how long was very long? One hundred years or two?

Chloe gulped and found her voice again. "I don't have any shirts that will fit you properly."

"I have another shirt," he said with another dazzling smile.

So much blood had drained from Chloe's head and neck during this whole ordeal that there would have been little for Gavin to feed on even if he wanted to. "At your secret hideout, I suppose?" she said, attempting a flirtatious twist to her words.

He didn't seem to notice and simply shook his head. "It's no secret."

"It is to me."

There were a few beats of intense silence with only her shallow breathing to fill the space between them. Then, as if coming to a final decision, Gavin took a few steps forward and squatted down onto the floor.

Chloe shrunk back against the counter, thinking he might spring forward. But instead, his hands grazed along the floorboards. Gavin's eyes were still locked on her face when his finger hooked into a knothole in the wood and pulled.

To her astonishment, not only one board came up, but several to reveal that there was a trap door hidden in the floor of her kitchen. Gavin opened the door wide, the invisible hinges making no sound at all.

What lay beneath her cabin was a dark cellar, too dark for her to even peer into. All she could make out were the few top steps that led down into the basement.

Chloe's jaw dropped. She'd never seen this before. There was no access to this basement anywhere else in the cabin and no window from the outside. But perhaps that's the way Gavin preferred it.

Stronger than the idea that this basement had been hidden from her all her life was the affirmation that Gavin had never been far away. He didn't have some distant shack that he slept in or a cave hidden in the side of the mountain. He was sleeping beneath her feet the whole time.

While recovering from her shock, Gavin descended into the darkness and came back a moment later wearing a tight fitting brown shirt that contoured his bulging muscles and broad shoulders.

He gently lowered the trap door, the edges blending so seamlessly with the rest of the floor that she couldn't see for sure where it was at all. Only the telltale knothole remained that gave away the location the hidden door.

She raised her eyes to meet his gaze, and Chloe could tell that he was enjoying this a little too much.

"How long has that been there?" she asked, her voice shrill with disbelief.

Gavin thought for a moment. "Two hundred and eighty-one years, give or take."

Chloe shuddered to think that it had been there that long and she'd never known. Had her aunt known? Did her mother know? Did anyone in their family know that a vampire had lived beneath them while they ate their meals and roasted marshmallows on the fire?

Without knowing how to accurately respond, and not wanting to offend him further, she turned away and used the crumpled up paper towels to wipe down the spilled coffee on the countertop.

"I hope this won't bother you too much," he said. From what she could tell, he hadn't moved, but she would waste no more of her time assuming she knew where he was at any given moment.

She gave a nervous, high-pitched laugh. "Bother me? Why would it bother me? I have a vampire as a roommate. I'm fantastic."

Chloe saw the error of her word choice and winced. She had the terrible habit of being sarcastic when she was clearly uncomfortable. Call it a defense mechanism, but to Chloe it was a nuisance and it pushed away people more often than not.

She quickly turned and saw that Gavin didn't take offense to her ribbing. In fact, his lips were pulled tight as if he were resisting the urge to laugh again. He was certainly in a better mood than earlier in the evening. That was possibly a perk of feeding.

Spinning to face him completely, she crossed her arms tightly over her churning stomach. "Listen, I'm really sorry about everything I've said over the past two nights. I know I've probably offended you, and I didn't mean to."

Gavin's expression shifted from amused to calm with a hint of something Chloe recognized as akin to admiration. "It's alright. I can only imagine what you must be going through."

She let out a tight breath and smiled. "Yeah, my aunt didn't exactly tell me about you in her will. Otherwise, I might have been a little more prepared."

A shadow passed over his face, and he was no longer smiling. "I heard about Mary Anne. You have my deepest condolences."

Chloe shifted her weight from one foot to the other. "How did you know?"

"I hear a lot through these floorboards," he said, tapping his heel on the wood to prove his point. "I heard about your aunt's passing when the realtors came to inspect the home. That's when I first heard you'd be moving in."

A sickening feeling came over her stomach. "How much do you hear?"

Gavin shrugged and his lips pinched together. "Not much. I can tell when you're walking around and having conversations on the downstairs floor, but nothing else." Why did Chloe not believe him? "And now it's my turn to apologize for my deplorable behavior earlier. Do forgive me?"

Chloe could only guess that he was referring to earlier when his eyes had turned a nasty blood red and he cleaned her cut finger. She scraped the bandage against her sleeve, not liking how sore and tender it still was.

"It's totally fine. I should have been more careful with the knife."

Gavin didn't reply but turned his gaze away to focus on some undefined spot on the wall. A tendon jumped in his jaw as he gritted his teeth together in what she could only describe as a deep self-loathing. He probably hated the way that he lost control, even for a moment. Regardless of whether he acted on such a temptation or not, he probably didn't like the fact that he was tempted at all.

It brought her back to what he'd said before about trying not to be a monster. Watching him stand there in her kitchen, handsome features and all, it was easy to imagine him as anything but a monster.

Chloe turned away and poured herself another cup of coffee. After glancing over her shoulder to make sure he wasn't right behind her, she turned and walked into the living room to turn on her laptop.

"I'm going to try and write a little tonight," she announced, unsure why.

"Wonderful. You haven't written anything in a while." The cheer in his words was notable.

"Nothing besides that little short story yesterday."

She heard Gavin's heavy footsteps lumber out of the kitchen and into the living room.

"That was rather devious of you, by the way."

Chloe grinned and perked up a bit at the off-handed compliment. "Why, thank you, sir," she replied in a horribly attempted British accent.

Once more, Gavin did not take offense and chuckled instead. At least he had a sense of humor, she thought. Maybe this cohabitation wouldn't be so bad.

While her computer was waking up, Chloe felt herself become hyper aware of Gavin and where he was in the house. First, he wandered across the fireplace to the window and stayed there for a while before sitting on the couch.

She wasn't quite sure why he lingered in the living room. There were a million places that he could be if he wanted to. But, instead of slinking down into the basement or hunting for rabbits out in the woods, he chose to be with her, somehow just content to be in the vicinity.

"So, you knew my aunt?" Chloe asked, referring to their previous conversation. He might have been fine with the silence, but she was not.

"Very well, actually," he replied.

When she opened up the word document for her novel, she heard him rise and draw closer.

Chloe tried not to read between the lines of his response, but it was too tempting. "How well?"

Gavin was standing behind her now, his hands slung in his pockets. "We talked a great deal on many topics."

She turned her head until her chin grazed her shoulder as she looked down to his knees, unwilling to meet his eyes and be trapped there. "Just talked?"

It took Gavin a moment, but then he realized what she meant and laughed. "Yes, I can assure you, all we did was talk."

Chloe inwardly let out a relieved sigh. If her aunt had gotten seriously intimate with a vampire, no wonder everyone thought she was losing her marbles.

Turning back to the word document, she refreshed herself with the events that took place in the chapter before. It felt like weeks since she'd sat down and cranked out a few paragraphs about her characters' love story.

But, as she began reading, she was painfully aware of how close Gavin was. He had taken another step forward and she could practically feel him leaning over her shoulder to read along.

His scent roiled around her once more, and the hairs on the back of her neck stood at attention. Her skin tingled pleasantly even though she couldn't feel his breath on her neck. In fact, he had no breath at all. It was quiet except for the muted din of crickets coming from outside, and all she could hear was the sound of her own breathing.

It had never occurred to her that Gavin wasn't really alive. He was a vampire, the living dead. He would have no heartbeat, no breath, nothing to make him validly living except for the fact that he moved and behaved as any living being.

Chloe had read in some mythologies online about vampires having no soul. But she already knew that couldn't be the case for Gavin. He was too caring and considerate not to have a soul.

The longer he stood there, the more intense her anxiety became. His nearness would make her come undone if she didn't break away. But she had almost no desire to. The moment felt so unnerving that she was willing to ask him anything as long as it would break the silence.

"When you were fixing the cut, I couldn't move."

The way it came out was more of a statement, but she meant it as a question.

"Yes, I am sorry about that as well," he replied with a sigh. Now she felt a hot gust of air blow on her exposed neck. Chloe tried to hold in her shivers. So he did have breath, but he didn't breathe. How was that possible?

"You did that to me?" she asked meekly. She wasn't reading anymore, merely staring at the bright computer screen, trying her hardest not to make any sudden movements.

"I did." She felt his face inch closer. "I knew if you had the chance to run, you would have. And I wanted the chance to help you."

Chloe swallowed. "And now?"

Gavin seemed to lurch minutely at the question. "I'm not doing anything now. I only use that particular skill when I'm... Well, it makes it easier than having to run after a meal. I'll just leave it at that."

She knew exactly what he meant.

"But, I promise," he continued, "that I will not use such powers on you again."

He relaxed as bit as he seemed to flow back into the task of reading. Chloe twitched her fingers, testing if he was lying to her about his sway over her body. They moved at her bidding, so she shakily reached out for her coffee mug.

She brought it to her lips, being extraordinarily careful not to spill. Just after one sip, she realized her mistake. The coffee was bitter, lacking the sweetener that she always added. In all the excitement, she forgot all about doctoring up her coffee so it was at least palatable.

Chloe's nose wrinkled at the taste. Gathering what strength she could from her need to have her cup of coffee, she stood from the chair and swerved past Gavin to retreat once more into the kitchen.

Gavin stayed in the living room, but only for a moment.

While she mixed in her usual dose of sugar, the spoon clinking against the inner walls of her mug, she sensed more than heard Gavin approach.

Standing there, her hands gripping her mug so tightly that the warmth seeped into her palms, a dangerous idea came to mind.

Chloe wondered if Gavin was putting on a show for her. He was so nice, so amiable and pleasant to be around that this couldn't be the truth. The only downside to his company was how undone he made her feel.

One common trait amongst all the myths about vampires she had learned was that they were masters of seduction. Women vampires were temptresses, and the men were dashing gentlemen up to the very end until they revealed their true intent for midnight lovers.

Would Chloe become one of those victims? Would the mask fall a second too late? What if, in the same way that he had manipulated her body, Gavin was distorting her mind to make her believe that what she saw was true? What if that handsome face was no more than a façade?

She wished that thoughts were like pencil sketches. Then, she could erase what didn't sit well with her and create a new image. But this new revelation couldn't be wiped away. There would always be that kernel of mistrust unless she was given a reason to believe that living in the same cabin with a vampire was completely fine; Or, as fine as it could be.

Chloe lifted her chin, and she heard an uncertainty in Gavin's steps. Could he feel her emotions in the same way that a predator could smell fear? Could he read her thoughts and know what it was she suspected?

Then, there was stillness. Chloe looked and saw him standing at the dividing line between the kitchen and the living room, staring at her with a perplexed look. He didn't seem angry or upset at all. Perhaps it was the shift in her stance that made him hesitant to trespass closer.

Hardly knowing what compelled her to ask, she said, "What?"

He shook his head as if coming out of a deep sleep. "Nothing. I..." Gavin paused, seeming pensive as he gazed at her. "You resemble someone I knew."

Chloe blinked. "Who?" Her fingertips pressed into the ceramic of her coffee mug, feeling the jagged ridges of the paint lines.

Gavin didn't answer. But he did take a few cautious steps forward.

Watching his slow swagger, Chloe forgot what it was she had been so concerned about. Yes, Gavin was handsome. And yes, he was a vampire. But wouldn't he have killed her long ago if he had really wanted to? He said so himself when she first found him in the living room the night before.

The idea was comforting and just the rational thinking she needed to fight away the mistrust she had felt moments before. Gavin wasn't her enemy here. He was her friend, someone who could keep her company at night while the rest of the world forgot that she had secluded herself away in this cabin. He was also someone to share her passion with. He obviously knew a lot about writing and literature. That was enough to earn her veneration.

The tension she'd felt for days about Gavin vanished. In its place was the surety that she'd, at last, found a new friend. It was a new life, a new adventure, and a new friend who happened to be a vampire.

Gavin came excruciatingly close, but Chloe wasn't afraid anymore. She trembled, but it wasn't from fear that he'd kill her. It was from the anticipation of what he might do instead.

She'd been so focused on his green eyes that she didn't see his hand reach out and snatch something from her robe pocket. She jerked back and watched him examine the small blue notebook.

It was one of many Chloe kept. One was in her purse, another by her bed upstairs, and another waiting on her dresser to be slipped into her jeans pocket when she went out. As a creative person and aspiring writer, she found it an effective habit to keep a notepad and pen on her at all times. She'd nearly forgotten that her robe pocket still contained any such supplies.

Gavin, his brows angled curiously, flipped open the thin plastic cover and began leafing through the ruled pages. Chloe watched him and sipped at her coffee, resisting the eager smile that wanted to burst forth.

She knew that some of the ideas contained in that particular notebook were from a few days ago when she came up with an alternate scene idea for the novel she was working on right now. They were changes that Gavin didn't even know about. Would he like them?

The answer came when Gavin made a face and began ripping out one page at a time. Chloe nearly choked on her coffee when he wadded them up in his fist and tossed them onto the counter.

"What are you doing?" Chloe shrieked, feeling as if she'd been indirectly defiled by the way he was destroying her ideas.

"These ideas are no good for your story," he simply said, still perusing through the contents of the notebook.

"Why not? I thought that hardware store scene would have been perfect!" Chloe defended, immediately setting down her coffee to try and salvage the tattered piece of paper from the counter.

"It's not realistic. You're forcing your characters together in a situation that would never happen."

Chloe was taken aback that Gavin presumed to know her characters better than she did. "And why would you say that?" she asked, smoothing the pages on her thigh.

Gavin flipped the notebook closed after tearing out almost every page with words written on it and looked up at her with a magnanimous expression. "Because, Ben Johnson is a banker, and he's already admitted that he knows little about the things that most men seem to know. This includes knowing how to repair a broken sink drain. Therefore, he would not immediately offer his help to Alleia."

Set back on her heels, Chloe was amazed. She'd completely forgotten that her male protagonist was a pretty useless excuse for a man when it came to repairing things. If she had added that scene, her readers would have immediately picked up on it. Either that, or she would have seen the mistake while revising the manuscript, and it might have thrown the book completely off.

Taking a bite of humble pie, she crumpled up the papers again. "You're right. How could I have missed that? I sometimes think of scenes that I'd like to add in my stories and just jot them down for later. But you're completely right. This scene isn't for Ben and Alleia."

Chloe raised her hand to toss the useless ideas into the trash when a hand clamped shut over her knuckles. The lack of frightening force was new to her and she relished the way his warm fingers gentle wrapped over hers.

Chloe flinched and looked up to meet his gaze again.

"If you like the idea, maybe you could save it for another novel," he suggested. "I'm sorry if I gave you the impression it couldn't be used at all."

The way he wadded up the papers to begin with had certainly made her feel as if her inspiration was worthless, but, she accepted his apology with a nod and began flattening the pages out again.

"You said you wanted to write tonight?"

Chloe nodded again and pocketed the somewhat repaired pages before taking up her mug again.

"I know I just proved that my assistance may not be viable, but permit me to help?"

She couldn't help but give him a tight-lipped grin. "I never did give you that answer about helping with Ben's part, did I?"

Gavin returned the smile, but he wasn't bashful about exposing his pearly teeth. "No, you haven't. But I wasn't going to bring it up."

Chloe's smile weakened a bit at the sight of his sparkling fangs. It was the only trait about Gavin that suggested he wasn't human, besides his pale skin, of course. And even though she had seen them before, they were quite daunting.

He noticed that her attention had been drawn towards his mouth and quickly pressed his lips together to hide them. "Are they as terrifying as you thought they would be?" he asked, a twinge of self-consciousness in his voice.

She shrugged her shoulders together as if to fight off a cold breeze. "They're not as long as I imagined."

Taking a step back, Gavin swept his arm out and then back across his stomach before bending low in a deep bow. "You have my word as a gentleman that I will never harm you."

When he rose back up, Chloe was on the verge of giggles. The bow, combined with his British accent and heart-stopping good looks, was too much to bear in one sitting. A sparkle came to his eyes as if he found her struggling face amusing.

It was what pushed her over the edge, and Chloe let out a string of giggles that she almost couldn't control. She covered her mouth and nose with the plush cuff of her robe to muffle the sound, but there was no hiding the one thing about her that she hated.

It was a genuine laugh, intermittent with moments where she couldn't breathe and strings of bubbling giggles. She hadn't laughed so hard in weeks, and she knew why. She'd never had a reason to feel happy until now.

Gavin waited patiently for her to settle down, his own facial muscles tight to suppress the urge to grin. But soon, even his control snapped, and she saw the fangs glisten in the kitchen light.

Funny how they both were trying to hide the one thing they must have hated in themselves, but in the end, it didn't matter. Chloe didn't totally mind his fangs, and he obviously didn't mind her dorky laughter.

She cleared her throat once her giggling had stopped and quickly walked away feeling discomfited. Gavin followed as she sat back down at the desk.

"So, what will we put Ben and Alleia through today?" he asked, clearly trying to change the subject for her sake.

Chloe thought it strange how now they were suddenly a team and this was their project. She wasn't alone anymore. It warmed her soul to know that Gavin was there to help.

He was so unlike Brent. Not only was Brent never really there when she needed him, but he hated her laugh and purposefully tried to not say anything funny to coax it out. Why hadn't she met Gavin sooner in life? Then, maybe she wouldn't have made so many awful mistakes.

Chapter 11

C hloe tried to hold perfectly still as she applied the black mascara to her upper eyelashes, her face pulled into an unattractive look like most women had while applying eye makeup. It had been a while since she'd had to bother about things like a beauty regimen, but tonight was special. At least, she would try to make it special.

She had no idea if Gavin would accept her invitation, but it was worth the shot.

It had been a week since they'd started working on the novel together. And in that time, she'd grown used to him. She had to admit that it had been a little unsettling for a few days.

He was no longer secretive about his comings and goings, and, on more than one occasion, he'd startled her by rising from the kitchen trap door without first announcing himself. After a while, he had gotten into the habit of knocking on the floorboards first before making an appearance each evening.

Chloe soon found confidence in his presence and felt safe knowing that he was there. Apart from the night she'd cut her finger, he had never displayed any sign of thirst or hunger towards her. Gavin always excused himself for an hour or so before they began writing well into the night. She assumed he was out to quench his vampire thirst instead of taking it out on her by accident.

Her schedule had been totally destroyed. She slept during the day, just as he did, and stayed awake all night. Chloe even began making her meals while Gavin wrote his parts in the novel and purchased blackout curtains for her room so the sun wouldn't disturb her sleep. With each passing night, she began to understand what it must have been like for Gavin to live in a world with no sun. She hated it and could feel the toll it was taking on her mental health.

Her tan was fading, and though she was not as pale as Gavin, Chloe still found it strange. What was worse, her powder foundation makeup no longer matched her skin tone. A few times, she took naps out by the creek just so she could get some sun exposure.

While applying her shimmering pink lip gloss, Chloe thought about how close she and Gavin had become. They were friends, to say the least, but there was always the underlying tension between them that Chloe had felt from the first day. Every kind gesture, every prolonged stare, every encouraging word was only fuel for the fire that burned within her for the vampire living in the basement.

She knew it was wrong—beyond wrong. It was obscene and morbid to think of Gavin as anything more than a friend and collaborating writer. Yet, she couldn't help but over analyze every detail of his posture and the sparkle in his amazing green eyes. Did they mean that he felt something, too? And what did that mean for her? What was in store for a woman who won the affection of a vampire? Her chest ached at the very thought that she could be a lover to something – someone – who didn't even have a beating heart. She didn't know how to feel about any of it.

Chloe remembered when Gavin had said she reminded him of someone he once knew. He had never mentioned the girl again, and Chloe had been too timid to bring her up. In fact, she'd been too timid to bring up anything related to the last nearly three hundred years of his existence.

Their conversations had been strictly focused on the novel they were writing together, nothing more, and nothing less. There were so many times she had wanted to ask him about things she didn't understand, such as why he lived in the basement, and why he hadn't moved on to live a life away from the cabin. Why did he only drink animal blood? Why did he look at her the way he did, his eyes so full of unexplainable emotion that made her feel weightless? And why, for someone who had been alive for close to three hundred years, did he know so much about things like how the washer worked and computers?

She refused to ask him any forward, possibly intrusive questions. She didn't want a replay of the first night they'd met face to face, and she had scolded him for freaking her out.

She hoped that tonight would make up for it all.

Chloe took a step back and looked at herself in the mirror, wearing a pair of faded, flair, hip hugger jeans and a black, long sleeve, V-neck, cashmere sweater top with a camisole underneath. It was certainly something different than she had been wearing for the past week and a half since she'd come to Carter Lake.

Her attire thus far had been restricted to pajamas and long jackets, with the exception of the night she had gone to Rosie's Bridge party. The top was form fitting; something that Gavin had not seen her in before. It wasn't too provocative but hugged her curves just enough to make anyone aware that she was all woman.

As a blush rose to her cheeks, she wondered if he would be blown away by her efforts to look presentable. Where they were going, no one would really see her, but Gavin would, and that was reason enough to dress up.

She brushed her hair one more time and checked the clock on the wall. It was just thirty minutes until sunset. If only it were enough time to do something better with her hair. Without regular beauty treatments apart from shampooing and conditioning in the shower, her hair had developed a mind of its own. Most of the evenings she spent with Gavin, she kept her hair up and out of the way in a bun or ponytail.

But now, letting it down, Chloe pondered what could be done about it. It was wavy and curled tighter at the ends than normal. She owned a hair straightener, but since her hair was so thick, it wouldn't do much to remedy the disaster unless she spent an exorbitant amount of time sitting in front of the mirror.

With a great sigh, she pulled out the flat iron and set to work, taming the superficial waves while leaving the ends to curl as they wished. The final result was not exactly what she wanted, but it was acceptable for a night out like this.

She slipped on a pair of fashionable black leather boots and made her way downstairs. Having had her cup of coffee before putting on lip gloss, she had no fear of ruining the look. She sat down on the sofa and tried to take her mind off of the night ahead by picking up Moby Dick and reading where she had left off so long ago.

All there was left to do was wait. Butterflies fluttered in her stomach. The feeling took her back to her high school days when she would grow anxious just at the thought of her crush coming around the hallway corner. Chloe felt childish. It was just an outing with a friend, nothing more. It wasn't like one date meant anything. It never did. But this was more than a date. It was a chance to get out of the cabin and take Gavin along with her.

The sun dipped below the horizon, and she flipped on all the lights downstairs in preparation for the darkness. Each slight creak in the wood made her grow rigid with expectation. But she relaxed after realizing it didn't mean Gavin was rising from his day sleep.

She checked the clock on the wall again and bit the inside of her mouth anxiously. If he didn't hurry up, they might be late. She did, however, account for his nightly feeding. But she at least wanted to propose her plan first before he hurried out of the kitchen door.

Finally, after a long wait, she heard his usual rap against the bottom side of the floor. The trap door in the kitchen opened without a sound and Gavin stepped into the light. He wore a black pinstripe, button up shirt with the first top few buttons undone and a pair of dark jeans. The shirt was not tucked in, unlike his usual custom of looking as if he were going to a job interview. But instead, the shirt hung out over his waist, and he was not wearing his usual coat. He constantly amazed her with his variety of wardrobe and style. Somehow, she had imagined that he only had one outfit to wear all the time.

He closed the trap door but hadn't looked to Chloe yet, even though she had snapped the book shut and sat up a little straighter on the couch with a bright smile.

When he finally laid eyes on her, Chloe watched Gavin's eyebrows arch in surprise.

"Good evening," he greeted. "Are you going somewhere?"

She beamed at him and nodded. "As a matter of fact, I am. And you're coming with me."

Gavin blinked and crossed the divide between the kitchen and living room. "I hope wherever it is we're going, you can take your laptop with you."

"Nope. No writing tonight."

Gavin gave her a blank stare as if she had just spoken in a foreign language. Surely he didn't expect her to write every night like a machine? She needed to get out just like anyone else. Chloe wasn't suffering from cabin fever just yet, but she felt that in another few days she'd be standing on the borderline for sure.

Then, as if a sneaking demon had latched onto her brain, she remembered Atlanta and Brent and how he'd treated her. But Gavin wasn't like Brent, right?

Slowly, Gavin nodded. "I suppose a break would be beneficial. But I won't be joining you, wherever it is you're going."

With that, he turned on the balls of his feet and strode towards the back door. Chloe, stricken by the urgent need to convince him, leaped up from the couch and pursued.

She even surprised herself when she was quick enough to place herself between Gavin and the door. Only when he stopped and went as still as a statue did she realize exactly what she was doing. Chloe was getting in the way of a hungry vampire and his path to a meal. She might as well have thrown herself atop the carcass of a deer while a pack of ravenous wolves gathered.

And she could tell from the ominous glint in his eyes that he was not amused by her bold move.

"Why won't you come with me?" she asked.

Gavin sighed heavily. "Isn't it obvious?"

Chloe shook her head. "No, it's not. Do you think you'll lose control and kill everyone or something?"

He did not find that comment funny either, and she saw his hands form into tight fists at his sides. "I don't know. I haven't been around a large crowd in centuries."

Chloe overlooked the way he said it so calmly as if he were talking about a few months rather than a few hundred years. She wondered if she would ever get used to how old he really was. "Would it help if I told you where we were going?"

"Where *you* are going. And no, it wouldn't. You can't sway me so easily."

She stepped closer and squared her shoulders confidently. "*We* are going to the movies. It's a drive-in movie, and I think you'll enjoy it."

Gavin's head tilted just the slightest, and she couldn't help but note the animal-like movement. "A movie?" he questioned, his lips parted.

"Yes. It's a movie my mom loved watching while I was growing up, and it's playing in town for tonight only. If you hurry up, we should be able to make it in time."

A few long moments of silence passed as Chloe began to wonder if she had won the battle. He seemed intrigued but still skeptical. If only she knew what exactly he was weighing in his mind, if she could really sway his decision. How far would she go to bribe him?

"A drive-in movie?" he clarified.

She nodded. "It's where you drive up in your car, and there's a speaker box where the sound feeds through, but the movie is projected onto this big screen. And the whole thing is in a big field. They also have a concession stand where you can buy drinks and popcorn."

Gavin shook his head in frustration as if he came to a decision that displeased him as much as it did her. "Too many people around. There's a reason I don't leave this house often."

"You never have to get out of the car," she reasoned, taking another step forward. She hadn't willingly been this close to him before. All the other times, he had trespassed into her space. But the tables had turned, and perhaps now he would know that she was too serious about this plan to let him reject her.

"I can strap you in with strings of garlic and hold a cross on you if I have to."

Gavin broke into a chuckle. "I'm not so sure that would hold me still for long."

Chloe didn't think it such a funny thing. The first few nights after she had discovered that he lived in the basement, she had placed a bulb of garlic under her pillow. And now he told her—in so many words—that it was useless.

"I'll do whatever it takes to make you comfortable while we're there. I just don't want to go alone."

It was an underhanded card to play, but Chloe laid it on the table anyway. She really wasn't afraid to go alone. She just wanted him to be with her. Although he had been alone for centuries, she didn't want him to suffer in that way anymore; no matter how willing he was to do so. No one deserved to be that isolated.

Gavin's expression softened, and after quite a bit of mental debating, he finally nodded. "Fine, I'll go with you. But please step aside."

She didn't have to be told twice.

"I'll be back shortly," he said as he disappeared into the cold, autumn night. He didn't have to declare his intentions for her to know exactly what he was going out to do.

Chloe shut the door behind him and did a silly victory dance before returning to the couch to read a little more.

As Chloe began to drive down the mountain, she could sense the tension in Gavin. He wasn't enjoying the tight turns down the winding road. Now, wearing his long coat, his body was hard to distinguish in the dim light. The lights from the dashboard illuminated his pale skin, and she could see the occasional wary glint in his eyes. Other than that, with his collar turned up to conceal his neck and much of his jaw, he resembled the shadow she had thought him to be the first night they had met outside the cabin.

"Easy on the leather," Chloe said laughingly. "This car is pretty new to me."

Gavin's hands were gripping his seat and car door so tightly, she thought something would rip or break off at any moment. When she spoke, his hands relaxed, and he apologized.

"Don't like cars?" she asked.

"Never been in one before."

Chloe's eyes went wide in surprise, but she wasn't sure why. Since he had lived through all of the technological changes of the world, she figured he would have experienced a little of everything by now.

"You've never ridden in a car?"

"Not once," he replied. "I never perceived the need to. I prefer to go down the mountain on foot. I always thought these infernal machines were a waste of time and money."

Chloe snorted. "How would you know that they were?"

She saw Gavin's eyes dart around in the darkness, latching onto subtle details outside of the jeep that caused him some sort of alarm. "I remember hearing conversations when they first came out. I remember your grandparents discussing how expensive gas was. In fact, that's been quite a frequent complaint amongst those staying in the cabin."

It was so strange to hear him talking about her grandparents like he knew them personally when she was sure that was far from the truth. Eavesdropping on conversations was not a way to get to know anyone. It was stalker-like behavior in her mind.

"What other things have you overheard?" she asked, eager to continue the conversation. This was possibly the first time they had ever discussed something outside of the novel.

Gavin opened his mouth but paused as if in thought. "I've heard about car accidents and how deadly they can be."

"And hiking down the mountain is any less dangerous?"

"It's simply more convenient."

Chloe tapped lovingly on the dashboard. "Well, this is more convenient for me." She ended the reply with a laugh, but Gavin did not return it.

He'd been fairly placid since they'd left the cabin. He had fed, that was for certain. The unreasonable grumpiness in his demeanor was gone. But what was left was something she never thought a vampire would so willingly display—Gavin was nervous.

It could have been a number of things. He had been vocal about his concern regarding being in a highly public setting. Or maybe he was worried about riding in a car, as he had already mentioned.

Something she had learned about Gavin was that he was openly expressive about many things but unwilling to explain himself. Years of living in darkness and solitude had left him without the social skills that normal humans needed. He lacked the mask, the shield of politeness to throw up in front of strangers.

There was a level of discretion when it came to interacting with others. If you were upset, you didn't show it. If you were sad, you bottled it up. Any sign of weakness and society would label you for life as an aggressive jerk or an emotional nutcase.

Gavin had no such skills, no talent in closing himself off and putting on a smile when he didn't feel like smiling. In that same way, he did not hide how terrified he was of riding in a car, or his unease about going into public.

And then there was the way he constantly slid a glance towards her, looking her up and down with the usual appreciation that men showed towards women. He probably thought she didn't notice, but she did. Just in the same way that Chloe thought he didn't notice when she checked him out.

When she came to the base of the mountain and turned onto the main road that split through Carter Lake, Gavin seemed to slump in the passenger seat. It was clear that he didn't want to be seen or noticed.

"Have you ever been to the movies before?" she asked. It was a silly question, but the thickening silence that filled the cab was suffocating. It had to break at some point; might as well be now. Maybe conversation would help calm him down enough to stop digging his nails into his car seat.

"No, I have not. But I've heard discussions about them."

Chloe smiled. "You sure hear a lot."

"Yes, I hear many things."

"Like what? What do you hear right now?" It might be a dangerous question. She'd read about how vampires and other monsters had heightened senses, but how much could he really discern? She imagined that there would be so much to hear and see that it would overload his senses. But, then again, the idea that someone could drink gallons of blood and not get sick was still a bit of a stretch on her imagination.

Gavin went quiet for a few beats then replied, "I can hear your heartbeat, your breathing, the engine, the sound of the tires against the road, crickets, the wind outside...and that man's horrible singing as he's taking a shower."

He pointed towards a small house sitting near the road with a few lights on. Being human, she obviously couldn't hear any of that. She was glad that she couldn't hear his singing either.

Chloe giggled and then turned back to the path ahead. "That must get annoying sometimes," she commented.

"It does. Sometimes, I hear things that I don't want to hear."

That alone made her mind wander, and she cringed to think of the things he might have heard coming from upstairs late at night, such as the disturbing conversations that had taken place in the kitchen, or the arguments in the living room that hadn't ended well.

It didn't take long for Chloe to find the turn for the road that led to the drive-in theater. The billboard, lit by only two out of four floodlights, was fading with age, and the paint was chipped practically all over. But she could find this place even in the dark and without the sign.

"My aunt used to take me here when we came to visit," she mentioned as she pulled up to the main gate where a little shack was selling the tickets.

Ahead was the enormous white screen and row upon row of speaker box poles and cars of every make and model waiting for the film to start.

In the meantime, short cartoons were being projected from a tall tower behind the shack. Off to the far left of the crowd of cars was the long building that housed the concession stand, and she could already smell the aroma of hot dogs and buttered popcorn drifting out into the chilly night air. Light shined through the concession window, and she could faintly see the silhouettes of a couple of people inside waiting for orders.

"I remember. You always came home, so excited after going to the movies. I could barely understand you through the childish babbling, but I knew you'd enjoyed it."

Chloe took a deep breath and let it out slowly. It was much easier to hear about her mother, aunt, or grandparents from Gavin. But after hearing him talk about her as a child, she didn't know how to respond. He'd known her almost all of her life, or at least known of her. It was like meeting an old friend of the family who knew her when she was too little to remember and talked about things she had no recollection of. But this was slightly different in the sense that she knew exactly what he was talking about, only she'd never known that he was there to witness it.

Not wanting the rest of the evening to turn awkward, she didn't press for more conversation just yet.

As she approached the shack, she rolled her window down and paid for two tickets in cash. The young high school boy smiled cordially, but when his eyes fell on Gavin, his lips turned down apprehensively.

Glancing over as she rolled past the shack to find an empty slot for her car, she saw that Gavin's eyes were fixed straight ahead, and they were anything but calm. She peered closely at his face as the light from the movie screen danced across his pale skin. She half expected his eyes to be red and black like she'd seen before, but Chloe was glad to see they were the normal green color she loved so much. He wasn't losing control. That was a good sign.

But his eyes were a pool of emotion that shined through no matter how hard he tried to hide it. She wondered how she could read him so well. His lips drawn in a tight line told her that he was uncomfortable. The way his brows were drawn low spoke volumes of his reluctance to be here at all. Yet, somehow, she sensed that he really was happy to be here. His muscles weren't nearly as tight as they had been before.

Such conflicting emotions, and Chloe hadn't a clue how she could sense it all so potently. Perhaps from years of having to read Brent, who was so volatile and impenetrable, she'd become more sensitive to others, especially enigmatic men.

She found a spot, most inconveniently located in the center of the crowd, and put her car in park. The bubbly music from the cartoon crackled through the speaker next to her, but other than that, the car was silent.

Chloe glanced at Gavin every now and then while the sketch-like cartoons played out slapstick comedies on the screen. He didn't move. Not even his eyes flitted around to follow the sporadic movements of the characters. She might as well have been sitting next to a mannequin.

"The movie's called *Laura*. It's about a homicide detective who falls for the girl whose murder he's investigating."

Finally, a flicker of confusion crossed his face. "If the woman is dead, how can he fall in love with her?"

Chloe didn't want to give away the plot, so she simply shrugged. "You'll have to wait and see."

Gavin went quiet again. Chloe snuggled herself deeper into the driver's seat and wrapped the flaps of her canvas jacket tightly around her.

"Are you cold?" he asked with hardly any emotion to suggest he was concerned, though Chloe knew differently.

"No, not right now."

Silence reigned once more for a few beats before a very humiliating sound rumbled through the cab of the jeep. Chloe's stomach chose that moment, of all times, to remind her that she hadn't eaten yet.

"You're hungry?" he asked, now revealing a twinge of worry.

She tried to laugh it off. "Just a little. But I'll be fine for a while. Normally my cup of coffee holds me over if I forget to eat."

"How can anyone forget to eat?" he asked with a sliver of amazement.

She shrugged. "It just happens. Especially if I get busy with doing something I'm passionate about.""Like writing?"

She nodded. "Yes, like writing."

Gavin turned to look at her. "But I've seen you eat at night when we're writing."

Chloe couldn't help but smile at the way he referred to their nightly activities as a partnership. What he said was true. But she cooked herself meals, not because she was hungry, but because she needed to take a break from him constantly hovering over her like a vulture waiting for her to spell a word incorrectly or make a terrible grammatical error in the sentence she was constructing.

She'd had enough invasive hovering with Brent to last her a lifetime. She didn't need it from Gavin. But it never bothered her in the same way. She wasn't annoyed with Gavin's watchfulness the way she was with Brent. Gavin only set her teeth on edge because of how near he was all the time. The anticipation of him doing something fresh out of one of her fantasies was nerve racking.

But she wasn't about to tell him that now.

"It doesn't happen all the time," she replied.

"I can go get –" he began. But she saw the way his eyes rose to the concession stand somewhere beyond the jeep, and she could tell that his mind was calculating all the cars he'd have to pass—cars filled with potential snacks if he so chose.

"It's ok," Chloe said. "I can wait a while, and if I get too hungry, I'll go get popcorn myself. You don't have to leave the car. I promised you wouldn't have to."

She admired the way he wanted to help her. It was cute and chivalrous of him to want to get her food, even though it'd be difficult for him and might cause others to be in mortal danger.

Gavin only nodded and looked back to the screen as it went completely black.

Chloe smiled and remembered times back in her childhood when her aunt had taken her to visit the drive-in. How her heart would pound when the screen went black, just as it did now. She'd known that the movie was starting.

The beginning credits began to roll. The white letters faded in and out over a backdrop, a portrait of the movie's namesake. Chloe marveled at her image, thinking how the definition of beauty had changed over the decades, but the old movie actresses of Hollywood would still be considered beautiful, even today.

"Is that Laura?" Gavin asked as his eyes drank in the beautiful painting above the fireplace on the screen.

Chloe then wondered if the whole movie would go this way. She was the type to be silent during a movie and not ask questions because she knew the answer would be revealed later. Gavin may be like Brent, always talking, making comments and asking questions that only interrupted important dialogue. She hadn't appreciated his commentary.

But right now, there was only the beautiful music playing, and nothing important was being discussed.

"Yep, that's Laura," she answered. "Isn't she gorgeous in that dress?"

Gavin tilted his head curiously. "I suppose."

Was he saying that so as not to insult Chloe or because he truly didn't find her looks remarkable? There were certainly enough characters in the movie who did find her stunning.

The credits faded away to a panning shot of a parlor room, ornately decorated with priceless trinkets behind glass cases and paintings tastefully hung on the walls. The grandfather clock was especially breathtaking.

The writer, Mr. Waldo Lydecker, narrated the opening lines of the film.

And immediately, she began to wonder if bringing Gavin to see this movie was the right choice.

The opening monolog spoke of how Laura died and the tragic emotional turmoil that the narrator was experiencing as a result. He talked about how losing Laura made him feel utterly alone in New York as if he were the only human being left.

And the shock of pain that crept up into Gavin's eyes was enough to make her want to turn the jeep around and speed back to the cabin.

What caused that pain? What was he remembering? Was he remembering his own death or the death of someone he cared for ages ago? Or perhaps it reminded him of losing Mary Anne. It had never occurred to Chloe that he would have lost a close friend when her aunt had moved away. Did they part on good terms, or had there been an argument? Chloe knew what it was like to lose a friend. She'd lost many just in the past few years, and it was never easy.

When she thought about it, Chloe knew exactly how Mr. Lydecker felt—alone, cut off from the world because of a tragedy that was out of her control. Although, their stories had completely different endings. Mr. Lydecker brought all of these misfortunes upon himself. Yet, Chloe wondered if she really was any different.

But as soon as the pain had flared in Gavin's eyes, it passed, and the movie rolled on. But for Chloe, it took a little longer to shake off the internal analysis.

Funny, she'd seen this movie several times, but this time was different than the others. She'd watched it with her mother, with Brent, with friends, and by herself. But she'd never watched it with Gavin. Maybe that was why it was suddenly special again, like introducing a piece of her childhood to someone with whom she wanted to share everything.

And this was not only the first time that Gavin had seen this particular movie. It was the first time he had seen *any* movie. Chloe felt that maybe she was doing him a service by reintegrating him into society, whether he liked it or not.

But, from her understanding of vampires, it might have been best to leave them in the shadows. They belonged there, not amongst the living, breathing people of the light. Chloe hated the idea that she couldn't share other things with Gavin like a picnic in a sunny meadow or a walk through a crowded mall while holding hands.

The thought of holding hands made her palms sweat and she became overly concerned with how her hands were positioned at the time. She wrapped them around her stomach, crossed them over her chest, and even gripped the steering wheel in an attempt to look relaxed.

Thankfully, Gavin didn't notice. He was too engrossed in the plot of the film. Or if he did notice, he didn't say anything.

"Lieutenant McPherson certainly is good at what he does," Gavin commented once while the movie character was interrogating one of the murder suspects.

Chloe didn't have a response. She just dumbly nodded.

Next were her legs. Should she try to cross them, or keep her knees clamped shut together beneath the steering wheel? Having her legs casually apart might send him the wrong impression. And if he had been raised in a society where propriety was king, it would certainly bother him.

In the end, she crossed her ankles above the pedals as best she could and stretched them out to avoid cramps.

Chloe chided herself for being so self-conscious. It wasn't a date. Gavin wasn't her boyfriend and never would be. This was just a chance to get out of the cabin and expose him to a bit of the new modern culture. Whether or not he would want to go again was another matter.

She was hardly paying attention to the film when Gavin said, "I would use an ink pen over a quill any day."

The odd statement drew Chloe's attention back to the movie screen where Laura and Mr. Lydecker were meeting for the first time in a flashback. Laura wanted him to endorse a pen for her advertising company, but the snooty writer was giving her a hard time, saying that he preferred to write with a quill dipped in venom, although Chloe recalled seeing him in the opening scenes, typing on an old fashioned typewriter while soaking in a marble tub.

"Oh?" Chloe knew that Gavin had grown up in a world where quills and inkwells were the only way that one could write. She would have thought that method would be the most comfortable for him since it was so familiar.

"Yes. I always found the dipping process tedious and sometimes frustrating."

"You write with pens a lot?" she asked.

"Indeed. I have a collection, which I must admit that I have amassed by stealing from residents of the cabin and in town."

Chloe blinked. "You've been into town before?"

Gavin looked at her and nodded. "Yes, but only briefly and infrequently. It behooves me to say that I have stolen and borrowed many things from people in Carter Lake."

"Like what?" she said with a slight smile. She already knew that he'd stolen things from her family when they had lived in the cabin, but never had she imagined he would venture out into town for anything.

"I have stolen necessary things like clothes, paper, and pens. But I only borrowed books."

"Why books?" she asked, angling herself in the seat to face him.

Gavin smirked. "I enjoy reading. It's one of the few pleasures in life that I have been able to retain through this existence."

"What's your favorite genre?" she asked, feeling her eyes widen with genuine interest. Finally, she was catching a peek at who Gavin really was.

A few beats passed as Gavin thought. "I don't know if you could count these as a genre, but I much enjoy Sir Arthur Conan Doyle's series about Sherlock Holmes, as well as Charles Dickens."

Chloe grinned, happy to find another person of like interests. She loved the classics, such as he described, but also any books from that century. Every line was like poetry back then, much different from the trash that was written nowadays. Chloe often wondered how novels with no plot or character development made it past the query stage of submission to publishers.

"If you don't mind," he muttered, "I'd like to continue watching."

By now, Chloe had almost forgotten where they were and the film that was still rolling. If they had been watching at the cabin from the comfort of the living room, she would have paused the movie so they could talk. But she didn't have that luxury here.

She cleared her throat, slightly embarrassed that she had almost become the kind of movie watcher she despised most; those who wouldn't shut up.

Chloe resolved to keep her mouth shut for the rest of the film, but that resolution was broken when Gavin made another remark.

"I don't like that Shelby character. He is much too presumptuous with Laura."

She could hear the disdain in his tone as if he believed Shelby Carpenter was a real person instead of a fictitious character in a movie.

"I don't like him either. And he treats Laura so terribly by running around on her."

Chloe knew what it was like to be in a poisonous relationship. When she had watched this same movie with Brent, he'd gone on and on about how he would never treat her with such little respect. Sure, he had never cheated on her. But he still broke her heart in the end.

"Simply deplorable," he said with a shake of his head.

She bit her lower lip as she thought things that were better left alone. But the more she watched how Shelby's character began to unfurl his true colors, the more she thought of Brent and the last year of their relationship; the fights, the screaming, and the way he had turned on her so suddenly. And she thought of how it had changed her, how she had defended him to everyone even though he didn't deserve it.

Chloe was just like Laura in a way—both of them saw the error of their choices too late.

It took a conscious effort not to open up the Pandora's Box in her mind and release the tainted memories of Brent and Atlanta. She could remember him and her old friends in passing, but never too deeply. She would be lost in despair otherwise, and she wasn't about to let that ruin her evening out with Gavin.

The movie was reaching its halfway mark now, and a big reveal was coming.

The detective had fallen asleep in Laura's apartment while stewing over the facts of the case. But he was awoken by Laura walking through the door.

Chloe watched the look of shock and bewilderment on Gavin's face and grinned.

"Is she a ghost?" he deliberated aloud. "Or is he simply dreaming? Surely, she can't be really alive. That woman identified her body."

Chloe shook her head. "Not tellin'," she said mischievously. Each of his suspicions was viable, but it would be revealed soon enough. She'd thought the same thing when she had first seen the movie as a young teenager.

What she didn't expect was for Gavin to turn to her with an expression like something was pressing on his mind. "You said once that you thought I was a ghost."

She heard the question in his statement and nodded. "Yeah, I thought you were."

"But why?"

Chloe sighed and drew her shoulders inward as if she were cold "I guess it was because I never saw you, and you left those notes all the time. And, from what I heard, my aunt thought the house was haunted. And then I found that land deed in the attic. I automatically assumed you couldn't be alive, so a ghost was the next logical thing to assume. I just connected the dots the wrong way, I guess."

Gavin nodded. "I can see how my behavior would have made you think that way. I apologize for the misunderstanding."

"It wasn't until I talked with my mom that she told me my aunt claimed you were a vampire. The idea would have never occurred to me otherwise."

It slipped out at the last minute, and Chloe wished she had worded it all a little differently. But Gavin didn't flinch at the word. He took it in stride and nodded.

"I heard your phone conversation that day. I'm sorry you had to find out that way."

It didn't surprise her that he had heard the conversation. She simply shrugged. "It's better than finding you out on the porch sucking on a robin or something."

Gavin chuckled good-naturedly at her joke. "I can understand that."

They exchanged smiles and went back to watching the movie, although Chloe found it hard to focus on anything but the subtle changes on Gavin's face at certain scenes. They'd gone from confused to pensive, then flickered with anger for the characters who deserved it. And towards the end, he displayed something that she hardly expected to see—envy.

When Lieutenant McPherson and Laura had an intimate moment in the interrogation room, Gavin looked as if he wanted that connection that they shared. Chloe knew how he felt. She understood completely and wished that she could fill that longing for him.

Chapter 12

The jeep pulled up to the cabin, headlights shining through the murky darkness ahead to illuminate the porch and front windows. Gavin still hadn't gotten used to the rough ride, and the tiny tear in the seat leather was a testimony to that. Yellow foam was beginning to stick out past the jagged edge of the fabric, but Chloe wasn't about to make him feel bad about it.

She cut off the engine and slid out of the jeep without a word. They hadn't spoken since the movie ended and they made their way back to the cabin. Both of them could feel the end of the diversion, though the night was still young. Chloe wasn't a bit tired after sleeping all day, and there was plenty of writing left to do.

She imagined that Gavin would be anxious to begin again, as he was every evening when he came back from his first feed after waking up. The way he obsessed over writing was almost disturbing and slightly oppressive to Chloe who longed for an extended break. Spending two hours away from the cabin wasn't enough.

Writing had never been an arduous task for her. She never regretted the choice she made to pursue her career as an author. But after several straight days of doing nothing but tap away at her laptop, the task was becoming monotonous. Perhaps it was true what they said—there was such a thing as too much of a good thing.

Chloe hiked up to the cabin along the gravel path, the cool night wind teasing her long wavy hair. As soon as she got inside she'd pull it all back so it wouldn't be in her way. Her efforts with the straightener did not last long without the added hairspray to make it all stay in place.

When Chloe glanced over her shoulder at Gavin, she found he wasn't in the jeep, but neither was he tailing close behind her like she expected. Instead, she marveled at the sight of him standing some distance down the hill, bathed in blue moonlight.

He was facing away from her, standing so still as he gazed out towards the creek, his long coat tails billowing in the wind like they had the first night they met.

"Where are you going?" Chloe called out. She didn't know what provoked her to ask. It was none of her business what he did. Perhaps he heard a deer grazing on the other side of the creek and wanted to venture out for another snack.

This was the second time she'd seen him in such a setting with the moon cresting in the midnight sky above and the crickets playing their usual song in the trees. And nothing had changed but the phase of the moon. He was still handsome, still alluring, and he still had an air of mystery about him that she couldn't penetrate.

Despite having known him for a couple of weeks, she really knew very little about him. Many questions still burned in her mind.

Gavin turned and looked at her, calmness in his expression that left an indelible mark in her memory. She would forever remember him this way—placid, tranquil, and so ethereally handsome.

"I thought I'd take a walk by the creek," he replied.

Chloe smiled, nodded, and turned away to ascend the porch steps, but his voice stopped her at the first tread.

"Would you do me the honor of having your company?"

She looked back and felt her heartbeat a little faster. When she had invited him to the movies, it was an attempt to draw him out of the cabin and into society, into her world. Now, he did the same for her, offering to share a moonlight walk in a place she had known so well in the daylight, but never by moonlight.

This was a night of firsts for both of them.

"Sure," she responded, as she carefully traversed the steep slope to catch up with him. She didn't need another twisted ankle, though it would have been nice to have Gavin carry her back up to the cabin again.

She joined him, and they walked down the hill together. After a short trek through the forest, they came to the creek.

It wasn't much different than in the daytime. The light from above sparkled on the waves like it did in Gavin's gorgeous eyes, and the same breeze rustled the leaves in the branches that hung over the stream.

How many times they must have come here by themselves, but never together. Along with the cabin, they had this creek and the mountains in common. Though they were so different in almost every way, they were still able to find some common ground.

Chloe cautiously came to the edge of the creek, her boots fractionally sinking into the mud as her eyes settled upstream. She wrapped her arms tightly around herself, letting her mind slip into a state of quiescent.

"Are you cold?" Gavin asked from somewhere behind her. That was the second time he had asked that tonight.

The timbre of his voice caught her off guard as she turned to see that he'd been staring at her from a few yards away the whole time.

She had to admit that her jacket was a little thinner than she'd like. "A little. But I'm alright."

Gavin seemed to ignore the second part of her response, and she watched as he slipped off his jacket, revealing the masculine body beneath. He approached her and deftly draped it over her shoulders, the tips of his fingers brushing against her as he released the garment.

The jacket was still warm and stained with his scent that engulfed her senses. Despite herself, Chloe shrugged into the sleeves that were far too big for her slender arms and hugged the flaps around her torso.

Gavin didn't shrink back into the shadows where he had been stalking, but stayed behind her, so achingly close. If she were to lean back, even a hair's breadth, she would have grazed against his chest.

She took a deep breath and let it out slowly, mist plumbing from her mouth and disappearing with the wind.

"Something on your mind?" he asked, his voice inviting and warm with affection as if he cared what she was really thinking.

It'd been a long time since someone actually cared what was going on inside her mind. Not even Brent wanted to hear her most secret thoughts, though she had asked many times on a daily basis.

But did she want to spill her guts to this man who had become her new and closest friend in the world apart from her family? She spent every day with him and yet she knew practically nothing. Yet, how much did she need to know before they bridged the chasm between them?

Her mind was a jumble of thoughts that she couldn't pin down anymore. If he knew what was going on in her mind, he would know that half of everything couldn't be articulated so easily in one night spent by a creek.

But Chloe felt compelled to try.

"I have a lot on my mind," she said simply as a test to see if he really wanted to hear it all laid out before him.

"Would it help to talk about it?"

Suddenly, she felt fear. Not fear of how silly she would sound carrying on garrulous about nothing that he should be concerned about. But fear of what would happen between them if she did tell him everything. Could she open up to him and there be no consequences?

Everything inside told her to keep her doors locked, to not let a single soul in. She didn't want to be hurt as she had been before. But there was a small voice urging her to open the gates and let this man in. He was different. Maybe he wouldn't hurt her.

Whatever the right course of action was, Chloe didn't know if she was taking it.

"Maybe," she said, a slight tremor in her voice despite how strong she tried to be in the face of all that lay before her tonight.

"Well," he said with a light tone, "I have a pair of ears that are waiting to be ensorcelled by your voice."

Chloe snorted, unsure of what he meant exactly, as she didn't know the meaning of the word "ensorcelled", but it sounded like a stab at flirting or flattery. She wasn't going to scold him for it.

"I have so many questions. I don't know how to ask them, where to really begin, or if I should bother asking them at all."

Gavin was still for a moment, then she felt a hollowness behind her as he moved away. She wanted to make a sound of protest, but only turned to see him take a few meandering steps downstream. His eyes were fixed on the slow current.

"I imagine you do have many questions. Feel free to ask. I will not withhold any answers."

Such invitation gave Chloe hope. She resolved to not make a muddle of this opportunity. Every question would be carefully worded.

Beginning with the most pressing question, she asked, "I know you're from England, but how did you come to be here in Georgia?"

Chloe saw Gavin's lips thin into a tight line. Recalling her words, she thought the question was structured well and without a hint of offensive tone. Maybe he was having second thoughts.

But he lifted his chin, and he raised his gaze to the trees on the opposite shore.

"I was born in Hatherleigh, in the county of Devon, in 1708. My father was a blacksmith, so naturally, I became one, too. I did well in the trade." He gave a slight shrug as if he weren't convinced of it.

A corner of Chloe's mouth twitched when she imagined him sweating away over a coal fire with a burning hot stick of iron in his fist.

"I had a brother who was a few years older than I. Before I left, he had two daughters and a son. I won't bore you with their names or appearances.

"I married young. She was the baker's daughter. We were of the same class, so it wasn't so uncommon."

Chloe hated the small smirk that came to his face. He was remembering his wife. A smoldering jealousy burned in her stomach for the woman whom she didn't even know. It was puerile the way she envied a woman who lived almost three centuries ago. She tried not to show her disappointment at the knowledge that he had been married once before. How could she expect him to have been a bachelor all this time?

But the hate was ephemeral as his new look of disgust glowered in the darkness. "But I nearly ruined us with dreams. We had a son to take care of, and I chased after a career as a novelist. Manuscript after manuscript was turned down, and our debt was mounting daily."

Chloe didn't know what hurt more, the punch in the gut that he had fathered a child, or that he had taken the same path she had in becoming a writer, and yet obviously failed.

"But we were given a chance at a new life. We were given a grant to come settle in Georgia, which had become a sort of debtors' colony in the New World. The journey across the sea was long, but we finally arrived in Savannah in February of 1733 on the ship called '*Anne*'.

"We were all excited. We built that cabin together, and I set my hand to becoming a fur trader. There was no chance for me to write, but we could build a new life—a fresh start for all of us, especially my son."

Chloe tried not to wince at the affection in his voice when he talked about his son. She should have been happy for him, but she wasn't. Not yet. It was like finding out her childhood crush had married and moved on with his life without her, but somehow in reverse. Gavin no longer looked like a shiny new penny, but a dingy coin that she couldn't define. Had three hundred years polished that past life away? Considering the way he smiled and spoke so fondly of his family, she doubted it.

Gavin heaved a sigh, and she saw the icy fog roll out of his mouth for the first time. There was a brokenness in his expression that brought her back to his story.

"My son was four years old and had gone to play in the woods. To this day, I don't know what happened out there. But, he came back with a deep gash in his arm, screaming that something bit him. We couldn't calm him enough to find out what exactly had bitten him.

"My wife cleaned the wound, but he got very sick with a fever. Then she and I both became sick with the same thing. It was an illness we had never known or heard of before, so we didn't know how to treat it."

Chloe saw his Adam's apple bob as he swallowed back the wave of emotion that clouded in his eyes.

"We were all too weak to move. As we lay in bed, I knew my son had slipped away from us. I remember my wife's last words to me were of love and that she always believed in my stories."

Chloe was so rapt by the story that she had to remind herself to breathe. Every nasty emotion she felt towards Gavin's family had been swept away in the creek's current.

She couldn't imagine his pain in losing everyone he held so dear to him. Her heart bled for him, and she would have let him drink what came out if it were possible. She would have given anything to make that pain go away.

"And I knew I had died. I can't tell you what made me so sure, but I knew. When I awoke, it was nighttime. My wife and son lay beside me. They were both cold and pale and dead. But I knew that something was not right with me. I felt things I had never felt before. I heard everything around me; I could smell things that no human could possibly detect.

"What disturbed me the most were the thoughts I had. When I sat up from the bed, I felt a need to seek blood. It took all my willpower to resist the impulse to feed on my dead wife and child."

Chloe wanted to beg him not to go on. She could infer the rest. He didn't need to explain. But her vocal cords wouldn't respond to her command. She just stood there, lips parted ever so slightly, wide eyes staring at Gavin as he continued explaining all the things she had not asked about.

"But I buried them in accordance to what I could do at the time. I fought off the need for as long as I could. When I discovered that sunlight burned my skin like a hot brand, I sought shelter in the food cellar.

"I tried to eat what was there, but I couldn't keep anything down. When night came once more, I couldn't fight it any longer. I fed on a beaver of all things," he said with an ill-humored laugh.

"As time went on, I learned what I had become. I heard of legends growing up about creatures that walked the night and drank blood. I don't know how this curse came upon me or why. If it was the disease my family contracted, I should have died with them, or they could have joined me in this eternal curse. But I, alone, survived. The world went on without me, and I've learned to cope with this as best I can. But I don't rejoice in this existence."

The vicious glint of his fangs on those last syllables curled over his lips made her blood run cold. "It's just like you said that night when I cut myself," she said, her voice meek and breathy. "You're a man trying desperately not to be a monster."

Gavin looked at her for the first time since he began his story. She felt torn apart by the absolute misery in his eyes.

Now she understood why he reacted the way he did to those first lines of the movie that night. He knew exactly how Lydecker, and all the others impacted by

Laura's death, felt knowing they lost someone they loved so deeply. But, unlike the movie, Gavin didn't have a happy ending. He would have no ending at all. His family wasn't coming back, and he couldn't join them so easily.

It was the most tragic thing she had ever heard.

"I'm so sorry, Gavin."

Her words were nothing more than a Band-Aid on a severed limb, but it was all she could offer him. He gave his best attempt at a smile as if she were the one needing comfort.

"You know what I miss the most?" he asked, coming towards her again with that soundless swagger that she adored.

"What?"

"The sun."

It sounded horribly cliché. Of course, a vampire would miss the sun. It was the one thing that he couldn't have besides a pulse. Yet, Chloe half expected him to mention his son, his wife, his old life in England; anything but the sun that she took for granted every day.

"It's nothing much. In fact, there are a lot of downfalls to the sun. You can be blinded by it, get a sunburn, and sometimes, it can get too hot. The sun is overrated."

Chloe said it all with a smile and flimsy gestures to amuse him. It worked, and he chuckled. But, when the laughter subsided, the tension of what they had been talking about settled in again.

"Do you have any other questions?" he asked, obviously trying to give them a reprieve from the previous topic.

After a few thoughtful seconds, Chloe asked, "You said you tried to make it as an author. Is that why you've been helping me?"

Gavin smiled. "That's one reason. But also because you can't imagine how bored I've been since the house has been empty. It's good to talk to someone again."

Chloe pressed her lips together to hold back the grin that so desperately wanted to shine through. She cleared her throat and continued, "This may be going a little out of order, but I saw the way your eyes turned red the other night when I cut myself. What brought that on?"

Gavin's eyes flickered off to the tree line for the briefest second, then back to her. "That would be the hunger. It was involuntary, I assure you. The change allows me to see heat."

"Like a snake or an infrared camera?"

He gave her a blank expression but then nodded. "Yes, I suppose so."

"Do you even know what an infrared camera is?" she laughed, remembering that he was centuries old.

"I believe I've read about them, yes. It just took me a moment to recall."

Chloe took a step closer, her boots squishing in the soppy ground. "And how do you know so much about modern technology? Is it from stuff you've read or from living in the cabin?"

Gavin wagged his head a bit in apathy. "It's a little of both."

"And I thought that vampires were supposed to be cold, but you feel very warm."

She'd completely forgotten her decision to be subtle in her questions, but it was too late when ill-chosen words came out. Gavin didn't seem to mind.

"I've only met one other vampire in my life, and he was just as warm as I am. I shook his hand, that's how I know. I don't know how to explain it to you. Perhaps it had something to do with our diet."

Chloe regrouped herself and took a moment to word everything perfectly again. "I figured out that you have super-speed and strength. Is there anything else you can do that's special?"

Gavin's lips puckered in thought for a while. "I have noticed I can heal remarkably fast. And, because of my predatory nature, I have extraordinary stealth abilities."

"I noticed that, too. You're really good at sneaking up on me." Chloe primarily remembered all the times she turned and he had magically appeared out of nowhere. Each time was still a shock.

Gavin smiled, probably remembering the same things. "Yes, and I do apologize for that. I have made an effort to be less sneaky."

With a shy smile still plastered on her face, Chloe began to think of her next questions. Of course, she wanted to know how any one person could be so smoking hot, charming, and smell so amazing. But, those questions were better left unasked and didn't really require an answer.

"If I think of any others, can I ask you on the spot?"

Gavin raised a hand and flattened it to his chest as he gave her a gentlemanly bow. "Of course, my lady."

Chloe blushed and giggled again, the same way she had in the kitchen that night he bowed to her the first time. "Stop doing that!" she exclaimed teasingly.

Gavin straightened. "Why?" he asked, a bit of a lilt to his tone.

"It's just too funny to see you bow and use that accent and everything."

"I'm glad I can amuse you," he replied with an air of playfulness.

Chloe thought to herself that he did much more than amuse her. She bit her lip and turned away to look across the creek. With the woods so shrouded in night, she could barely distinguish the silhouettes of the trees and bushes.

It was a calm night, and she was more than glad that Gavin had suggested this walk. Even though they had unsettling conversations, she was glad that the subject hadn't turned to her. It would have been fair that Gavin ask questions in return, but he didn't seem as prying and curious as she was.

"Are you tired?" he asked.

She shrugged. "Maybe a little."

"I know you've been sleeping through the day so you can stay up at night."

Chloe had never tried to hide that fact from him. But she also knew that she was not indefatigable. She hadn't gotten quite used to his cycle after living years under the system that the rest of the world operated in for the most part.

And she hadn't been tired until he mentioned it. Without meaning to, she yawned and covered it with the cuff of his jacket.

Gavin chuckled and moved away. "Come. That's enough night air for you."

Chloe agreed and fell in behind him as they walked back up the hill to the cabin.

The climb reminded her of the night they first met, and she asked, "When I twisted my ankle, the next morning it was completely fine. Did you do that?"

Gavin grinned back at her. "I did. It's something I learned years ago with your aunt. I helped the arthritis in her knees."

"And when I got sleepy that one night when I tried to stay up waiting for you, did you make me go to sleep?"

Gavin gave her a slightly more sheepish smile. "Yes, I did."

Chloe snorted. "That explains why I never had trouble sleeping when I came to visit. Did you make the whole house fall asleep like that?"

He shrugged. "I had to. If your aunt or grandmother had been up late cleaning the kitchen, how else would I have gotten out unnoticed?"

It was a peculiar idea that Gavin had so many supernatural abilities. She wondered if he caused the sleepiness she felt now, but she shrugged it off when they reached the back deck.

Chapter 13

G avin had excused himself for a moment after escorting her inside the cabin.
And that was fine with Chloe. It gave her time to fix some fresh coffee to
ward off the sleepiness that had overwhelmed her so suddenly.

As she poured water into the coffee maker, she recalled how Gavin hadn't even
mentioned anything about working on the story since they first left the house for
the movies. Even when she was showing how tired she was, he didn't insist that
they go inside to continue on to the next chapter.

She also thought about all he had said by the creek. It was a dizzying amount
of information to process. She'd never be able to look at him the same way again.
All those disgraceful thoughts and fantasies about Gavin made her feel ashamed.
How could she think of him in such a way when he had lost someone dear to him
so tragically?

It wasn't as if it were an ex-girlfriend that he hated. If that were the case, she
wouldn't feel a bit of remorse for the way her heart beat faster at the thought of
him. Or the way her palms sweated and hands trembled when he came too close.
Perhaps this new knowledge that Gavin was a widower would help in curbing
those unwarranted emotions that raged within her.

Chloe took a deep breath, fixed her cup of coffee, and walked to the desk to start
up the laptop. Another night of hard work lay ahead, and she hadn't the time to
mourn over vain hopes about Gavin. Her heart wanted to break over him, but
the pieces were too sore and minuscule from the last catastrophe in Atlanta. She
should have been prepared for this kind of disappointment.

As she was booting up her laptop, she heard Gavin come through the back
door. She didn't bother to look up, knowing he would be at her side the moment
he saw her sitting in front of the computer.

But, as she navigated through the folders on her hard drive to pull up the novel in progress, she heard a noise coming from the fireplace. Chloe turned to see Gavin carefully placing logs on the iron grating inside the firebox.

Slightly nonplussed by his actions, she watched in silence. Once the logs were placed to his liking, he knelt down by the hearth where she had left some old newspapers she had used for packing and began stuffing the open cavity below the logs.

But she found her voice when he struck a match.

"What are you doing?" she asked.

"I thought it would be nice to have a fire going. Would it bother you?" he asked, looking up at her with the lit match held tightly between his fingers.

She shrugged and tried not to think about how handsome he was. "No, it wouldn't bother me."

He then leaned down and angled the flame under the kindling paper until it was set ablaze. Gavin shook the match to extinguish the flames and tossed it on the stone hearth before moving around the coffee table.

It was then he looked up and saw what she was doing. Both exchanged confused looks until he broke the silence.

"I thought you wanted a break tonight?"

Chloe blinked away her mild shock. "Can you read minds?"

Gavin smiled but shook his head. "No, I can't. I just assumed from your desire to go see the movie that you were getting a little tired of being cooped up here."

Chloe grinned playfully. "For a man who hasn't spent a lot of time with people, you sure are good at reading them."

He gave a nonchalant gesture and sat down heavily on one side of the couch. Flames began to slowly overtake the logs in the fireplace, and that empty spot beside Gavin was beginning to look warm and inviting.

However, she knew that the safest place would be as far as possible from him. She wasn't afraid of him but of what she would do in a moment of weakness. Chloe turned away and began to refresh her memory of the story plot. Writing was the last thing she wanted to do, but it seemed the most logical course of action. It just might be the thing to distract her from the crushing disenchantment about what she and Gavin could have had.

That is until Gavin shattered her resolve with one simple question.

"Would you like to join me?"

Chloe squeezed her eyes shut so tightly she could feel her eyelashes touch the upper part of her cheeks. Common sense told her to stay at the desk, but everything that ached and burned for companionship urged her to join him.

With a pitiful sigh, she stood—coffee mug in hand—and sat down in the armchair about five feet away from him. This was a reasonable compromise. She curled her feet up onto the cushion, and she realized with a twinge of embarrassment that she was still wearing both of their coats.

Setting the mug down on the hearth, she stripped both layers down and hung them over the back of the armchair before resuming her comfortable position.

Chloe took one sip and glanced at Gavin over the rim of her mug. His arm was stretched out over the back of the sofa while the other was leaned against the armrest. It was a perfect pose, one worthy of the front cover of a magazine or romance novel cover. But what drew her attention most was the way his eyes were solidly fixed upon her.

She could almost see the flicker of fire glow in his eyes that sparkled like emeralds. And that soft smile spread across his lips made her want to melt, and her core went tight with anticipation.

Combined with the way he stared at her, the subtle scent of wood smoke, and the residual smell of him on her shoulder, it was enough to drive her mad.

She fought back any foolish ideas with the image of him cuddling with another woman from the eighteenth century. They probably had romantic moments like this all the time. Chloe's chest ached with the sharp pain of bitterness towards the situation.

She looked away and gazed into the building fire until her eyes burned from the brightness and heat.

"I remember," Gavin began softly, "years ago, when you and your aunt would roast marshmallows past your bedtime."

Chloe knew any more talk of her childhood and what Gavin thought he knew of it would push her over the edge. She didn't reply but ran a hand over her forehead and down her flushed cheek. The movement suggested exasperation, but it didn't deter Gavin from continuing.

"Your aunt loved to sit in that chair and read late into the night with a fire just as this. After we became more open to each other, she read aloud to me."

Chloe closed her eyes. She didn't want to hear about her aunt, either. She was over her period of mourning for the woman who had so influenced her life. All that was left was to honor her memory by succeeding in this new one Chloe had created.

Silence reigned once more, except for the crackling and gentle roaring of the fire. Chloe could still feel Gavin's intense gaze set upon her.

"Once before," Chloe said, her voice thick, "you said that you didn't hear much from the basement. But the more you talk about things from the past, the more I think you were lying."

"I suppose I was. The truth is that I hear many things; things I don't mind hearing, and things that I wish I could forget."

Chloe let her arm drape across her chest, her hand resting upon her collarbone. With her legs pulled close and her coffee mug resting on her knee, she appeared as if she were trying to hide or shield herself.

"What kind of things?" she asked, refusing to let her gaze deviate from the glowing embers.

It was a while before he replied. "I've heard laughter. I've heard hateful words spoken in a moment of pain that would be regretted later. I've heard rejoicing. And I've heard much sorrow over the years, living here with your family."

Chloe wasn't surprised. All of those things were the typical traits of a family. They loved and hated. But in the end, they came together as a strong unit should. Chloe wondered about the fate of her family. Her aunt had not married or had children, and she was the only child of her parents. If Chloe ended life as a spinster and childless just as her aunt, what would become of the cabin that had been passed down through their family?

"I've heard you cry at night," he said. His voice was gentle, almost musical in the way he spoke something so profound as if it were something simple.

Chloe raised her eyes and looked to Gavin. The smile was gone, replaced with a thin line of concern.

Yes, she had cried at night. She had often woken up with tear stains on her pillows. Her dreams were not pleasant, and lying alone at night with only her regrets and doubts to keep her company, it was hard not to get emotional.

Chloe's defenses began to weaken. But she would not break. She wouldn't do that anymore, not for anyone.

"Why did you come to live here?" Gavin asked. There wasn't a hint of malice or annoyance in his tone. He didn't ask it because he didn't want her there. He asked because he was curious. She wondered when she had given her permission to ask such questions.

Chloe sniffled and rubbed her thumb against the handle of her coffee mug. "To be a writer," she said flatly.

"But surely you could have done that where you were before?"

Chloe snorted, putting up her defenses once more to deflect the seriousness of the conversation. "No, I couldn't have."

"Why?"

Gavin was pushing her buttons, trying to pry out what she didn't want to talk about anymore.

New life. New adventure. No more past. It was the mantra she had repeated to herself over and over, but it never really took hold. She still saw practically everything through the lens of what happened in Atlanta; through what happened between her and Brent.

Maybe if he understood, he'd back off about it.

Chloe took a breath and let her gaze fall to the rug underneath the coffee table. "I guess since you told me about your old life, I can tell you about mine."

Gavin was attentive, stone-still as he waited for her to begin.

"My family lived in Atlanta. My mom and dad met in Carter Lake, got married, then moved there to start a family. Mom never liked this small town. My aunt stayed behind. When I was little, as you know, we visited a lot.

"But, as I got older and mom started limiting the trips, I got side tracked with my own life. I made friends and spent time with them rather than with my own family. I grew up, graduated and moved out. I worked odd-jobs through college and finally landed a job as a receptionist at a dentist's office."

Chloe shifted uncomfortably. "One day, a patient walked in, and he was very charming. We went out a few times, and we thought we were a good match. Brent was a successful businessman and owned his own apartment. I had been rooming with my best friend from high school for years.

"When we got serious, I moved in with Brent." Chloe swallowed hard. "And that's when it all started. I didn't notice it at first. I thought he was just trying to be romantic. When I wanted to go out with the girls, he begged me to stay home, and we'd watch movies on the couch or cook dinner together."

She sighed. "But then it got worse. I hadn't seen my friends in weeks. He even took away my phone when I tried to text them while we were spending time out together. My family tried to reach out to me about reunions, but Brent insisted that we couldn't take a weekend off to drive down to Carter Lake or anywhere else I wanted to go.

"One of my friends from college happened to be a guy, and when Brent saw that I'd been texting him, he overreacted and told me to cut him out of my life because I could only have room for one man."

"And that man was him," Gavin added in something akin to a growl.

Chloe nodded. "Yeah. And one by one, I lost my friends. They stopped inviting me out, saying that I was flaky and too absorbed in my relationship with Brent. I never told them the truth, that he practically kept me in a cage. The only place I was allowed to go was work and home unless he was with me."

She took a shuddering breath, fighting the tears that pressed against her eyelids and threatened to ruin her mascara.

"I never knew someone could be so controlling, so demanding. I thought it was just his way of showing he loved me. But then one day, I talked back. I don't even remember what we were fighting about when he hit me."

Chloe immediately felt the wave of anger pulsate off of Gavin. She wasn't sure whether to be frightened by it or gratified.

"That night, I realized that I couldn't be with him anymore. That night, while he slept, I packed my bags and left. My parents had already bought their RV and were half way across the country at the time, but I was able to stay with one old friend. I explained everything, and she took me in as a refugee, so to speak."

Chloe pulled her legs in tighter, her socked feet gripping the edge of the cushion. "Brent was furious, of course. I broke up with him over the phone, and that was the last I heard of him. I changed jobs, got a cheap apartment on the other side of town, and a couple of weeks later, my aunt passed away and gave me this cabin."

Chloe lifted her gaze up to the wood planks on the ceiling. "I guess I'm here to escape from Atlanta, from Brent, and everything else. I couldn't rebuild any of the bridges that I'd burned over the years, but I figured I could make some new ones here."

It sounded terribly poetic, and Chloe wished she could have been writing that down. Gavin didn't speak for a while, probably still boiling with rage over the way she'd made Brent out to be the bad guy.

But it wasn't all Brent's fault. She had let him control her the whole time. She could have stopped it from the beginning, but she did nothing. All because she thought she loved him. But that wasn't love, at all. Chloe wasn't sure what it was anymore.

"I cry at night because I'm lonely. I miss my friends, I miss my family, I miss my aunt. But, most of all, I miss the way this cabin was when it was so full of all those things I don't have anymore. This place just isn't the same."

Her throat grew tight as her overwhelming sadness came forward. But Chloe sipped her coffee and pushed back the demons once more. Even though he had heard her cry at night, she wouldn't cry for him now. She refused to even look him in the eyes.

"Not to take away from your misfortune, but I get lonely, too."

Chloe swallowed her coffee and let the tepid liquid warm her. "I can't imagine being cooped up here for centuries with no one to talk to."

"It wasn't so bad in those years your aunt was here." Gavin's tone was reflective and thoughtful. "I can't recall a time when only one person lived here. It's always been a couple or a family, but never one solitary person."

Gavin stretched out his long legs, his feet tucked under the coffee table. "When I realized that your aunt was alone, I decided to reveal myself to her. She reacted much in the same ways you did. She was scared, apprehensive. But, then she warmed to my company, and we became good friends."

Chloe let out a gust of breath. "Did you have any idea why she left?"

Gavin nodded gravely. "She said everyone thought her crazy. And she began to believe the same. It was heartbreaking to hear the things that she said. She denied that I was real, saying that I was just in her mind. When she told me that she was leaving, I didn't want to believe her. But then I woke up one night, and she was gone."

Chloe grimaced and finally lifted her gaze to his face. "You've had so many people leave you."

Gavin looked at her with such an expression that made every muscle quiver with longing. "You have, too."

It was then that she saw how similar they were; how similar they had always been.

Gavin fled from England to start a new life in Georgia. Chloe moved from Atlanta for the same reason.

Gavin had watched people come and go with each passing generation, leaving him alone and friendless in the end. Chloe had to suffer the loss of every friend she had ever had, as well as being estranged from her family, only to dump her abusive boyfriend and begin a life alone in the mountains of Georgia.

But they had each other. They had this cabin. And they had their passion for writing. If only they had met in another time and under different circumstances.

Chloe saw their stories collide like two tragic trains in the night. But instead of carnage and destruction, there was something she didn't want to believe was possible—hope.

Chloe turned away before she lost herself in his gaze and sipped one more time on her coffee. She couldn't crumble under this new truth. Not now.

She didn't know what to do now. She could continue to sit here and endure awkward silence while the one man who understood her, stared a hole through her, she could get up and write, or she could go to bed.

But none of those seemed appealing at all. Her mind was too muddled to churn out the words she needed to form sentences and much too active to go to sleep. But sitting here in front of the warm fire and an even warmer company was too much to handle.

"I need some air," she stated before rising on unstable limbs to make her way into the kitchen.

"Chloe, I didn't—" was all she heard before shutting the back door behind her.

The cool night air soothed her hot skin. And even though she didn't have a jacket on, the weather was pleasant enough.

Chloe leaned against the rough wood railing that enclosed the deck and gripped her mug between her hands, which now served as they only solid thing to ground her in this moment of turmoil.

She realized how silly this all was. But, Chloe couldn't get past the crippling fear. This man made her feel things she never wanted to feel again. It was all too fast and too deep. And she couldn't find a way to slow down or climb out.

It was easy to know Gavin from a distance. But this night proved that he had so many levels of who he really was, and she couldn't take that first step. She knew, without a doubt, that she would drown.

But it wasn't only Gavin who got too close. Chloe allowed him in, and she hated herself for it. Chloe felt vulnerable, her nerves raw from the sudden exposure to the scrutiny of this man she had met less than two weeks ago.

A single tear slipped down her cheek, chilling her skin on the way down. It was therapeutic to cry. But how much could she allow herself?

Chloe wasn't given the chance to find out before she heard the back door swing open slowly. She didn't turn around and hoped that Gavin would just pass her by and slink off into the forest for another meal.

But he didn't. Like a good friend, he came up beside her and leaned against the railing, mimicking her posture. She was thankful that he kept his distance, their elbows at least a foot or so away from touching.

"Chloe, I'm sorry if I upset you. I shouldn't have pried."

She shook her head, tendrils of hair flickering with the movement around her jaw. "It's nothing."

Then he did something unexpected. He snickered. "You sound just like your aunt when you say that."

Chloe met his gaze and almost against her will, she gave him a strained smile. The thought occurred to her that perhaps instead of shutting out his anecdotes about her late aunt, Chloe could have been more open to them. Maybe they could make up for the lost years she had so carelessly thrown away. Gavin was the one who was closest to her until she left, the one who she'd confided in. If anyone knew about her, it would be Gavin and her mother.

"Tell me more about her."

Gavin gave her a devilish grin. "If you come back inside, I'll talk about her all night."

Chloe tilted her head and found his charms irresistible. The pain, the fear, the anguish she felt before didn't seem so intense when he was around.

It was ironic how the man who made her feel so much could make her so calm. He was her poison and her antidote. He was the thing that could kill her, but then restore life to her tired bones. He conjured the storm and then quieted it all at the same time.

Such conflicting emotions made no sense to her, but, perhaps in time, she could decode them and understand what this all meant.

She nodded and they went back inside to sit by the warm fire.

—

It was well into the night, and Gavin was still rattling on about Mary Anne and Chloe's ancestors.

After Chloe agreed to come back inside, Gavin avoided any intimate conversation involving her old life in Atlanta and her abusive ex-lover. Gavin wasn't sure he could talk sensibly on the subject as he still felt his blood boil with rage over the way Chloe had been treated. If he could have done anything about it, he would have. Gavin had strict moral boundaries when it came to killing humans, but for this, he would have made an exception.

Gavin was surprised when Chloe agreed to join him on the couch. He'd had the distinct impression that she was no longer comfortable with him after they came back from the creek, and he knew exactly why.

Explaining how he became a vampire must have struck a chord in her that she did not expect. For a while, he suspected that she regretted asking the questions that weighed so heavily on her mind.

But he was even more surprised when a few hours had passed and she scooted closer to him on the sofa. When she leaned her head against his shoulder, he was too terrified to move. If he showed any discomfort or unease, she might have moved away and taken the radiant light of her company with her.

Gavin never wanted to be any farther from her than this. He wanted to feel her body against his, giving her warmth so freely for all eternity.

It was a miracle that he could keep his voice steady enough to continue his stories about Mary Anne. But, he did so for hours, listening to the sound of his own voice and the crackling of the fire, intermittent with tiny giggles and softly spoken questions from the beautiful woman leaning on his shoulder.

When he checked the clock on the wall, he was disturbed to find that it was nearly four o'clock in the morning. It had been a while since he heard anything from Chloe.

When he peeked down, he saw that her eyes were shut, and she was breathing steadily in deep sleep. He smiled, admiring her flawless, peaceful face half nestled into the fabric of his shirt.

With his arm slung over the back of the couch, he let his hand drop down to gently caress her upper arm and shoulder. Instead of waking her up, Chloe burrowed deeper into his side and laid her hand across his abs.

Gavin's lips separated as he watched her for a while, waiting for her to snap out of her dream world and realize the nightmare she had curled up against.

An immeasurable amount of time passed, but she didn't budge. Gavin became entranced by her heartbeat, slow and steady, but strong just like her family line. He could also smell her blood, so near.

It would have been easy for him to bite through her tender flesh and make a meal of her right then and there. The squirrel he had fed on before they went to the movies was satisfying enough for a few hours, but he had felt the nasty effects of hunger close to midnight. Normally, he tried to find a more substantial meal to hold him over while they worked on the novel, but there was not enough time.

If they stayed together like this for much longer, he might do something he would come to regret.

Being careful not to jostle her, Gavin slipped his arms around her and swept her up into his arms the way he had the night they first met face to face. With her limp body cradled against his chest, he carried her up the stairs to her bedroom and gently laid her down atop the mattress.

Gavin then pulled the covers up over her body and tucked them tenderly under her chin, much like he used to tuck his child into bed so long ago. But this woman that lay before him held a special place in his heart that almost superseded the memory of his son and late wife.

It was a horrible reality. His family should have been the shining glory of his human life. But the years had not been kind to his heart and their memory. With each passing day, their faces became no more than ghosts, shadows of an ancient time that he could barely remember. Only events and fleeting details were retained somehow.

He remembered his wife's voice and her quirks. He remembered how his son was fascinated by insects. He remembered the taste of burnt bread and salty dishes that had been ruined by his late wife's cooking.

But Chloe was slowly working her way through his mind and consuming his heart. The sadness of his loss became blanketed in her warmth. The bitter memories were chased away in the glow of her smile. The demons of his past fled at the sound of her laughter. Her eyes, so full of acceptance and eagerness to be with him, were all he dreamed about during the day and all he wanted to see when he awoke at sunset.

Staring down at her now, realizing how much she truly meant to him, he felt fear creep through his body. He was growing too close.

It was only a matter of time before he hurt her, either emotionally or physically. There would come a moment when he wouldn't be able to control himself, and he would take her blood or worse. It had been his fear when he revealed himself to Mary Anne, and now again with Chloe.

But what else could he do? A bond had been formed between them. She might not feel it, but he certainly did. He felt it like a tether, an unbreakable cord that grew strained each dawn when he had to crawl back into the cellar and sleep the day away while she remained upstairs in her own bed.

Gavin ran a hand over his face and pressed his fingers into his eyes, feeling the mounting fatigue hit his system a little harder than usual. The sun was coming, and soon, he would need to leave her again.

Looking back down at Chloe, he sighed and combed back a thick strand of hair from her cheek, letting his fingertips drag across her skin. He watched her shiver and stretch beneath the quilt.

He quickly withdrew his hand, hoping he didn't wake her. But she rolled onto her side and curled up once more as if nothing happened. And that's what he should be—nothing more than a passing shadow in her life. He couldn't linger and complicate things for Chloe.

Gavin straightened and walked away, feeling his heart tug back towards the woman who had consumed him so quickly and suddenly. If only there was some way to cure this curse of love.

Chapter 14

C hloe sat in front of her laptop, staring blankly at the open document as if it were the epitome of all that was evil in the world. With her chin propped up in her hand, she sighed.

This shouldn't be so hard. It was just a scene. However, it was the most pivotal scene in the whole book. And somehow, in her plot notes, she didn't detail at all how to approach it, and it was too far back for her to remember what was going through her head at the time.

It was a gap that she wasn't sure how to fill.

But not only that, she was exhausted. The night before, she had stayed up listening to anecdotal stories about her aunt and her family before she was born, and all the families that came before.

She was amazed at how much Gavin could remember. But she was even more amazed how fast time had flown. Before she knew it, somehow she had fallen asleep and woke up in her bed the following afternoon by her rumbling stomach. She hadn't eaten the entire evening before, so she went all out to prepare a meal she could snack on all night.

However, this scene was not what she wanted to linger on all evening. But here it was, a little past sunset, and she still couldn't figure out the right approach.

Chloe didn't want Gavin hanging over her shoulder while she typed out this scene, either. It'd be far too embarrassing. But, it appeared that it might be unavoidable. Gavin had already woken up and left through the backdoor for his "morning" feed a little while ago with very little ceremony.

Chloe hoped that nothing was bothering him. With the way she'd leaned against him last night without invitation or permission, she wouldn't have been surprised if he was a little upset. No woman in the era he grew up in would have engaged in such behavior.

The stories he told last night were merely a diversion from the awkward and sensitive discussion that came before it. Chloe welcomed them. It kept her from speaking too much, and he never asked her to share childhood memories in return. She had shared too much as it was.

Chloe hated the way she behaved, but at the end of the night when she apologized for reacting the way she did, Gavin brushed it off as nothing. It took a lot out of her to open up the way she did, but he still understood somehow. Either that or it wasn't a big deal to him.

He would be back soon, and she still didn't know where to start. And Gavin would come in, asking her about what came next in the plot like he always did on the nights they spent writing together. It was a conversation she didn't want to have, but there was no way to skip this scene and carry on.

She'd downed two cups of coffee, but the solution still eluded her.

Then the back door opened, and she knew it was too late. A gust of cold wind swept into the living room and ruffled a bit of her hair. Gavin shut the door loudly behind him.

"It's quite windy outside," he informed her. "I'm glad they decided to show the movie last night, rather than tonight."

Chloe made a muttered sound of acknowledgment but continued to glare at the computer screen. Her efforts to focus were to no avail, especially when Gavin came up beside her and shoved his hands into his coat pockets.

The scent of pines still clung to his clothes, but it did little to mask his otherworldly fragrance that made her head light.

Chloe debated on asking him to build another fire in the fireplace tonight but decided against it. Wrapped up in her flannel pajamas and sitting so close to him, she was warm enough.

A few moments passed before Gavin finally broke the silence.

"Something troubling you?" he asked, his southern English accent shining through once more to make her heart beat a little harder.

Chloe groaned and rubbed her cheeks in despair. "I can't figure out this scene."

There was a hint of a laugh in Gavin's throat when he asked, "What scene is that?"

Instead of speaking it out loud, Chloe pulled up her plot document and pointed to the bullet point that was not crossed out. Gavin leaned over and peered at the words.

Then, as he read them, he nodded in understanding. "Ah, that one. I was wondering how you would approach it. I didn't see any connecting points."

"Exactly," Chloe said, her tone laden with exasperation. "I don't remember what I was thinking when I made it, but everything afterward hinges on this scene, and everything before it seems to lead up to it fine. Like you said, I just don't have a connection."

How could she possibly make her characters kiss when she didn't even know the circumstances that would lead up to it?

"Well, let's think of how it could happen."

Gavin walked away and began pacing the floor, very slowly and methodically as if each step led him closer to an answer for them.

Chloe turned around in her chair and draped her arms over the back. "I could have them in the middle of a conversation, and from the content, they decide to kiss."

"Or," Gavin added, "It could be spontaneous. Like one grabbing the other in a moment of intense passion."

A blush rose to her cheeks at hearing Gavin speak that way. To him, this must be just another scene; something to get through and move on so the book could be finished. But to her, it meant much more.

This kiss scene would seal their bond, in a way. It was the moment when Ben and Alleia would realize their true feelings for each other. It meant that the rest of the book would be focused on fueling that relationship and working towards a common goal.

Chloe refused to take it lightly.

"But, do you think either character would act so impulsively?" she asked. "I mean, Alleia is a little too shy for it, and Ben thinks that she doesn't love him back."

Gavin scratched at the stubble on his jaw. "It would certainly be out of character for both of them. Alleia would not make that move without coaxing, and Ben wouldn't do it for fear of rejection."

"Then it has to be as a result of a conversation. They both like to talk. It'd make more sense."

Gavin nodded in agreement. "Yes. So, where are they when this scene starts?"

Chloe glanced back over her shoulder at the computer. "It's set on the beach. She went out to think, and he happens to be walking his dog out there."

"Very good. Who will initiate contact?"

She shrugged. "I guess he would since he found her. What would he say?"

Gavin paused and stood between the sofa and coffee table, his chin tucked down on his chest, deep in thought. Chloe knew this look well. He did this when he was getting into character.

In the process of writing, both of them had subconsciously channeled their fictional counterparts, role-playing their scenes back and forth in an effort to make it all truly believable. It was a wonderful method, and Chloe enjoyed it. These parts were fun to write, as opposed to the pages of reflection that she wrote while Gavin relaxed in the armchair, waiting for her to finish so he could take over and write his own parts.

She never knew writing with another person could be so fun and just as fulfilling as writing alone. Gavin was a blessing in many ways, but this was the greatest way.

He lifted his head. "He probably wouldn't initiate contact so willingly after their last conversation. I presume she's on the beach, thinking about everything she had said to him."

Chloe nodded. She and Alleia were so similar in the way that she often said things she didn't mean. "Yeah. She was a little too open with him, and it turned awkward, remember?"

As soon as she said it, she remembered how their own experiences seemed to mirror what was happening in their story. The only difference was that Alleia dumped all of her problems on Ben in a moment when he didn't want them or need them, and he unloaded on her in a not-so-pleasant manner.

Gavin nodded. "And Ben's still feeling guilty about the way he behaved, so he wouldn't approach her readily."

After a few beats of silence, Chloe exclaimed, "What if Ben's dog ran up to her, and when Ben called to him to heel, he didn't budge."

Gavin bobbed his finger, a gesture she was familiar with as well. He did that when he believed she was onto something. "Yes. I've read that dogs can sense a human's emotions. If Alleia is upset, Spike will notice and go to her."

Chloe scooted to the edge of her chair. "Right! And when Ben can't call him from a distance–"

"He'll have to approach her and–"

"That starts the conversation."

Chloe was beaming, thrilled to no end that she and Gavin were on the right page, literally.

She turned around and began furiously tapping away on her keyboard, fleshing out the scene up to the first point of dialogue, which would be for Ben. In the meantime, Gavin continued to pace, probably playing out how he imagined the kiss would go.

Chloe was still nervous about it. She wondered if he was thinking about his first kiss with his late wife. Would he try to recreate it, or stay true to the story and only let the emotions of that moment in his life bleed through to Ben's character?

When she was finished, she glanced back over her shoulder and saw that Gavin's expression was hard and pensive. It sent a cold shiver down her spine to think he was fully into character now, prepped and ready for the serious task ahead.

"Ready?" she asked.

Broken from whatever dark thoughts he was brooding over, Gavin looked up and nodded. "Ben says, 'I'm sorry if he disturbed you.'"

Chloe typed out the dialogue but did not turn around as she recited what Alleia would say in reply.

"No, he didn't bother me. He never has."

This was a contradictory statement to how she reacted to Ben's dog the first time they met. Their first conversation was an argument over whether Spike should stay in the coffee house with Ben while he ordered his drink, or leave the dog tied up outside. Alleia's first words to him had been cold and harsh, calling him out for bringing a filthy animal into a restaurant establishment.

Gavin thought, then said, "What are you doing out here by yourself?"

Thus it continued where Gavin would speak and Chloe would type. The only sounds in the cabin were her quick hands working the keyboard, Gavin's light footsteps across the floor, and their make-believe conversation.

"I was just–" Chloe cut herself off for a moment. "Alleia wouldn't openly admit to what she's thinking, would she?"

"I suppose not," Gavin replied. "She can make up some excuse."

"But she hates lying, especially to him."

"But is a lie worth it to avoid another deep conversation? Also, is she still ashamed of her outburst from before?"

Chloe nodded in agreement. "Yeah, I guess you're right. She says, 'I was just... on my lunch break and thought I'd come and enjoy the view.'"

Gavin laughed.

"Do you want Ben to laugh, too?" Chloe asked.

"No. I was just thinking about how terrible of a lie that was."

She turned in her chair to look at him. "How so?"

Gavin's eyes sparkled with amusement. "From what your plot outline says, it's a Tuesday. She doesn't work on Tuesdays. And Ben would know it. Also, her work is not within walking distance of the beach."

Chloe admitted that she could see the silliness in the lie. "Well, because she hates lying, she doesn't do it often, so she can't think of a convincing one on her feet like that anyway. Plus, maybe it would get Ben thinking that something was wrong."

"But he won't call her out on the lie. He's trying to avoid how he behaved before."

Chloe nodded and added that extra narrative commentary before waiting for him to give her the next lines.

"Ben looks at her with concern. He asks, 'Are you ok?'"

Chloe paused after typing the dialogue, trying to debate what Alleia should say. Gavin was right in saying that she wouldn't dump on him again like she did before. But the girl had no one else to talk to. Her family had deserted her after the supposed scandal, and her friends didn't want to have anything to do with her. Alleia was alone.

"Alleia replies, 'It's nothing, really.' And she turns away to watch the water."

"I know that look. You're not alright."

"I just have a lot going on right now."

"Maybe talking will help."

"It never helps."

"Do you want her to push Ben away?" Gavin asked.

Chloe shook her head. "No, but she's not going to spill her guts so easily without a little reassurance."

Gavin paced a little more and then sighed. "Ben says, 'Talking always helps. I talk to Spike a lot.'"

"About what?"

"Ben shrugs. 'All sorts of things. It helps to get it out of my head.'"

"Alleia laughs. 'What could you possibly need to talk about? You don't have any problems.'"

"She's being snappy again," Gavin added out of character. "Ben sighs. 'I have a lot of problems. But I talk about them so other people don't have to deal with my being a sourpuss.'"

Hearing Gavin say the word sourpuss in his British accent brought a soft giggle out of Chloe. "Alleia's not laughing. I am... Alleia would be slightly offended by that. Did you mean for him to imply that everyone has to put up with her attitude unnecessarily?"

She could hear the smile in his voice. "If it gets her to open up, he'll say just about anything."

Chloe bit her lip and imagined if she were in Alleia's place. Would she take the bait and bare her soul? Would she reveal her darkest secret? If she had a chance to go back in time to last night with Gavin, Chloe wouldn't have made herself so vulnerable.

But was it worth it for Alleia?

"Alleia seems nervous but then takes a deep breath and says, 'I've been thinking about us.'"

It was a serious moment for her star characters, but Chloe couldn't help but revel in the emotional chaos to come. It certainly would be a fun scene to write, just not to experience. She'd had enough of that to last a lifetime.

"What about us?"

"Everything. What you mean to me and why I feel this way. I can't stop thinking about you all the time, and I want to drown myself in this ocean just to make the madness go away."

The cabin was filled with a warm, dense intensity that even made Chloe feel a little breathless.

"I know what you mean."

"You do?" Chloe caught the surprise in her own voice.

"Yes. Do you know what it's like to dream the same dream every night and wake up to realize it might never come true?"

Chloe swallowed hard. "Yes. This may sound crazy, but I always feel on edge when you're not around. It's like–"

"Like I want you to be there when I turn the corner but hate the agony of realizing you're not there."

She didn't understand why, but Chloe's fingers had a difficult time typing out the words correctly.

"Exactly. You're just saying all of this to make me feel good, aren't you? You don't really know what this is like. I'm just wasting my time," Chloe recited. "Alleia turns and tries to walk away."

"Ben takes her arm and turns her around. 'No. I'm not just saying things. I might have before, in the past, but not now. I think about you. I dream about you. I've talked Spike's floppy ears off every day about you. You say I don't understand, but I do. You don't know how much I do.'"

Chloe detected the breathy tone as if he were reaching his own breaking point. She turned to make sure Gavin was alright and saw him standing much closer to her than he had before. Now, with his feet firmly planted at the end of the sofa, she could see the odd mix of terror and conviction in his eyes.

He was really getting into character.

She turned back to the computer and typed out more narrative, mirroring Ben's expression with Gavin's.

"Alleia is a little shocked and says, 'I had no idea.'"

"I've spent so much time perfecting this stoic appearance. I never wanted you to know because I had no idea if you felt the same way. You're shy and abrasive sometimes, but that's what I adore about you. I've never met anyone like you in my whole life. Other girls are flimsy and weak, so shallow that they could be mistaken for a wading pool. But you're like a drinking well. Deep and sometimes dark, but I long to see how deep you can go, and if you'll permit me, to refresh myself in your soul."

Chloe held in her grin, pressing her lips tight together as she tried to type out his speech as quickly as she could. This was getting good. Now she was glad that she got Gavin's input on this scene rather than conceal it from him.

"I didn't know you were so poetic."

"There are many things you don't know about me. And every day that passes, I want to share everything with you. I've never been more candid with anyone. But I get the feeling that you don't care to know. You sometimes act like you don't want to have anything to do with me."

"Alleia shakes her head," and Chloe did too. "No, that's not it at all. I want to know more about you. I have from the very beginning. I just didn't know how to talk to you, how to communicate."

Chloe heard Gavin take a few steps forward. "I'm always here for you. You say the word, I'll be there, and we'll talk all night and all day if that's how you want it. I can't stand to be parted from you; to have you leave me, as everyone else has. I can't stand the loneliness anymore."

Suddenly, the truth of their conversation dawned on Chloe.

Ben had a family, he had friends, he had a pet dog, and coworkers that would fly to the moon and back for him. What Gavin said didn't match up with his character.

Gavin wasn't playing anymore.

Chloe turned in her seat to meet his emerald gaze, fierce and full of an emotion that she hadn't seen before. Unrequited longing for the one he looked upon now.

She opened her mouth to stop him, to break whatever spell it was that she had inadvertently cast on him. But he didn't. He only continued on, his words tumbling out a little faster than before.

"Before, my world was dark and full of death and despair. I didn't want to continue that way. I couldn't take the silence, the loneliness. I needed someone. And then you came. It was as if the sun had come back after centuries of night, but you didn't burn me. You stayed and accepted me. You gave me hope. I could never repay you for the miracle you've worked for me."

Chloe somehow found the strength to stand, and she rushed towards him, hands raised to stop his mouth from confessing anymore. It was too much.

Gavin grabbed her wrists before she could. "Please, Chloe. Don't turn me away now," he begged.

Where was this coming from? Gavin had never led her on to suggest any of this was truthful. How long had he been playing himself and not Ben? What he said about keeping up a stoic face, was that Gavin? It was convincing enough.

But how could this man, this vampire, stand in front of her like this with such a pleading expression, asking her for the thing he must have been craving for centuries—a friend, a companion, someone to love and protect. He didn't have to say it for her to read it in his eyes.

Chloe felt confused and troubled all at once. Never had a man thrown himself at her like this. Brent never did. Their relationship was slow, gradual. It was months before they really opened up the way that Gavin did now.

The longer she stared up at him, her eyes wide with fear, she realized that this is what she had wanted all along. She needed Gavin just as much as he needed her. But where was this terror coming from? Was it fear of the future? The present? His past? Hers? How far would this go? How could it work?

In a moment of reckless abandon, Chloe denied the doubt and fear. She wanted to be the woman Gavin deserved. Chloe knew she could never replace his late wife, but he wanted her to try. He wanted her.

And then, it was like the floodgates had opened. Before Chloe could stop herself, desperate tears and words poured out.

"I could never reject you. Yes, I was scared at first. But it wasn't necessarily of you. I was scared of how I'd make it through this whole thing in one piece. I don't want to be hurt again. I told you how Brent used me and helped to destroy my life. Now, at rock bottom, I didn't want to chain myself here.

"This was supposed to be my new life, my new adventure. I was going to start fresh and make things right again. When I found you, I thought maybe I was about to get on the same train I should never have gotten on in the first place."

The tears flowed a little heavier now. "I feel things for you that I never felt with Brent. I don't even know if this is right. All I know is if you left me today, I don't know how I could recover."

Gavin reached out and used his thumb to wipe away the moisture on her cheeks. His touch was soft and warm. "I will never leave you, as long as you still want me here."

Chloe felt intoxicated by his words, entranced by his nearness and everything he was. "I will always want you here." Then, an unwelcoming thought entered her mind.

This was all happening so fast. How had they gone from mere friends to declaring their deepest feelings for one another? It wasn't natural, but it still felt right somehow.

She said, "Are you making me feel this way?"

Knowing that Gavin could do such remarkable things as healing her twisted ankle, make an entire household fall asleep, and make her as immobile as a deer in headlights, it wasn't a far-fetched idea that he could plant ideas in her head to mold the situation to his liking. He might be able to make her fall for him so fast that she wouldn't know how it happened.

Gavin shook his head. "I can't control your mind. I can only control your body in some ways."

She knew he spoke the truth.

Chloe didn't understand how it had come to this, and somehow, she didn't care. The way he looked down at her, with such affection and need in his eyes, she could have died now and gone contented to heaven.

But Gavin decided to give her one more thing.

He bent down towards her, and she closed her eyes as their lips touched. The heat would have made her melt into a puddle on the floor if Gavin's arm hadn't wrapped around her waist to hold her up.

His fingertips pressed into her ribs, pulling her in tight against his body. She could feel every contour of his body, every sinuous line that seemed to match perfectly with her own.

Explosions of intense passion filled her core, making her knees tremble. His lips played against hers, grazing in ever-so-gentle movements. Shocks surged through her body, setting her blood on fire, traveling from her core to her fingertips.

Chloe swooned, the noise muffled against his mouth and lost in his own groans of pleasure. Her arms somehow found their way to wrapping around his neck, her fingers tangling in his thick dark hair. His free hand was splayed between her shoulder blades, drawing her closer still.

His scent filled her nostrils, and it was all she wanted to smell for the rest of her life. She wanted to wake up to this smell, go to sleep to it, and spend every waking moment just like this.

Gavin's tongue slipped between her lips and explored her mouth, tempting her to tease as he did. And Chloe obeyed, though she found it hard to avoid his sharp incisors.

As their kissing grew more passionate, Chloe began to feel that subtle ache low in her belly grow as well. It begged her for release, an end to the repression that had existed since the first day Chloe had laid eyes on Gavin.

Gavin sensed the need and began to kiss around the curve of her jaw and to her neck. Every touch sent sparks through her body, driving her mad with longing. Chloe had never felt this desire so furiously with anyone, not even Brent.

But Chloe was thrown from her climb to ecstasy when she felt the prickly edge of teeth glide across her skin. It wasn't painful, but firm enough to cause alarm.

The promise of sex was shattered and replaced with a new threat of death.

The fangs broke the thin skin, and Chloe felt a tiny droplet seep out. Gavin's moist tongue slid over the tiny cut, and Chloe let out a short cry of distress.

Gavin went rigid and his lips closed over his teeth, sheathing the weapons he had just used on Chloe.

The next few seconds were a whirlwind.

Gavin let go of Chloe and moved away with such force that she fell on her knees. Unable to support herself, she watched in horror as Gavin screamed out in rage and slammed his fist against the stone around the fireplace.

She heard it crack and a sprinkling of dust fell to the hearth.

Gavin gripped the wooden mantle, bracing himself against it with his back turned to her. His back shivered with convulses. And though his head was down, she could hear him breathing heavily. Each exhale was accompanied by a guttural sound, like a growl.

Chloe didn't have to know much about vampires to know that he was fighting the urge to feed on her. After touching the tiny cut, she found that it was much smaller than she originally believed and pushed herself up with the help of the nearby sofa arm. A tiny smear of blood appeared on her hand, but the wound barely hurt at all. What was injured the most was her trust in him.

She wasn't sure if she should speak and try to comfort him or run for shelter. No, she couldn't run. They had just finished telling each other they wouldn't leave. Fleeing now would make her a liar.

Chloe gathered her strength and approached the volatile vampire. He didn't appear to sense her approach in any way, and when she lightly touched his arm, he went still again. No convulsing, no breathing, nothing. Like a stone statue, he stood there, half leaning against the mantel. She couldn't see his face.

"Gavin, it's okay," was all she could whisper. Chloe didn't even know why she said it. Of course it wasn't ok that he had almost killed her and drank her blood. But what could she tell him instead?

He didn't break his promise, and that's what mattered.

"No, it's not," he grumbled.

"Nothing happened. We're ok."

"*Nothing*" was a relative term. He had tasted her blood, and he probably craved more. That wasn't "nothing". But he had enough control to pull back before things got worse.

Gavin straightened up and met her own tortured gaze with his. Only, his eyes were not as she expected. They were red with hunger as they had been that night in the kitchen when she cut herself. Her heart seized in her chest for a fraction of a second.

"You don't understand. I want to be with you so badly, but it can't happen. Look at me."

"I am," she said. "And I'm not afraid. We can make it work."

Again, she wasn't sure why she said it, but it just seemed right to say. It was the truth. They could make it work somehow, someway. If they thought hard enough and tried, they could. Anything was possible. He had given her hope and encouragement when she needed it most, and now she would do the same for him.

Gavin shook his head, every muscle in his body tense. "I could never forgive myself if I hurt you."

"But you won't hurt me." Chloe wasn't totally confident in that statement and he could tell.

"You don't know that." His voice dropped a few octaves, deep and growling.

"Yes, I do. You pulled back now even after..." She barely had the courage to say it.

Gavin's hackles rose. "But I didn't want to. Your blood-" His eyes darted down to her bleeding neck and fixed there for longer than she was comfortable with. She covered her neck with her hand and flinched when he took a lunging step towards her. But he stopped, hands balled into tight fists, so tight that she saw black blood drip from between his fingers as nails dug into his own flesh.

"Gavin, we can make this work."

Gavin laughed, but it was a laugh of incredulity, completely empty of humor. "No. This can never work. I want you too much. It's not safe."

Chloe watched him standing there, the two halves of himself warring against each other in the battle that had been going on for almost three hundred years. The slightest wrong move would give one of them the advantage. But she was the equalizer, the secret weapon to end the fighting.

She removed her hand from her neck and took a step toward him, extending her palm to him, fingers trembling. Gavin eyed her skin stained with glistening blood droplets. His tongue peeked out between his lips in an obvious sign of thirst, but he did nothing more.

"You see?" she whispered. "You're strong. I'm offering myself to you, and you still won't take it."

"But I want to," he whimpered. "I want to so badly."

She couldn't imagine what he tasted in her blood. Was it like a heroin high? A shot of whiskey to an alcoholic? Sugar candy to a child? She might never understand how blood made him reach this point of desperation.

Chloe cautioned another step closer, and Gavin angled himself away like he was ready to flee. But step after step brought her closer, and still he did not take her bait. Not until she was close enough for him to feel her breath on his face.

His nostrils flared, taking in the scent of her blood, but she could see the humanity in his vampire eyes. He still had control. She offered her hand up to him once more, raising it up to the level of his chin.

Gavin's entire body shuddered, but he kept his eyes fixed on hers. "Why are you doing this?"

"To prove a point," she replied coolly.

Gavin glared at her. "That I'm nothing more than a monster? I'm on the edge between taking you and killing you, and you push me this way?"

Chloe blinked in amazement at his words, trying to grasp their meaning. Did her blood serve as an aphrodisiac? Gazing deeper into his vampire eyes, she saw it there plainly. The lust for blood and lust of the flesh were powerful.

"You're not a monster, Gavin," she whispered, hoping the softness of her voice would ease his torn soul.

His hands shot out and seized her by the arms. Chloe let out a tight breath at the sudden movement but did not struggle against him. His hold on her was not so tight that it might cause bruising later but firm enough to keep her from running away.

"Then why do I smell fear in you?" he snarled, and she wasn't sure if he was angry at her or at himself.

"I'm not afraid of you," she replied. "I'm afraid I can't have you."

However he chose to perceive her response, it worked. His hands relaxed and fell from her while his handsome face was marred with confusion and inexplicable rage.

Before he had a chance to run away, Chloe lunged at him and pressed her lips against his to prove that he was not the object of her fear and neither was the threat of death. She didn't want to die, especially by Gavin's hands. But if this helped to prove that she was completely committed to whatever this was they shared, then it was not in vain.

Gavin returned the kiss, but would not touch her otherwise, even though her hands pressed him against her, holding him there so he wouldn't flee.

When she finally released him and took a step back, Gavin braced one hand against the wooden mantel to steady himself, his red and black eyes rolling. She waited while he recovered from the shock she had inflicted upon him. It might not have been necessary, but now he knew that he could consciously control himself if he wanted to.

Chloe also hoped that this proved to him that she trusted him completely. Even bleeding and vulnerable, she gave herself to him in the most dangerous way possible without a second thought.

"And what about years from now?" he said, his voice a little louder than it had been before, rose in frustration against the situation more than her. "You'll grow old, and I won't."

Chloe hadn't thought about that before, but it wasn't an important detail in the heat of the moment. "That's not a big deal."

"It is to me." He spat. "I don't know if I could handle seeing you waste away in your old age while I can do nothing to stop it."

It was then that Chloe got the idea. With a trembling hand, she pulled back her collar to expose the soft flesh of her shoulder and side of her neck that was still slightly bleeding. "Then let me spend eternity with you."

It was a rash decision, an impulsive move that would change her life forever. But she wasn't thinking about that anymore. All she could think of was making this all better.

A disgusted grimace was joined with his response. "I can't. Even if I knew how it worked, I wouldn't let you throw your life away like that. You have a family, a potential career. I couldn't ask you to join me in darkness."

Again with the poetics, Chloe thought. She let her pajama shirt pop back into place. "Then join me in the light," she offered flippantly with a shrug. She didn't mean for him to take it seriously. Nowhere in any of her studying had she seen any mention of a cure for vampirism besides death.

Gavin shook his head again, as she expected. "No, it's imposs-"

Then, a look came over him, washing away the despair and hopelessness. Whatever idea passed through his mind, he liked it, and it latched on tight.

"Wait," he said, dropping his arms to his side and staring off into space with a vacant gaze. She could see gears turning in his eyes, still red hot from hunger and lust.

A long silent moment passed before Chloe began to lose her patience. "What is it?"

Gavin blinked, and his eyes swiveled around the floor and the room as if he were looking for something. "I don't know why I hadn't thought of this before."

"Haven't thought of what?" Chloe whined, hating that he was keeping her in suspense.

Finally, he looked at her, and she could see a small smile appear on his face, the first genuine one she had seen since before their kiss.

"I told you that I had met another vampire once before. He didn't stay long, but we did talk quite a bit. He was born a vampire, unlike me. When I explained to him that this curse was brought on by an illness, he envied me. He said that I could be human again."

It was the solution to their problems. "How?" she asked hastily.

"He said that my condition was caused by a virus I contracted while I was sick. My wife and son did too, but they were too weak to accept it, and that's what killed them. The virus is like a parasite, but there's a way to starve it out and cleanse it from my body. I can't feed for seven days, and at the end of the seven days, I have to drink pure vinegar. It purges my system, and I can be human again."

She threw her arms out in an exaltation of joy. "Great! We'll start today, and in a week, you'll be human again!"

The wary look on Gavin's face made her joy go sour.

"It's not that simple," he said. "Since then, I've tried to reach seven days and I could only get to four without difficulty. After that, I normally become unconscious of my own actions, and I go out and feed. I'd need to be locked in the cellar from the outside. I've never had anyone to help me."

"My aunt wouldn't help?"

"She was too frightened of the dangers that came with keeping an uncontrollable monster under the house."

It was understandable, and if Chloe hadn't felt so passionately for Gavin, she would have told him the same. But that was far from the case. She wasn't sure how it had come to this, but she was willing to walk through hell itself to make this work. Besides writing, she had never been so determined about anything in her life.

"We can do this, Gavin. I know we can. I'll do anything."

Gavin looked at her, studying her expression as if he were searching for any hint of mocking or joking. Perhaps he thought that she wasn't serious.

Chloe charged towards him, prepared to do whatever was necessary to convince him. But, he was ready for her this time and held her back.

"No, Chloe," he demanded. "If we're going to go through with this, you cannot get too close."

She let out a huff and gave him a pleading look. "I just showed you that you could control yourself."

"I've had a meal already tonight. I'm not starving like I would be after three days." He lifted his chin as if he were asserting his dominance. "You must keep a safe distance from me and refrain from any interaction that might bring out the beast in me."

Chloe wasn't sure if he meant the monster that craved blood or the lustful carnal beast that wanted to take her. She smiled and nodded in agreement. "I'll try" she teased.

None of this made a lot of sense. Her heart, once shattered and slowly mending back together, seemed a little more whole now, knowing that Gavin did care for her. If he was willing to give up immortality and practical invincibility to grow old with her, then surely he wanted her as more than a plaything to feed on.

Chloe couldn't comprehend the sudden changes. A month ago, she was alone and miserable. Tonight, she stood before a creature that, by all scientific logic, shouldn't exist, professing all she had felt for him since they met just a short time ago. She hardly knew exactly what was happening or why, but there was no use fighting it anymore. They wanted each other, needed each other. And Chloe knew that in a week's time, this would all just be a bad memory, a stepping stone on the way to a brighter future for both of them.

Chapter 15

Chloe suspected that day two of Gavin's detox program would be much like his first. Sure, he was a little grumpy all night while they worked out the rest of the scene on the beach for the novel, but he was tolerable.

She sat on the sofa, waiting for him to emerge from the basement. Her fingers scratched at the ceramic mug in her hands, her eyes anxiously staring at the empty fireplace. Gray ashes remained from the other night when Gavin had lit a fire, and she had been too lazy to sweep them away. They were a reminder of that night, and if she could help it, they would sit there until the world ended.

Clad in her flannel pajamas and favorite robe, this night seemed a little colder than usual. The chill seeped through her wool socks and made her toes slightly numb. Even with her feet curled up on the sofa cushion, it was hard to ignore the drop in temperature. All she could think was that it never got this cold in the city so early in the season.

Silent seconds ticked by, and she began to hum. It was something she did to fill the air with something other than the ringing silence or crickets from outside. Chloe hummed the tunes with no precise melody in mind. It was just a string of pleasant noises to distract her from the fact that it was two hours past sunset, and Gavin was still in the basement.

Her mind replayed the events of the night they last kissed, the night that he tasted her blood and all the effects from it. The memory continually popped up at the oddest moments, both in the hours that she slept and the hours she was awake.

She remembered the hungry, lustful glint in his eyes and the way his whole body went rigid and tight with control. She'd never seen anything like it before, and she hoped not to again. Pushing Gavin to the edge of insanity was the last thing she wanted to do.

But that kiss, so soft and full of every emotion that needn't be explained with words. Chloe tried to push away the bad consequences of that kiss, but they would be forever linked in her thoughts.

She regretted nothing, and if she kissed him again and he lost control as he did before, she would still regret nothing. Kissing a vampire might have been the most thrilling and most satisfying thing she had ever done. Nothing could compare.

She wasn't sure why Gavin's kiss was more addictive than Brent's. Perhaps it was the raw need behind every sinuous move of his lips against hers, or the way he held her so close as if she would fly away with the wind that had wailed outside the cabin. Whatever it was, she couldn't wait another five days for such a kiss again.

If it weren't for his constant state of discontent and irritability, Chloe might have risked another kiss upon that mouth that had tasted her blood. But he wouldn't even let her close and refused to touch her. Under other circumstances, she would have been offended. But she understood all too well that things could go so terribly wrong if the kiss got out of hand.

Chloe's long-suffering paid off when she heard the familiar sounds of Gavin opening the hatch in the kitchen. She turned and watched as her vampire stiffly climbed his way up and out into the fluorescent light.

She smiled at first, glad to have him here at last. But, when he turned to look at her, her smile faded.

Gavin looked terrible. If it were possible, his skin was even paler than usual, and his eyes were rimmed with dark circles as if he hadn't slept in days. He was still gorgeous in the same way he had always been, but there was a sadness written in the lines of his face that hadn't been there the day before.

Chloe rose from the sofa and set her cup down before coming to him. "Are you ok?" she asked. It was a silly question. Of course, he wasn't.

Gavin sighed and shut the hatch rather heavily. The sudden bang of wood on wood made her jump a bit. But she refused to run from him, even when he looked at her with a gaze laced with a brooding, inexplicable resentment.

She took a tiny step back and waited.

"I'm fine," he replied. But the sharp blade of hate was in his voice.

How could he speak to her like that? Chloe tried to convince herself it was the hunger. He had warned her from the beginning that it would be like this. She'd even had a taste of it that one night that seemed a lifetime ago when she had stood between him and his next meal.

Just when she thought her heart was on the mend, she felt it crack a little. It was enough to make her want to give him anything he desired, even her own blood. She'd even give him her own blood if it would make this bad attitude go away.

Gavin rubbed his hand over his face and grumbled sleepily. "I'm sorry," he said, obviously picking up on her reaction to his venomous words.

Chloe shook her head and wrapped her arms around her midsection. "It's alright. I understand."

Gavin bared his teeth at her. "No, you can't understand this," he snapped.

Her hands began to shake, even pressed against her ribs. There was no point in arguing. It would just make him more upset. Chloe stood there, waiting for anything; another apology; a gentle gesture that told her everything was and will be ok; anything to ease her sudden doubts.

She tried to think about the end goal. In less than a week, he'd be human, and this would be a memory to look back on and laugh.

Gavin ran his fingers through his hair, which now seemed a little more unkempt than usual. Frustration radiated from him, but he wouldn't look at her now. His eyes wandered, and she wondered if he was trying to distract himself.

She could only imagine how hard it was for him to be in the same house with her. It must be like a starving human who sat at a Thanksgiving feast but couldn't partake.

"What can I do to help?" she asked, her voice carefully soft and meek. Any hint of aggression might set him off again.

Gavin's mouth opened quickly as if he would respond with another biting answer, but he stopped himself and walked around her, keeping his hands occupied the whole time. He wiped his mouth on his palm, scratched at his dark eyebrows, pinched his nose and huffed air out at the same time, and all manner of other fidgety movements that left her wondering if he were about to have a psychotic breakdown.

After taking a few restless turns around the living room, he turned to her and said, "I need to be busy."

Chloe nodded, trying to process what that meant. "Ok. We can work on the novel if you feel up to it."

He shook his head and waved off her offer. "No, no. That only keeps me occupied while we're discussing the plot. But when you type, I have nothing to think about. I need to think. My mind needs a diversion."

She shrugged. "Would reading help?"

"It would," he replied tirelessly, "but I've read nearly every book in Carter Lake."

"Then we'll get you more."

"Where?" he asked in exasperation. "There are no bookstores."

"You've heard of libraries, right?"

"Of course, I've heard of libraries," he growled. "But there isn't one anywhere near here."

Chloe took a few cautious steps forward. "I remember passing by one on my way to Carter Lake. I know where it is, and it's probably only an hour's drive away."

Gavin turned a fierce look at her. "Then why are we just standing here? Get dressed!" he barked.

Even through his anger, she found what he said slightly amusing. She smiled, much to his annoyance, and went upstairs to slip on a pair of jeans and a t-shirt.

After an hour of enduring Gavin's harping on her driving skills as they sped down the darkened highway, they came to the library Chloe had mentioned. She cut off the engine and stared at the blackened windows. It was almost ten o'clock, and she should have known that the library would be closed.

Chloe grimaced to think how Gavin would explode. But as soon as she leaned over to turn the key that was still stuck in the ignition, she heard him open the passenger side door and slide out.

"Where are you going?" she called out as he briskly walked around the front of the jeep.

"Where do you think?"

Chloe had almost had enough of his attitude, but she held onto the fact that he wouldn't be this way forever. She slid out of the car and jogged to catch up with him at the glass front doors.

"The library is closed," she said in hushed tones. Looking around, there were no other stores or residences nearby to see them. The library was safely tucked away on a back road far from the main strip of the town that was a little bigger than Carter Lake. There might have been no reason to be so cautious.

Gavin ignored her comment and pulled out something from his jeans pocket. She was nonplussed to see it was a Swiss Army pocket knife set, complete with a corkscrew and nail file, along with a number of other doodads. Chloe couldn't understand why a vampire would need such a tool but wasn't about to ask.

He flipped out a sharp picking tool and began working on the door lock.

"Gavin, we can't just break in!"

"Please be quiet so I can hear the locking pins."

His voice was oddly calm and level, which might have been the only reason Chloe decided to do as he said. They were committing a felony, and if a cop happened to roll by, there was no explaining their presence there.

Just as she was wondering if breaking into a library would constitute a fine or night in jail, Gavin twisted the antique doorknob and pushed open the heavy oak door.

Inside was dark, with the only exception of a backroom light that hadn't been turned off and a few green dots that belonged to computers sprinkled between the rows of tall bookcases. The only light to aid their way came from the orange glow of the street lamps in the parking lot that beamed through the windows that stretched from the floor to the ceiling.

Gavin walked inside while Chloe rushed out to the jeep to retrieve her laptop.

When she came back and softly closed the door behind her, the library was deathly silent. Her footsteps on the tile foyer floor echoed off the high ceiling as she made her way towards a studying desk.

"Gavin?" she called out, his name reverberating off the walls.

"I'm still here," he replied from somewhere in the far back of the library.

Chloe began to make her way in that general direction to look for a place to settle down. But after a few steps past the history section, something flew past her, followed by a gust of wind that whipped her hair over her face.

She tried to find her balance and brushed her hair away to look for what had almost hit her.

"Was that you?" she hollered, a slight warble in her voice as she tried not to laugh at herself.

"Yes, I apologize. I didn't know you were standing there." Gavin was a few rows behind her now in the reference section where all the encyclopedias were kept.

Chloe turned and hurried to catch up, but as soon as she did, the blur that was Gavin flew out of the aisle and across the divide between the fiction and nonfiction sections.

She stood perfectly still, not wishing to be run over again.

"Are you going to pinball around like that all night?" she quipped.

"Possibly," was his only response.

She wanted to groan in frustration. Chloe hoped that this trip would also be a bonding time for them. She imagined that he could sit across the table and read while she wrote in the novel for a little while. That didn't appear to be what he had in mind at all.

However, she didn't want to hinder him from doing what he needed to do. Already she could sense the lack of tension in his voice. There was plenty here for him to read that would keep him distracted from the hunger that must be endlessly gnawing at him.

Chloe found a table somewhere in the central part of the library and began to set up her laptop, mouse, and hard drive. While she waited for the computer to wake up, she peered down the shadowy aisles.

She couldn't see Gavin in any of them and gave up the attempt after a while.

As she typed out the next scenes that did not include Ben, Chloe saw the faint wisps of movement in the corner of her vision. There was no method to Gavin's roaming. He sporadically whisked from one section to another without pattern.

When it did happen that Gavin was within sight of where Chloe sat, she turned and watched him in fascination. He didn't read like she, or any other human on this planet, did. He flipped through the pages of a thick tome, reading each page that was densely packed with words as if there were only one sentence there. She watched him finish off a heavy novel in less than five minutes. Then, he placed it back on the shelf and moved on to somewhere else.

"Are you really reading everything?" she asked once.

Gavin replied from some bookcase behind her, "Yes, I am. I'm a fast reader."

She laughed. "I think that's an understatement."

Chloe watched the time crawl by slowly, and her progress in the novel went even more slowly. She found herself sidetracked by keeping tabs on where approximately Gavin was in the library; so much that it was hard to concentrate on the task at hand. Every time he moved, her eyes darted around to see where he went and which section he was reading from now.

Midnight tolled, and with only a few pages written, she wondered if she should get up and read a little herself. It might be more productive, and Chloe had been meaning to see if they had a copy of Wuthering Heights she could pour herself into.

But as she was about to rise from her seat, she saw Gavin walking towards her. His eyes were fixed on the pages of a book, and his mouth was twisted in horror and disbelief. His steps were slow and lumbering as if he were walking in a daze.

Chloe glanced at the title and sucked in a tight breath. It was a book she hadn't read before, but many of her friends had raved about it years back. It was a gruesome tale of murder and bloodlust, with the vampires as the star characters.

A library was a treasure trove of knowledge and adventure. It was a place where anyone could walk in and travel across time and space, slipping into someone else's shoes and living a life that they never could. It was part of the reason she wanted to become an author. She wanted to give that thrill to others and share the story that was inside her.

But if she had known that the library had such books stored on its shelves, she would have never brought Gavin here at all. Chloe chided herself for forgetting that such books existed. It was only a matter of time before Gavin found them here.

He stepped up to the edge of the table and turned one page with such aching slowness that Chloe wanted to weep. The motion conveyed less apprehension and more utter shock at the words his eyes drank in.

After a few agonizing moments of silence as he continued to read, Gavin shut the book. He wasn't even half way through. Without lifting his gaze, he pulled out one of the chairs at the desk and sat down heavily.

All the anger that had been there only hours before was gone, leaving only a sad emptiness in his expression. Chloe didn't know what to say to him. There would be no way to curb the hurt he must have felt.

"It's no wonder you were afraid of me," he whispered, his voice barely audible. If it weren't so silent that Chloe could hear a pin drop, she might not have heard him at all.

She pushed aside her laptop and swatted the book out of his hands before gripping his fingers with a boldness that only a lover possessed for the one they cared so deeply about. His skin, which she hadn't touched in days, was ice cold, much different from the usual warmth it gave. Was he chilled by the book he just read or was this an effect of the detox?

"You aren't like them," she said, wishing her voice hadn't turned so brusque. Chloe had to make him believe that what she said was true.

Gavin looked at her, a flicker of self-loathing behind his gaze. "How am I not? I'm still a monster; an abomination amongst humanity."

Chloe shook her head. "You're not like them because you're not a murderer."

Gavin squeezed his eyes shut and turned away. "Yes, I am."

She huffed. "You've killed animals. I'm sure some animal rights activists would call you a murderer, but it's not the same as killing a human being."

"But I have killed a human."

A chill shot through her veins, and her stomach retched. She'd never known Gavin to lie. And the pain and regret in his voice told her that he wasn't this time, either.

She swallowed and asked, "When?"

It took a while before his eyelids cracked open, but he wouldn't look up at her. "A long time ago. It was during your Civil War. The fighting had come close to Carter Lake."

Chloe could sense his struggle, reliving the memories he had hidden from her. She understood why he kept this a secret. It was the root of all his self-loathing, the pivotal point in his existence that made him question his own humanity. She didn't have to listen to the whole story to know that this is when he considered himself a monster, not when he had to bury his family and hide from the light of the sun in his own cellar.

"After a battle, I was in the woods, and I came upon, what I believed to be, a dead soldier. I had found many before. Especially in the war for colonial independence before your family took possession of the cabin. I was always careful to check for a heartbeat. If there was none, I..." He paused, but he didn't have to finish his sentence for her to know what he meant.

So hers was the not the first drop of blood he had tasted.

"This time, I was careless. The soldier wasn't moving, and I hadn't fed yet. By the time I bit down, it was too late." He swallowed hard, his lips twisted in disgust. "I felt his pulse while I drank, but I couldn't stop. It was like nothing I'd ever tasted before. Human blood is so different from that of an animal's."

Gavin breathed a heavy sigh. "When it was over, and I realized what I had done, I tried to kill myself. But even after a hundred years, it was still all new to me, and no matter how hard I tried, I couldn't."

Finally, he met her stare, and Chloe's heart was gripped with grief when she saw the tears form in his beautiful eyes.

"I'm just like them, Chloe. I'm a monster."

Chloe stood up and moved around the table, driven by a need to comfort him somehow. She came up behind him and wrapped her arms around his shoulders and neck and hugged him tight.

She understood what Gavin had done, but she didn't care. It was an honest mistake and a poor decision. Heaven knows, she had made poor choices, too. Maybe none of them involved killing a person, but a mistake was a mistake, and it was too long ago to dwell on it so heavily. That abandoned soldier may not have survived his wounds anyway.

All that mattered to Chloe was that he was here, with her, and his suicidal attempts had failed. If he had succeeded, they would have never met.

So much death lingered around him, but it had not managed to destroy him.

Gavin shivered, but her lips spread into a smile when she felt his hand lay across her forearm.

"You're not a monster to me, Gavin. You never will be. You feel remorse for the things you've done. Those characters didn't. That's what sets you apart. You still have your humanity. And I'm glad you didn't kill yourself. If you had, I would never have met you."

Gavin leaned his head against hers, and she could see a bit of a smile on his lips. It was the first she'd seen in days.

They stayed like that for a while, just holding each other until the pain faded away into the dark recesses of his subconscious. Chloe knew it would come up again, but for now, it was gone. She'd been able to do something that he could never do for himself—cope with the past.

The moment was broken when Gavin went rigid. It was the same motionless state as when he had bitten her a few nights ago while they kissed.

His fingers clamped down on her arm.

Chloe jerked her head away to look at his face. Even in the dim light, she could tell that his eyes had changed again. A black and red gaze was fixed hungrily on her wrist.

For a fleeting moment, she was scared, but not for herself. She was scared of Gavin falling off the wagon so soon. It was only his second day. If he fed, even a drop or two, they would have to start all over again.

However, after such a moment of emotional weakness, Chloe wanted to cater to him just this once. They could start again just as easily as before. Humanity could wait a couple of more days, couldn't it?

Instead of pulling away, Chloe drew her soft flesh closer to his mouth. She was like a mother spoiling a child, but Gavin had suffered enough.

"I don't mind," she whispered in his ear as if she were giving her consent to something much more meaningful than a midnight snack.

She watched Gavin's face contort with emotions as each one segued into the next almost seamlessly; confusion, relief, hesitance, longing, anger, and finally fury that could be compared to that night when he tasted her blood for the first time. No doubt, he was remembering how her blood had sent him into a euphoric state and how terrible he felt afterward.

Instead of accepting her offer, he released her arm and bolted away, disappearing into the library. Chloe couldn't even tell which direction he'd fled. She spun around and looked at the front door, but it stayed shut. Gavin hadn't left, she was certain of that.

Her own feelings conflicted with one another as she sat down behind her computer. Chloe felt pity for Gavin, but she was also proud. He could have fed, but he hadn't. He was much stronger than she had anticipated.

Shame crept in, deriding her for being so weak and giving into his temptation. No amount of reasoning could rationalize her effusive behavior.

Chloe resolved that she would have to be strong from now on, strong like he was. It would only get worse from here, and the hunger would be even more consuming. If she gave into him on the fourth day, there was no telling if he would take only a sip or drain her dry without restraint.

But she couldn't belabor the issue any longer. They wouldn't have to start over. And there were five days left on this journey. Chloe only hoped they would both make it out in one piece.

Chapter 16

Even after two and a half cups of coffee, Chloe had a hard time keeping her tired eyes open. The drive down the mountain had proved a little dangerous due to her heavy exhaustion. But, the fridge was empty, and the grocery store closed at six o'clock.

What was more debilitating than the fatigue was the bright sunshine. Chloe never realized how accustomed she had become to the dark of night. Even the light that fell across her left arm while she was driving seemed to sear her skin a bit. Chloe saw a lot of aloe in her future if she stayed out in the afternoon sun for too long.

This would also be her first time interacting with people since committing herself to staying up with Gavin every night.

It was day three of his detox program, and after last night's near disaster when she offered him her blood in a moment of weakness, Chloe knew she had to tread softly today.

Carter Lake was buzzing with activity. Families were out in the streets with their children, shopping and spending their Saturday together. It reminded Chloe that she hadn't talked to her mom or dad in a while. Each time she wanted to call, it was at an ungodly hour for them, and she knew they wouldn't answer the phone.

It was then that she realized that Thanksgiving was approaching. Two weeks away. Main Street was generously decorated with fall colors on the lamp posts. Pumpkins, hay bales, and scarecrow men were on nearly every bench and street corner. Signs everywhere advertised Pumpkin Patch excursions and turkeys for sale.

Chloe hadn't given much thought to holiday celebrations or plans, but she suspected that her mother would want to arrange something.

That thought made her cringe. How would Gavin deal with that? By then, he would be human. Could they explain the truth to her mother or tell unending lies about how and when this handsome Brit had appeared?

That was a bridge she would cross when they came to it. For now, all she was concerned about was the present and just five nights ahead.

She parked in front of the grocery store and pulled out her long list from her back pocket. She hoped that no one would notice her red eyes or the way her feet dragged a little as she walked.

The grocery store hadn't changed, except for the holiday decorations sprinkled here and there. Grabbing a cart, she began.

While passing down can after can of vegetables into her cart, she couldn't help but catch snippets of words from the conversation down the aisle.

She looked, her attention diverted for the moment, at two older women who wore concerned looks.

"Can you believe they found her there in the ditch? Dry as a bone, bless her heart," one said, clicking her tongue worriedly as she pressed a bony hand to her rouged cheeks.

At first, Chloe thought they might have been talking about a stray animal. But as the conversation continued, she realized that was not the case.

"How are her parents doing?" the other asked, leaning so far forward that her string of pearls dangled down from around her neck.

The first woman who seemed a little younger than the other shook her head. "Not good I'm afraid. They were already having marital issues, and with this, I'm not sure how long they'll stay together."

"That's just terrible," the second exclaimed.

The curiosity bug bit Chloe, and she approached the two women with her cart.

"I'm awfully sorry," she began, "but I couldn't help overhearing. Who was found in a ditch?"

The two women didn't seem the least bothered by her intrusion. Chloe's first impressions of them were rather stereotypical. The women looked like out of place in a grocery store. They might have been more at home in a beauty shop, the way they gossiped and by their flamboyant fashion tastes.

The second and older lady angled to face Chloe, including her in the conversation. "You haven't heard, honey?"

Chloe shook her head. "I haven't been to town in a while."

The younger lady said, "They found Susie Hopkins dead in a ditch out on Old Mill Road just on the outskirts of town."

"Oh, that's terrible."

Murders happened all the time in Atlanta, but she had never expected that kind of tragedy to come to Carter Lake. Such crimes were devastating to a small community like this where everyone knew everyone and families were connected in all sorts of ways.

"She's the third one in the last month."

If Chloe had been drinking anything, she was sure it would have shot out of her nose. "Third?" she asked, her eyes wide and jaw slacked.

"Yes, ma'am," said the younger. "And it's the same with all of them, bled dry and their neck and shoulders torn to bits. The police think it's a rabid animal, but the county and state aren't giving us all the details if that's what it really is."

"I personally think," the older butted in, "that it's someone murdering these poor children. If it were an animal, they would have been eaten, not left to bleed out. And, I heard that there was practically no blood at the crime scene at all. It's like someone let them bleed out somewhere else before dumping them there."

"Sheriff Lemasters isn't telling the community anything. Darlin', are you gonna be ok?"

Chloe felt light headed and nauseated. To these ladies, she must have looked either pale or green around the gills. The way they talked about the murders, the blatant detail, and things that should have been considered taboo, it was too much.

It took her a moment to realize they were speaking to her and she replied with, "Oh, yes, I'm fine. It's just so horrible. Did you know the families?"

One snorted a laugh. "Of course, we know their families. Everyone does. They're holding a memorial service tonight for Susie at the school gymnasium. It starts at seven. Will you be there?"

Chloe paused and then shook her head. "No, probably not. But I'll pay my respects later. I have other plans I can't break."

It was a lie she had used before many times with her friends in Atlanta. It was a typical excuse, one she had rehearsed time and time again until it sounded perfectly believable. It came in handy now when her mind couldn't lock down on any solid concept.

She excused herself and hurried away on her jelly legs to continue her shopping.

But no matter how hard she tried to focus, her thoughts kept going back to what the ladies said about this new rash of murders.

Bled dry. Neck and shoulders ripped apart. Found in a ditch. No blood at the scene at all.

It was too gory, too strange. Chloe agreed it couldn't be an animal. Animals don't drink blood, and if the body was in a fair enough condition for the children to be identified, this was no rogue bear or coyote.

But, a senseless murderer wouldn't leave such a mess behind. Wouldn't it be a single knife wound or gunshot? And it wouldn't explain the victims being bled dry.

The idea she wanted to avoid couldn't be denied. If she had heard about these murders weeks ago when they first happened, she wouldn't have even considered it. But after learning that there are more things out there that go bump in the night, Chloe imagined the worst.

What if Gavin was not the only vampire in Carter Lake?

Chloe sat on the edge of the couch cushion, waiting for the sun to set. She'd sat there several times before while patiently waiting for Gavin to appear. But she had never been this nervous.

Her hands were fidgeting in her lap, and her mind was in a million places. After coming home from the grocery store, she made herself some baked chicken and rice for dinner, but only took a few bites. Her stomach was so tied in knots that she was afraid to eat too much.

She wasn't worried about Gavin being the murderer. She knew for a fact that he wasn't. Gavin spent the whole of last night with her, so there was no way he could have killed that girl. Plus, his obvious grumpy behavior during the detox was proof that he hadn't fed.

It was the thought that something else was lurking out there in the woods and would probably kill again.

Finally, dusk fell over the mountain. Every little noise made her heart skip a beat, thinking it was Gavin coming up to the hatch in the kitchen floor or another vampire snooping around her cabin outside. She went deathly still each time and listened, but nothing more.

Chloe groaned in anguish and held her face in her hands. Sometimes, she wished she could go down there herself and drag him up. It would save both of them time. However, she knew that Gavin was too volatile during his detox. She wondered if he would be as grumpy on this night as he was the night before.

Finally, Chloe was sure she heard him and rushed to the kitchen. Still fully dressed from the trip to town, she squatted down by where she believed the trap door was. Even after all the times she saw him come up, she couldn't find the seams in the wood that differentiated the door from the floor. And she couldn't determine which knot in the wood belonged to the hatch door, either.

The door tilted up no more than a few inches and bobbed there for a moment as if Gavin were struggling to lift the wood. Chloe lent him a hand and pulled up the door, flooding Gavin and the few stair treads behind him with fluorescent light.

Gavin was in a sorry state. He was still extremely pale compared to normal, and, if it were possible, it appeared his face had aged half a decade while he slept. What's more, he wasn't angry anymore. The scowl that seemed fixed on his face was gone, and in its place was a bone-deep weariness. Chloe felt tired just by looking at him.

She felt pity for him, knowing that he was suffering for the chance to be human. But it wasn't only that. He suffered so that they could have a chance at being together.

Chloe felt a new level of appreciation for Gavin as she watched him literally crawl up the slanted ladder on his hands and knees. He was truly trying. This wasn't some half-hearted attempt to appease her. This was what real commitment looked like. Yes, he was doing it because he was sick of being a vampire, but the benefits were wide reaching for both of them. He was willing to make the change and endure the consequences. Brent would have never done that for her.

Once his upper body reached the kitchen floor, Gavin stretched out his torso along the planks of wood and nestled his head in his folded up arms. His other half was still resting against the stairs.

Chloe smiled despite herself. "Good morning," she whispered cheerfully.

Gavin grunted but didn't move. Still holding the trap door suspended over his body, she gave a short giggle.

"Are you going to climb the rest of the way out of there or do I have to drag you?" she asked. She kept her tone playful as if she were talking to a child. Chloe was enjoying this a little too much.

Gavin turned his head to face her and gave her a sleepy smile, his eyes minimally open and one eyebrow arched. She grinned, admiring how handsome he was despite the detox effects and exhaustion that was so prevalent in his eyes. He couldn't be feeling any better, but he certainly was in a more pleasant mood than yesterday.

It took him a few tries, but Gavin managed to pull himself up and out of the trap door and fully into the kitchen. At first, the vampire laid flat on his stomach, but then after much struggling with his own lethargy, he rose to a sitting position and leaned back against a set of cabinet doors.

Chloe closed the hatch and sat in front of him, watching his head and eyes roll as he fought the sleep that tried to overcome him. All the while she smiled, thoroughly amused.

"You gonna be ok?" she asked.

Gavin mumbled an affirmative before opening his eyes as wide as he could to see her clearly.

"Did you not sleep well?"

He cleared his throat and replied, "I slept fine, that's what's the matter. When I sleep too deeply, it's often difficult to wake back up."

"I'd offer you some coffee if I didn't think it would kill you."

Gavin smirked and let his eyelids droop a little. "It probably would."

"Is there anything I can do?" Chloe knew that question was a dangerous one, especially since she asked it yesterday and nearly got her head chewed off.

Gavin barely had the energy to shake his head. "No. Just give me a moment."

Chloe didn't have a moment. Though this spectacle put a smile on her face, her heart was still full of anxiety.

"I was in town this afternoon, and I heard a couple of older ladies talking about something that's been going on in Carter Lake for a while now."

Gavin, through his fatigue, gave her his undivided attention. His brows furrowed together as he must have picked up on the worry in her voice.

"There has been a string of murders. Little kids are getting torn apart and left in ditches." She paused to observe the strange mix of confusion, worry, and odd fascination in his expression. "Each one was bled dry with lacerations on their neck and shoulders. One girl was found this morning."

"That's terrible," Gavin commented, and she could detect the genuine sentiments in his words.

Chloe took a deep, steadying breath and leaned her elbows on her knees. "Gavin, could this have been done by a vampire?"

He didn't respond at first but gazed at her with that same muddled look as if he were still processing what she had told him.

"It's possible. Though, I haven't seen another vampire feed. You forget, I haven't been out in the world as much as I am able to. I've stayed on this mountain for centuries."

"That one vampire you met before, how long ago was that?"

Gavin shook his head. "That was over half a century ago. He's not around anymore. And even if he was, he made it very clear to me that he wasn't the type to do what you're describing."

Chloe bit her lips thoughtfully. "Is there any way we would be able to tell if a vampire did it?"

Gavin shrugged. "I'd have to see the body or go to the place the vampire has been. I remember the one I met before had a distinct scent that is unlike humans or animals."

"If a vampire was in an area, could you smell it?"

"Most assuredly, I could."

Chloe nodded and smiled. "Great. We'll go tonight. The ladies told me where they found the girl."

She stood up and grabbed for Gavin's hand, but when she tried to pull him up with her, he didn't even budge. Chloe looked back at him and saw the same amusement in his smile as before when he laid half in the basement and half in the kitchen.

"Didn't I say I needed a moment?"

Now it was Chloe's turn to plop down on the floor and Gavin to laugh at her silliness in a loopy, half asleep way.

The drive down the mountain with Gavin was not like their first. He was more relaxed and not as panicked as before. The grogginess from the detox might have acted as a tranquilizer to his nerves. She wasn't sure if she preferred Gavin exhausted like this or grumpy.

Chloe assumed this extended bought of tiredness was a result of malnutrition. She remembered days when she had gone without eating before. The first stage was irritability, and then the second was fatigue. If she didn't get food in her system, Chloe would drag her feet all day, completely miserable.

It was with this recollection that Chloe realized that Gavin's detox side effects were not much different than how hers would be if she hadn't eaten in a while. But she didn't turn into a creature that couldn't control her actions.

Chloe then remembered that this was his third night. Gavin said before that on his fourth night, he became unconscious and hunted whether he wanted to or not. That meant this might be their last night together before she had to lock him away.

She turned to look at the way the bright moonlight shined off of Gavin's features. After this night, loneliness would be her new companion. How would they manage being apart for four whole nights? It was something she hadn't considered before when they originally concocted this plan. They had spent so much time with each other over the past couple of weeks that it would seem strange to not have him lurking around the cabin.

Turning her attention back to the twisting roads at the base of the mountain, Chloe sighed. "How's tomorrow going to work?"

"What's that?" Gavin asked, his voice cracking a little with sleepiness.

"Tomorrow. It'll be your fourth day. What do I need to do?"

Gavin shifted under his seat belt as if he were trying to get comfortable. "I won't be able to come out of the basement. I suggest that, sometime during the day, you find a way to lock me in."

Chloe remembered seeing padlocks at the hardware store and nodded. "Ok, but what about on the seventh night?"

He was silent for a moment, probably thinking, then said, "I'm not sure. I may be very weak by then. Either that or more determined to feed."

Chloe came to the first stop sign at the main road that led into Carter Lake and turned left. There were no cars out, and very few house lights were still on this late.

"How do I protect myself from you in case a lock doesn't work?"

A few beats of silence later, Gavin replied, "I'm really not sure."

Chloe felt a sliver of fear snake through her core at his answer. How could he not be sure? "What about garlic? Silver? Wooden stakes? Crosses? Holy water?"

As she rattled off all the possible stereotypical weaknesses of vampires, Gavin grew frustrated and cut her off with a sharp gesture. "I told you. I don't know, Chloe."

When she looked over, Chloe saw that he was rubbing his forehead, and his eyes were squeezed shut. She wondered if he was having another temptation spell. As they passed the worn-down gas station on the left, Chloe began to debate whether or not she should turn back around and leave this for another time.

But, knowing that this was the last night he could wander amongst the living, and after becoming human, he wouldn't have the supernatural sense of smell, this was their only chance to find out if this was really a rash of vampire attacks or a rabid animal.

"Gavin?"

"I'm fine."

"You don't look fine."

"I'm just..." he began. Chloe heard the annoyance in his tone, and she didn't know if it was caused by her or if it was self-directed. "I'm wondering if this was a bad idea."

Chloe no longer felt fear but a twinge of panic. What did he mean? That going into town was a bad idea? Trying to become human? Or trying to have a relationship with her?

In a moment of blind, emotional turmoil, Chloe began to second guess all of these things herself.

Yes, going into town with a hungry vampire might not be the smartest thing in the world, but it was for a good reason. Chloe romantically hoped that perhaps they could solve these murders together and save lives. If it was a vampire, they could fight it off or perhaps reason with it. If not, then Gavin was the best man for the job to find whoever, or whatever, was killing the children of Carter Lake.

They had gone head-long into this detox process without any planning, either. Chloe was sure that neither of them had thought this through. All they knew was the end result, and that was all that mattered. But there were too many risks. Her late aunt might have been right in denying Gavin the accountability partner he needed.

Chloe didn't know how to defend herself, and Gavin seemed just as clueless. Over the years, he'd probably only learned how he couldn't be killed rather than how to kill him at all. What would she do when it came time to feed him the vinegar on the seventh day? There were so many ways that this could go wrong, and she could end up the victim of his ravenous hunger.

And where did that leave them? If Gavin stayed a vampire, would he still want to be with her, a mere mortal human? Chloe knew her own heart. She wouldn't abandon him just because things didn't go their way. But would he want to put himself through the heartache of watching her grow old and die just like her Aunt Mary Anne?

The thought of Gavin leaving made her want to pull over to the shoulder and cry over her steering wheel with him as a witness in the passenger seat. Luckily, she was stronger and less impulsive than that.

"What do you mean by that?" she asked, trying to control the subtle tremor in both her hands and her words.

Gavin passed a hand over his eyes. "I don't know. I'm tired, and my mind isn't all there."

Chloe wanted to breathe a sigh of relief, but all sense of that fleeting emotion was gone when she saw the road sign for Old Mill Road. She turned onto the street, which was vacant on either side and stretched on into the night. The road had ditches on both sides and trees beyond, but Chloe could see no houses or any other sign of civilization.

Gavin looked out of the windshield. "It may be better if we go on foot from here," he said.

Chloe nodded and pulled the jeep to the side of the road, put it in park and killed the engine.

The night air was cold, and Chloe was thankful she had grabbed a heavier coat than she had been wearing into town earlier. Gavin, however, only wore the same long coat and a single button down shirt as he always did.

Gavin walked ahead of her, his steps rather loud and grinding against the asphalt. The detox made him careless as to who heard him or not. Chloe hugged the flaps of her coat tightly around her chest and followed after him, being careful not to interrupt his concentration.

He spoke not a word until they came to one section of the road. He stopped at the point where trees ended and an abandoned field of cotton plants began. With his chin tilted up towards the clear starry sky, he sniffed.

"There's been blood here recently," he stated softly.

Chloe looked around her as an owl hooted overhead. "Human?"

"Yes. But there are many other scents, too." Gavin slowly meandered towards the opposite side of the road.

"Vampire or animal?" Chloe asked as she trailed behind him.

"I most certainly smell an animal," he replied.

Chloe had hoped for a moment that there was no real danger. The authorities could easily deal with a rogue bear or even a cougar if that's what killed the children.

"But nothing large. I smell squirrels and deer mostly."

Once again, she was crestfallen. "Anything else?"

Gavin hopped down into the ditch and bent down around the base of some pines on the other side. "I smell the police and chemicals that I presume they used for cleaning." He breathed in deeply, and Chloe got the humorous depiction in her mind of him behaving like a bloodhound.

"Any vampires?" Chloe didn't want to continually mention the worst case scenario, but it was the only reason they were out there in the chilly night at all. She was thankful that no one seemed to be traveling out this late, either.

Gavin crouched down and sat there for a moment as if to get his bearings.

"It's very faint, but I do smell a vampire. Not one that I'm familiar with, of course. It's so faded that I won't even be able to track it."

Chloe's shoulders slumped, and she felt as if she'd be sick right there on the side of the road. There was a vampire in Carter Lake; a violent, child-murdering vampire. She cursed under her misty breath.

Gavin stood and stared down the road in the direction of the cotton field. Chloe watched him, waiting for anything. But his expression gave her no clues as to what he was thinking exactly. The detox had made him even more closed off to her.

She wanted to grab him by his coat lapels and demand more information, but she knew that he had none to give. What he told her was all he knew.

Chloe pressed her slightly chapped lips together and tried to hold in her impatience, but it was too much.

"We need to go after it and stop it," she declared, feeling a righteous indignation burning inside of her. If he wouldn't react to this horrible truth, then she would.

Gavin turned to her, and she could see his dark eyebrows pinching together over his nose in the dim light. "Go after it? I can't track it. And how will you kill it? I'm not sure if that stake through the heart bit works at all. Next to that is sunlight, but there's no way we could trap it until dawn."

Chloe teetered on the edge of the asphalt, looking down at Gavin who was still standing in the ditch.

"I don't know. All I know is that we know what's been killing these kids, and we can't just walk away. We have a moral responsibility to do something about it." Chloe waved her hand off in the general direction of town. "You know the police will just think that I'm crazy and won't believe a word of it. We have to take matters into our own hands."

Gavin smirked. "Although I have always admired the vigilante approach to these kinds of matters, it's a purely romanticized ideal that has too many consequences. We are ill prepared, and I am in no condition to either fight it or defend you."

Chloe began pacing a few yards in each direction, mulling the situation over in her head and coming up with a plan. Just as Gavin was climbing his way out of the ditch, she approached him with her proposal.

"We can't track it. But it'll need to feed again, right?"

Gavin nodded. "Theoretically, yes."

"Then we lure it out with a potential meal and catch it off guard. You can hide in a tree and I'll try a little bantering back and forth, and when it least expects it, you drop down and stake it through the chest."

Gavin narrowed his eyes at her curiously as if she had grown two heads. "Are you insane? There's no way I'll allow you to be used as bait for a vampire who is obviously skilled in killing humans."

Chloe shrugged. "What other choice do we have? The vampire won't go after you. And if it does, it'll probably just see you as a threat and try to kill you. If you stay hidden and just drop from the tree, it's minimal effort. No fighting or defending necessary."

Gavin took a bounding step towards her. "And what if it won't have anything to do with your badinage scheme and go straight to attacking you? What am I to do then? You could be dead by the time I reach you."

She understood the risks, but somehow, they didn't seem as dangerous as what Gavin was making them out to be.

"If we don't at least try, then the vampire will kill more children; maybe all of them." Chloe was so close to Gavin now that she could reach out and caress his lips if she wished; so close and yet so far away. "You may not kill them yourself," she continued, "but you will seal their fate if you don't do something to stop it."

Gavin glared down at her. She could see that he was thinking it over, weighing the options in his mind. Chloe didn't mean to force him into this decision. She didn't want to manipulate him. But, somehow, she knew that he understood that this was the right thing to do. They were throwing caution to the wind, but unless he had another idea, this was the best course of action.

Finally, defeat settled in, and Gavin nodded. "Fine." He raised a cautioning finger. "But, you must do exactly as I say. Failure to do so will cost both of our lives."

"Both?" Chloe blinked.

"If you die, I will die, simple as that."

His voice was calm and even as if he were stating a fact of the universe that could not be disputed. However, Chloe could see the eddy of feeling in his eyes when he said it, and she knew it to be true. She had to stay alive for his sake, at least.

He turned and trudged back towards the jeep, leaving her with nothing but the implied loyalty and devotion he felt for her. It was all conveyed in that guileless statement, and Chloe would never forget it.

Chapter 17

Chloe put one foot in front of the other, slowly wandering over the mountainside. The cabin was far behind her now and over the creek where she'd played as a child.

She replayed the moment when she had crossed over that strip of water with Gavin by her side, a little more awake than he had been an hour before. He had explained to her exactly what to do.

But now, standing under the light of the waning moon above that filtered through the dense canopy of leaves, Chloe couldn't remember a thing. All she could think of was how alone she felt out here.

Her role was the bait for the vampire that had been terrorizing Carter Lake, and she knew that Gavin was somewhere in the treetops above her. But, she heard nothing, saw nothing. Even the animals that normally pierced the night with their mating calls seemed to be conveniently missing.

It was as if she were the only person on the face of the planet; the only one left after some apocalyptic disaster that left her untouched. This must be how Gavin had felt after burying his wife and son; so alone, so empty.

But she couldn't think of that now. She had to stay alert and ready for when—or if—the vampire showed up.

They were fools to go through with this plan without properly preparing themselves. With Gavin in his weakened state and both of them totally clueless as to what could kill another vampire, they were up a creek without a paddle and at the mercy of the current. But to Chloe, there was an urgency to stop this menace before it killed any more innocent children.

"Wow, I can't believe how lost I am," she said rather loudly. She was playing to the vampire that might be within earshot, but even Chloe had to admit that her statement was filled with more truth than she liked.

"It's cold and a little creepy out here. Can anybody hear me?" she screamed the last supplication, hoping to lure the predator towards her. She was easy prey.

Keeping her head on a swivel, she continued to walk, her feet shuffling through the fallen autumn leaves on the forest floor. It was the only sound she heard besides the wind rustling the leaves that still clung to branches overhead.

Every tree looked the same, every bush and fallen log blurred together in the darkness. Figures and paths were distorted by her poor night vision. It was impossible to tell which way was north or if she had been going in circles this whole time. She wasn't even sure if Gavin was still following her.

Chloe tried to keep her heart light, thinking about how this exact scene would have been so corny in a horror film. From an audience standpoint, everyone would know that she would die somehow. What fun would it be if she escaped? Chloe was glad this was not a movie.

"Hello?" she called out with her hands cupped around her mouth to help project her voice.

"Hello."

The deep voice came from behind her, far too close for comfort. And it wasn't Gavin's.

Chloe let out a startled shriek, jumped and turned to see who the voice belonged to.

Standing in front of her was a man clad in all black. He would have blended in with the night around him if it weren't for the pale glow of his exposed arms and face. His features were sharp, his physique strong but slender. Long golden hair, comparable to freshly harvested corn, was pulled back into a ponytail that draped down his back. Dark brown eyes leered down at her, supplemented by a sly Casanova smile.

Chloe backed away slowly as the man raked his eyes over her body obviously sizing her up. He matched her step for step, keeping barely a yard of distance between them.

"What's a beautiful lady like yourself doing out in the middle of the woods?" he asked. His accent was American but lacking a southern dialect. He sounded more like he belonged in the New England states like Boston or New York.

Chloe cleared her throat to make up for the long pause before she replied. "I decided to take a walk and got lost. I live on the mountain. I guess I should have carried bread crumbs with me."

She laughed feebly at her own joke, but the man's expression showed no hint that he even knew what she meant by that.

"Perhaps I could assist you home? I know this mountain well."

Chloe gave him a half hearted smile and stopped backing away. He also stopped. "I'm not sure which direction I came from."

"I know the way to town from here," he said. "When we reach there, can you find the way back?"

Chloe feigned a deliberation, scrunching up her lips as if she were thinking it over. She couldn't remember what Gavin told her to say. Was she supposed to accept any offered help or decline it? Was she supposed to stall for time or simply wait until Gavin made his move? Why hadn't he made his move already?

Finally, she nodded. "I think I can manage that. Which is the way to Carter Lake?" she asked, trying to sound cheerful and genuinely thankful for his assistance. But all the while, she wondered how many other poor girls had fallen in this same game.

The vampire grinned, showing his teeth but careful not to reveal his sharp incisors just yet. He was savoring this, playing with her. He'd gain her trust first and then move in for the kill.

He gestured in one direction. "Town's this way."

Chloe wasn't sure if he was telling the truth but nodded and began to walk that way. The vampire followed close beside her as if he were a loyal dog keeping pace with its owner.

"My name is Terrance. What's yours?" he said, offering his hand to shake.

Chloe was thrown off by the gesture and jerked back a little, half expecting him to reach out and grab her. But he was calm with no hint of malice. Was it always his custom to get to know his dinner before devouring it? For any normal person, it would have made the job of killing more difficult. Perhaps it wasn't the same for vampires.

She hesitantly took his hand and shook it. His skin was cold as ice, just like she had suspected a vampire's would be. But Gavin's touch had been warm before the detox. How long had it been since this vampire had fed? Or was this because he took the life of a child and drank their blood? "Chloe," she replied.

Terrance nodded as if he approved of her name and her openness. "That's a beautiful name; a beautiful name for a beautiful girl."

Chloe looked away. "You should know I have a boyfriend."

Terrance chuckled. "Am I not permitted to administer compliments to taken women?"

"I suppose you can, but I'm just making you aware that you'll get nowhere with me," Chloe added with a simpering smile. And just like that, she was flirting.

Terrance approved of this as well. "If you have a boyfriend, why is he not out here with you?"

She sighed and came up with a fake story off the top of her head. "We had a fight. I came out here to cool down and think things through. But I'm going to take him back, so don't get any ideas."

He chuckled. "I'm glad to hear you worked things out."

Terrance, if that was his real name, moved branches out of the way for her and made sure her path was unobstructed. The journey was silent for a while, and Chloe began to get worried.

Where was Gavin? Why hadn't he attacked yet? Did he get lost somewhere or fall asleep in the treetops? And if he was waiting for the perfect moment, could Terrance detect his presence? Surely a vampire could tell when another one of their kind was near. And even if he couldn't sense Gavin, then he could have smelled or heard him in the trees.

Chloe had to put her anxiety on hold when Terrance turned to her and asked, "You look familiar. Have we met before?"

She purposefully avoided meeting his piercing gaze that was burning a hole through her. "No, I'm pretty sure we haven't."

"Then perhaps I know a relative of yours." A few beats of silence passed, and then Terrance snapped his fingers. "I know!" he exclaimed with much ebullience. "Are you related to Mary Anne Hilton?"

Chloe stopped dead in her tracks and looked at Terrance with a mix of horror and confusion. How could he know her late aunt? There was no doubt this vampire was the one killing the children in Carter Lake, but that had only been going on for a month, and her aunt had moved out of the cabin years ago.

Was it possible that this vampire had visited the area before? And what was her aunt doing by associating with both Gavin and Terrance? Or maybe, Chloe thought, this was the old vampire that Gavin had met with previously. Perhaps that was why Gavin hadn't attacked yet. He might know this vampire and trust him.

She didn't know what compelled her to say, "Yes, she was my aunt."

"Was?" Terrance questioned, tilting his head curiously.

Chloe crossed her arms tight over her stomach. "She passed away over a month ago."

Terrance clicked his tongue a bit and shook his head. "That's a shame. She was a nice, old woman. You have my deepest condolences."

With that one sentence, Chloe knew this couldn't be Gavin's old acquaintance. Whoever that vampire was left the area a half a century ago, and from what Gavin said never came back. Her aunt would have been a young lady back then, not an old woman.

Something wasn't right, and Terrance wasn't telling her the truth. She didn't expect him to, but it made Chloe uneasy all the same. However, she had to keep playing along. If Gavin was still waiting for the right moment, she had to bide her time.

"Thank you. We were really close."

Terrance began to lead the way back along the path. "I know what it's like to lose a close family member. It's never easy."

He lifted a curtain of pine branches and let Chloe pass on ahead. But when she stepped through, she froze.

Before her was a cabin, and not just any cabin. It was her cabin. And sitting on the gravel path was her black jeep. The scene was bathed in moonlight, but it didn't seem quite real.

She'd wandered much too far into the woods to have arrived at her cabin this soon. Terrance stepped up beside her.

"Is this your home?" he asked casually as if he already knew that it was.

Chloe looked over her shoulder from the direction she had come and saw the sparkling waters of the creek. She knew for a fact that she hadn't waded through the creek to get to where she was standing now.

This wasn't right.

Chloe looked back to the cabin and felt her heart thud loudly in her chest.

"Is something wrong?" Terrance asked, moving to block her vision.

Her face must have portrayed her shock and confusion. She pointed a shaky finger over her shoulder and looked around wildly for Gavin or an explanation.

"Yes, something's wrong," she replied. "This is my home, but there's no way I can be back here again."

"Why not?"

The vampire took a few languid steps towards her, and she countered by retreating the same number of paces.

"I was walking for hours. There's no way..."

Chloe didn't want to finish her sentence, afraid that she'd reveal her real reasons for meandering through the woods. Terrance didn't react to her sudden hysteria.

Something in his eyes told her that the game was over. He was moving in for the kill.

Chloe turned and sprinted toward the creek, but she didn't get far before colliding with something solid. She fell backward, bruising her hands on the ground as she caught herself.

Terrance loomed over her, his eyes blazing red and black in the darkness. She scrambled to crawl away but suddenly found that she wasn't able to move at all. It was the same inexplicable immobility that she had experienced when Gavin bandaged her finger.

She remained frozen in place, one hand raised in an awkward twist from when she'd tried to crawl away. Her muscles ached, but she couldn't pry herself out of the position. Not even her eyes would shift in their sockets.

She heard shuffling footsteps in the leaves as Terrance approached her.

"I was wondering how long this would last. I suppose my hopes were too high. This could have been very amusing if you had continued to play along."

She saw his dark leather boots come into view. Terrance crouched down low and twisted his head so he could meet her fixed gaze. His long golden hair hung down, disturbing the bed of leaves there.

"Stand up," he commanded.

Chloe wanted to reply with some sarcastic quip, but her mouth wouldn't obey. Instead, her body obeyed him. Her movements were not her own as she pushed herself up and rose stiffly to stand tall in front of him.

If she were able, she would have been trembling with fear. She couldn't run, couldn't scream, and if Gavin were anywhere close by, he would have saved her by now. Was it possible that Terrance took care of Gavin before he even met up with her? In his weakened state, Gavin probably wouldn't have stood a chance against a stronger vampire.

And he was stronger, Chloe could tell that much. Out of her periphery, she saw the image of her home disappear and blur like a mirage. It was all an illusion. But how much of any of this was real?

Terrance stood up and circled her like a predator would while sizing up his prey. She could feel his leer traveling up and down her frame in a hungry, lustful way.

"You must be wondering a thousand things right now," he said, his voice lilting and poetic. It would have been soothing in other circumstances, and if it belonged to anyone else.

"Did you think you were clever? Did you think I'd be too blind to see your intentions?" Terrance sounded genuinely insulted. But how could he have known their plans?

"Oh, and don't worry. Your boyfriend is fine. He wasn't hard to take care of." He leaned in close and whispered in her ear, "That means we won't be disturbed."

Chloe was horrified by what he could possibly mean by that.

He raised his hand in front of her face and curled his fingers so one nail caught under her chin. He pulled, and her body was led to turn and face him. They were close, her chest grazed against the front of his shirt with each deep breath. Chloe would have rather stopped breathing than be under his spell this way.

His finger traced along her jaw, down the side of her neck and made its way down her shoulder and in between her breasts. Chloe wanted to shudder, to scream and beat him with her fists. She didn't even want to look at him, but her eyes wouldn't close.

"Don't worry, I won't force you. I'll make you want it, beg for it. If it will help, I can do this."

Terrance's face melted away to be replaced with Gavin's. But she knew it wasn't him. It could never be him. The smile, the emerald eyes, they all looked like Gavin's, but Terrance could never replicate his warmth, his kindness, and sincerity.

"Or would this suit you?"

Gavin was gone, and the man who stood before her was someone she never wanted to see again. Brent's hazel eyes gazed down at her with that laughing expression he'd always had. Terrance even simulated Brent's cologne.

Chloe couldn't respond. The only thing she could think about was if Gavin was truly ok. What had Terrance done to him?

Terrance dropped the charade and was standing before her once more. Chloe knew this had to be a mind trick. Was he reading her thoughts and memories? It would explain the mirage, but Gavin said that he couldn't manipulate her mind. Was this vampire so much stronger than Gavin that he had unlocked new abilities?

"I suppose this will be better. Then, it'll be me you want and not either of those buffoons."

Rage boiled in her chest. Yes, Brent was a terrible man. But she couldn't stand to have anyone talk about Gavin with such disrespect.

"Don't you dare talk about him like that," she growled.

Terrance staggered backward, baffled by her sudden outburst. Chloe was surprised herself.

She clenched her hands into fists and tried to force them higher, but their movements were slow and halting. The mesmerism was still too strong to resist, even against her temper.

Terrance became annoyed and held his palm out to her. She froze once more.

"You have a strong will. But mine is far stronger." He came forward, his red eyes still blazing. "I think it best we skip the appetizers and move onto the main course."

Her neck muscles went lax, and Chloe's head lolled to one side, baring her skin for Terrance's fangs. Just before he moved in for the bite, she saw them flash in the moonlight, growing long and sharp in preparation for the meal he was about to devour.

Chloe squeezed her eyes shut, bracing herself for the death that would follow. Would it be quick? Would it drag on for hours? Would she die as soon as she was bled dry or would it take longer than that? Chloe didn't want to find out.

All at once, before his teeth sank into her neck, she thought of her family and old friends in Atlanta. What would they think when they found out she had been murdered in the mountains? Her parents would mourn her, of course, but would anyone say she deserved it? She made the choice to come out here after all. She could have faced her problems in Atlanta, but instead, she'd fled.

Chloe wondered if she made the right decision.

But then she thought of Gavin and the kiss they'd shared, and she knew that it was all worth it to have known him, even for a little while.

Chloe didn't welcome death, but she would submit to it, knowing that her life was made a little brighter by a creature of darkness; by a man so desperate to not become a monster.

"Get away from her!"

That voice, so familiar and yet so distant, shattered through the forest. Chloe looked to see Gavin standing not too far away, poised for attack with his hackles raised and head ducked low like a wolf growling at an enemy.

Terrance lifted himself up and turned to see who it was that had interrupted his meal. Chloe knew that his fangs hadn't found purchase in her neck. She was still untouched but couldn't move.

Instead of being angry, Terrance laughed. It was a booming, maniacal laugh like a villain who had seen his master plan unfold perfectly before him.

"Ah, so you've decided to join the party."

Terrance, his fangs still a menacing length, moved to stand behind Chloe, using her as a shield. "We were just getting started. I'm sure there's enough to share."

"Don't touch her!" Gavin bellowed. She could see, even in the darkness, his eyes glowing the same red as Terrance's.

Chloe could see there was something different about Gavin. She couldn't put her finger on it exactly, but there was an aura about him that didn't seem right. Was he one of Terrance's illusions, too?

No, he was real. But there was a subliminal difference in his voice, his stance, the way his face was pulled tight with rage. Something had happened that Chloe couldn't even begin to guess.

"Or what?" Terrance asked mockingly. She felt the tip of his nail prick the side of her neck. She gasped but was still unable to move. "What can you possibly do? I know you're weak. You're starving yourself."

Chloe whimpered as that nail dug deeper into her neck and sliced downward. A low, guttural growl emanated from Gavin that seemed to vibrate the very ground where they stood. The forest shook with his fury.

"Don't be a fool," Terrance continued. "You can't change what you are any more than a tiger can change his stripes or a whale can walk on land."

Gavin took a strong step forward, but he was still hesitant. And Chloe knew why. She was bleeding now. She could feel the warm liquid ooze out from the cut on her neck. And Gavin's eyes, the eyes she loved to gaze into so much, were locked onto those few droplets that seeped down her skin.

She didn't have to guess what kind of a battle raged inside him. He was hungry, but he didn't want to drink her blood. He knew how savory it tasted, how it gave him a high like animal blood could never give him. Gavin vowed to never hurt her, to never use his fangs upon her flesh. He had once, but it was an accident. This was all Terrance's plot, a purposefully crafted plan to lure Gavin into killing her. Chloe had full confidence that Gavin had the control to resist the temptation, to hold the urges at bay for her safety's sake. It wasn't the fourth night yet, and he still had control.

But then he took another step toward them. And another. He showed little sign of stopping as his defenses began to weaken.

"You care for this human," Terrance said. "But you crave her blood. I can tell. You craved it from the moment you first saw her bleed."

Gavin paused and peered at his opponent in the darkness. "How did you–"

"How did I know? Can't you…" Confusion was laced in their villain's words. Then he chuckled. "Oh, right. I forgot. You're new to this. Well, perhaps not very new, but you have had no mentor."

Terrance began to pet Chloe's hair with his free hand, while the other gripped her shoulder. "You probably don't know how to read a human's memories. Nor do you know how to replicate them so that they relive those moments. It's a handy trick when you're in the mood to play with your food. Not many of our kind have this hunting ability. But since you're older than I am, I half expected you to know."

A cold hand caressed her cheek. "All you need do is touch their skin, and it's laid out before you like an open book."

Gavin's anger vanished, and in its place was an odd fascination. Chloe wanted to cry out to him, to tell him not to listen to Terrance. What the vampire said was completely true. She had been a victim of it firsthand, but this was exactly what Terrance wanted. Gavin was playing in perfectly, and he couldn't see it.

"Come, brother. Drink. Nourish yourself, and I will teach you as my mentor taught me. There is so much you need to know. But you will learn none of it from this human and her love for you."

Chloe felt hot breath on her neck and then a slimy tongue glide across the cut. The saliva stung her open wound, and she managed to wince. Terrance pulled back and let out a satisfied breath as if he had just taken a sip of a refreshing beverage.

"Now I see why you wanted her. Her blood is delicious." Terrance gathered a handful of her hair and yanked at her scalp to further expose her bleeding neck. "You've tasted it once before. Now try it for real this time."

Her worst fear came true as she saw Gavin walk toward them, no longer poised for battle, but an eager participant in the pleasures that Terrance offered him. Chloe wanted to weep for Gavin and mourn all they stood to lose. If he drank her blood, there was no turning back.

Not only would Gavin fall off the wagon and lose what little ground he had gained in the detox process, but he might not have the control to resist her after he drank from her so deeply. Knowing Gavin, he would feel utterly guilty for his actions. This wasn't like killing an unknown soldier who was wounded in the middle of nowhere. She was his muse, his inspiration. Chloe knew better than to call herself his girlfriend. It was far from the truth. They were not lovers, for they never confessed it or reveled in its sins. Chloe didn't know what she meant to Gavin exactly besides being a companion, an accountability partner, and friend.

She closed her eyes, unwilling to witness the last betrayal by someone she cared for so deeply; someone she loved.

Chloe could tell she had been sandwiched between the two men. With Terrance behind her and Gavin in front of her, she was trapped. Even if she could move, there was no way she could escape.

Gavin's scent filled her senses, sending her into the involuntary dizziness that came with his presence. She felt a trembling arm wrap around her waist and pull her in tight, his torso a rigid wall of strength against her supple form.

At any other time, in any other place, she would have leaned up to kiss him. But instead, he leaned down to kiss her, only, not on the lips as she would have liked. One last gesture of affection would have made this moment a little less bitter.

She heard Terrance make comments of approval, urging Gavin to do the job.

Gavin bent his head down, his lips and nose stroking around the cut and underneath her jaw. Her core came alive with sensations she couldn't begin to describe. Passion and longing made her whole body ache and tremble outside of the spell that Terrance had over her.

Despite herself, Chloe let out a sigh, letting both of the men know that she was enjoying Gavin's caresses. Each tantalizing stroke of his tongue and movement of his lips on her skin were filled with emotion. He wanted to do this, to bring her to the edge of madness the way only he could.

Gavin's other hand grabbed her wrist in a vice. Didn't he know that she would never run from him even when he was about to take her life?

But seconds went by, and she knew by the lack of pain in her neck that Gavin had not tasted her blood yet. He hadn't bitten down. He hadn't taken the bait.

As soon as she realized this, he went rigid.

The next moments were a blur.

Gavin took advantage of his hold on her and used his inhuman strength to propel her away from both himself and Terrance.

Chloe went flying to the side and tumbled through the leaves and foliage before sliding to a stop a safe distance away. Sounds of hissing, roars, growls, and battle ensued where she had been standing. But the forest around her was spinning too fast to allow her to focus on anything.

Chloe felt her neck first and touched the sticky blood that was caked around her wound. Terrance's hold over her was broken, freeing her body and mind to her own will.

When the dizziness passed, she looked up to see Gavin and Terrance fighting the way only immortals could, with blinding speed and extraordinary strength. There was no way to keep track of their movements or determine who was winning the fight. She couldn't even distinguish if the cries of pain were from Terrance or Gavin.

Chloe felt a bursting pride for Gavin. He'd stayed strong and confronted temptation under the worst conditions. It was all a trick. This whole scheme was a trick. Everyone was deceiving everyone else. Who won in the end, she couldn't tell.

When her legs decided to work, she used a nearby tree to help her stand and watch the battle. The suspense was terrible. If only her eyes could keep up with the action.

But one thing was certain. She couldn't just stand around and wait for the victor to claim her.

Chloe fought the fog of fear in her mind and thought hard. What could she do? What did she have at her disposal to help Gavin? What could she, a mere mortal human, do to inhibit an experienced vampire like Terrance?

Her expression was one of grim determination as she pulled her set of keys from her pocket. Years ago, Brent had advised her to get a pocket knife. But, she never knew how to work them, so she bought this instead.

It was a rather dull device that hooked onto her keychain. With a simple flick of her finger, she could flip out a curved blade to use for scouring or opening an envelope. She hoped it would be effective enough.

Taking a deep breath, she rolled up her sleeve and dug the tip of the blade into her wrist. The edge was so dull that it took a lot of pressure to break the soft, white skin. But when she did, it bled just enough to make her convulse a bit. Self-mutilation was at the top of her list of things that made her skin crawl.

Chloe pocketed her keys and ran towards the warring vampires. They were beginning to slow down. Gavin was becoming weaker, and she saw his opponent issue blow after successful blow. Terrance wasn't tiring at all.

She waited, flexing her wrist so the blood would continue to dribble out. Her feet flitted back and forth, looking for an opening so she could charge in. But the two were moving so fast and sporadically.

Finally, Terrance knocked Gavin to the ground and sent him rolling through the twigs and leaves. His dark hair was disheveled and some of his clothes were ripped, but Terrance was in a similar state.

He charged towards Gavin and planted his foot on his chest. He was preparing for the final strike.

Chloe ran up and launched herself at Terrance's back. He shouted at first, but when she reached around and pressed her bleeding wrist to his lips, he went silent.

He thrashed at first in an attempt to get her off, but his thirst got the better of him.

Fangs sank into her wrist, and she felt the blood begin to drain out of her. It was the strangest, most indescribable feeling as if her very life force was being sucked from her soul.

Chloe meant it only as a distraction, but the longer that Terrance hung on, the more she began to fear that this was about to backfire on her. Gavin needed the chance to recover and attack while Terrance was unguarded. It was the only way.

First, her muscles began to ache and spasm. Then her head throbbed with excruciating pain. Then came the fatigue, the feeling like she could sleep for a thousand years, all while her veins felt as if they were collapsing in on themselves, empty and pulsing in a search for the lifeblood that was no longer in her body.

Consciousness began to slip from her when she heard a great, inhuman cry. The last thing she remembered seeing was Gavin's face, distorted with animalistic rage, and red eyes focused on Terrance. Chloe heard a gut wrenching shrill cry as she tumbled to the forest floor and had the feeling of being soaked.

The scent of blood was everywhere mingled with sulfur and death.

But before she could find out whose blood it was that she smelled, her eyes rolled back in her head, and everything went blacker than the night.

Chapter 18

Gavin stood in a pool of his enemy's blood, his chest and arms drenched in the same dark liquid that caked the ground around his feet. Blood dripped from his lips and rolled down his chin to join the rest. The ground here would be forever stained by the death of this vampire. Nothing would grow through the seasons for centuries to come.

How did he know? Because when he ingested Terrance's blood, he also took upon himself the memories and knowledge that his enemy possessed. He saw the faces of his prey as they were in the throes of death. He saw places and people he had never laid eyes on before. He didn't possess his power and skills, but Terrance held true to his promise that he would somehow teach Gavin all that his mentor taught him before.

So much knowledge, and so many facts and images flashed through his mind. All he could do was stand there and process it all little by little.

His senses were aflame, and for several long, agonizing moments, he could neither see, hear, or smell anything. It was as if for a moment, he didn't exist. He was lightweight and floating with a rekindled strength that he hadn't known before.

The world moved on around him, and with one less evil being in the world, the animals of the night emerged from where they had been hiding to once again fill the forest with their calls and daily activities.

But Gavin couldn't go on as before.

In the span of just a few days, he had tasted the blood of his love and the blood of the one he hated. He had never met Terrance before, but after he deceived them in the cruelest way, Gavin had never hated anyone more in his life. Not even himself.

Once his mind began to quiet and adjust to all that had happened, he became aware of himself and the one heartbeat that lay close by. Though his eyesight was strained and blurred momentarily, he could make out Chloe's figure lying in the grass.

Terrance's blood was splashed over her body, just as it was on his, but not near as heavily.

He'd never intended to kill Terrance and take his blood. But here he stood, his hunger gone, and the detox plan ruined by this one battle. How could he tell Chloe? What would she think of him now? Would she still think he wasn't a monster? He was thankful that she was unconscious so she couldn't see him this way.

But as his hearing tuned to the sounds around him, he heard that she was more than just unconscious. Her heartbeat, once strong and rhythmic, was softening, and its pounding was more sporadic in her chest.

One sniff of the air told him that she was not well. Terrance had drunk deeply from her but did not kill her.

With halting steps, Gavin sloshed through the blood and carnage towards Chloe. He did not feel the usual compulsion to feed as the hunger was gone. Since he had tasted her blood, he wanted nothing more than to take her and know her in the way that was forbidden to them.

All he ever wanted was to taste one drop, just one sip from her each day. And to kiss her deeply, feel her body in his hands, touch her soul somehow.

But seeing her lay here, motionless and on the brink of the abyss, he wanted none of that.

He listened to her shallow breaths and watched her chest spasm as if her lungs were trying to expand but lacked the strength.

Gavin pushed back the fear of losing her. If he let it consume him now, he would never be able to do what was necessary to keep her alive. Instead, he clenched his jaw tight and scooped her into his arms.

With inhuman speed he navigated his way up the mountain, whizzing past trees and shrubs until he reached the cabin. Paying no mind to the way his boots tracked in dirt and residual blood left on the soles, Gavin brought Chloe inside and up the stairs.

Like a machine that cared only for her wellbeing, Gavin laid Chloe down onto the floor of her bedroom and stripped off her soiled clothes before tucking her into bed.

The wound on her neck was deep but no longer bled as it did when Terrance had first cut her. The same went for her wrist, but Gavin would not let them fester in the open air.

He retrieved her first aid kit from downstairs and bandaged both her wrist and the cut on her neck as tenderly as if she were awake to feel every touch. Checking her pulse with his keen ears again, he found that it was growing fainter. She wouldn't last much longer without more blood circulating through her body.

Gavin stood there for a moment, watching her and wondering.

Terrance had given Gavin so much through his blood. One thing was the knowledge of how to create another vampire. A human must be in a state, just like Chloe, and ingest a bit of the vampire's blood. Gavin had the full knowledge of how to sire another vampire, and Chloe could be his first convert.

He remembered that Chloe had offered her neck to him that night they first kissed, inviting him to change her into a bloodthirsty creature like him. He had refused, but things had changed. Chloe was about to die unless he saved her.

Gavin lifted his wrist to his mouth and let his fangs pierce the skin, making black blood ooze from his veins. But when he bent low to let Chloe drink, he stopped.

Chloe had been so willing to join him in the dark. It might be the one way they could be together for all eternity without having to worry about growing old and dying the way humans did. Perhaps this would be easier than Gavin going through detox.

But Chloe had a family. She had a future. He couldn't let her throw it all away and become a vampire like him.

Gavin cursed his momentary foolishness and held his bleeding wrist to his chest, waiting for it to heal.

If Chloe did not become a vampire, how else could he save her? He racked his brain until he found the answer. Last night, he had read through a medical book describing the process for a blood transfusion. It was simple enough, but he needed fresh human blood for that.

There was a clinic in town, he remembered. They were sure to have something akin to a blood bank. If he took her there as she was, they would ask too many questions. He had to go alone to retrieve supplies.

Taking one last sniff of Chloe's wounds to make sure he would be able to distinguish her blood type amongst all the others he had to choose from, he made his way out the door, not bothering to change shirts or wash up. If he played it right, no one would even know he was there.

The first thing she heard was the crickets, such a familiar sound. Then she felt the pain, the throbbing achiness in every part of her. Chloe squeezed her eyes shut tighter, but even that couldn't block it all out.

Soft sheets were under her and a warm, heavy quilt on top. Her fingertips moved along the stitched surface, and she breathed in the earthy scent of wood. It was warm but not too warm. Even with her eyes closed, she could tell a light was on to her left, probably the lamp on her nightstand.

Chloe moved her arm a bit to try and find the edge of the bed, but something pulled at her skin and stung a bit, inhibiting her movements. When she opened her sore eyelids, she could feel the bits of crust that had collected in the corners tumble down her cheeks.

She blinked a few times until the misty clouds didn't obscure her vision anymore and then looked down at her arm. Just below her elbow was wrapped in tight bandages. Her opposite wrist was bound in the same way with white gauzy dressing.

With another tilt of her head, she confirmed that the only light in her bedroom came from the lamp beside her. Then she heard a stirring to her right.

She saw Gavin, sitting in the armchair that once resided in the living room but which was now drawn up close to her bedside.

He looked surprisingly well. He no longer looked as sickly as he had when he'd begun to detox. He was still pale but not as pale as he had been, and everything about him seemed to shine, from his eyes to the health of his hair, he appeared radiant.

Gazing into his smiling green eyes, it all came back to her. She remembered blood, a scream that she would have expected to come out of a cougar, the pain, and the feeling of being drained dry like a straw sucking up nothing but air at the bottom of an empty cup.

Most of all, she remembered the fear.

With sleep still lingering like a fog over her mind, she couldn't speak just yet. But Gavin's warm and encouraging smile was enough. He seemed relieved.

"You're awake," he stated, almost as if he needed to tell himself rather than her.

Chloe took a deep breath, though her chest ached with protest. Gavin took up her hand and held it between his warm palms. Her skin must have been cold, judging by how extraordinarily hot his felt against hers. It took her a moment to realize that his hands were that warm, so different than when she last felt them.

"What happened?" Chloe asked, her voice cracking a bit in an effort to speak.

Gavin shifted to the edge of the chair seat. "You've been asleep for days."

Chloe took in his outfit–a black, long sleeve shirt that looked soft and inviting, and she could see a bit of the jeans material that covered his thighs. Then she took an assessment of herself. If her memory was correct, she wasn't wearing this pair of pajamas out in the woods when they confronted that vampire.

The vision of a face, noble and topped with long blonde hair, came to her mind.

"Terrance," she muttered.

"You don't have to worry about him. He won't be bothering anyone in Carter Lake again, or anywhere else for that matter."

She looked up at Gavin's face, so bright with confidence and an underlying twinge of guilt. "You...?"

But she didn't need to finish it. Chloe might not have been the sharpest tool in the box some days, but she could put two and two together. Terrance was dead, and Gavin was the one who killed him.

The blood she saw just before passing out wasn't hers. It was Terrance's. Chloe couldn't say she was disappointed. The town was safe, and the children had been avenged by the same type of creature as the one that killed them. It seemed ironic in hindsight.

"My clothes..."

"I changed them. Under the circumstances, I found it necessary."

Chloe didn't want to think too deeply about the fact that Gavin had seen her practically naked. It wasn't a huge concern of hers at the time.

Using what little strength her long rest had given her, Chloe tried to push herself up, but Gavin touched her shoulder. He was gentle enough, but it felt as if she had been stabbed with a fistful of pins.

"Don't sit up. You're still weak from the transfusion."

Chloe let herself slide back down as she gave him a look of utter confusion and horror. "Transfusion?"

Gavin nodded, appearing a little grim now. There was something he wasn't telling her.

"What happened? Tell me everything. Please?" she begged.

He cleared his throat and leaned his elbows against the edge of the mattress, her hand still clasped in his.

"After you passed out, I..." His Adam's apple bobbed as he swallowed down the harsh emotions. "I killed Terrance, then I saw how badly you were hurt. If I hadn't done it, you would have died."

"I brought you back to the cabin and then went to the clinic in town. I read about blood transfusions once and how they saved lives. I broke into the clinic and took the supplies I needed. The only way I could tell which type of blood you needed was by the smell. I never noticed before, but human blood types smell different from one another.

"I came back after also grabbing a medical book from one of the doctor's homes and performed the transfusion. I admit, it was crudely done under these conditions, but it proved successful." He gave her a weak smile. "I've been waiting for you to wake up every since."

Chloe turned her head to scan around the room and she now noticed the pile of used hospital equipment in the corner. An unrepressed smile came to her lips as she thought of all the trouble Gavin had gone through for her.

A million things could have happened to him, but he took the risks for her anyway. Chloe ignored the knowledge that he stole from a hospital. The supplies could have been used on someone else more worthy of being saved, but Chloe was too tired to argue or reprimand him.

But her smile faded when the rest of her thoughts caught up with her. She gazed up at Gavin's face and saw he was still pale. He was still a vampire. But, if she had been asleep for days, that meant...

"You cheated," she said. She wasn't angry, she wasn't offended. Only concerned.

Gavin quirked one side of his face and nodded. "I had to. You were bleeding so much, and I refused to partake the way that Terrance did."

Chloe also remembered how he had played a part toward both her and Terrance. He pretended like he would bite her neck where Terrance had cut it, but he didn't. Not even a lick. Well, he licked plenty, just not any of her blood. Her stomach went tight when she thought of the way he held her so close and caressed her waist.

"What did you do then?" she asked.

Gavin opened his mouth to answer her, but then shook his head. "It's best if I don't tell you."

Chloe peered at him worriedly. "You didn't feed on a nurse, did you?"

The tension in the room broke when he let out a soft chuckle. "No, not a nurse. Not a human."

If his nighttime meal had been an animal of some sort, what was the problem in telling her? Unless it wasn't an animal. Chloe's eyes went wide.

"Terrance?"

Gavin didn't respond, only pressed his lips into a thin line and stared. He didn't have to speak a word to tell her that her assumption was right. Terrance had made himself useful by dying. Not only was the town safe, but Gavin had gotten the strength needed to save Chloe.

"And you feel ok?" she questioned.

He nodded. "Yes, I feel fine."

But there was an underlying tremor in the way he said it. No, he wasn't all fine. Something else happened, but he wasn't telling her. She leveled a look at him.

Gavin tucked his chin low and avoided eye contact while he explained, "I really am fine. I just wasn't prepared for how his blood would affect me."

"How did it affect you?"

He lifted his head, his eyes wandering around the room as if looking for a way to explain exactly what he felt. "I wasn't aware that if a vampire drank the blood of another vampire, he would also take on their knowledge."

Chloe blinked. "So you know everything he knew?"

Gavin sighed. "In a manner of speaking, yes. I also shared in his experiences, such as places that he's traveled and things that he's done."

She paused to reflect on that for a moment. "Does that mean you experienced when he killed those children?"

Gavin wouldn't answer her. And in his silence, she knew the answer. Yes, he experienced the thrill of killing an innocent child.

"What else did you learn?" she asked.

He shifted uncomfortably in his chair. "I learned everything his mentor had taught him. But I didn't find out the one thing I want to know so desperately."

"What's that?"

He looked up at her with eyes full of despair. "How to survive the seven days without blood. There is no easy way about it, Chloe."

Somehow, she knew that to be true all along. There was no quick fix to anything. There never was. There was nothing but hard work and patience on the journey to getting what they both wanted. But she accepted that, and all they could do was to move on.

"Did you feed tonight?"

"I've fed every night while you've been recovering. I've had to."

Chloe nodded in understanding. She couldn't expect him to continue the detox program with her lamed up in bed.

Gavin brought the back of her hand to his mouth and kissed her skin affectionately. "I've stayed with you every night, except when I had to leave briefly to eat. There were some moments when I could barely hear your heartbeat."

She was touched by his declaration of devotion and concern.

"Thank you," she whispered as her eyes began to water with sentiment.

Gavin smiled and leaned over to kiss her forehead. She must have looked a mess, having not showered or washed her face in days. Yet still, he showed his affection for her. Brent never even wanted to be in the same room with her when she was sick with seasonal allergies because of how disgusting she looked with a puffy nose and swollen eyes.

He settled back in the chair and asked, "Are you hungry?"

Her stomach answered him back almost immediately and he grinned.

She giggled. "Do you even know how to cook?"

"I won't lie. I can't. My wife always took care of that, and I never saw the need for such a skill afterward. However, I can procure a snack if it's already made."

Chloe felt the all-too-familiar sting at the mention of his late wife but brushed it off. "I guess I can go for a granola bar from the pantry."

Gavin nodded and left the bedroom. She could hear his footsteps all the way down the stairs and the sharp smack of the pantry door hitting the cabinet frame in the kitchen. He was back at her side in no time at all, opening the orange and gold wrapper for her.

She took each bite gingerly, chewing slowly until the movement no longer hurt so badly. It was surprising to acknowledge, but even her teeth hurt a bit. All the while, Gavin sat and watched her. Surely there was something better for him to do, but when Chloe thought about it, there truly wasn't. His whole world revolved around her now. If she wasn't so important to Gavin, he wouldn't have been so attentive.

"Is there anything I can get for you?" he asked.

Chloe wondered about that for a while. She wanted to check her phone and laptop for any messages. Her mother may have called sometime in the last few days and might have been just as worried as Gavin.

Or, she could ask for a book out of one of the many boxes and have Gavin read to her while she dozed off again. Then again, sleep seemed like a tempting idea.

But instead, she replied, "Can you join me?"

Gavin blinked back the puzzlement and his eyes roamed up and down the length of the bed. "I beg your pardon?"

Chloe felt a warm blush rise to her cheeks. Had she asked the wrong thing? They'd shared an intimate kiss, and he'd sent her spiraling into a cycle of longing twice already, and yet, lying next to her in a bed was a foreign concept all of a sudden?

"You don't have to if you don't want to," she corrected quickly. "I was just... I don't know what I was thinking."

Chloe pressed her chilled palm to her forehead and clamped her eyes shut in embarrassment.

"No, no," he replied. "I'm sorry. I didn't mean it to come across that way. I..." he sighed. "The last time I was in a bed with a woman, I was with my wife."

Chloe waved her hand at him but couldn't bear to see the look on his face. "No, I totally get it. Just forget I said anything."

How could she have been so insensitive? Of course, he would have apprehensions about climbing under the covers with her. If she weren't such an invalid, she would crawl away in shame.

All she wanted was to be closer to him, to feel him near and know that everything would be alright. But she'd have to settle with distance for the time being. Evidently, their relationship wasn't as deep as she originally thought. They were both still struggling with hurts, and it would take time. Chloe just wished it wouldn't take so long.

Gavin grabbed her outstretched hand and kissed the heel of her palm, his lips like silk against her skin added to the scratchy texture of the stubble of his chin against her fingers.

"Just get some rest, Chloe."

With her eyes still closed, she nodded and let her head fall to one side. Sleep came astonishingly swiftly.

Chapter 19

W hen Chloe awoke next, her senses were met with something strange. She could tell it was still night time. Even the blackout curtains couldn't block out all of the sun, and she couldn't see any stripes of light across the walls or hardwood floor.

The lamp was still on by her side, but the room felt empty and void. Gavin wasn't there, the chair at her bedside vacant.

But what was even stranger was the aroma that filled the cabin. The air was permeated with the scent of spices and of cooking meat. She could even hear the faint sizzle of a frying pan coming from downstairs.

Her body wasn't nearly as sore as it had been when she last remembered, but her limbs were still stiff from being in bed for so long. She pushed back the heavy quilt and swung her legs over the edge of the bed. Her feet were covered in a pair of warm wool socks, no doubt slipped on by Gavin himself, so the task of shuffling across the floor proved easier.

Supporting herself against the wall and railing, Chloe made her way down the stairs. The living room and kitchen were lit, illuminating a very peculiar sight in the kitchen.

Gavin was there by the stove, his long sleeves rolled up past his elbows, and both of his hands were busily stirring a few pork medallions around in an oily cast iron skillet. Steam wafted up from the pan, carrying the delicious smells to her at the foot of the stairs.

She could see a pot of boiling water on one of the back eyes, and past the hanging towels on the handle, she could see the oven light was on. The counter was littered with spice bottles and the usual mess that comes with cooking.

A smiled as she watched him cook. She didn't even care what he was preparing. It was just too adorable to see him try.

Gavin looked up from the cast iron pan, and his eyebrows shot up as if he were surprised to see her standing there. After setting down the rubber spatula and pan, he hurried towards her, taking bounding steps across the length of the house.

"Are you well?" he asked. "You shouldn't be up so soon." He took her by both elbows to support her, even though she was perfectly able to stand by herself.

To have him so close, touching her, and his scent mingling with that of sizzling pork, it was heaven.

Chloe loved how he was fussing over her, and she shook her head. "I feel fine," she replied laughingly. "What are you making?"

Gavin glanced over his shoulder. "I found a recipe book in the cabinets and picked a few of the dishes you marked with the color tabs. I hope you don't mind."

How could she ever mind anything he did for her? She grinned, her cheeks aching. "No, I don't mind one bit."

Gavin broke into a beaming smile and led her to the sofa. "I'm almost finished if you can wait a few minutes more."

She nodded and settled herself down on one of the cushions, curling her legs up behind her. Gavin retreated back into the kitchen and resumed his task under her watchful eye.

"I thought you said you couldn't cook," she said.

"I did," he called back over the hissing of cooking juices. "But the recipe is fairly simple, so I figured I'd have a go at it."

"I'm so proud of you," Chloe giggled. Her tone was teasing, but the words were sincere.

She watched as he flitted around the kitchen, cleaning up messes here and putting away things there, all the while monitoring the meal at the stove. He didn't move at lightning speed as she half expected him to, but Gavin strode from one end of the kitchen to the other with an efficient stride. He reminded her of a chef operating in his natural habitat of a bustling kitchen.

Taking a deep breath, she asked, "So, your wife did all the cooking?"

Posing such a question was like shooting herself in the foot. Not only was she bringing up a time before he was a vampire, which may have caused unwanted flashbacks, but also, Chloe was reminding him of his late wife. Even though she was dead, Chloe felt slightly jealous and threatened by this woman's memory. She had the one thing that Chloe never had. His wife was his first; his first love, his first wife, the mother of his first child. And Chloe was just a girl who happened to be at the right place at the right time. Yes, Gavin said he wanted Chloe now, but it would take a while before she fully replaced his late wife, if she could be replaced at all.

"Yes, she did. Janette loved to cook. Or, more specifically, bake. Roland loved her Eccles cakes in the morning for breakfast. If we didn't watch him carefully, he'd eat them until he became sick."

Despite the obvious fondness he displayed for his former family, Chloe smiled. "What are Eccles cakes?"

Gavin turned to her, spatula in one hand and a dishrag in the other, and a sparkle in his gorgeous green eyes. "Oh, they're fantastic little pastries. They're like little rolls filled with currants and topped with butter and sugar. Janette didn't get to make them often because the cost of making the filling was quite exorbitant for our income, but they were a treat to have when we could afford them."

Chloe felt a pang of bitter jealousy again. The way he spoke his wife's name, with as much tenderness as he spoke hers, was almost unbearable.

"Perhaps I can try and make them for you sometime."

Gavin smiled and nodded. "I'd like that." Then he turned back to cooking.

Chloe wasn't sure if that was the right thing to say. Yes, she wanted to prove that she could be just as good as Janette had been, but what use was there in competing with her? Would it even matter?

She angled herself away from the kitchen and stared at the fireplace. It was now clean of ashes, probably dumped out by Gavin sometime while she was unconscious. Chloe half wished that he would prepare another fire like he had on that night that felt so long ago.

Wrapping her arms around her stomach, she felt the coarse bandages on her wrist. Chloe fingered the gauze, thinking about the nights that would follow. There were many things to discuss, but she had no idea where to begin.

Gavin came in and presented her with a dinner plate and cup of hot coffee. She graciously took them and sipped the scalding liquid to find that it was perfectly sweetened with her usual dosage of sugar and cream.

When she turned to thank him, Gavin was already in the kitchen again, cleaning up the dishes and putting away the excess food in the refrigerator.

Looking down at her plate, Chloe saw a slab of seasoned pork chop accompanied by a side of boiled cabbage and baked apples that seemed to be generously smothered in cinnamon and sugar.

Taking up her fork, she tasted each dish. The apples were superb, though she suspected that he had probably mistaken the initials for teaspoon as tablespoon and applied far too much seasoning. The cabbage was adequate, though it lacked the extra helping of salt that she normally added.

Chloe was the wariest about the pork chops for one specific reason, and after one bite, her suspicions were confirmed.

"I noticed you didn't add garlic," she stated.

Gavin went still in the kitchen. "Yes, well, I wasn't sure how I would react to cooking with it."

Chloe nodded, completely understanding his apprehension on the matter. She would have been nervous, too.

"So, you have no idea how garlic affects you?" she asked with a mouthful of moist apple slices.

"I detest the smell, but otherwise, I don't know."

Chloe tilted her head. "But I thought when you drank Terrance's blood, you learned all that he knew?"

Gavin leaned his hip against the counter and shook his head. "All I know is that it's something vampires should steer clear of. Terrance was careful enough to adhere to that rule, so I have no idea how it will affect me."

She nodded again and used her knife to cut off another piece of meat. "We should probably find out at some point."

Gavin didn't reply but continued to move around the kitchen. She heard pots, pans, and utensils all clanging together before the sound of running sink water drowned out almost everything else.

She recognized the meal he prepared, but it still wasn't as good as what her mother had made when she was younger. The dish she remembered was all baked together in one pan rather than separate. Not even Chloe could make it the same way her mother did so long ago. If her parents ever came for Thanksgiving, she'd have to add groveling to her list of things to do with them so that her mother would make this same dish. And hopefully, by then, Gavin would be able to enjoy it, as well.

She shoveled the food into her mouth, feeling the ravenous hunger take hold. Even if it was totally bland and tasteless, Chloe would eat it.

Gavin finished the dishes and wiped down the counters before returning to the living room. He flopped down beside her on the sofa and propped his feet up on the coffee table. He wasn't wearing shoes, she noticed. However, his feet were clad in the same wool socks that hers were. Same color, same pattern.

"Are you wearing my socks?" she asked incredulously.

Gavin glanced between her face and his feet. "No, not at all. Your aunt gifted these to me years ago."

Chloe blinked. "They look just like mine."

"Did Mary Anne give you wool socks, too?"

Thinking about it, she nodded. "You know what? I think she did." Chloe extended her short legs and gripped the edge of the coffee table with her toes to display her own socks. Sure enough, they looked identical.

"Maybe my aunt bought yours at the same time she bought mine," she remarked. What a strange thing it was to share something so simple with Gavin; a pair of socks given to each of them by the same person.

"I doubt she ever thought these socks would be in the same room together again."

They stared at each other's feet, flexing their toes and rolling their ankles like silly children. Gavin bumped his foot against hers, and she giggled.

"You know what I've been thinking about?" she said. "What if my aunt really did think they would? She made me the heir to this cabin, knowing full well that you were here. She must have wanted us to meet."

Gavin nuzzled his toes against hers. "That might suggest she truly believed I was real. Did she know about what was going on in Atlanta?"

Chloe shook her head. "Probably not; not unless my mom told her. I hadn't talked to my aunt in a long time. Now I'll never get to."

A hesitant but strong arm wrapped around Chloe's shoulder and drew her in close to him. She breathed in his scent, his clothes slightly aromatic with the odors of residual spices and herbs from cooking. Still, he smelt glorious.

She sighed and nestled into his shoulder, letting her cheek rest against his collarbone while her nose burrowed into the base of his neck.

Silence ruled over the living room for the longest time, and Chloe felt as if she might go to sleep to the gentle caresses of his foot against hers until he spoke again.

His voice was thick with emotion. "Perhaps Mary Anne wanted us to meet because she knew she couldn't be there for us."

Chloe opened her eyes. "What do you mean?"

"If your aunt knew you were going through troubles, she wasn't the type of individual to intrude into your personal matters. And with myself, she couldn't help me through the detox process. And when she moved to Savannah, Mary Anne might have thought that we could do some good for one another. That is if she recanted her beliefs that I truly did not exist."

Chloe understood his logic. They could do for each other what her aunt could never do herself. It made sense. How such a woman could think ahead so well was beyond her.

"So," she began cautiously, "does that mean we still want you to be human?"

Gavin shifted to look at her with bewilderment. "Of course. Why wouldn't we?"

Chloe shrugged and wiggled closer, their knees nearly touching. "I don't know. We just rushed into it last time without a lot of planning. After the fourth day, how will I protect myself if the worst should happen? And then, what about the seventh day? Who's to say that you won't be a raving madman? And how do we know it will even work? What if it kills you?"

Gavin edged away from her and shifted in such a way so that he faced her completely. Taking her face between his hands, he gazed into her eyes with a fierce determination. "It will work. I have every confidence that it will. As for the dangers, we will figure something out."

She could have drowned in his eyes, so warm and beautiful. Her heart rose up in her chest, and despite her mild fatigue, she wanted to throw herself at him and let come whatever may happen.

"You still want to be human?" she asked breathlessly.

Gavin bent his forehead against hers. "I want to be with you." His breath was sweet and intoxicating.

"That's not what I asked."

He smirked. "But that's my answer. As I am now, I feel we could never be together in the ideal way. If I were human, we could." The corners of his lips fell a bit. "Unless you're having second thoughts."

Chloe clasped her hands over his and squeezed his fingers together. "No, not second thoughts. I just don't want us to rush into it again. We need to be more prepared."

Gavin tried to move away, but Chloe refused to let him. Breaking free of his hold, she leaned forward and kissed his lips. Such a kiss, she hoped, would prove to him that she was still committed, still willing to help him through the change and be there as his partner.

She knew that he had specifically requested they never kiss this way again. It was dangerous, given what happened the first time they gave into their mutual passion. But she didn't care. There was no hunger in him to tempt him now.

He kissed back with equal passion and tangled his fingers in her hair behind her head. His thumb glided along the edge of her jaw. Chloe felt the kiss warm and soothe her frazzled and aching nerves, centralizing it all to the one place he had never touched. Yet.

But before they could get carried away, Gavin had enough clarity of mind to pull away. Chloe shuddered as their lips slowly disconnected, brushing against one another like the waves of the ocean receding from the sandy shore.

Gavin gave her one more short, but mollifying, kiss and let her fall against his chest with a sigh. She never wanted to move from this spot, not even if judgment day were raging outside. The sky could catch on fire for all she cared as long as Gavin stayed locked in her embrace.

His hand passed down her slightly matted and oily hair in long strokes that would have soothed a wild mountain lion. Chloe closed her eyes and let sleep take her once more.

Chapter 20

C hloe stood with her hands on her hips, smiling smugly down at her meager collection scattered across the coffee table. Now, fully recovered from the blood transfusion, she was ready to begin the detox again with Gavin. All he needed to do was come upstairs and they could get started.

She heard the hatch door in the kitchen rise as Gavin dragged himself up the steps to emerge. She turned and gave him the warmest, encouraging smile she could muster. The easiest way to give a cat a bath was to make it feel like they weren't going to take a bath at all.

But after one look, she could tell that Gavin wasn't fooled. He raised an eyebrow and looked her up and down. He was as handsome as usual in a pair of worn out jeans and hunter green shirt that matched his eyes almost perfectly.

Sometimes, she wondered if he thought anything of her flannel plaid pajamas. At least now, she had taken a shower and looked more presentable as compared to the last few days. However, Gavin may not have cared in the least about Chloe's appearance. He had seen her a total mess, and he'd seen her all dolled up for a night out, and he was still undeniably attracted to her.

"What's going on?" he asked warily.

She dropped her arms to her sides and knew the game was up before it even started. "I'm feeling much better today, and I thought we could start on preparations for the detox." She tried to keep her tone hopeful.

Gavin wasn't as enthusiastic. He looked tired and not in the mood for anything other than a quick, satisfying meal and perhaps a nap. But he grimly nodded and closed the trap door before joining her in the living room.

When his eyes fell across the coffee table, he froze and would not look back up at her. "What's all this?"

Chloe edged closer to him, hoping that her feminine presence would pacify whatever annoyance he may have about the experiments to come.

"They're Holy items. A few are mine, but I found others in the attic among my family's old heirlooms. I thought we could test each one out first and see if they affect you at all."

Gavin gave her a sideways glance and frowned. "What else will we be trying this evening?"

Chloe reached around and pulled a folded up piece of notebook paper out of her back pocket. "Well, a lot of these we obviously can't try because they may be too deadly."

"Such as?" His tone was laced with the usual morning grumpiness that came with not eating first thing.

"Sunlight, decapitation, stake through the heart, those sorts of things."

Gavin took a deep breath, his chest expanding in exasperation. "Very well. Let's get this over with."

Chloe grinned. "Sweet! So, are you ok with this being your first night for detox?"

Gavin rubbed a hand over his stubbled cheek. "I suppose tonight would be as good a time as any."

She knew this wasn't easy for him, but she appreciated his effort. Chloe had no doubt that he still wanted to go through with the detox. Gavin was just grumpy, and this would persist for another night or two, at least. Beyond that, she didn't want to think about it.

Chloe stuffed the note away and moved toward the coffee table. She had nativity and Easter scene figurines of Jesus, a Holy Bible bound in black leather, several different styles of crosses and crucifixes, as well as a glass of water that he would surely ask about momentarily.

"Alright, so first, do you feel anything just being near this stuff?" Chloe asked, gesturing out to the relics.

Gavin stepped up to the edge of the table and shook his head. "No, I don't."

She picked up the Bible and presented it to him. He stared at the gold embossed letters on the grainy leather cover before looking up at her through his dark eyebrows.

"You're supposed to touch it," she explained.

He sighed and slapped his hand over the Bible, letting it rest there. He didn't scream, hiss, or even wince. Nothing happened. When Gavin looked back up at Chloe with that same tired expression as if he were bored out of his mind, she pulled it away and went on to the next item.

He saw and touched item after item, but nothing happened. And he didn't even seem surprised.

Chloe was slightly disappointed. These would have been some of the easiest tools to use in defending herself if something should go awry, as well as the one thing she spent the most time preparing for him tonight.

"Is that glass supposed to be filled with Holy Water?" Gavin asked after being presented with a ceramic figurine of Jesus.

Chloe picked up the glass and dipped her fingers in it. "Yes. I read that Holy Water is supposed to sting at least and burn like sunlight. I know I'm not a priest, but I blessed it myself." She drew her dripping fingers from the glass and turned to him. "Are you ready?"

"Ready for-"

Before he could finish, Chloe flicked the water at his face. Gavin's face wrinkled from the surprise, but his flesh did not burn or even become reddened by the droplets that ran down his cheeks and the tip of his nose.

"Anything?"

Gavin ran his hand over his face and cleared his throat in aggravation. "No, nothing."

Chloe sat down on the sofa, slightly dejected by the failed tests, and set down the glass on the table. She pulled out her notes and used a tiny pencil to put a strike through each of the different relics she had listed.

Propping her elbows on her knees, she went down the list for him. "Ok, so does sunlight affect you?"

Gavin began pacing around the living room, his hands thrown casually in his jean pockets. "Yes, it does. It burns my skin."

"Do you know if it's just the intense light or the ultraviolet rays? I'd have to go to Atlanta for it, but they make lamps that imitate sunlight."

"I'm not sure. All I know is that the sun burns my skin, and with prolonged exposure, my skin will start to burn away. If the sunlight reaches my blood, it's even worse. After ten minutes at the most, I'd be dust."

Chloe felt her hands tremble at the very thought of Gavin enduring so much pain. Her eyes followed him around the room. "How do you know?"

Without looking at her, he replied, "Through Terrance's blood, I witnessed another vampire from ages ago burn in the same fashion."

She grimaced and tried to block out the mental picture that was forming in her mind. No, sunlight wasn't a reasonable tool.

"Ok, we won't go that route. Even if it is the ultraviolet rays and I could get my hands on one of those lamps, I'm not one hundred percent sure it would work."

Gavin nodded and passed around the arm of the sofa. "Very well. What's next?"

She turned back to her notes. "Decapitation."

"That works," he said quickly.

"How do you know?"

He chuckled, a rather humorless sound. "What creature do you know can exist with its head severed from its own body?"

Chloe gave him a single nod. "Good point." And she struck a line through. "Drowning," she stated.

Gavin shook his head. "That doesn't work at all."

She sighed and rubbed her fingers against her temple. "You've tried?"

"Yes. Once. I washed up miles downstream, completely unharmed. Next."

Hearing about all the ways that Gavin had tried to kill himself was not the way she wanted to spend her evening. She couldn't possibly put herself in his shoes and understand the kind of desperation he must have felt to want to rid the world of one more vampire. Just to imagine that he despised his own life that much caused her heartache.

Chloe slashed through that method. "Fire. When I researched it, I read that vampires are supposed to be afraid of fire or their skin catches on fire and it spreads quickly, causing death as if they were in sunlight."

A wry smile came across Gavin's lips. "Catching on fire is bothersome, but it doesn't have the same effect as you read about."

"You've tried to set yourself on fire?" she asked dryly.

"No," he replied with a snicker. "I was building a fire for your aunt one evening, and some of the kindling fell onto the hearth. When I picked it up to put it back in the firebox, it singed my hand and caught my sleeve on fire. A quick rinse in the sink and it was fine. I didn't even get hurt, really."

Chloe smiled, only because he was able to laugh at himself. She put a line through the word and moved on. "Oh, this might be promising."

She stood up and pulled out the necklace she had put on before he came up from the basement. It was a small heart-shaped pendant that gleamed in the fluorescent light.

Gavin made his way towards her and peered at the piece of jewelry. "Silver?" he questioned. Chloe nodded. "I'm not a werewolf, Chloe. Or do I have to explain the difference?"

After unclasping the back of the chain, she held it out for him to take. "I know the difference, but this is one thing you share in common with werewolves, I guess."

Gavin raised his hand and reached out, but when skin met metal, nothing happened.

"Anything?" she whined.

"No. And I find it a little offensive that you're saddened by that."

Chloe pocketed the necklace. "If we can't find a way for me to defend myself against you, then the detox isn't going to work; unless you're perfectly fine with me killing you instead."

Gavin didn't find that amusing at all. "I told you, we will find a way. Even if we can't tonight, we'll keep trying. I wouldn't force you to go through with this if I knew you wouldn't be safe."

He leaned down and gave her a quick peck on the lips. Her knees wanted to buckle, but Chloe stood firm. After she recovered from swooning, she pulled out the note again.

"Next thing is running water."

A frown formed between his eyebrows. "Running water?"

"Yeah, like you can't cross a river or stream."

"I've crossed over the creek many times."

She shrugged. "What about running tap water?"

Gavin dropped his chin. "Do you not remember me washing the dishes last night? Not only that, but I have taken plenty of showers, so modern running water will not affect me."

Chloe looked bemused. "You've taken showers?" He nodded. "With me in the house?"

Gavin scrunched up his face in such a way that told her he very well did take showers in the house without her knowing. But she didn't want to think of that now. She waved her hands to brush the issue aside and marked it off on the sheet. They were running out of ideas quickly.

She frowned. "I don't know if this would really help for every scenario, but vampires are rumored to be pretty polite when it comes to being invited into a home."

Gavin shook his head. "Absolutely false. I mean to say, I am polite, but I don't require an invitation to go anywhere. I've broken into almost every home in Carter Lake looking for things I need."

Chloe nodded. "Right. And you broke into the clinic, too." With an exaggerated flourish, she scratched that off the list. "And the best has been saved for last—garlic. "

Gavin scowled. "What did you have in mind to test this?"

Chloe hurried into the kitchen and pulled out a bulb of garlic from the pantry. Already, Gavin stood up and backed away, wrinkling his nose at the smell when she was no more than a few feet away.

"Is it really that bad?" she asked before taking a sniff for herself. There was the hint of an odor, but nothing as nasty as what he made it out to be.

"Imagine a sweaty shoe after a dog has defecated in it, and you might have a closer idea as to what I'm smelling."

Chloe bit her lip. This certainly may turn out to be the key to keeping her safe during the detox. "But, do you think this would be a useful weapon?"

He shrugged and rubbed his nose. "If I'm hungry enough, I'm not sure."

Bouncing the garlic in her hand like a baseball, she walked slowly across the living room floor. Gavin retreated, always keeping a piece of furniture between them.

"This has to be an effective weapon, though. Just a bad smell isn't going to cut it." She looked up at him and stopped. "Let me see if it burns your skin."

Gavin shook his head and covered his nose and mouth, resembling a stubborn child who didn't want to take his medicine.

Chloe grinned and began chasing after him. She giggled as he tried to scramble away, knocking over chairs and stubbing his toes on furniture legs. After a while, she knew they were getting nowhere.

She chucked the garlic bulb at him and nailed him right in the cheekbone. He cried out in anguish and backed up against a wall, still holding his face. Chloe rushed over and examined his skin but couldn't see any sign of a rash, burn, or abrasion. For a moment, she thought it would be a viable weapon. It was much easier to chuck garlic bulbs at him all night than to risk killing him with a stake.

"I didn't appear to hurt you," she said.

Gavin sneezed into his hand and wiped at his watering eyes. When he looked down at her, she saw that the whites of his eyes were bloodshot like he'd been crying.

"You ok?" she asked.

He nodded, small locks of hair that came loose during the chase bobbed with the motion. "Yes," he said, sounding horribly congested.

Chloe leaned forward and peered up his nose to see that it was clogged with mucus. "I want to try something," she said.

Gavin groaned. "What more could you possibly do? I thought that was the last of it."

She left him there and went to the kitchen. Scavenging through her spice rack, she found what she had been looking for and came back. She held it out so he could read the bottle label.

"Garlic powder?" he moaned.

"I bet I could fashion little bombs with garlic powder loaded inside. If you get too close, I can throw it at you and that may stop you from attacking me. I just need to see if this has the same effect as the whole garlic."

Gavin was not as thrilled as she was. The last effects of the garlic on his face were finally wearing away, and he looked normal again, apart from the weariness he felt from not feeding.

But he didn't complain this time. He steeled himself and waited for the test.

Chloe honestly was not going to enjoy this any more than he was. If the powder did what she suspected it would do, the results would not be pretty. But it was the only way to make sure she had an effective tool for the days to come.

She unscrewed the lid and saw him go rigid at the release of garlic odor. She backed up a pace or two and then flung the shaker in his direction, making the sandy shaded powder dust his entire face and down the front of his shirt.

The spice added a splash of color to his complexion, but that was the only good thing it did for him.

The garlic worked the same way as tear gas used for crowd control during riots and military gas mask training.

Gavin began to cough heavily. His eyes, even though they were closed, were leaking heavily and turning the powder on his cheeks into caked mud. Mucus drained from his nose and dribbled down his lips.

He rubbed at his face to get the spice off, but it only made it worse. When his face began to swell, Chloe grabbed his arm and dragged him upstairs, spouting apologies the whole way, even though she had done it on purpose.

Gavin sneezed, coughed, and sputtered as she led him into the bathroom. Chloe frantically turned on the tub faucet and stripped off his shirt. At any other time, Chloe would have been turned on at the sight of his bulging muscles, but she was too concerned with the fact that his face was turning beet red. The garlic powder must have gotten clogged in his sinuses somehow.

Gavin, still incapacitated by the effects, let Chloe guide him to the running water and stuck his face underneath the faucet. She held him there and began wiping his skin to get the powder off. There was no risk of drowning him, so even when he tried to pull back, Chloe kept him locked in place. The dull, golden powder dropped in clumps onto the tub floor and washed down the drain.

Once she knew the spice was gone, she released him to continue his own cleansing, blowing his nose under the water and rubbing at his eyes and lips. Chloe stood back by the sink and crossed her arms, anxiously waiting for him to stand up and declare he was fine again. When she had thrown the garlic in his face, she'd had no clue if the effects would be long lasting.

After what seemed like an eternity, he stood up, water dripping all over the tile floor and down his chest and abs to dampen the tops of his pants. He groped for a towel and she hurriedly handed him one from the rack on the wall.

After drying his face and torso, he turned to her and tried to open his eyes. But from the way he squinted and the veined redness around his pupils like before, she could tell he still wasn't out of the woods yet.

He sniffled and swayed a bit. Chloe ducked underneath one of his arms and brought him into the guest bedroom and the double bed inside. She hadn't spent a lot of time in this room since she moved in, except to store all of her boxes of books that Gavin had moved upstairs from the living room in the early days of their first attempt at detox.

Navigating through the maze to get to the bed, she was thankful he wasn't too disoriented; otherwise, she would have been staggering and stumbling under his weight. Chloe let him tumble down onto the mattress, and she heard him let out a sigh of relief.

"You think you're going to be ok?" she asked, lifting his long, muscular legs up on top of the quilt.

Gavin sniffled again and coughed. "I think so," he grumbled.

Chloe's motherly instincts prodded her to take his temperature, make chicken noodle soup, and give in to any demands he may ask of her. But instead, she knelt by the side of the bed and continued reeling off apologies for what she'd done to him.

"I had no idea it'd be that bad. I didn't even think that much got on you. It was a successful test, but I don't even know if I want to use that stuff on you again."

Gavin lifted a hand blindly and placed it firmly on the crown of her head. With his eyes still leaking a bit and squeezed shut, he said, "No, you must use this to defend yourself in the last days of the detox. It may be the thing that saves your life."

Arguing would get her nowhere, so Chloe admitted defeat and nodded, though the thought of him killing her, draining her body dry of blood to satisfy his hunger, was not something she wanted to imagine or fret over. She wanted to believe that everything would be fine and that she wouldn't even have to use the garlic powder.

His hand slid down, and she kissed the back of it before placing it on the quilt. The room was dark, but she could see his outline from the light that slanted in through the hall door. This room didn't have blackout curtains, so some pale moonlight streamed in and fell across the floor and numerous boxes that were scattered around. It'd be a quiet place for him to recover for an hour or so, but no more.

"I'll let you rest," she said before standing to leave.

Gavin grabbed her hand before she had a chance. She looked back and saw his eyes cracked open, gazing up at her with such a pleading expression that she would have given him the world if he asked for it.

"Stay with me?"

That, she could do. Chloe nodded and was about to pull up a box of books to sit on when he gave a strong tug on her hand, leading her to crawl into bed with him.

At first, settling in beside him seemed awkward, and Chloe's movements were clumsy as she tried to get comfortable. After a few minutes of grunting and hushed apologies for bumping knees and elbows, she found herself snuggled against his bare side with one hand resting on his powerful chest.

There was no heartbeat, no steady rise and fall that came with breathing. If it weren't for the intense heat his body exuded, Chloe would have thought she was touching a lifeless corpse.

Neither of them spoke for a while. The only sounds she heard were the crickets outside and Gavin's occasional coughing and sniffling. The congestion wore off soon enough, and when Chloe glanced up to check, he looked completely normal again, as handsome and alluring as ever.

She could hardly believe she was lying here with him in such an intimate way. When the roles were reversed and she was the invalid in bed, he refused to join her. Why the change of heart?

The room was too dark for her to see much of anything, but she could tell his eyes were closed. She wondered if he was asleep. But, she'd never seen him sleep before, so she wasn't sure how to tell precisely.

Instead of disturbing him, Chloe let her fingers trace random shapes and patterns along the smooth surface of his pale skin, admiring the hard muscle underneath.

She drank in his scent until it made her lightheaded. Chloe couldn't recall a time when she had been this close to him with so little clothes. There was that time he had to change shirts, but at the time, she dared not to get too close to him. Even then, he was still something wild in her mind, and she had no idea of the true humanity that lay beneath.

Now, lying here in the dark with him, the musty smell of the bed quilt enveloping them, Chloe couldn't help but let her mind wander to places that were out of the question for the time being.

But, the memory of what he'd told her the other night snapped her out of the gutter. Gavin hadn't wanted to join her in bed because of his traumatic memory of waking up to his dead wife nearly three centuries ago.

What had happened to make him want differently since then? Certainly, it was nothing Chloe had done. Was this another side effect of the garlic? Did it somehow affect him mentally?

"You're quiet," he remarked through the darkness.

Slightly startled to hear him speak after such stillness, she tensed and readjusted her position. "Just thinking."

"About what?" he asked, his voice lacking the congestive sounds that were so prevalent before.

Chloe slowly let out a breath. "You, mostly."

She could almost feel his smile. "What about me?"

"About why we're lying here together. I thought you didn't want to do something like this."

Gavin's arm around her stiffened a bit, then relaxed as he replied gently, "I originally didn't want to."

"Why?" she asked, trying to keep the offense out of her tone.

He didn't reply for a moment, but then said, "I was afraid of something happening that should not happen."

"Biting me?"

"No," he replied. "Something that I've wanted to do before but dared not to."

He was dancing around the answer, and after some thought, Chloe believed she understood what he meant. That night when he took her blood, he said that he wanted to take her in the carnal sense of the word.

"And you don't right now?"

He gave a huff of a laugh. "The garlic has put me out of sorts." He tilted her chin up so their eyes could meet. "Though you are still beautiful in my eyes, I don't think I'd have the heart to do anything at the moment."

Chloe didn't know whether to be flattered or appalled. Coming from such a traditional upbringing, it would seem strange that Gavin would want to do something as taboo as make love to her out of wedlock.

He gave her a warm smile, and then she laid her cheek back onto his chest. "I was also thinking about that night in the woods with Terrance."

His body went tense, and Chloe knew she was treading on unstable ground.

"What about it?" he asked, his voice strong and serious.

Picking her words carefully, she replied, "Terrance told me you were well occupied. I thought he might have hurt you, but then you showed up. What happened? Weren't you following me?"

"I was. Or, so I thought." Gavin was slow to speak as if he were choosing his words so carefully. "He used his power of manipulation against me, and when I found that I was following nothing more than an illusion, it took me a while to find you again."

"When did you know it wasn't me?"

A tremor, like a shiver, passed through his body, and she felt it transfer to her own, rattling her very bones with the intensity of it. "I saw you being attacked and torn apart by some animal I couldn't describe or detect. I heard your screams, and I could even smell the blood and carnage below me as it happened. But when I jumped down, the beast ran away. I held you in my arms as you were dying, but there was nothing I could do.

"Then, I realized it wasn't you."

"But how?"

Gavin tilted his head down, his lips so close to her hair that she felt the fine strands move with each word he spoke. "It only took me a few seconds to realize that this illusion wasn't complete. The figment I held in my arms did not feel like you. It looked like you, smelled like you, but it lacked your spirit. As soon as I figured it out, the illusion was gone, and I was alone. I retraced your scent and found you with Terrance."

Chloe remembered how he looked when he came upon them. Matching that with his story told her that he must still be reeling from the shock of seeing her die. There was a distinct change in him that night. He confused her at every turn. Every moment was a guessing game of what was going through his head. It reminded her of the mean trick he'd played on Terrance.

Along with the memory came the phantom sensation of his lips and tongue caressing the skin on her neck. So gentle, so seductive, and yet it was all a show for Terrance. Chloe had truly believed that Gavin was going to drink her dry, but it had been a plot to make Terrance believe he was winning.

His arms encircled her tighter, and Chloe nestled herself in. "You had me scared that night that you really would bite me. I could tell you were hungry."

Gavin kissed the top of her head. "I made a promise that I would never hurt you, and I intend to keep it as long as I am able to."

That was not a solid promise. He couldn't guarantee that he would never bite her, but he could promise that he would try not to. He'd only broken his promise once, but the situation had gotten out of control, and she forgave him easily for it. And that promise was all she wanted. All she could hope for.

Chloe smiled, and they lay in the bedroom for a while longer. They didn't speak as they simply enjoyed each other's company. The only hint that Gavin was still awake lay in the graceful movement of his fingers as they stroked along her shoulder. His touch further soothed her nerves until she was ready to fall asleep completely.

"What are you thinking?" she asked dazedly.

Half expecting no reply at all, she was a little surprised to hear him say, "I'm thinking of a lot of things."

Chloe shifted and stared up at the underside of his jaw that was dark with stubble that never seemed to grow. "Name one."

Gavin's eyes cracked open, a speckle of light reflecting in his glistening eyes. A smile appeared. "I was thinking about one time when I was sick back in Hatherleigh. Janette and I had been married for only a few weeks, and I contracted a cold. I refused to rest, but she was constantly pestering me." Then he chuckled. "It took one good sneeze, and I completely botched an order of horseshoes before I realized she was right."

Chloe found herself smiling as well, even though she still felt the green monster of jealousy rear its ugly head. To hear him talk so fondly of his wife was like having a knife lodged between her ribs.

"You must miss her a lot," she said. "You talk about her a lot."

Gavin shifted beneath her. "Does it bother you?"

Chloe sighed, wishing she could lie to him. "Honestly, it does."

"Why?"

Chloe sat up and stared at him, deciding whether or not to spill her emotions out to him one more time. "It's like you talking about how much you love an ex-girlfriend while you're in a relationship. It's hypocritical." She swallowed and looked away to avoid his pained expression. "I know you love Janette and your son, probably more than anything else in the world. But, I don't understand how you can talk about them so much when I'm around."

She might have sounded like a jealous girlfriend or a spoiled child. There was no reason that she should feel upset. It must be a natural thing to think about his old family all the time.

Gavin touched her arm. "I didn't realize it bothered you so much." An uncomfortable pause stretched on before he said, "I talk about them often because I'm afraid I'll forget them."

She looked back at him, trying to keep the hurt out of her gaze. "Forget them?"

He nodded. "After years, centuries, my memory of them is fading. Thinking of them, reminding myself of the times we shared together, helps me to hold them there a little longer. Since you came, I have thought more of you than anything else." His thumb grazed tenderly along her arm as he spoke. "I've thought of you so much that I think of them less, and I can't remember as much. If I mention them to you, it's because I'm still trying to hold on."

Chloe bit her lip and turned away, unsure of how to feel. She was the reason he talked about his family so much. She was the reason that he was beginning to forget about the love he had for two people who have been dead for centuries. Part of her wanted Gavin to forget all about his family, to let him release that hold he had on them. Another part felt guilty for making it so much worse for him.

"So, I'm never going to stop hearing about your dead wife and son?" Her words came out a little harsher than she expected, the pain bleeding through.

She felt more than saw him flinch at her choice of words. "I don't know what else to do, Chloe."

She took a deep breath and nodded. "I'm sorry. I'm sure you miss them a lot."

He was quiet for a few beats, then replied, "Not as much as I used to."

Chloe's eyebrows pinched together in puzzlement as to what he meant. When she turned back to face him and Gavin saw her expression, he continued, "When I was alone, I missed Janette and my son more than I could possibly bear. But since I first laid eyes on you, it hasn't hurt as much." If it were possible, Chloe was only more confused. "You remind me of her, of Janette."

Blinking back the alarm, Chloe asked, "I remind you of her? How?"

Gavin grinned and rolled his head on the pillow so he could get a better look at her face. "Your eyes. You both have the same eyes. They're mostly hazel, but they tend toward a dark green shade on the outside and a striking auburn ring around the pupil."

Nimble fingers grazed along the skin over her cheekbone as he regarded her with an affectionate gaze. Chloe felt chills crawl up and down her spine at his gentle touch.

"Not only that, but you two are so similar in your mannerisms. The way you walk and move, your choice of words and the way they dance off your tongue. You could tell a person to go to the devil with such charisma they would enjoy the trip."

At that, she laughed and buried her face in his chest to hide the blush rising up her neck.

"Having you around is almost like she's here again."

Chloe was no longer amused. She gave him a serious look and asked, "Is that why you kissed me before? Is that why you want to be with me like you say you do?"

Gavin watched her closely as she shifted toward the edge of the bed. If she stood up to leave, she knew he would stop her.

"No, that's not why."

"You just said that I reminded you of your late wife and–""I know what I said," he calmly interjected, "but I think you misunderstood what I meant."

Chloe didn't like to be told that she misunderstood anything. She understood quite a bit. Brent always did that to her, and it only made her more upset. "Do you want to be with me just because you're lonely then?"

"No, that's not entirely why either."

"Then why?"

"I've told you why."

Chloe scoffed. "You mean what you said the night we kissed? Because I accept you as you are?"

Gavin looked pained at her harsh tones. "That's part of it, yes."

"You're giving me a lot of mixed signals here, and I need a solid answer. Do you want me because you want your wife back, too?"

The silence was unnerving, and Chloe couldn't read him. She couldn't tell if he was actually thinking of the answer or letting her figure it out for herself.

Then he said, "Janette is dead. I've come to terms with that. I know I can't have her back. I also know that you're not Janette, and you never will be. You have her eyes and a few things that remind me of her, but you're not her. If I wanted my wife, I wouldn't want you. Does that make sense?"

Chloe didn't trust her voice to answer. She only turned away and brought her knees up to her chest to hug close. What he said did, in fact, make sense. There were still differences between Chloe and Janette, she was sure. Janette must have been far prettier and gentler in nature. In her mind, Chloe imagined Gavin's late wife to be a perfect angel.

What she couldn't stand was the idea that Gavin was settling for her just because she was convenient. If he had his pick of women, dead or alive, Chloe wasn't so sure that she would be his first choice.

Gavin sat up and placed his hands on her shoulders from behind. His piercing gaze was hot against her back, and it made her nervous.

"You're still not convinced," he stated, so sure of the truth.

Chloe shook her head but refused to look back at him.

"How can I convince you that what I say is true?"

There really was no way, and Chloe knew that. She had to do something that she hadn't done in months—trust. She'd trusted Brent once, and he'd ruined her life. She never wanted to be used again.

Brent hogged her attention and stole her away from her friends and family simply for her companionship, and she wasn't so convinced that Gavin wanted something different. She wanted to be unconditionally loved and accepted for who she was, not for what she could give. It was a tall order, one that she was sure no man could fulfill.

She didn't want to think that love was a selfish emotion. With only her experiences with Brent to guide her in what love meant, Chloe was clueless. For someone who aspired to write romance, she knew nothing of the concept.

Chloe took a shaky breath and rubbed at her misting eyes. Gavin's grip tightened and he pulled her back down with him. Resuming her position from before, she hid her face in his shoulder, but kept her arms close to her own chest instead of his, creating a barrier between their bodies.

His fingers gently raked back and forth along her shoulder blades to comfort her.

A choice had to be made that night. Chloe could assume that Gavin was lying and only wanted her around for her company and as a reminder of his late wife. Or, she could believe what he said was the truth and let it go. Yes, she wasn't his first. But he was choosing to make her his last. That had to count for something.

"Tell me," he said softly. "Are words enough to convince you?"

Chloe sighed. "I don't know. Words are good for some things. And you haven't lied to me, not really. I shouldn't have any reason to not believe you."

"What if I said that I love you?"

Chloe looked up at him in wonder. His entire expression told her that, just like before, he was not lying. Not only did he show honesty in his eyes, but she saw the one flicker of emotion that had always been there that she had never been able to decipher.

She'd never seen this look in Brent's eyes. No man had ever looked at her in that way. But, searching her memory, she had seen it before. Her father had that same look when he watched her mother washing dishes in the kitchen late at night. She saw that same look on a man who held his fiancé close while they walked down the street. An older gentleman who had been married to the same woman for fifty years had that same look when he kissed the back of his wife's hand in public.

How could she have missed this before? In the chaos of detox, vampires, and late night writing sessions, she never thought to really think about the way he always looked at her. And that look, that soft gaze full of love, had been there since the first day.

"You love me?" she questioned, her voice in a gentle whisper.

He nodded. "Yes. I love you. I've loved you since you wrote me that letter."

"But you hadn't even seen me before then. How could you love someone you've never formally met?"

"I don't know. All I know is that I can't stand being apart from you. I dream of you each day, and you're all I think about. I want to help you succeed in everything you set your mind to and make you happy, nothing more. If that's not love, then I don't know what is."

Chloe watched his face before replying, "I want all those things for you, too."

Gavin kissed the top of her head, but Chloe never returned his sentiments in any other way before she laid her head back down onto his shoulder. For now, she wasn't sure if she could speak those words he had so freely confessed to her now.

Chloe chose to let her doubts go. Instead of dwelling on things that would only ruin the moment, she let herself be taken captive by his warmth, his masculine scent, and his comforting presence. Who would have thought that such a dangerous beast like a vampire could be a source of tranquility for someone like herself? They were both damaged, both broken in their own right. And yet, they might be perfect for one another.

Chapter 21

C hloe felt Gavin's hand fall heavily on her shoulder and shake her roughly.

"Chloe, wake up!" he demanded.

Her eyes snapped open. She must have fallen asleep on the desk in the library some time while Gavin was occupying himself with reading. The second day of the detox was upon them and, as before, Chloe drove them to a library in another town far away from Carter Lake so he could be distracted from his bloodlust.

However, the library looked slightly different than it had when she'd dozed off. It was much brighter as dawn's light was peeking through the window blinds. Gavin was out of the direct line of the windows, but that wouldn't last for long.

Panic surged through her, and she began frantically packing up her laptop. "I'm sorry, Gavin," she said. "I didn't expect to nod off like that."

"I completely lost track of time myself. I suppose that's a good thing."

Chloe stood from the desk and shouldered her bag. "Not when it's going to put us late in getting back home." She glanced out the window. There was no way they could get to her car without Gavin being singed by the sunlight.

"I can make it to your jeep," he assured her. "But I'm not sure how I can survive the trip back."

"It's about two hour's drive," she said as she looked around for something to cover him with. The jeep had been a blessing for Chloe when she'd first moved to Carter Lake. Now, with no trunk to stow him in, she wished with all her heart that she had not traded in her sedan. Even if he crouched down on the floorboards, sunlight would still find him through the windows.

She rushed around the library, looking for anything like a tarp or blanket while Gavin hid behind a bookcase in the shadows. When her eyes lifted momentarily to check the angle of the rising sun, Chloe spotted a quilt hanging on the wall over the children's area.

Disregarding the laws of men, she grabbed a chair to stand on and yanked the dusty tapestry down from where it was pinned. She would return it the next night or maybe when the detox was over.

She came to Gavin with the quilt, and he didn't have to be told twice how to use it to his advantage. Taking careful measures, they exited the building with the quilt draped over Gavin's crouched body and ran to her jeep. There was no telling when the staff would be coming in to open up the library.

Chloe heard Gavin grunt and hiss as she tried to hustle him into the back of her jeep.

"What's wrong?" she asked, fearful that there was a tear somewhere in the quilt.

"Some sun is coming in through the stitches. I'm alright."

Chloe grimaced and helped him onto the floorboard, covering him up as best as she could. The drive back to Carter Lake was a fast one, but the sun was winning this race. The light that came through her windshield was nearly blinding to Chloe who hadn't stepped foot out in the sun in so long. She could understand why Gavin both feared it and missed it. The sun gave life, but in this case, it administered nothing but death and pain for him. If they survived this detox, Chloe vowed that she would help Gavin to enjoy the daylight once again.

Chloe's jeep slid to a stop in front of her cabin, the wheels skidding against the pebble driveway. After snagging one of her nails on the seat buckle when she nearly ripped it off to get out of the car, Chloe threw open the back door.

"You ok, Gavin?"

The quilt moved a little as he was preparing to wiggle his way out of the back seat. "Yes, I'm fine."

He sounded slightly breathless, but she couldn't decide if it was from the fast ride home or if the sunlight was leaking through the quilt a little more than he was letting on.

Chloe helped him from the car, but after taking only a few steps, the quilt suddenly fell from Gavin's body. He groaned and hissed as the light engulfed his skin. Wisps of smoke rose from his face, and even though it had only been a few seconds, Chloe could smell the charring flesh that he tried to conceal with his arms.

She ducked down and snatched the quilt from the ground. It was only then that she discovered that a corner of the fabric was snagged on one of the seat mechanisms. In her haste to cover Gavin again, she was sure that she tore some of the threading that held the quilt together, but she didn't care. Gavin's safety was a greater priority.

Gavin whimpered and had a slight limp as they hurried towards the front door. Chloe fumbled with her keys as she jammed them into the locks, the sound of her own heartbeat and rapid breathing loud in her ears.

"The cellar," Gavin rasped when they stepped foot into the living room.

Her fingers scraped against the wood planks, contracting a couple of splinters in the process before she found the right seam and lifted the hatch to the cellar.

Helping Gavin down the dark steps, she was submerged in a cool darkness that she had never experienced before. Gavin had never permitted her access to this area. Under the circumstances, it was understandable to allow her here this once.

Once their feet hit the solid wooden floor, Gavin rushed deeper into the darkness and let the quilt fall away. Chloe couldn't see him at all as she stood in the faint light that beamed down from the open hatch.

She listened to Gavin's shuffling footsteps and heard the faint squeak of springs as if from a mattress. Unsure of what else to do, she climbed up the ladder a short way and closed the hatch but did not leave the cellar.

"What are you doing?" Gavin asked, his tone a little gruff and impatient.

Chloe didn't respond but pulled out her phone with trembling hands and turned on the flashlight feature. A pale blue light washed over half of the cellar, which she found to be little more than the size of her bedroom upstairs.

In the far corner, she saw Gavin's form sitting on a carved wooden bed frame. From the old colonial styled details, she could tell that it must be the bed that he and his wife once shared.

Off to the side was another piece of furniture, a writing desk. It was simply made, probably from the same era as the bed, with a single chair pushed underneath. On top of the desk were piles of parchment pages. Some were tinged with a golden hue, others as white as any modern sheet of copy paper. An ink pen rested atop a work in progress.

The floor beneath her was planked wood just like the rest of the cabin, but some planks were warped with age. The air in the room, along with being comfortably cool, was slightly damp, probably since they were half underground. The walls were also made of wooden paneling with white grooves between each wide plank. She wondered if they were the original boards that made up his home almost three hundred years ago.

"Chloe, you shouldn't be down here," he warned.

She paid him no mind. Yes, it might be dangerous, considering that he hadn't fed in two days, and her blood was racing enticingly through her veins. But this was the first glimpse she'd gotten into his private life, the life she had wanted to see for so long.

When he'd told her about living in the cellar, she hadn't been sure what to expect. Ironically, she thought that his space would be elaborately decorated with all the finer things and have several levels that he was free to roam during the daytime. But that was not the case. The cellar was simply that, a cellar. Wine or produce could easily have been stored here, but no, this was the home of a vampire in hiding.

Not only was it his home but the place where he listened in on all of her conversations and the conversations of her family for generations. Just as he had told her before, he listened to their fights, their parties and celebrations, their lamentations, and everything in between. She could picture him reclining on the bed and simply finding entertainment in listening to the humans who dwelled above. She could imagine him penning away masterpieces at that tiny desk and mourning over the fact that no eyes would ever read them.

Chloe marveled at the number of hours, days, years, he had spent within these walls. No wonder he wanted to be human. After three centuries in this place, she'd do anything to get a little more freedom.

Walking softly, as if the cellar were some ancient shrine or holy place, she made her way to the desk and examined the contents.

"What's all of this?" she asked, talking in a near whisper.

"My manuscripts. Please don't disturb them." Gavin sounded a little more like his normal self.

Ignoring his request, she reached down and picked up one of the top sheets in the pile. The handwritten cursive was distinctly Gavin's. In some places, there were lines striking out a few words, and then in other places, whole sentences with corrections had been scribbled in the margins.

Chloe's eyes scanned through a couple of lines before Gavin was at her side. The wind generated from his quick movements blew a few papers off the desk, and they drifted to the floor. He seized her wrist and squeezed until she dropped the manuscript page.

She turned to look up at his face, the light from her phone illuminating patches of burnt skin that were slowly healing. A tight breath escaped her lips, brought forth from the shock of his assault and the sight of his disfigured face gradually morphing back into the handsome man she knew.

But his eyes were not the same. They were full of a rage that she couldn't give a name to. It was neither from hunger nor the fact that she had disobeyed him. It was something else entirely.

After gazing up into his fiery green eyes, she finally realized why he glared at her in such a way.

"What are you afraid of?" she asked.

The hard lines on his face softened, and his grip eased around her wrist. "I am not afraid."

"Yes, you are. Is it because I almost read your manuscript? I'm sure it's not bad."

Gavin let out a sigh and shook his head. "No, it is."

Chloe searched his face for the truth, but all she could do was speculate. "Has no one ever read your work? Not even Janette?"

This time, he lowered her arm and twisted his hand around so their fingers would interlace. He appeared to struggle with the words for a moment, wrestling within himself what exactly to tell her.

"No. No one has ever read my work. Not Janette and not even a publisher."

"But I thought you said you couldn't get anything published? I assumed that meant you had tried."

He shook his head. "I was always too fearful to hand my work over to anyone. Janette tried to convince me to solicit it somewhere, but I never did. She asked to read it herself, but I wouldn't let her."

Chloe stepped closer. "But, why not? Didn't you trust her?"

Gavin looked pained at the accusatory question. "Of course, I trusted her. I wouldn't have married her if I hadn't."

"Then why didn't you let her read it?" she asked a little more urgently.

Gavin's free hand balled into a fist and began to shake. "Because, I didn't want her to hate it and have her stop believing in me. If she thought I had no talent, she might not have supported me so strongly in my passions."

The corners of Chloe's mouth twitched with a smile that she wanted to give him, but was afraid it would come out as mocking or condescending. "If she loved you like I believe she did, then she wouldn't have stopped supporting you for anything."

Gavin stared into her eyes for what seemed like ages, the two of them standing together in the silence of the cellar while the rest of humanity went about their morning. But in this dark place, Chloe felt as if she was in another world, and Gavin was the master of that world.

She could hardly believe what she was saying. In her mind, Chloe had never liked Janette for the pure fact that she had been married to Gavin. But here she was, reassuring Gavin that what Janette felt for him was special and unconditional.

Defending the woman who seemed like the enemy altered Chloe's opinion of her. Suddenly, she wasn't a threat anymore. If Gavin had never let her read his manuscripts, perhaps what they had shared wasn't so special after all. It gave Chloe hope that maybe one day, she could be better than Janette and that Gavin would love her even more completely than he had ever loved Janette.

But her eyes fell to the bed behind Gavin. If it really was their bed, Chloe was reminded of something else that she had not been able to share with Gavin yet. How many times had they done what married couples do in that bed? Was their son conceived in that bed?

All of a sudden, she felt like an intruder. She wasn't a vampire like he was, and yet here she was, stranded in the darkness, his darkness that he'd been creating for years with his sorrows and regrets and memories of his former family. She hadn't felt it when she'd first come in, but now it was suffocating.

"Maybe I should go," she said as she turned away. But Gavin's hand held her back from taking another step.

"No, don't go."

How could she resist his plea that was so full of the loneliness he had suffered for years? She stood still, the only thing connecting them were their joined hands and some spiritual bond that had formed somehow in the time they had known each other. It bridged the darkness, and for a brief moment, Chloe felt a light in her heart because of it.

She looked back at Gavin, and even in the dim light, she saw his tortured gaze in the shadows. His eyes, darkened as they were, begged her to stay. And this wasn't his powers of manipulation. This was a genuine, subliminal call for her company, her acceptance, her love. And she would give it freely.

Chloe went back to him, her phone lowered so the light shined on their feet and legs. Their bodies somehow gravitated closer to one another until they were nearly touching. Her breath quickened, and heart pounded against her chest. She was sure that he could not only hear it but feel it, too.

Unsure what prompted her to say such a silly romantic thing, she whispered, "It beats for you."

Gavin didn't ask for an explanation before he snaked one arm around her waist and brought her closer. Their torsos pressed together, and she could feel every contour of his strong body. She couldn't tear her eyes away from him.

She didn't know whether it was fear or passion that surged between them. Her body began to quiver, and an ache developed low in her belly.

Memories of the night in the woods flashed back to her. He had held her in the same way. Was this lust or hunger she saw in his eyes?

The need to survive spurred her to step backward, but he refused to let go. She whispered his name before his lips consumed hers.

Warm and tender, he kissed her, and the fear ebbed away. Her eyes drifted shut, and she dropped her phone, landing in such a way that the light bulb landed face down onto the floor. Darkness swallowed up the room as Chloe used her free hand to rake through Gavin's hair.

"I love you," she finally whispered, professing to him and to the world the thing she had been so apprehensive to say from the beginning. To love a vampire, a powerful creature of the night, seemed such a morbid thing. Yet, holding him close and feeling his hands caress her so tenderly, it felt like the most natural thing in the world. How could this love that blossomed in the night be wrong in any way?

Their kiss intensified, the passion mounting between them and ready to boil over. His mouth moved along her jaw and down her neck. A moment of panic flared in Chloe's chest before his lips and tongue sent her into a deeper level of ecstasy that made her forget everything. Nothing else in the world existed except for them and this cellar.

Before she had time to even think about it, Gavin's shirt was on the floor, and hers joined it. Their skin touched, and it was a glorious feeling. Even in the chilly cellar, they kept each other warm. The manuscript and the conversation they'd started were quickly forgotten as Gavin and Chloe moved closer to his bed, still enraptured in each other. Kisses and caresses abounded as they expressed their true emotions in ways that words could not.

Chapter 22

When Gavin awoke, his senses were on fire. The darkness seemed as bright as the sun. The sounds of bugs crawling along the planked floors were like bear claws scratching at the walls. The smell of the grass and trees outside somehow penetrated the walls of his dwelling place to reach his nostrils. And his skin, oh his skin was alight with sensations he hadn't felt in centuries. And above it all, he felt refreshed, somehow alive although he knew that he was dead.

And when he turned to look at Chloe, sleeping soundly beside him with her arm draped over his body, he knew exactly why. Memories of their lovemaking and overflowing passion came back to him in an instant.

A well of emotions came rushing in, and he wasn't sure whether to feel ashamed for having known her in the Biblical sense before marriage, elated that she would trust him enough to be intimate, or terrified that she was getting too dangerously close so far in the detox period.

He reached out and touched her cheek, savoring the softness of her flesh. He had her to thank for making him feel this way. Only she could have awakened that part of him once more. How could he feel ashamed of it?

A new sound echoed in the darkness with them—a heartbeat. His eyes dropped to the fragile skin on her neck, and he could see the veins pulsing beneath. An instinctual urge threatened to ruin the joy he felt. His mouth watered and stomach quivered in the first unbearable pains of hunger.

He felt his fangs grow behind his lips and eyes morph to display his bloodlust. It would be so easy to take her now while she slept so vulnerable in his bed. But his love for her stood as a wall, impenetrable and strong in the face of this curse he bore. How long would such a barrier stand?

Being careful not to wake her, Gavin slipped off of the bed, and he dressed himself in the clothes he had shed so eagerly. He listened and could hear the night owls making their usual twilight calls. It was safe for him to leave the cellar. But he could not feed.

Looking back at Chloe, he saw her shift under the blankets. He admired her body, remembering how it had felt in his arms and against his body. The lust of the flesh had somehow merged with his lust for blood, and the desire to take her, both her body and for sustenance, was almost too much to control.

Just one touch from her would set off a chain reaction that he would not be able to stop. He had to distance himself from her somehow, not only for his sake but also for hers. He could not bear the sight of her dead body limp in his arms. Fear gripped his chest while hunger assaulted his core, both battling for a say in what he should do.

Chloe had no dreams during that sleep, only a deep slumber that replenished her strength when she awoke. But even when she opened her eyes, she was still in darkness. The blackness was so complete that she couldn't figure out if her eyes were truly open.

But the one thing she could sense was how empty the bed was. She reached out to the other side, but all she felt were sheets and air. Rolling over, she tried to peer into the darkness, but it was no use. She could see nothing.

"Gavin?" she mumbled, her voice still thick with sleep.

When she heard no reply, she threw her feet over the side of the bed and probed around the floor for her clothes. When she found her phone, she used it to inspect the cellar. But Gavin was nowhere.

Chloe's nerves twisted with disappointment. After everything they had done, she thought Gavin would have stayed by her side until she woke. It would have been the chivalrous thing to do; at least that's what she had always believed.

She began to wonder if their lovemaking had been as wonderful for him as it had been for her. Perhaps it wasn't, and Gavin couldn't stand to be near her for another moment longer. Chloe didn't want to believe it, but her nerves were a little too raw right not to think rationally.

Then, her mind jumped to an entirely different conclusion. What if the hunger had gotten the best of him? Gavin had never gone more than three nights without feeding, and this was his third night.

Chloe quickly got dressed, rushed up the stairs, opened the hatch and climbed out. When she turned to the living room, she saw Gavin sitting on the sofa. She let out a sigh of relief. At least he hadn't left her.

But there was a rigidness about him that alarmed her. He didn't turn to greet her but blankly stared into space with a cold expression as if he were angry or too deep in thought.

Chloe approached slowly as if a sudden move would spook him.

"Gavin? Are you ok?"

He didn't respond. Chloe hugged herself tightly and stopped just at the arm of the sofa, watching him for any sign that he'd heard her. He didn't move; he didn't blink. It was as if he were a statue—cold and lifeless.

"Gavin?" she whispered, terror filling her to unimaginable levels. Silence was the worst thing in the world to her. Silence meant that he was shutting her out and communication was broken somehow. What happened that she wasn't aware of?

Chloe moved to sit down next to him, but Gavin suddenly bolted from the sofa and reappeared by the front door, moving faster than her eyes could travel. And for the first time, he looked at her. She could see the fear there, a real fear that was tearing him apart from the inside out.

She took another step towards him, and Gavin mirrored the move, stepping as far from her as possible.

"What's wrong? What did I do?" she implored.

Gavin shook his head. "You did nothing wrong."

"Then why are you running away from me?"

"I..." he swallowed, "I don't want to hurt you."

Now she understood. Gavin must be struggling with his hunger still, but he wasn't in the mood for squirrels or rabbits tonight. Chloe's hand unconsciously moved to her neck and felt for any puncture wounds. Finding nothing, she was thankful his self-control had held out for this long.

"You wouldn't hurt me," she stated as calmly as she could, almost as if she were trying to convince herself. They had been so close last night, and so much could have happened while she'd slept.

"Then why did you just check your neck?"

Chloe pressed her lips together in shame and bowed her head. "I'm sorry. I–"

"You thought I had done something to you in your sleep."

She looked back at him and shook her head. "No, not really. I... I don't know why I did it."

"Don't lie to me, Chloe. I know when you're lying."

She took a deep breath, knowing that his raised voice was completely normal. Three days into the detox, he was going to be grouchy. Instead of arguing, she said nothing for a long time as the tension built between them. Who would be the first to talk about what had happened in the cellar?

"You think I don't trust you?" she asked, trying to keep the timidity out of her voice.

"I don't trust myself anymore."

She could sense the anguish in his words. "You seemed to do a fine job yesterday."

Gavin's eyes squeezed shut for a moment before answering. "I don't understand what kept me from accidentally killing you. None of that should have happened."

Chloe managed to take a few steps forward without him retreating in turn. "I'm glad it happened."

He shook his head. "I was completely out of line. I wasn't thinking straight."

Chloe closed the gap between them and placed her hand on his cheek. But his skin wasn't nearly was warm as it usually was. Gavin flinched at first then stood still under her touch. His jaw clenched tight, and his eyes closed, as if he were trying to block out something unpleasant. Chloe knew exactly what it was but tried not to be afraid.

"I wanted it, too."

Gavin opened his eyes and revealed them to be the bloodlust color she had seen before. She refused to shy away from those eyes which served as a fair warning that she should back away. Even if she died tonight, she would die with the pleasure of knowing Gavin's love.

"You can't stay here."

"I'm not going anywhere," Chloe contested.

"It's not safe."

"It never has been."

Gavin took her hand in his and pressed it between his palms. "Go to the inn just a few miles down the mountain. Stay there until this detox is all over. I'm begging you."

Chloe shook her head. "I won't leave you. We're going to see this through until the end, no matter what that end is. I have the garlic powder."

"What if it's not enough?"

"It will be enough," she insisted, bringing his hands to her chest. "We will get through this, and I'm going to be by your side every step of the way."

Gavin shook his head. "I won't be responsible for your death."

"We've been through this already, Gavin."

He bowed his head and then looked around the room, knowing that she was perfectly right. They had gone over this so many times already. Yes, it was dangerous. Yes, he could hurt her. But he had enough control to make it through, and she was the only one who could see that somehow.

Then he turned to her and said, "Lock me in the cellar."

"But it's only the third day. You've made it through this far without being locked away. Can't we wait one more day?"

Gavin shook his head again, red eyes following her. "I can't risk it. I can't risk you."

He leaned forward as if he wanted to kiss her but then had second thoughts and pulled back. Chloe wouldn't let him retreat and met his lips with her own, his body stiffening until she released him.

The pure energy that radiated from him was enough to make her a little more hesitant. The wildness in his eyes, and the lust that was ready to consume him, was so evident that it seemed to take on a power of its own.

"If you want to be locked away, I'll trust your judgment." She swallowed the lump in her throat that didn't want to budge. "But I'm not leaving you."

As if in a daze, Gavin finally nodded. "Promise me you will do whatever it takes to keep yourself safe. I don't care if it means killing me."

"I could never kill you, Gavin." Chloe leaned closer and settled her head on his shoulder, their hands still joined between their bodies. She could feel the subtle motions of Gavin's head moving toward and away from her as if in a physical battle with his own temptations.

It broke her heart to know that he was struggling this way. Like an addict coming down from a high, he was reaching the point where he would be inconsolable, nothing more than a raving mess of a man and beast. If only she could talk to someone who had been through this before and had come out of it alive. If only there were some blog or tutorial to guide her on this journey.

She lifted her head and looked him square in the eyes, watching how the red in his irises swirled and seemed to pulsate with his hunger.

"I will lock you away on one condition."

"I don't know if you can afford conditions at this point, Chloe." His breath was wispy and hushed as if any loud noise might make his condition worse.

"I will lock you away if you let me read your manuscripts."

Gavin dropped her hands and backed away, a look of incredulity plastered on his gorgeous face.

Yes, she knew exactly what she was asking for—not only the manuscripts but his unconditional trust. They had exposed themselves to each other just hours ago in the most intimate way that any creatures could. It didn't seem too demanding to want his trust, too.

Whether he believed it or not, she trusted him. Why else would she kiss him when his eyes were warning her to stay away? But would he return the gesture and let her do something that not even Janette had been privileged to do?

Raking his hands through his dark hair, he paced near the base of the stairs. His steps were stuttered and clumsy, so unlike him. The need to feed must have been taking a harsher toll earlier than either of them had expected. He hadn't behaved this way the last time. Had their lovemaking accelerated the effects somehow?

Finally, he waved his hands in defeat. "Fine. You may have them. But I don't want to hear your opinions regarding them."

Chloe smiled very wickedly. "I will tell you what I think of them, whether it's good or not."

Gavin wasn't in the mood to argue and stormed towards the hatch in the kitchen. "Do you have a lock?"

Chloe followed him, not willing to let their last encounter be this brusque and unfeeling. "I think I can take one off of the back door and fix it on. There's no time to go to the hardware store this late at night."

"Good. Do it as soon as you're able."

He opened the hatch and quickly disappeared into the void. While Chloe fished out a screwdriver from one of the kitchen drawers, Gavin returned with his arms full of the manuscripts he so prized. She could tell by the way he clutched them so tightly to his chest that he was still not fully willing to part with them.

She approached him once more, cautiously. When their eyes met, she saw that the crimson hunger had relinquished possession of his eyes, leaving the tender forest green that she loved so much.

Her eyes stung with impending tears as she stared at him, knowing that this would be the last time she saw him for at least four more nights. It really wasn't such a long time, but she had grown accustomed to his presence. Those eyes were always there, watching her, keeping her safe, and reminding her that she was wanted. Now, all she would have were the wonderful memories and the hope that there would be more days to follow.

And she could see that he wasn't thrilled about the arrangement, either. If it were possible, she saw his eyes mist over with tears just as hers were. Or perhaps it was a trick of the light.

Gradually, he loosened his hold on the manuscripts and handed them over to her. Chloe took them into her arms with the utmost care, showing him that his life's work, all three hundred years of it, were in capable hands.

"Whatever happens, whatever you hear, do not open that hatch until the seventh dawn."

She nodded, her throat too tight to speak the loving words that she wanted him to hear.

"Keep garlic in your bedroom. If I manage to break free, that should keep me at bay."

These were all things that she knew and understood. Gavin was simply stalling, waiting until the last possible moment before locking himself away in the dark that he'd lived in for so long.

"Can I ask you one thing?"

"Anything," Chloe managed to choke out.

Gavin stepped closer and reached out to stroke her cheek. "During the night, can you read to me? Or try to speak to me? I may not be able to talk back, but I can hear your voice. Perhaps it will make the next few nights easier."

Yes, easier for him, but not for her. She knew what it was like to have one-way conversations. They weren't at all pleasant for someone who was lonely. But if it would soothe Gavin's hunger, then she would give it a try.

"I can."

Gavin's hand slipped behind her neck and pulled her in for one more kiss to release the tension between them. It reminded Chloe of the love they made and how she wanted more. Every fiber of her being wanted to hold him as she had before and feel his caresses. Her cheeks grew hot as her mind wandered, but he pulled back before she had the chance to unleash her desires. And she could see the desire in his eyes as well.

"Just a few more days," she whispered, hoping he would take it as a promise.

Gavin nodded and slowly backed away to the hatch again, their eyes never deviating from one another. And as he climbed down the ladder and closed the hatch behind him, she felt a tug on her heart. It was so strong and totally unmistakable that she had to keep herself from weeping aloud. She had to be strong for him, for whatever relationship they have or would have when the detox was done.

It might have been silly to miss him already, but Chloe couldn't imagine another moment passing without him close by. Granted, she had thought the same about Brent at one time or another, but never did her heart ache so badly as to have him leave this way.

She couldn't dwell on such hurts now, though. She had a job ahead of her. After setting down the manuscripts on her writing desk, she turned on the coffee pot to brew up a batch of comfort and set herself to finagling a lock latch to keep the beast in the cellar from escaping.

Chapter 23

C hloe rubbed her bloodshot eyes. Staying awake both day and night with only a few hours of sleep was taking a harsher toll on her than she had anticipated. Just two more nights and they were home free.

At sunset each day, Chloe would go to the hatch door and talk to Gavin. Most of the time, she rambled about her book ideas or childhood memories that had taken place in the cabin. That first night that Gavin was locked away was not nearly as bad as she thought it would be. He was still conscious enough to talk back and ask questions to keep himself occupied. But the next night, she was not so lucky. All she could hear below the floor was the muffled pacing of footsteps and grumbles that didn't sound quite human. Since then, her voice had gone unanswered, and Gavin had been completely unreachable.

That is, except for the few hours of sleep she forced herself to have after sunrise each morning. In those hours, Gavin's spirit came to her in dreams that kept her teetering between being asleep and awake. She would see his eyes and hear his voice mumbling incoherent things that she wished she could understand. But they were mere memories. She knew that, but each time she woke in her bed, she was sure that she felt him in the room somehow. The echo of his presence was too strong to be mistaken for anything else.

When she climbed out of bed each morning, she made an extra strong batch of coffee and sat down at her computer to continue the work that Gavin knew nothing about.

Being extra careful to decipher his handwriting, Chloe took each page of his manuscripts and transferred them into a word processor on her laptop. No publisher in their right mind would accept a couple century's worth of notes and rough drafts.

Chloe hadn't told Gavin about her scheme, mainly because she was afraid of his reproaches. She knew that after the detox was done, he would find out and probably be furious with her for going behind his back in this way. But after the book became a bestseller, perhaps he would forgive her.

On the other hand, this might cripple whatever shred of trust he had in her. Chloe understood what a momentous and terrifying thing it must have been for Gavin to give up his manuscripts like that. Then again, maybe it wasn't trust that had made him hand over the papers but his pure desire for her to be safe. It was a comforting thing to know that he valued her more than his own confidence in his work. There was no telling how this betrayal would affect their chances at a future relationship.

Chloe gave a languid sideways glance towards the pile of papers she had yet to copy and sighed; nearly half way through. Hopefully, Gavin would at least appreciate the effort she was putting out for his sake.

Many times during the process, she wondered why she was doing this at all. Gavin had said that he didn't want to submit his work to a publisher, and here she was trying to make it happen anyway.

She understood his apprehensions and fears, but they were only another sign that he was truly passionate about becoming an author. Like he had once told her, if a writer was too prideful, they might as well just give up. To the eyes of the artist, nothing was good enough for the eyes of the public. Only when they fully accepted that fact could they hope to achieve greatness.

And she had total confidence that Gavin would be great. It was evident in his stories. The way he used words was like an art form which put the great literary masters to shame. Her work was nothing in comparison to this piece of gold stacked on her desk.

But Chloe couldn't think about the future just yet. There were too many variables, and if one small thing changed, her entire life would be drastically different. All of it hinged on whether Gavin would survive the detox or not. And it was too soon to tell.

What she needed right now was to get out of the cabin somehow. Over the last few days, she'd taken a break by going down to the creek as she let her tired eyes rest on the beauty of nature that surrounded her. That wasn't going to be enough this time. She hadn't heard another voice beside her own since Gavin's humanity had slipped from him the other night.

Part of her debated about going into town to talk to Miss Rosie, but she would be too tempted to bring up Gavin, and the old woman reminded her too much of the aunt that she'd lost. Her need for human contact had even made her consider taking a trip to the hardware store to talk to Bob, the man who had bought her sedan. Chloe wasn't sure what they would have to talk about, and a conversation with a mere acquaintance would not satisfy her need.

This new level of loneliness made her realize how foolish her decision was to move up to the remote mountains. She wondered, if this all fell through if she could get in touch with the realty company so they could continue leasing the cabin to vacationers. Chloe pressed her fingers against her eyes as she tried to rub out the image of Gavin lying lifeless on the cellar floor.

How had she expected to live like this in the first place? Chloe missed her family and old life back in Atlanta too much. How could she have predicted that this life change would be for the best? Her resolve to be a recluse cracked under the ache in her chest, the yearning for company. Gavin had been there since the first day, and she'd never had to think about being alone until now.

Chloe stood up from her desk and stretched her stiff limbs, willing life and warmth back into them as she hobbled to the kitchen. Glancing out the window, she saw what a nice day it was outside. It was such a nice day that she wanted to share it with Gavin, or anyone at this point.

She sighed and walked aimlessly back into the living room. Picking up her cell phone, she scrolled through her contact lists, searching for any old friends who might still want to talk to her. Surely someone would be open to even a shallow conversation about shoes or the newest fashions. Normally, Chloe despised that kind of talk, but as she had already admitted to herself, she was desperate.

When she reached halfway through the alphabet, she saw her mother's phone number and couldn't hit the dial button fast enough. Chloe sat down on the sofa, anxiously waiting as the other line kept ringing and ringing. She knew that her parents would be headed this way to celebrate Thanksgiving with her. Hopefully, they were in an area that had a signal or weren't too busy sightseeing to chat for a bit.

The call went to her mother's voicemail. Chloe let her mother's automated message drift around her mind, closing her eyes to envision her mother there with her, giving the instructions to leave a message after the tone. She had heard it so many times before, but it sounded so much sweeter and cheerful now than ever before. It had been a long time since she had heard anything so light and happy.

When the tone came, Chloe almost forgot it was her turn to speak.

"Hey mom, it's me," she began. "I just thought I'd call to see how you were. We haven't talked in a while, and a lot has happened that I want to tell you." Chloe paused, quickly weighing the consequences of what she would say next.

"I met a guy in town. He's really great, and I want to tell you all about him. Call me back."

Chloe tapped the red circle and ended her message. Leaving that message did little to soothe her. Now she was even more eager to hear from her mother.

The decision to mention Gavin might have been a mistake. What could she possibly tell her? That he was a vampire now, but in a few days, he might not be? That he ate squirrels at midnight but had gorgeous eyes and a gentle heart?

No, Chloe would have to lie through her teeth and tell her mom everything else about Gavin that her parents would see when they came for the holidays. Chloe didn't like lying to them, but this time, it was an absolute necessity. It wasn't like she was trying to hide a broken vase or bad report card. There was a line she couldn't cross when it came to revealing who Gavin was. As far as they would know, he came from England and aspired to be a writer just like she was.

But then, what if Chloe told her parents all about Gavin and he didn't make it through the detox? What would she tell them when they arrived, hoping to meet their future son-in-law and instead finding a brokenhearted daughter? They were still reeling from the last breakup with Brent.

Chloe held her head in her hands and was a little surprised to feel that her palms were nearly ice cold. Maybe it was all the typing, or the fact that she hadn't turned on the heater since she'd arrived. Fall was in full swing, bitterly cold winds and all. And soon, it would be winter, and there would be snow to shovel. It was hard to imagine the coming seasons without Gavin. She couldn't bear it.

Maybe it was the loneliness playing tricks on her, or the exhaustion that seemed to permeate her bones, but Chloe heard something familiar coming towards the cabin. It was a car engine, revving up the steep incline as the tires ground against the gravel drive. Then, a car door opened and slammed shut.

She stood up and went to the door, needing to see if her senses were fooling her into believing she had a visitor. Maybe it was her parents or Miss Rosie from town. Either way, she was far too excited for words to know that soon, someone would speak to her and chase away the loneliness.

But, when she opened the door, all the over abounding joy gave way to terror. It wasn't her parents or anyone else she wanted to see stepping up onto the porch.

A man, tall and attractive, stood before her, darkening her doorway. The sunlight behind him seemed to make his blonde hair glow, and his hazel eyes were bright and happy to see her. She could not return the expression.

"Hey, Chloe," he greeted. His voice was just as she remembered, though she had never wanted to hear it again.

"What are you doing here, Brent?" she asked, trying to keep her tone level and unoffending.

"I've come to see you and this house you bought."

"I didn't buy it," Chloe corrected, a little bit of venom seeping through. He never liked it when she corrected him. He always said he knew exactly what he was talking about. But at this point, she didn't care what he liked or didn't like.

"Whatever," he replied with a shrug of his shoulders. "I still came to see you."

"How did you know where I was?" Chloe knew for a fact that she hadn't told Brent about her aunt's passing. In fact, she was sure that she had never told him about Aunt Mary Anne at all.

"Cindy told me you moved to Carter Lake, so I went asking around."

Chloe's lips scrunched with disgust. What right did he have to go asking for her around town? Not only would there be rumors all over the place, but he shouldn't have tried to find her in the first place. What would everyone think of her? If he talked to Miss Rosie or Bob at all, what would they think of her now with some strange guy marching into town asking where she was like a stalker?

Then, at the same time, she cursed her old roommate, Cindy, in her mind for leaking such confidential information to her ex-boyfriend. Brent had probably spun some pathetic story to get the truth out of her.

"You're not welcome here. Please leave my property before I call the police."

Realistically, it would take nearly fifteen minutes for any cop cars to make it up the mountain, if they could make it up at all. And by then, Chloe was liable to strangle Brent—or throw him into the cellar.

Brent tossed his head back and gave a huff of a laugh. "Come on, Chloe. I just want to talk. I came all this way from Atlanta to-"

"And you can go all the way back and think about why I'm turning you away now."

His face went cold like it often did when he was about to lose his temper. "The least you could do is tell me why you up and left to move out into the middle of nowhere just to spite me."

Chloe's eyes went wide. "You think I moved out here to spite you?" she cried, remembering how he had always made everything she did into some attack or offense. "My aunt died and left me this house."

He shrugged his shoulders again, his neatly pressed shirt crinkling with the motion. "Couldn't you have sold it or something?"

Chloe waved her hand towards the inside of the cabin. "This is part of my childhood, Brent. I wouldn't just sell it."

Brent made the same gesture, but it was filled with disdain like this piece of her history was nothing more than a pile of garbage. "You never told me about this place. How could it mean so much more to you than Atlanta and all your friends? You know you left all of them behind, too."

Chloe balled her hands into fists, feeling a fireball kindle inside her for her ex's ignorance. "What friends, Brent?" she shrieked. "You know damned well I have none now because of you!"

Brent's pale eyebrows angled downward into a scowl. "I can't believe, after all this time, you're still blaming me for something I didn't do."

"You did do it, Brent! I told you this already. You forced me to stay home with you when I promised to–" Chloe stopped herself, knowing that this argument would lead to nothing.

She threw up her hands in surrender and turned to close the front door. "I'm not getting into this with you. Leave!"

But Brent was too quick and blocked the threshold with his body, keeping her from locking him out. "No, I'm not leaving. And I'm going to set the record straight with you," he said, pointing an accusing finger in her face just like he had done the night she left. "You made a choice to stay home with me. You could have gone."

Chloe batted his hand out of the way. "No, you manipulated me and made me feel that if I left, you'd be all alone without me. You played on my feelings, knowing if you put on that face, I'd feel guilty and stay."

Brent scoffed. "I didn't do anything like that!"

"Yes, you did!" Chloe yelled, knowing that there was no one to disturb on this side of the mountains but the birds and squirrels. "Every time I needed to be somewhere, you gave me those sad eyes and pouted, saying 'Ok, if you have to go, I guess I'll just be here watching the movie by myself'," she mocked.

"Was it wrong of me to want to spend time with you? We're a couple, and that's what couples do."

Chloe couldn't help but laugh and wag a finger at him with the best sassy attitude she could muster. "No, Brent. We're not a couple. Couples build each other up and support one another no matter what. We broke up. I'm not spending any more time with you. I wasted years of my life, catering to you, and I'm done."

She made another attempt to close the door, but Brent's hand smacked the face of the door and held it open.

"When are you going to get it through your thick skull that I love you? I just want to be with you. Is that so wrong?"

Chloe could feel her face turn red with rage. "No, what's wrong is you pinning me against the wall and forcing sex on me when I needed to go to my friend's college graduation!"

"I don't recall you ever saying that you didn't want it."

"I let you take me because I felt like I had to make up for not being there when you wanted me."

"And that was an even trade. What was the problem?"

Her eyes went misty with angry tears. "The problem was that she wouldn't speak to me again after I told her that I missed one of the biggest moments of her life because my boyfriend wanted to do me on the kitchen counter!"

"Then she wasn't a very good friend. She should have understood."

Chloe's jaw dropped in disbelief. After all of this time, he still thought he was in the right. This arrogant and selfish man in front of her was still convinced that she was the offender here.

"Listen, I didn't come to argue." He held up his free hand in petition. "I came here to take you back to Atlanta with me. I just got a promotion and a fat bonus check. I want to take you to Hawaii so we can work things out."

Even now, Brent was trying to steal her away from things she really wanted to do and the place she needed to be. She just told him that her aunt had died and this place held a special place in her heart. There was no way she was going to leave, especially for him.

And she knew exactly what would happen once they got to Hawaii. He'd leave her to go off and do his own thing, ignore her during dinner to stare at some blonde across the room, accuse her of things she didn't do, and then make her feel like all their problems were her fault.

No, not this time. Not ever again.

"I'm not going anywhere with you, Brent." Her voice was oddly calm now but still filled with pure defiance.

"Why not?" he asked, his voice so full of hope. "It's warm in Hawaii this time of year. It'll be great."

Chloe bit her lips together, once more debating whether or not to tell the truth. "I'm with someone, Brent. I'm not leaving him for you."

Brent donned a look of disbelief and shook his head, looking around for some explanation as if he hadn't heard her correctly. "You wasted no time, huh?"

"What's that supposed to mean?" she asked, propping a hand on her hip.

"I never took you for the type to rebound that fast."

Once again, Chloe had to decide on a moment's notice whether or not to tell someone else about Gavin. Brent had no right to know about her personal life and especially about Gavin. But maybe, just maybe, this would be the thing to push him over the edge and show him that he had absolutely no chance with Chloe. Not now, not ever. And Gavin would be the tool she'd use to get him off the mountain and as far away from her as possible.

"Compared to you, he's a god," she began, letting her words float to Brent with sensual inflections as if Gavin were there right now, pleasuring her in a way that Brent never could.

"Oh?" he said, egging her on for more, all the while, murder brewing in his eyes.

"Yes. He's charming and ruggedly handsome. His body is chiseled and strong. Oh, you should see him naked, too," she swooned. "And best of all, he actually cares about me. He has since the first day we met. He believes in my writing and wants me to succeed, whether he is by my side or not. He's twenty times the man you ever were."

Chloe didn't see Brent's hand come soaring her way before it made contact with her face.

"So, you've turned into a slut? I should have gotten more use out of you before you went and screwed everything up."

She covered the deep red mark on her face with her hand as she felt her skin tingle and slightly swell from the impact. Her ears were ringing, but she heard him quite clearly.

Chloe marveled that Brent picked just one thing from her speech rather than listening to the whole. If he had ever loved her, Brent would have respected the fact that she'd found a better man and left. But now, his fragile pride was being attacked, and he couldn't take that.

"I demand you leave, Brent. I'm not going with you, and I never will." All anger left her tone, leaving an even sound devoid of malice or anything else that he could use against her. She had tried that before and it only fed his ego. She had learned in Atlanta to let herself go blank, even when every stubborn nerve in her body told her to rebel against this asshole and everything he had done to her. All she would give him were words. Goading his pride obviously wouldn't work, and she was out of ideas.

"I'm not leaving without you. This new boyfriend can go to hell for all I care."

Brent seized her wrist and began pulling her out of the doorway and down the porch, his fingers bruising her flesh. As thin as he was, he was still able to throw her around. It took a moment for her to realize that she was halfway to his truck before she acted, thrashing against him violently.

She screamed and scratched at him like a wild animal, the heels of her slippers digging into the dusty gravel beneath her feet. All the while, Brent kept grumbling threats against her and her new lover, practically ignoring the fact that she was fighting him the whole way.

When Chloe realized she was at the passenger side door, she opened her mouth and chomped down as hard as she could on the hand that gripped her wrist. She felt the skin give way and her teeth sink in. The iron flavor of blood grazed over her tongue as Brent hollered out more obscenities.

His hold loosened just a bit, and she was able to break free. With all the clumsiness and gracelessness that was typical of her, Chloe scrambled back up the driveway to the porch, panting and whimpering the whole way.

She faintly heard Brent trying to charge after her, but somehow, she managed to get back into the cabin and shut the door before he had a chance to get to the porch. Her trembling fingers worked the numerous locks, and Chloe was thankful for the precautions she had taken in her first few days at the cabin.

Backing away, she heard Brent banging his fists on the door as he ordered her to let him in. With heart racing and mind frantic, she tried to come up with a plan.

Going out the back door would solve nothing. He would find his way around soon enough. Upstairs was a dead-end street if he broke down the door, and she knew that he would. Brent may not be strong, but when he wanted something, he found a way to get it.

If she couldn't go out, and she couldn't go up, the only other way was down. Chloe rushed towards the hatch door in the kitchen and stared at the padlock for a moment.

Was it worth it? Would she be safe?

Chloe heard the wood on the front door crack, and she didn't have to think twice. She snatched the padlock key from the kitchen counter and quickly let herself down into the cellar.

She waited on the ladder, trying to calm her breathing, holding it if necessary. Not a single sound came from the darkness around her. All she could hear was her thrumming heartbeat and the commotion that Brent was making above her.

He shouted at her, and then the front door came crashing down. She flinched as she listened to him shout and scream, turning over furniture, and tearing up her home. Her thoughts went to her laptop and Gavin's manuscripts. Their futures, their lives' work was on that desk.

She could stand Brent's insults, his abusive, controlling personality; she could even take Gavin staring at her with his hungry vampire eyes. But she couldn't stand the thought of losing everything they had worked so hard for.

Chloe leaned her head against one of the rungs on the ladder and tried not to cry, listening for the crunch of metal or shredding of paper. Brent's heavy footsteps trailed up the stairs, and some of his rampage was muffled by the distance.

Slowly, she lowered herself down the ladder and sat against one of the walls, drawing her knees to her chest and trying desperately not to panic.

She wasn't terrified by the fact that she was in a dark cellar with a sleeping vampire that hadn't eaten in days. No, she felt that she was far safer with Gavin than the monster that was tearing his way through her cabin right now.

Brent's words echoed in her mind about how it was her own fault for losing her friends in Atlanta. He had a point that it had ultimately been her decision to stay with Brent when she'd needed to be somewhere else. She could have had a backbone and turned him down.

But she knew for a fact that it wasn't her fault that he'd hit her. That was his choice, and a man who made those kinds of choices had no business being in her life. She would never regret her decision to leave him behind in Atlanta. She just wished that he wasn't a few feet away, tramping around upstairs in her home.

Chapter 24

Gavin woke from his comatose sleep, and with his consciousness came the agonizing pain. It was the same pain he had endured before, but each night was worse than the one before. His bones were on fire; his flesh tingled and was sensitive to every little touch. His brain and organs felt as if they would explode, especially his stomach. And throughout his parched veins was a throbbing ache that often came with the hunger that had plagued him for the last three centuries.

His senses were attuned in a way they had never been before. But each sound, each overpowering scent was an assault on his mind and body. The darkness used to be his sanctuary, but now it had become his prison, locking him away from the very thing that could relieve his suffering. And he wasn't thinking about blood. He wanted Chloe.

Nothing else brought him relief in this time of suffering except the sound of her voice, her strong heartbeat, the sound of her blood rushing through her body. Everything told him that she was alive, and he took heart in that fact. As long as Chloe was alive, there was hope for an end to this.

Gavin had often wondered, while he waited for her to come to the hatch and talk to him like she usually did in the twilight hours, if she had left him or abandoned what relationship they could have when this was all over. But as soon as her melodic words drifted down through the cracks in the hatch door, he felt the pain lessen, if only a little.

Letting Chloe take the manuscripts was perhaps the second hardest thing he had ever had to do, rivaled only by the decision to go through this detox. He felt naked and exposed without his life's work as if a piece of him was missing and in the hands of someone else.

He didn't fully trust Chloe with his work, but it was the only way to pacify her the night after they'd made love. He wanted her safe, and if that meant having to feel this momentary hollowness in his soul, then he would rather be in this cellar for decades.

On this evening, even before he opened his eyes, he knew that something was not right. Too many smells and too much tension stirred in the cabin above. He only heard one heartbeat, and it was closer than it had been on the previous nights.

His keen nose first singled out Chloe, her sweet magnolia-scented body wash was unmistakable amongst the other odors. But then he picked up another. It was more of an echo, a shadow of a scent that was stale and only a few hours old, but it was all over the cabin above him and the property outside.

It was a terrible scent. Car fumes, city smog, and a twinge of alcohol made up the bulk of it, and it was all covered by a veil of expensive cologne that reeked of unnatural chemicals. It burned his nose and made his eyes water.

He tried to ignore the stench and focused on why Chloe seemed so near. She seemed much nearer than even if she were lying on the hatch door, and it scared him.

When Gavin opened his eyes and pushed himself up from the mattress, he was shocked to see Chloe sitting there against the far wall near the ladder. He examined her figure hunched over her propped up knees, asleep and peaceful where she was.

Joy and fear mingled in his heart at seeing her there. The sight of her and her beautiful face, motionless in sleep, was a bright spot in the darkness of this horrible detox.

But the reason for his fears became all too apparent when the scent of fresh blood reached his senses. No, Chloe wasn't bleeding, but with his olfactory senses exponentially amplified by his hunger, Gavin sniffed the air and smelled her blood in her veins.

The monster in him came alive; the starving beast they needed to kill came out in full force like a dark storm cloud over his mind. It took only seconds for Gavin to lose himself completely to the thirst.

He tried to fight it, to rebel against the nature of this disease that had tormented him for centuries. But it was no use. The hunger was too strong, and his body far too weak to resist anymore. It had been many nights since he'd had a meal, and the vampire in him would not settle for passing one up now.

"Chloe."

The voice snapped Chloe awake after spending hours down in the cellar. Her neck and back were stiff from being bent over her knees when she fell asleep. The last thing she remembered was Brent still rummaging around upstairs, looking for her and probably her purse.

She was sure there would be a chaotic mess to clean up after her ex-boyfriend finished tearing up the cabin. From the silence above her, she knew that Brent was gone now. But how long had she been hiding?

"Chloe," the voice said again.

She looked in the direction of Gavin's voice but couldn't see him in the complete darkness that surrounded them. There was no movement, no breathing except for her own, but she knew that he was there.

Gavin's voice sounded so strange and yet oddly pleasant. The last time they had talked, his voice had been strained by the hunger and the struggle for control. But the way he said her name now reminded her so much of when he was fully fed and contented.

As she slowly rose to her feet, she hoped that, against all odds, they were over the worst. Gavin himself said that he had never made it this far in the detox and wasn't sure how he would react. Perhaps, just like hunger in humans, after a certain time, he just became numb to the urge.

"Gavin? Are you ok?" she asked, her heart banging loudly in her chest. And she knew that he could hear it pumping away, skittering around like a jackrabbit while she tried to remain calm.

"Yes, I'm perfectly fine. Come closer."

Chloe caught something in his words that didn't seem right—a quiver that she couldn't quite describe or explain. Was it the hunger, or joy that she was close by?

But she would take no chances and took a step back. That's all she managed before a feeling came over her that was all too familiar. It was the same mystic pull that had held her in place when she had been under Terrance's control in the woods.

All of a sudden, Chloe couldn't move, not even blink. Her body was not her own anymore. This wasn't Gavin. This was the monster that possessed his body. Gavin would never have used his powers against her.

And then she saw them—two tiny stars in the darkness gliding toward her without a sound. Gavin's eyes, she was sure. Or his fangs. But where the light source came from that reflected off his eyes or teeth, she didn't know. All she knew was that he was coming closer, and there was no way to escape this hungry vampire.

"Gavin, snap out of it," she whispered, fear stealing her voice.

He didn't respond, and the diamonds in the dark were upon her now, and she could feel his body so close to hers. Even now, she held onto the hope that this was a farce, a joke, or that this was only a momentary rash of insanity that he would snap out of soon before he did something that he would regret for the rest of eternity.

"Gavin, please! Don't do this."

His hands reached out and wrapped around her arms just below her shoulders, his fingers shaking as they squeezed her flesh. It was only then that she knew he was fighting the hunger. If she just kept going, kept reminding him of who she was and what they wanted.

"Gavin, I know you can hear me. Remember when we kissed. Remember when we made love. Remember what you promised me. I love you, Gavin. Remember!"

His physic hold over her body began to weaken, whether from the toll that hunger was taking on his body or her persuasive words. With much effort, Chloe reached out, and her hand met his cheek, just under one of the diamonds that seemed to twinkle back at her.

"Think of the sun. Think of how fun it will be to sit by the creek. I promise we'll go on a picnic as soon as you're free of this. Won't that be fun?"

Gavin shivered under her caress. He was getting distracted, and that's just what she wanted. His skin felt cold and damp with perspiration. Was it possible that the hunger was making him ill? Or was this the human part of him fighting off the vampire disease?

"But we just need a few more days. You can last that long. I believe in you. I love you, Gavin."

The two diamonds disappeared and she could hear him shudder and tear away from her just before he let out a cry of anguish that sounded inhuman. Chloe thought she made out his plea for her to run, but she wasn't about to sit around and ask him to repeat that.

She hurried toward where she thought the ladder was, stumbling in the dark while Gavin turned over his writing desk. The crunch of ancient wood made her cringe, thinking of such a beautiful piece of furniture being destroyed like that.

Her hands touched wood and clutched the rungs. Chloe frantically crawled up the ladder and opened the hatch. The amber light of sunset flooded the cabin and beamed down around her, providing sanctuary against the raging vampire in the cellar. By the vicious hisses behind her, she guessed that the rays must have singed Gavin, but only a little.

Chloe didn't even glance behind her when she threw the hatch down. Her hands, alive with fear and urgency, grabbed for the padlock and latched it just in time before Gavin charged the trapdoor, nearly bucking her off.

She scrambled away to the kitchen cabinets and leaned against them, watching the hatch door rattle and jump with his efforts to escape. Obviously, the beast inside him wasn't thinking about the sunlight that had just burned him seconds before.

Placing a hand over her racing heart, Chloe waited until Gavin quieted and slunk back down the ladder. She could still hear him pacing like a hungry lion trapped in a cage. Her face broke out in a cold sweat when she thought of how close she had come to death.

No, they weren't out of the woods yet. Not by a long shot.

All the doubts she might have had that he loved her were killed in that moment. If he didn't truly love her, he wouldn't have fought himself as hard as he had.

Chloe almost wanted to believe that she was just a convenient companion, a replacement for the wife that he'd lost so long ago. But she was so much more. She was the woman who he was willing to risk everything for, even his life, for the chance to grow old with her. Even when a monster lurked just beneath his skin, he fought it back to keep her safe and refused to give in. He was so much stronger than she could have ever imagined.

It took her a moment to calm down enough to take in her surroundings.

Brent had trashed the cabin, but his truck wasn't out in the drive anymore.

The sofa was tipped on its front, and the cushions spilled out over the fireplace hearth. The kitchen was a veritable catastrophe with broken mugs and dishes scattered across the floor. And just as she'd feared, so were Gavin's manuscript pages. From her vantage point, they all appeared to be intact and not ripped to shreds by Brent's rampage. She was thankful that she had numbered the pages on that first night. Her computer was on the floor but was also in one piece.

She reached up and used the edge of the counter to lift herself to her shaking feet, her system still in shock after facing Gavin and death itself. Funny how many times she had come so close to dying since she'd met Gavin, and it wasn't getting easier.

Retrieving the broom and dustpan from the utility closet under the stairs, she swept up the broken pieces of glass and ceramic. It was then that she realized her clothes were filthy. Crouching down on the dusty floor of the cellar and being dragged down the gravel drive had left her slippers and pajamas covered with a thin layer of dirt.

But Chloe didn't care. There was too much to set right, and there was too much upstairs that she didn't want to look at just yet. She was sure fragments of clothing would be everywhere, and she didn't even want to think about her books. Thankfully, she kept her prize copy of Jane Austen stashed away where no one would find it. It was hard to weigh what would be the worst tragedy: her book torn to bits, or her laptop destroyed beyond repair.

Setting her mind to cleaning would take her focus off of her brush with death and the disaster that Brent had left in his wake. With luck, this was the last she would see of him. And if she did ever see him again, Gavin would put him in his place.

After struggling with the sofa, she managed to get it turned back right side up and the cushions back in place. As she stooped down to gather together the manuscript pages, she heard her phone go off.

It was her mother's ringtone.

Chloe rushed around, following the sound of her phone and pleading for it to keep ringing so she wouldn't miss the chance to talk to her mother.

She found it underneath a small pile of parchment pages and quickly tapped the green button.

"Mom?" she answered a little too frenziedly,

"Hey, baby!" her mother replied cheerfully, her voice full of the motherly love she had missed. "Is everything ok?"

Of course, her mom would notice her tone immediately. Chloe took a deep, muted breath and nodded even though her mother couldn't see. "Yes, I'm alright. How are you and dad doing?" she asked.

While her mother prattled on about the few trips they had taken in the past week or so while Chloe had been disconnected from the world, Chloe glanced around at the chaos and realized she couldn't talk to her mom while the place was a mess.

Still listening to her mom, she slipped on her boots and stepped out the backdoor. The evening air was chillier than she expected, but she wasn't sure if she had any jackets in good enough shape to put on yet. The upstairs remained unexplored.

Chloe leaned her arms against the porch railing and gazed out over the woods, letting her mother's rambling take her far away from the cabin. It was good to hear her mother so happy, so carefree. It was a state so different from how she felt right now. All her life consisted of was panic, fear, unexplainable passions, and an out-of-reach hope for a future that wasn't set in stone yet. All she knew was that she was in love.

"But enough about me," her mother finally said. "Who's this man you met?"

Chloe had almost forgotten that she had told her mother about Gavin. Under any other circumstances, she would have been willing to rattle on for hours about her handsome vampire lover. But in her current state of mind, she wasn't so sure she could form the right words.

"His name's Gavin," she began, hoping that her mother would simply ask questions that she could answer rather than have to come up with things to say. She also hoped that her mom would not make the connection between her Gavin and the Gavin that her aunt had raved about years ago. If anyone asked, it was a coincidence.

"That's a nice name. What does he do?"

Of course, her mother would be concerned with how her boyfriend made a living. It was only natural. Chloe paused to think of an excuse. "He's a... a writer."

"Oh, really? That's nice. Maybe he can get you in touch with some publishers."

Chloe rubbed her cheek and realized how tired she really was. "He's not published just yet. But he will be. He's going to be submitting his manuscript in the next week or so. We're just working on the finishing touches."

"Oh, you're both working on the book?"

Chloe shifted weight from one foot to the other. "Well, kind of. I'm doing some editing work for him."

"And what's he doing?"

Chloe bit her lip and searched her exhausted mind for a viable answer. "Well...Nothing right now. He's recovering from a... a bad fall."

It was all she could think of.

"Oh, the poor thing. Is he alright?"

"Yes, he's ok. He'll be up and about in a few days. I'm taking care of him in the meantime."

Her mother took a deep breath. "So, you're editing his book and nursing him back to health?" Chloe agreed. "But how is your novel coming?"

"Uh... Well, I haven't had a lot of time to work on it lately. A lot has been going on."

Her mother grumbled the way she always did before she was about to give her blunt, honest opinion about something she disagreed with. "Chloe, I know you must like this guy a lot for you to drop your own novel to help him out, but I can't help but wonder if this guy is going to be just another Brent."

Chloe leaned her forehead against her arm and sighed. "He's nothing like Brent, mom. Brent never helped me with anything in my life. Before Gavin had his fall, he was helping me with my novel, too. I was having problems writing the male's part, and he gave me the input I needed."

Her mother was quiet for a few beats, probably unsure of how to respond to her daughter's comeback. Chloe understood why her mother would think that way about Gavin, but she was totally wrong in every way.

Gavin would never have trashed the cabin the way Brent did. Then she remembered how he'd turned over the writing desk in the cellar during his fit of rage against himself.

But Gavin would never hurt her like Brent had. Except he almost did. He almost did worse.

Chloe gritted her teeth in frustration. No, Gavin was not like Brent. They were completely different men, and she had far more in common with Gavin than she'd ever had with Brent.

But, there was a nagging voice in the back of her mind that whispered lies to her, telling her that she was making the same mistake again. It was only a matter of time before Gavin turned out to be just like Brent. He would prize and value her so highly that he would want to be the only one to spend time with her.

What would happen when Gavin became human and they got married? Gavin might not be comfortable around other people, and if Chloe wanted to go to town to visit people like Miss Rosie, maybe he would keep her from going by bribing her with working on their newest novel to trap her in the house. What if he became just as manipulative and controlling as Brent? What if he hit her the same way Brent had when she'd tried to leave?

Tears stung her eyes, and she lifted her head.

"Mom, Gavin is the most wonderful thing to happen to me. He cares about me. He appreciates me. He's talked about how he's willing to do just about anything to keep me safe and happy. We've had beautiful moments together that terrified me and thrilled me all at the same time. I've never known anyone like him, and I'm sure I'll never meet anyone nearly as good as he is."

Normally, she would never talk to her mother in such intimate detail about her boyfriends, but Chloe wasn't only trying to convince her mother of Gavin's trustworthiness. She was also trying to remind herself why she was going through all of this trouble for a man she had only met a few weeks ago.

There was so much more that she could tell her mom. Like how Gavin was so beautiful in his brokenness but determined to heal her own hurts; and how he had a conscience and a sense of chivalry. Gavin was smart, funny, and sensitive. He had a bigger heart than anyone she knew, even if it wasn't beating yet.

She heard her mother stir on the other end of the line as a long silence filled the air between them.

Then she said, "I'm glad you've found someone who makes you happy, Chloe. Will we get to meet him over Thanksgiving?"

That was only a few days away.

Chloe knew better than to believe that this was her mother admitting defeat just yet. She wouldn't release her doubts until she'd met Gavin in person, and that was something Chloe couldn't guarantee. If Gavin didn't make it, what would she tell her parents then?

"Yes. Absolutely."

"That's wonderful. I can't wait."

The rest of the phone call went as it usually did, with her mother talking about plans and trips in the future, as well as little frustrations with their RV and her father's bad habit of not asking for directions. It was the little things that Chloe missed so much. She wanted anything that would keep her mind off of what was to come during the next few days.

After their phone call ended, Chloe looked down at her phone and saw nearly a dozen missed calls, voicemails and text messages, all from Brent. She erased her phone log and read through each text. Some of them were accusatory remarks towards Chloe and her new lover. Others were threats upon her life or new home. A few were sweetly worded apologies for the nastier of the voicemails he left for her to listen to. And the final one was a brief notice that he was back in Atlanta and would not bother her again.

Chloe didn't bother listening to the voicemails. She knew exactly what they all said and she didn't want to be barraged with insults and threats. She had enough to worry about and once she cleaned up the cabin, she wanted no more reminders of Brent's sudden invasion into her life. He said he would move on, and so would she.

Chapter 25

G lancing at the clock, Chloe knew the time had come. The golden light of dawn was just sifting through the trees outside as the sun made its descent over the mountain to fall on the cabin. But the kitchen was still dim.

Chloe had been preparing her eyes for the job by walking around in almost total darkness on this last night of the detox. She needed her sight in peak condition when she climbed down the stairs into the cellar. A small lantern sat on the floor just by the hatch door that she would use, but it would only allow for a small amount of light, and that's the way she wanted it. There was no reason to wake Gavin before it was time.

Standing there with the bottle of vinegar in one hand and a bag of garlic powder in the other, Chloe tried to calm her nerves. She had prepared for this moment for days, practicing her efficiency at pouring the vinegar and making the garlic bombs they had discussed. But nothing could emotionally prepare her for what she had to do.

She felt like a wound-up spring inside, twisted and tense but unwilling to release. Her arms and fingers refused to still themselves, and she began to doubt her ability to use them. What if she dropped the vinegar? What if she threw the garlic bomb in a hasty moment and missed completely? One small mistake would lead to their deaths.

When Gavin awoke, there would be no do-overs. Yes, she could run back upstairs and hide, but how much of a time window did they have before he died from starvation?

And then the bigger questions remained: What if this didn't work? What if the vinegar killed him instead of cure him? What if it only intensified the hunger and he wasn't able to control himself? What if he killed her?

Chloe gripped the neck of the vinegar bottle a little tighter as her sweaty palm slipped over the smooth glass, but she still managed to keep a good hold on it.

Time was passing all too slowly, the minutes seeming like hours. She looked at the clock once more and knew that she couldn't delay this any longer.

Stuffing the vinegar bottle under her arm, she picked up the lantern and unfastened the lock on the hatch. She opened it and listened for any grunting or predatory pacing in the cellar. Nothing.

Taking a stealing breath, she climbed down the ladder and flipped on the electric lantern. A dim, blue light illuminated the cellar. At first, all she saw from her place at the bottom of the ladder were fragments of dismantled furniture, scattered in chips across the floor along with what appeared to be ripped up fabric, cotton stuffing, and mattress springs.

Steadying herself, she scanned the rest of the room. All the exquisite furniture that she had loved so much had been destroyed in Gavin's animalistic fury the other night. The pieces of what might have been a trunk were also thrown helter-skelter across the cellar along with articles of men's clothing.

When her lantern light fell on the far side of the room, she found Gavin sleeping. He was propped up in the corner, his head leaning against the wall.

Chloe let out an involuntary gasp when she saw how haggard his face appeared. Deep, dark circles hung under his eyes that seemed to reach halfway down his cheeks. His skin, if it were even possible, was paler than before, almost ghost-white and sheer to the point that she could see blue veins beneath his skin. His hair, once a dark shade, now appeared gray and aged from the stress of the detox, the follicles thinning and damaged. If a doctor could have evaluated his condition, he might have declared Gavin borderline emaciated and severely malnourished.

Chloe swallowed and set the lantern down on the floor before slowly creeping her way towards the vampire. She took the vinegar bottle and shakily began to unscrew the cap, all the while keeping a vigilant eye on Gavin.

She was no more than a few feet away when she saw his eyelids flutter and twitch. With the garlic powder ball in hand, she froze and watched him, her every muscle bunched and ready for a fight if it came to that, though she wouldn't throw the garlic unless it was absolutely necessary.

But Gavin didn't attack. Not exactly. He opened his bloodshot eyes, his pupils dilated to their fullest. They rolled around in his head unable to focus on anything just yet. His parched and cracked lips parted ever so slightly. His head rolled against the wall until he was able to face Chloe.

She stiffened and watched as his eyes fixed on hers. Her lungs seized, and she tried to breathe again but couldn't. She didn't think this was his mesmerism powers. If it was, she wouldn't have been able to lift her fist that held the garlic.

No, this was the feeling of her heart breaking over Gavin's distressing condition. She couldn't stand to see him like this.

His chin lifted a bit, and his tongue darted out between his lips as if pleading her for a drink. Of what, she couldn't tell. But by the way his body lay limp on the floor, Chloe knew that he was too weak and exhausted to move.

She took another step, and Gavin didn't react. Her feet moved slowly across the floor, narrowing the gap between them. All the while, Gavin only stared up at her with wide eyes, wordlessly beseeching her for relief.

When she was within arm's reach, she noticed something strange.

He was breathing. His chest rose and fell with shallow breaths, a sign that life was returning to this corpse whose heart hadn't beat and lungs hadn't filled with air in centuries.

Chloe wanted to grin and jump for joy that this detox was actually working. But they weren't out of the storm yet. There was still one last thing to do.

She began to mumble a short prayer, a supplication to God that this would all end well and that Gavin would gain his humanity back. Just before she whispered an 'amen', Gavin's hand shot out and grabbed her ankle.

Despite herself, Chloe let out a short shriek and jerked backward. The garlic powder bomb fell from her hand and landed halfway across the cellar. Chloe lost her balance and fell to the floor. Some of the vinegar shot into the air and spilled onto the floorboards, filling the air with its pungent scent.

But Gavin did nothing. His fingers, still wrapped around her ankle, were feeble, and Chloe was able to easily kick her way out of his grip.

Her bosom heaved with each breath as she watched him sit in the corner, his eyes fixated on her, but there was no sign of hunger or malice. The monster within him that thirsted for blood was too weak. When the host's body failed, so would the parasite.

Chloe waited a long moment, their gazes locked. Then she glanced down at the bottle of vinegar. There was only a small amount left in the bottom after that fall. But it would have to be enough.

She crawled forward on her hands and knees and sat beside Gavin. His mouth opened, fangs bared for her to see. They were nearly as white as his skin and glistened in the lantern light. She wondered how Gavin was aware enough to know what she needed from him without having to ask.

With a shaky hand, Chloe raised the bottle and tipped it down so the vinegar would pour into his mouth. The liquid gushed from the rim and rolled over his tongue.

At first, all he did was wince and shudder, probably at the unsavory taste. Once the bottle was empty, Chloe sat back and waited, her heart thumping so hard behind her ribs that it hurt.

Gavin closed his mouth and his eyes, seeming to be waiting as well.

Then, the stillness between them was shattered as Gavin cried out. It was breathy at first and then grew louder and shriller like a banshee. Chloe scuttled away and covered her ears against the screech after dropping the empty vinegar bottle.

Gavin's limbs convulsed, and his head thrashed above his shoulders, his skull bashing against the cellar walls, but that pain must have been nothing compared to what he felt everywhere else.

Like a scene from a horror movie, Chloe watched Gavin's body writhe in agony as the vinegar worked its way through his system. Tears spilled from her eyes, knowing there was nothing she could do to ease his pain.

It must have been only minutes on the clock as his body shuddered in constant seizures, but it felt like much longer. As Chloe watched, she began to see a change.

Gavin was no longer just screaming but gasping for air, his lungs coming to life again. His body mass slowly returned; his arms and core filling out with the muscle and flesh that he'd lost during the detox. The dark shadows on his face faded away, and even in the bluish light of her lantern, she could see some color return to his cheeks. He was no longer pale like a vampire but richly tanned like the blacksmith and fur trader he'd been when he was human.

His eyes opened, and she could see the color of his irises beam through the darkness. His pupils were mere tiny dots in the center of his eyes. It was hard to see precisely because of his thrashing about, but Chloe could swear she saw the fangs begin to recede into his gums.

But the worst was yet to come. Gavin's arm reached out to her, his fingers bent into gnarled angles, and she could hear the joints crack.

"Chloe!" he called out, his voice hoarse through the screams.

She stifled the whimper that rose in her throat but wouldn't move towards him. Yes, the detox was almost complete, but she dared not get too close.

Instead, she clasped his hand in hers and held on tight. His fingers closed over hers, but his strength was sporadic, at once so tight that it bruised her, and then almost so loose that it fell from her grasp.

Soon, the screams became wheezes. Out of Gavin's mouth came gurgling sounds like he was choking or about to vomit. Black liquid, as thick and putrid as stale blood, spilled over his lips and down his chin to stain the front of his shirt.

Chloe gasped and covered her mouth and nose against the smell of death coming out of Gavin. After a few seconds of listening to him choke on the vile substance, Chloe couldn't take any more.

She grabbed him by the collar and pulled him down so his head was bent low. The liquid poured out faster and into a puddle on the floor beside them, seeping into their clothes and between the cracks in the floorboards.

Gavin coughed and sputtered until there was nothing more to eject from his system. Chloe reached out and tried to wipe his chin but pulled away when he fell forward onto the floor, curling up to shiver and continue his seizures.

This time, though, there were no more screams, only raspy breaths and wheezes, his eyes wide open but unfocused. Chloe bent down low beside him and rubbed his back, thinking it would somehow ease his suffering that was coming to an end. The evil had been expelled from his body. All that seemed left were the aftershocks of his transformation.

Examining him one last time, she found him to look completely human. But there was still one last test.

Chloe stood up and hurried to the ladder. The sun would be up by now and the cabin full of pure sunlight. With her heart full of both joy and dread, she threw open the hatch and let the light pour in, chasing away the darkness and the centuries of living in agony.

The light fell across the floor and made its way to Gavin's face. For the first time, Chloe saw his eyes reflect the sunlight he had so longed to see again.

But instead of smiling and basking in the glow of the morning, Gavin let out one last scream.

Chapter 26

C hloe sat back at her desk and stared at the final page of her manuscript. Months of work were finally at an end, and it was a blissful relief. Her first novel was finished and ready for the first round of edits. She knew that the worst was still to come, but at least it was all out of her and on the paper.

"Everything all right?" he called from the kitchen.

"I just finished," she proclaimed with a satisfied air.

His heavy, rather loud footsteps came bounding in from the kitchen area, and Chloe looked over to see him wiping his hands on a rag.

Gavin was just finishing up the dishes from preparing their picnic lunch.

He smiled his usual toothy grin and came up behind her chair to examine the page. His forest-green eyes skimmed over the paragraphs, and he nodded his approval.

"Very nice. I was wondering if you were going to change the ending," he remarked, his British accent rolling melodiously off his tongue.

Chloe shrugged nonchalantly. "I just thought this was a better way to wrap up their story."

Gavin's wonderful masculine scent filled her nostrils as he bent down and kissed her cheek affectionately. "I'm glad. Are you ready to go out to the creek?" he asked, resting his hands on her shoulders.

"Absolutely. Just let me get my coat."

Despite the warmth of the sun beaming down outside, it was still quite chilly. When Chloe turned in her seat, she looked up to regard Gavin as he walked back into the kitchen to pack their picnic bundle. She watched as his hands deftly folded the thick blanket and set it on the kitchen counter beside their basket.

Even now, after all of the changes they had been through, he was still as handsome as he was when they first met. And even though it might be too soon to tell, her fears of Gavin becoming another Brent was a thing of the past. Everything was in the past, and all that awaited them was a bright future—bright as the day.

It took Gavin turning back to her and catching her stare to make her realize she hadn't even moved to get her jacket.

"Are you well?" he asked.

She nodded and stood to go to the coat closet. "Yeah, I'm fine. Sorry."

"That's the third time I've caught you staring like that in the last week. Are you quite sure?"

Chloe giggled and slipped her arms into the sleeves. "Yes, Gavin, I'm just fine."

Once they'd gathered their lunch and blanket, they stepped out the back door and onto the porch.

"I don't know why I let you drag me outside into the cold every single day for lunch," she told him as they walked down the steps. "You know, it's going to snow soon. What will we do then?"

Gavin grinned and tilted his head to the sun. "Then we will have to don our thicker coats and bring a shovel to make a path to the creek."

"And what if the creek is frozen over, genius?" she laughed.

"We don't take these picnics for the creek."

Yes, Chloe knew that quite well. Every day, rain or shine, they went to have their lunches outside in the middle of the daytime. Gavin hated the night and often went to bed as soon as the sun dipped below the tree line, only rising with the crack of dawn. He had told her once that he never wanted to see the stars or moon again unless they were sparkling in her eyes.

Chloe followed Gavin to the creek, both of them being careful not to slip on the dead autumn leaves that practically covered the hillside by the cabin. The creek was not yet frozen over, but she knew it was only a matter of time. And Gavin hadn't experienced a human winter in a long time. His resolve to go to the creek, even in the dead of winter with three feet of snow on the ground, would crumble when his fingers went numb.

He spread the blanket, and they sat down together as they did every day. And just like every day, Chloe unpacked their lunch while Gavin gazed across the creek. She knew exactly what he was doing.

He was watching how the light danced on the water and through the thick canopy of trees above. The look of fascination in his eyes was the same look that Chloe had the first time she had come back to the cabin after having been away for years. He had been here a thousand, maybe a million times before, but never had he been able to witness this place in the splendor of day.

"Isn't it glorious?" he whispered in amazement.

Chloe admired his childlike wonder and did not scold him for it. To see his gorgeous face, tanned and bathed in the glow of sunlight was enough for her. He was happy, and that's all that mattered.

"Yes, it is."

She leaned against his shoulder, holding their turkey sandwiches in her hands and offered one to him. Gavin tore his eyes away long enough to eagerly take the sandwich and chomp down into the bread.

Chloe had seen Gavin eat so much lately, but she would never shake the mental image of him feeding on a squirrel or bird instead of a sandwich or salad.

"Better than blood?" she teased him.

He rolled his eyes, having heard this question far too many times. It was becoming quite an old joke for him, but not for her. "Yes, Chloe. Much better than blood."

She giggled and bumped her shoulder playfully into his ribs.

A few moments passed in quiet reflection, both of them admiring the lovely late autumn afternoon when Chloe's phone vibrated in her pocket.

"I thought you left your phone at the cabin?" Gavin asked as she wrestled it out of her jeans.

"I wanted to keep it close in case mom called to say they were getting close to Carter Lake. They're coming to visit again."

When Chloe's parents came to celebrate Thanksgiving, she wasn't sure what to expect of their reaction to Gavin, especially since it would be his first interaction with other humans besides herself and Aunt Mary Anne. They absolutely loved him and planned to come for a longer stay around Christmas time.

But when she checked the caller ID, she saw it was not her mother who was calling. It was a number she didn't recognize. Normally, she would reject the call, but this was not the usual time. She was expecting an unknown caller ever since the day she'd snuck a copy of Gavin's manuscript in the mail to a publisher in Atlanta.

After the detox and the time it had taken Gavin to adjust to being human again, Chloe admitted to him about copying down his whole manuscript. At first, he was rather perturbed by her deceit. But after she told him how much she loved his story, he changed his tune a bit, and they came to a mutual agreement to make the best effort to get it published. Chloe knew these things would take time, but no one had sent back a rejection letter yet, so there was a good chance this was the call they were waiting for.

She pressed the green button and answered.

"Hello, I'm trying to reach Gavin Caras." a man's voice said on the other end of the line.

Chloe threw a sideways glance at Gavin and nodded. "Yes, he's right here. One second." She pulled back the phone and pressed the speaker button so she could hear what the man had to say.

"Hello?" Gavin said after Chloe's mute promptings. He had never talked on a phone before.

"Yes, is this Gavin Caras?"

"Yes, it is."

"Hi. My name is Alex Henderson, and I'm with Sunshine Publishers. I just wanted to give you a call and let you know that we read your manuscript and thought it was absolutely amazing."

Chloe wiggled happily in her seat and opened her mouth in a soundless squeal while Gavin smiled widely, the widest she had ever seen drawn across his face.

"The style was refreshingly classic and so mature. My boss hasn't seen that kind of writing in years, and he loved it immediately. We're working up the details now, but we will be in touch in a few days to go over them with you if that's okay."

It took a moment for Gavin to get over his speechlessness before he replied, "Yes, that will be perfectly fine. I'll be awaiting your call."

After a few parting words, Chloe ended the call and embraced Gavin.

"You did it, Gavin!" she exclaimed.

Gavin still couldn't speak but pulled back and kissed her sensuously on the lips, his hands caressing her body. Since his return to life, Gavin often surprised her with such spontaneous expressions of love.

When she asked why, he only told her that he didn't know what else to do when he was so abundantly joyful. It only seemed natural to let his happiness spill out to her. As a result, she shared in his gladness and rejoiced with him.

In the heat of their love, Chloe couldn't help but remember their first kiss that night in the cabin while they worked on her novel. And she realized something so important that she wondered how she could have possibly it missed before.

If she had never come to the cabin to become an author, and if she had never sat down and written those first few pages of her novel, Gavin would have never made himself known, and he would have never become an author himself. They would have never met if not for their mutual love of writing and literature. They would have never known what true love was if they had never come together for the sake of their passions.

Afterword

Dear Readers,

I hope you have enjoyed reading about Chloe and Gavin's struggle to be together and find their true passions.

Passions has been a stretch for me because I don't particularly care for vampires, and this will be the only novel I ever write where the main conflict includes a vampire. I have vampires featured in other books, but they aren't in the limelight like Gavin is.

The inspiration for such a story came from some deep-rooted desire to be a full-time, stay at home writer. That and I'd love to own a cabin out in the middle of the woods where I could spend the weekends while I could write distraction free. Not only that, but I had this creepy scene in my head of a girl sleeping and a man watching over her late at night. But, this wasn't in a perverted way. He was protecting her as he had always done ever since she was a child. I expanded that idea and wondered "What if this guy was immortal in some way, like a vampire, and he knew her because he lived in the attic or basement or something?" And there were the planted seeds that grew into this challenging novel. I hope I have done the characters justice and not stepped on any toes of vampire lovers out there.

If you enjoyed this story, I'd love to hear it! Leave me a review on Goodreads!

Check out some of my other titles!

Until next time, happy reading!

- Sheritta Bitikofer

About the author

Sheritta Bitikofer is an author of paranormal and historical fiction. She lives for the deep, engaging stories that enthrall readers from cover to cover. As a wife and mother of eclectic tastes, she can be found roaming Civil War battlefields, haunting her local coffeeshop, or relaxing with a plate of chili cheese fries.

Follow her for upcoming novel releases
www.sherittabitikofer.com

Also by Sheritta Bitikofer

Bewitching Darkness
Bewitching Hearts
<u>The Decimus Trilogy</u>
The Beast of Verona
Amber Ashes
Saving the Beast
<u>Redemption Duet</u>
The Rose
The Lion
<u>Wolves in the Open</u>
Highland Howls
Silver Screen
Mourning Moon
<u>Standalones</u>
Escape
Clouds
Passions
By The Book

www.ingramcontent.com/pod-product-compliance
Lightning Source LLC
Chambersburg PA
CBHW060546260626
47161CB00003B/1069